The Two Dianas
Vol. III

by
Alexandre Dumas

The Two Dianas
Vol. III
by Alexandre Dumas

Copyright © 2024

All Rights reserved.

No part of this publication may be reproduced, stored in a retrieval system, or transmitted in any form or by any means, electronic, mechanical, photocopying or Otherwise, without the written permission of the publisher.
The author/editor asserts the moral right to be identified as the author/editor of this work.

ISBN: 978-93-68094-72-2

Published by

DOUBLE 9 BOOKS

2/13-B, Ansari Road
Daryaganj, New Delhi – 110002
info@double9books.com
www.double9books.com
Tel. 011-40042856

This book is under public domain

ABOUT THE AUTHOR

French author and playwright Alexandre Dumas is best known for his romantic novel La Dame aux Camélias (The Lady of the Camellias), published in 1848. Giuseppe Verdi adapted it into his opera La traviata (The Fallen Woman), which debuted in 1853. Other notable works by Dumas include a number of stage and film adaptations, which are usually titled Camille in English-language adaptations. The playwright Alexandre Dumas père ("father"), the author of classic works including The Three Musketeers and The Count of Monte Cristo, was the father of Dumas. Dumas received the Légion d'honneur (Legion of Honour) in 1894 after being accepted into the Académie française (French Academy) in 1874. The illegitimate child of tailor Marie-Laure-Catherine Labay (1794–1868) and novelist Alexandre Dumas, Dumas was born in Paris, France. His father gave him official recognition in 1831 and made sure the young Dumas attended the Collège Bourbon and the Institution Goubaux for the greatest education available. The elder Dumas was then permitted by law to remove the child from his mother. The younger Dumas was driven to write about sad female characters by her anguish.

CONTENTS

CHAPTER I
WHEREIN IT SEEMS AS IF THE MISUNDERSTANDINGS WERE ABOUT TO BEGIN AGAIN 9

CHAPTER II
A CRIMINAL'S SPEECH AGAINST HIMSELF 17

CHAPTER III
JUSTICE 25

CHAPTER IV
TWO LETTERS 35

CHAPTER V
A PROTESTANT CONVENTICLE 42

CHAPTER VI
ANOTHER TRIAL 54

CHAPTER VII
A PERILOUS STEP 62

CHAPTER VIII
THE IMPRUDENCE OF PRECAUTION 68

CHAPTER IX
OPPORTUNITY 76

CHAPTER X
BETWEEN TWO DUTIES 83

CHAPTER XI
OMENS 89

CHAPTER XII
THE FATAL JOUST 94

CHAPTER XIII
A NEW ORDER OF AFFAIRS 101

CHAPTER XIV
RESULTS OF GABRIEL'S VENGEANCE 107

CHAPTER XV
CHANGE OF TEMPERATURE 115

CHAPTER XVI
GUISE AND COLIGNY 124

CHAPTER XVII
REPORTS AND DENUNCIATIONS 131

CHAPTER XVIII
A SPY 137

CHAPTER XIX
AN INFORMER 145

CHAPTER XX
A CHILD KING AND QUEEN 153

CHAPTER XXI
END OF THE ITALIAN JOURNEY 160

CHAPTER XXII
TWO APPEALS 169

CHAPTER XXIII
A PERILOUS CONFIDENCE 174

CHAPTER XXIV
THE DISLOYALTY OF LOYALTY 182

CHAPTER XXV
THE BEGINNING OF THE END 188

CHAPTER XXVI
THE FOREST OF CHÂTEAU-REGNAULT 195

CHAPTER XXVII
A GLIMPSE AT THE POLITICS OF THE
SIXTEENTH CENTURY 201

CHAPTER XXVIII
 THE TUMULT OF AMBOISE 207
CHAPTER XXIX
 AN ACT OF FAITH 213
CHAPTER XXX
 ANOTHER SPECIMEN OF POLITICS 222
CHAPTER XXXI
 A RAY OF HOPE 229
CHAPTER XXXII
 WELL-GUARDED SLUMBER 234
CHAPTER XXXIII
 A KING'S DEATH-BED 240
CHAPTER XXXIV
 ADIEU, FRANCE! 248
CONCLUSION 256

CHAPTER I
WHEREIN IT SEEMS AS IF THE MISUNDERSTANDINGS WERE ABOUT TO BEGIN AGAIN

Arnauld du Thill was not at once taken back to the dungeon which he occupied in the conciergerie of Rieux. He was taken to a room adjoining that where the court was sitting, and was left alone for a few moments.

It might be, they told him, that after questioning his adversary, the judges would desire to hear him further. Left to his own reflections, the crafty scamp began by congratulating himself upon the effect he had evidently produced by his clever and bold speech. Brave Martin-Guerre, notwithstanding the righteousness of his cause, would surely find it hard to be so persuasive.

At all events Arnauld had gained time. But on thinking matters over more carefully he could not conceal from himself that he had gained nothing else. The truth which he had so audaciously distorted would finally overwhelm him on all sides. Could he hope that Monsieur de Montmorency himself, whose testimony he had dared to invoke, would take the risk of using his position to shield the avowed misdeeds of his spy? It was doubtful, to say the least.

The result of Arnauld's cogitations was that he gradually relapsed from hope to anxiety, and all things considered, said to himself that his position was not the most encouraging in the world.

He lowered his head under these discouraging thoughts, when some one came to take him back to prison.

So the tribunal had not thought best to question him further after Martin-Guerre's explanations! Another cause for anxiety.

All this, nevertheless, did not prevent Arnauld du Thill, who noticed everything, from observing that it was not his ordinary jailer who had come to take him, and was with him at that moment.

Why the change? Were they redoubling their precautions against his escape? Did they hope to make him confess? Arnauld determined to be on his guard, and said not a word during the whole walk.

But behold! another cause of amazement. The room to which this new custodian conducted Arnauld was not the one he ordinarily occupied.

The latter had a barred window and a high chimneypiece, which were lacking in the other.

However, everything bore witness to the recent presence of a prisoner,—crumbs of bread still fresh, a half-emptied cup of water, a straw pallet, and a half-opened chest within which could be seen a man's clothes.

Arnauld du Thill, who was well used to restraining his emotions, made no sign of surprise, but as soon as he found himself alone, he hastened to overhaul the chest.

He found nothing but clothes in it; nothing else to indicate its owner. But the clothes were of a color and cut which Arnauld seemed to remember. Especially two jerkins of brown cloth, and yellow tricot breeches, which were neither of a common shade nor shape.

"Oho," said Arnauld, "that would be strange!"

Just as night began to fall, the unknown jailer entered.

"Hallo, Master Martin-Guerre!" said he, laying his hand familiarly upon the pensive Arnauld's shoulder in a way to signify that the jailer knew his prisoner very well, even if the prisoner did not know his jailer.

"What is the matter, pray?" Arnauld asked this very friendly official.

"Well, it's just this, my dear fellow," the man replied; "your affair seems to be looking brighter and brighter. Who do you suppose has obtained leave from the judges, and now asks of yourself the favor of a few moments' conversation?"

"My faith, I can't imagine!" said Arnauld. "How should I know? Who can it be?"

"Your wife, my friend; even Bertrande de Rolles herself, who is beginning to see, doubtless, which one of you has the right on his side. But if I were in your place, I would refuse to receive her,—that I would."

"Why so?" asked Arnauld du Thill.

"Why?" repeated the jailer. "Why, because she has denied you for so long, of course! It is quite time for her to come over to the side of justice and truth, just when to-morrow at the latest the decree of the court will proclaim it publicly and officially! You agree with me, do you not? and I will send your ungrateful spouse about her business without ceremony."

The jailer took a step toward the door, but Arnauld stopped him with a gesture.

"No, no!" said he, "don't send her away. On the other hand, I want to see her. In short, since she has obtained leave from the judges, show Bertrande de Rolles in, my dear friend."

"Hum! Always the same," said the jailer. "Always easy-going and good-natured. If you allow your wife to reassert her former ascendency so quickly, you take a great risk. However, that's your business."

The jailer withdrew, shrugging his shoulders compassionately.

Two minutes later he returned with Bertrande de Rolles. It was growing darker every instant.

"I will leave you alone," said the jailer, "but I shall come to take Bertrande away before it is quite dark: those are the orders. So you have hardly a quarter of an hour; use it to quarrel or to make up, as you choose."

And he left the cell again.

Bertrande de Rolles came forward, shame-faced and with bent head, toward the pretended Martin-Guerre, who remained seated and silent, leaving it for her to begin the conversation.

"Oh, Martin!" said she at last, in a weak and hesitating voice, when she was at his side; "Martin, can you ever forgive me?"

Her eyes were wet with tears, and she was literally trembling in every limb.

"Forgive you for what?" replied Arnauld, who did not propose to commit himself.

"Why, for my stupid mistake," said Bertrande. "Of course I did very wrong not to recognize you. But was there not some excuse for my mistake, since it seems that at times you were deceived yourself? So it was necessary, I confess, to make me believe in my error, that the whole province, Monsieur le Comte de Montgommery, and justice, which knows everything, should prove to me that you are my true husband, and that the other is only a fraud and an impostor."

"But let us see," said Arnauld; "which is the acknowledged impostor,—the one whom Monsieur de Montgommery brought hither, or the one whom they found in possession of Martin-Guerre's goods and name?"

"Why, the other!" replied Bertrande; "the one who deceived me so, and whom during the last week I have still called my husband, stupid, blind fool that I was!"

"Aha, so the thing seems to be pretty well established now, does it?" asked Arnauld, with emotion.

"*Mon Dieu*! yes, Martin," Bertrande replied in some confusion. "The gentlemen of the court and your master, the worthy nobleman, told me just now that they had no longer any doubt, and that you were surely the true Martin-Guerre, my dear, good husband."

"Ah, indeed," said Arnauld, whose cheek paled in spite of himself.

"Thereupon," continued Bertrande, "they gave me to understand that I would do well to ask your forgiveness, and to become reconciled to you before they pronounce judgment; so I asked and obtained leave to see you."

She stopped a moment, but seeing that her pretended husband gave no sign of replying, she went on,—

"It is only too certain, good Martin-Guerre, that I have been very guilty toward you. But I implore you to reflect that it has been entirely involuntary on my part, as I call the Holy Virgin and the child Jesus to witness! My first mistake was the not having unmasked and discovered the fraud of this Arnauld du Thill. But could I imagine that there could be such a perfect resemblance in the world, and that the good God would amuse Himself by making two of His creatures so exactly alike? Alike in feature and in form, but not, it is true, in character and heart; and it was that difference which should have opened my eyes, I confess. But why? Nothing warned me to be on my guard. Arnauld du Thill talked to me of the past just as you yourself would have done. He had your ring and your papers, and not a single one of his friends or relatives suspected him. I acted in good faith. I attributed the change in your disposition to the experience you had gained in your extensive travels. Consider, my dear husband, that under the name of that stranger it was you whom I always loved, you to whom I submitted joyfully. Consider that, and you will forgive me for the first mistake, which led me—without intending it or knowing it, so help me God!—to commit the sin for which I shall pass the remainder of my days asking pardon from Heaven and from you."

Bertrande de Rolles again paused in her justification to see if Martin-Guerre would not speak to her and encourage her a little. But he remained persistently silent, and poor Bertrande, with sinking heart, continued,—

"Even if it be impossible, Martin, for you to bear ill-will toward me for this first involuntary wrong, the second, unfortunately, deserves beyond question all your reproaches and all your anger. When you were not at hand, I might mistake another for you; but when you had presented yourself, and I had leisure to compare you with the other, I should have recognized you at once. But consider whether even in that matter my conduct does not admit of some excuse. In the first place, Arnauld du Thill was, as you say, in possession of the title and name which belong to you, and it was extremely repugnant to my feelings to admit a supposition which would make me guilty. In the second place, I was hardly allowed to see you and speak with you. When I was confronted with you, you were not dressed in your ordinary dress, but were wrapped in a long coat which hid your form and your gait from me. Then, too, I was kept secluded almost as closely as Arnauld du Thill and yourself, and I hardly saw either of you except before the court, always separately and at a considerable distance. In the face of that terrifying resemblance, what means had I of determining the truth? I made up my mind, almost haphazard, in favor of him whom I had called my husband just before. I implore you not to be angry with me for it. The judges to-day assure me that I was mistaken, and that they have abundant proofs of it. Thereupon I come to you, penitent and abashed, trusting only in your kind heart and the love of former days. Was I wrong to rely thus on your indulgence?"

After this direct question, Bertrande made another pause; but the false Martin still remained dumb.

Surely, in thus renouncing Arnauld du Thill Bertrande was adopting a curious method of softening his heart toward her; but she was acting in perfect good faith, and committed herself more and more irrevocably to that view which she believed to be the true one, in order to touch the heart of him whose forgiveness she supposed herself to be imploring.

"As for myself," she resumed humbly, "you will find my disposition much altered. I am no longer the scornful, capricious, ill-tempered virago who made life such a burden to you. The cruel treatment which I have undergone at the hands of that wretched Arnauld, and which ought to have condemned him in my eyes, has had one good result, at least,—in bending and taming my spirit; and you may expect to find me in future as easily managed and obliging as you yourself are gentle and kind-hearted. For you will be gentle and kind with me as you used to be, will you not? You are going to prove that now by forgiving me; and then I shall know you by your good heart, as I know you already by your features."

"So you do recognize me now, do you?" said Arnauld du Thill, at last.

"Oh, yes! indeed, I do," replied Bertrande; "but I blame myself for having waited for the judgment and decree of the court."

"So you do recognize me?" said Arnauld, persisting in his question. "You do realize now that I am not that intriguing scoundrel who had the assurance to call himself your husband no longer ago than last week, but that I am the real, legitimate Martin-Guerre, whom you have not seen before for many years? Look at me. Do you recognize me now, and acknowledge me as your first and only husband?"

"To be sure I do," said Bertrande.

"By what marks do you recognize me?" asked Arnauld.

"Alas!" said Bertrande, frankly, "only by the outward appearance of your person, I confess. Were you beside Arnauld du Thill and dressed like him, the resemblance is so exact that very likely I could not tell you apart even now. I know you for my true husband because I was told that I was to be taken to him, because you occupy this cell, and not Arnauld's, and because you receive me with the calm severity which I deserve; while Arnauld would be trying still to abuse me and deceive me—"

"Wretched Arnauld!" cried Arnauld himself, harshly. "And you, weak and credulous woman—"

"Don't spare me!" was Bertrande's rejoinder. "I much prefer your reproaches to your silence. When you have said to me all that you have at heart—for I know how kind and indulgent you are—you will soften toward me and forgive me!"

"Very well!" said Arnauld, in a somewhat milder tone. "Don't be downhearted, Bertrande; we will see."

"Ah!" exclaimed Bertrande, "what did I say? Yes, you are, indeed, my own dear Martin-Guerre!"

She threw herself at his feet, and bathed his hands with her honest tears,—for she really believed she was talking with her husband; and Arnauld du Thill, who was observing her distrustfully, could find no excuse for the least suspicion. Her expressions of joy and penitence were not ambiguous.

"Very good!" Arnauld muttered to himself; "you shall pay for all this some day, ingrate!"

Meanwhile he seemed to give way to an irresistible impulse of affection.

"I am weak, and I feel that I am yielding," said he, pretending to wipe away a tear which was not there; and, as if in spite of himself, he breathed a kiss upon the lowly head of the fair penitent.

"What ecstasy!" cried Bertrande; "he has almost forgiven me!"

At this moment the door opened, and the jailer reappeared.

"Humph! Made it up, have you?" said he, testily, as his eye fell upon the sentimental tableau presented by the happy pair. "I was sure of it,— you're such a milksop, Martin!"

"What's that? Do you blame him for his kind heart?" said Bertrande.

"Ha, ha! Come, come!" said Arnauld, laughing in the most fatherly way.

"Well, as I said before, it's his business," replied the unmoved jailer; "and it's my business now to carry out my orders. The time has expired, and you cannot stay a minute longer, my weeping beauty."

"What! must I leave him already?" asked Bertrande.

"Yes. You will have time enough to see him to-morrow and all the rest of your days," was the reply.

"True, he will be free to-morrow!" rejoined Bertrande. "To-morrow, dear, we will begin again our peaceful life of former days."

"Postpone your caresses till to-morrow, too," observed the fierce jailer, "for now you must leave."

Bertrande kissed once more the hand which Arnauld du Thill held out to her royally, waved a last adieu to him, and preceded the jailer from the cell.

As the latter was closing the door, Arnauld called him back.

"May I not have a light, a lamp?" he asked.

"Yes, to be sure, just as you have every evening," said the jailer; "that is, until curfew,—nine o'clock. By our Lady! we don't treat you as harshly as Arnauld du Thill; and then, too, your master, the Comte de Montgommery, is so generous! You are well taken care of to oblige him. In five minutes I will bring your candle, friend Martin."

The light was brought to him very shortly by a turnkey, who withdrew at once, wishing the prisoner good-night, and reminding him anew to extinguish it at curfew.

Arnauld du Thill, when he found himself alone, quickly removed the linen suit that he wore, and clothed himself no less speedily in one of the famous suits, composed of a brown jerkin and yellow tricot small-clothes, which he had discovered in Martin-Guerre's chest.

Then he burned his former costume piece by piece in the flame of his candle, and mingled the ashes with those which were lying on the hearth.

It was all done in less than an hour; and he was enabled to extinguish his light and go virtuously to bed even before the curfew tolled.

"Now, we will see!" said he. "I seem to have been beaten before the court; but it will be very pleasant to succeed in deriving the means of victory from my defeat."

CHAPTER II
A CRIMINAL'S SPEECH AGAINST HIMSELF

We can readily understand that sleep hardly visited Arnauld du Thill's eyes that night. He lay stretched upon his straw litter, his eyes wide open, entirely engrossed with reckoning up his chances, laying plans, and marshalling his resources. The scheme he had devised, of substituting himself for poor Martin-Guerre once more, was an audacious one doubtless, but its very impudence endowed it with some chance of success.

Since luck favored him so marvellously, should he let his own audacity betray him?

No; he quickly adopted the course he was to follow, and left himself free to adapt his movements to events as they might shape themselves, and to unforeseen circumstances.

When day broke, he examined his costume, found it unexceptionable, and devoted himself anew to acquiring Martin-Guerre's gait and attitudes. His mimicry of his double's good-natured demeanor was so perfect as almost to be exaggerated. It must be confessed that the miserable blackguard would have made an excellent comedian.

About eight o'clock in the morning, the cell-door grated on its hinges.

Arnauld du Thill suppressed a startled movement, and assumed an air of tranquil indifference.

The jailer of the night before reappeared, introducing the Comte de Montgommery.

"The devil! now the crisis is at hand!" said Arnauld du Thill to himself. "I must be on my guard."

He waited anxiously for Gabriel's first word when he should look at him.

"Good-morning, my poor Martin-Guerre," Gabriel began.

Arnauld breathed again. The Comte de Montgommery had looked him straight in the face as he called him by name. The misunderstanding began again, and Arnauld was saved!

"Good-morning, my dear, kind Master," he said to Gabriel, with an effusiveness of gratitude which was in truth not wholly feigned.

He had the assurance to add, —

"Is there anything new, Monseigneur?"

"The sentence will be pronounced this morning in all probability," Gabriel replied.

"At last! God be praised!" cried Arnauld. "I long for the end, I confess. There is no conceivable doubt now, — nothing more to fear, is there, Monseigneur? The right will surely triumph?"

"Indeed I hope so," said Gabriel, gazing at Arnauld more intently than ever. "That villanous Arnauld du Thill is reduced to desperate remedies."

"Is he really? And what infernal scheme is he hatching now?" asked Arnauld.

"Would you believe it?" said Gabriel; "the impostor is trying to renew the old confusion."

"Can it be?" cried Arnauld, with uplifted hands. "What is his pretext, in God's name?"

"Why, he has the assurance to claim," Gabriel replied, "that after the hearing was at an end, yesterday, the jailers made a mistake, and took him to Arnauld's cell, and you to his."

"Is it possible?" said Arnauld, with a capitally feigned gesture of surprise and indignation. "What proof does he give in support of that impudent statement, — upon what does he base it?"

"This is what he says," said Gabriel. "It seems that he, like you, was not taken back at once to prison yesterday. The court, when they withdrew to consult, thought that they might desire to question one or both of you further; so the guards left him in the vestibule below, as they left you in the courtyard. Now he swears that was the cause of the error, and that it had been the custom to leave Arnauld in the vestibule and Martin in the courtyard. The jailers, when they went to take their respective prisoners, naturally confused the one with the other, according to his story. As for the guards concerned, they are the same ones who 'have always had charge of the two, and these human machines only know their prisoners, without being able to distinguish their persons. He bases his new claims upon such absurd reasons as those; and he is weeping and shrieking and asking to see me."

"Have you seen him, Monseigneur?" asked Arnauld, eagerly.

"My faith, no!" said Gabriel. "I am afraid of his tricks and his wiles. He would be quite capable of deceiving me and leading me astray again. The blackguard is so bold and clever withal."

"Ah, Monseigneur defends him now!" rejoined Arnauld, feigning discontent.

"I am not defending him, Martin," said Gabriel; "but we must agree that his brain is full of expedients, and that if he had applied himself to earning an honest living with half the skill—"

"He's an infamous villain!" cried Arnauld, vehemently.

"How severe you are upon him to-day!" replied Gabriel. "But I was thinking to myself as I came along, that after all he has not caused anybody's death; that if his condemnation is pronounced in a few hours, he will surely be hanged within a week; that capital punishment is perhaps an excessive penalty for his crimes, and that in short we might, if you choose, ask for mercy to be shown him."

"Mercy for him!" Arnauld du Thill repeated with some hesitation.

"It requires thought, I know," said Gabriel; "but come now,—you have thought about it; what do you say?"

Arnauld, with his chin in one hand, and rubbing his cheek with the other, remained for some seconds pensive without replying; but at last, having made up his mind, he said firmly,—

"No, no! no mercy! That will be much better."

"Oho!" replied Gabriel, "I did not know you were so vindictive, Martin; you are not generally so, and only yesterday you were pitying your adversary, and would have asked nothing better than to save his life."

"Yesterday, yesterday," muttered Arnauld, "yesterday he had not played us this last trick, which is to my mind more shameful than all the others."

"That is very true," Gabriel remarked. "So you are very decidedly of the opinion that the culprit should die?"

"*Mon Dieu!*" replied Arnauld, with a sanctified air, "you know, Monseigneur, how my soul revolts at violence and revenge, and all deeds of blood. My heart is torn to be compelled to yield to so cruel a necessity, but it is a necessity. Consider, Monseigneur, that so long as this man who resembles me so closely is still in the land of the living, I can never lead a peaceful, happy life. This last bold stroke which he has just struck shows that he is incorrigible. If he is sentenced to be kept in prison he will escape;

if he is banished he will return, and therefore I shall always be anxious and in torment, expecting every moment that he will come back to worry me, and unsettle my whole life again. My friends and my wife will never be sure that they really are dealing with me, and suspicion will always be rife. I must always be on the watch for renewed struggles and fresh attacks on my identity. In short, I can never say I am really in possession of my own personality. Therefore I must in my grief and despair do violence to my character, Monseigneur; I shall doubtless mourn all the rest of my days for having caused the death of a fellow-creature; but it must be, it must be! To-day's imposture removes my last scruples. Arnauld du Thill must die! I yield to necessity."

"So be it, then, he shall die," said Gabriel. "That is to say, he shall die if he is condemned, for judgment has not been pronounced yet."

"What do you say? Isn't it certain?" asked Arnauld.

"It is probable, but not certain," was Gabriel's reply. "That devil of an Arnauld addressed a very crafty and convincing speech to the judges yesterday."

"Cursed fool that I was!" thought Arnauld.

"While you, on the other hand, Martin," continued Gabriel, "you, who have just demonstrated to me with such admirable eloquence and conviction the necessity for Arnauld's death, could not, you will remember, find a single word to say before the court yesterday, nor could you adduce a single argument or a single fact to aid in the triumph of truth. You were confused and remained almost dumb, in spite of my urgency. Although you had been informed as to your adversary's arguments, you did not know how to meet and reply to them."

"The reason is, Monseigneur," was Arnauld's response, "that I am at my ease with you alone, while all those judges frightened me. Besides, I confess that I relied upon the righteousness of my cause. It seemed to me that justice would plead for me better than I could for myself. But that seems not to be the case with these men of the law. They want words, nothing but words, I can see now. Ah, if it could only begin again, or if they would hear me even now!"

"Why, what would you do, Martin?"

"Oh, I would pluck up a little courage, and then I would speak. It would not be a difficult matter by any means to demolish all the proofs and allegations of Arnauld du Thill."

"I tell you that would not be an easy matter!" said Gabriel.

"Pardon me, Monseigneur," replied Arnauld; "I can see the weak points in his strategy as clearly as he can see them himself, and if I had been less timid, and if words had not failed me, I would have told the judges—"

"Well, what would you have told them, pray? Just tell me."

"What would I have told them? Why, nothing could be simpler."

Thereupon Arnauld du Thill set to work to refute his speech of the evening before, point by point. He unravelled the events and the mistakes of the double existence of Martin-Guerre and Arnauld with so much the more facility, because he had tangled them up himself. The Comte de Montgommery had left certain matters still obscure in the minds of the judges, because he had been unable to explain them to his own satisfaction, but Arnauld du Thill elucidated them with marvellous clearness. The result of his discourse was to show Gabriel the two destinies of the honest man and the rascal as clearly and sharply defined and distinguished, for all the confusion there had been in. regard to them, as that between oil and water when put in the same vessel.

"Have you then been collecting information at Paris on your own account?" asked Gabriel.

"Without doubt I have, Monseigneur; and in case of need I could furnish proofs of what I say. I am not easily excited, but when I am driven into my last intrenchments, I can make energetic sorties."

"But," Gabriel continued, "Arnauld du Thill invoked the testimony of Monsieur de Montmorency, and you do not reply to that."

"Indeed, I do, Monseigneur. It is very true that this Arnauld has been in the constable's service, but his was a disgraceful employment. He must have been a sort of spy for him, and that fully explains why he attached himself to you, to follow you about and watch your movements. But though such people are employed, they are not acknowledged. Do you suppose that Monsieur de Montmorency would choose to accept the responsibility for the doings and sayings of his emissary? No, indeed! Arnauld du Thill, perched at the bottom of the wall, would not really dare to call upon the constable; or if he did venture in despair of his cause, Monsieur de Montmorency would deny him. Now, to sum up—"

And in his clear and logical resume, Arnauld successfully demolished, bit by bit, the edifice of fraud which he had so skilfully constructed the preceding day.

With such facility in argument, and such a flow of words, Arnauld du Thill would have made a very distinguished advocate of our times. He had the misfortune to live three hundred years too soon. Let us have pity on his shade!

"I believe that all this is unanswerable," he remarked to Gabriel when he had finished. "What a pity it is that the judges cannot hear me again, or that they have not heard me now!"

"They have heard you," said Gabriel.

"How so?"

"Look!"

The door of the cell opened, and Arnauld, entirely bewildered and somewhat alarmed, saw the president of the tribunal and two of the judges, standing grave and motionless on the threshold.

"What does this mean?" asked Arnauld, turning toward Gabriel.

"It means," replied Monsieur de Montgommery, "that I suspected my poor Martin-Guerre's timidity, and wished that his judges, without his knowledge, should hear the unanswerable speech they have just heard."

"Wonderfully well done!" rejoined Arnauld, breathing freely once more. "I am a thousand times obliged to you, Monseigneur."

Turning to the judges, he said in a tone which he tried to render bashful, —

"May I think, may I hope, that my words have really established the justice of my cause in the enlightened minds which are at this moment arbiters of my destiny?"

"Yes," said the president; "the proofs which have been furnished us have convinced us."

"Ah!" said Arnauld du Thill, triumphantly.

"But," continued the president, "other proofs, no less certain and conclusive, compel us to state that there was a mistake yesterday in remanding the two prisoners to their cells, — that Martin-Guerre was taken to yours, Arnauld du Thill, and that you are now occupying his."

"What! — how's that?" stammered Arnauld, thunderstruck. "What do you say to it, Monseigneur?" he added, addressing Gabriel.

"I say that I knew it," replied Gabriel, sternly. "I say again, *Arnauld*, that I desired to make you out of your own mouth furnish proofs of Martin's innocence and your own guilt. You have forced me, villain, to play a part which I abhor; but your unparalleled insolence yesterday made me understand that when one enters upon a struggle with such as you he must use the same weapons, and that frauds can only be conquered by fraud. However, you have left me nothing to do, but have been in such haste to betray your own cause that your cowardice has led you on to meet the trap that was set for you."

"To meet the trap, eh?" echoed Arnauld. "So there was a trap, was there? But, in any event, you are abandoning your own Martin in my person; don't deceive yourself about that, Monseigneur!"

"Do not persist, Arnauld du Thill," interposed the president. "The mistake about the cells was contrived and ordered by the court. You are unmasked beyond a peradventure, I assure you."

"But since you agree that there was a mistake," cried the irrepressible Arnauld, "who can assure you, Monsieur le President, that a mistake was not made in executing your orders?"

"The testimony of the guards and jailers," said the president.

A Criminal's Speech against himself.

"They are in error," retorted Arnauld. "I am really Martin-Guerre, Monsieur de Montgommery's squire, and I will not submit to be convicted in this way. Confront me with your other prisoner, and when we stand beside one another dare to choose between us,—dare to distinguish Arnauld du Thill from Martin-Guerre, the culprit from the innocent! As if there had not already been confusion enough in this cause, you must needs add to it. Your conscience will prevent your coming to any such conclusion. I will persist to the end, and in spite of everything, in crying, 'I am Martin-Guerre!' and I defy the whole world to give me the lie or to produce facts to contradict me."

The judges and Gabriel shook their heads, and smiled gravely and sorrowfully at this shameless and unblushing obstinacy.

"Once more, Arnauld du Thill," said the president, "I tell you that there is no longer any possibility of confusion between Martin-Guerre and yourself."

"Why not?" said Arnauld. "How can he be recognized? What mark distinguishes us?"

"You shall know, miserable wretch!" said Gabriel, indignantly.

He made a sign, and Martin-Guerre appeared upon the threshold.

Martin-Guerre without a cloak! Martin-Guerre mutilated, and with a wooden leg!

"Martin, my good squire," said Gabriel to Arnauld, "after miraculously escaping from the gallows which you helped him to ascend at Noyon, was less fortunate at Calais in avoiding an act of vengeance which was only too justifiable, intended to punish one of your infamous deeds: he was hurled headlong into an abyss in your stead, and compelled to suffer amputation of one leg; but by the mysterious working of the divine will, which is just when it appears most cruel, that catastrophe has now served to establish a point of distinction between the persecutor and the victim. The judges here present can no longer be deceived, since they may now recognize the criminal by his shamelessness, and the innocent man by his disfigurement."

Arnauld du Thill, pale and overwhelmed, and crushed beneath the terrible words and withering glances of Gabriel, no longer tried to defend or to deny himself; the sight of poor crippled Martin-Guerre rendered all his lies of no effect.

He fell heavily to the floor, an inert mass.

"I am lost!" he muttered,—"lost!"

CHAPTER III
JUSTICE

Arnauld du Thill was, indeed, lost beyond recall. The judges at once met for deliberation, and within a quarter of an hour the accused was summoned before them to listen to the following decree, which we transcribe literally from the records of the time:—

"In consideration of the examination of Arnauld du Thill, called Sancette, alias Martin-Guerre, now confined in the conciergerie at Rieux:

"In consideration of the testimony of divers witnesses, to wit, Martin-Guerre, Bertrande de Rolles, Carbon Barreau, etc., and especially that of Monsieur le Comte de Montgommery:

"In consideration of the avowals of the accused himself, who, after trying in vain to deny it, finally confessed his crime:

"From which said examination, depositions, and avowals it appears:

"That said Arnauld du Thill has been duly convicted of fraud, forgery, false assumption of surname and baptismal name, adultery, rape, sacrilege, larceny, and other crimes:

"The court has condemned, and does now condemn and sentence said Arnauld du Thill:

"First. To do penance in front of the church of Artigues, on his knees, clad only in his shirt, with head and feet bare, having a halter about his neck, and holding in his hands a torch of burning wax:

"Secondly. To ask pardon publicly of God and the king and the outraged law, as well of the said Martin-Guerre and Bertrande de Rolles, husband and wife:

"And this done, said Arnauld du Thill shall be delivered into the hands of the public executioner, who shall cause him to be led through the streets and public places of the said village of Artigues, still with the halter around his neck, until he shall be before the house of said Martin-Guerre:

"There to be hanged by the neck upon a gallows to be erected to that end on that spot, and his body to be afterward burned.

"And, in addition, the court has discharged from custody said Martin-Guerre and said Bertrande de Rolles, and does now remand said Arnauld du Thill to the judge of Artigues, who will cause this decree to be carried into effect according to its form and tenor.

"Given at Rieux the 12th day of July, 1558."

Arnauld du Thill listened to this anticipated judgment with a gloomy and sombre air, although he repeated his confession, recognized the justice of the decree, and showed some repentance.

"I implore God's clemency," said he, "and the pardon of mankind, and am disposed to meet my fate like a Christian."

Martin-Guerre, who was present at this scene, furnished fresh proof of his identity by bursting into tears at the words of his arch-enemy, hypocritical though they might be.

He conquered his ordinary bashfulness so far as to ask the president if there were not some means of obtaining mercy for Arnauld du Thill, whom he freely forgave for the past so far as he was concerned.

But good Martin-Guerre was informed that the king alone had the right to interpose, and that for such an extraordinary and notorious crime he would surely refuse to exercise his right of pardon, even though the judges themselves should ask it of him.

"Yes," Gabriel muttered to himself; "yes, the king would refuse to show mercy. And yet he may well need that mercy should be shown himself! But in this case he would do right to be inflexible. No mercy! Never any mercy! Justice!"

Martin-Guerre's thoughts probably did not resemble his master's; for in his absolute need to forgive somebody, he at once opened his arms and his heart to the penitent and humble Bertrande de Rolles.

Bertrande was not even put to the trouble of repeating the prayers and promises which in her last very useful blunder she had poured out upon the forger Arnauld du Thill, when she believed she was speaking to her husband. Martin-Guerre gave her no time to lament anew her errors and her weakness. He cut short her first attempt to speak with a loud kiss, and carried her off, triumphant and delighted, to the blissful little house which he had not seen for so many years.

In front of that very house, which had at last reverted to the hands of its true owner, Arnauld du Thill, a week after his conviction, suffered the penalty which his crimes so well deserved.

Folks came from twenty leagues around to be present at the execution, and the streets of the wretched village of Artigues were more densely thronged that day than those of the capital.

The culprit, it must be said, showed a certain amount of courage in his last moments, and at least ended his shameful life exemplarily.

When the executioner had cried aloud to the people three times, according to custom: "Justice is done!" and while the crowd was slowly melting away in horrified silence, within the house of the victim of the culprit's wiles a man was weeping, and a woman praying; they were Martin-Guerre and Bertrande de Rolles.

His native air, the sight of the locality in which his youth had been passed, the affection of his kinsfolk and his old friends, and, above all, the loving attentions of Bertrande, in a very few days banished from Martin's face every trace of unhappiness.

One evening in this same month of July he was seated under the vine at his door, after a peaceful, happy day.

His wife was within, busy with her housekeeping cares, but Martin could hear her coming and going, so that he was not alone; and he looked off to the right at the sun, which was just setting in all his glory, giving promise for the morrow of as beautiful a day as that which had just passed.

Martin did not see a horseman who rode up on his left, and dismounting, approached him noiselessly.

He stood a moment observing with a grave smile Martin's attitude of dreamy and peaceful contemplation. Then he reached out his hand, and without a word touched him on the shoulder.

Martin-Guerre quickly turned, and rose with his hand to his cap.

"What! You, Monseigneur!" he said, with much emotion. "Pardon me, I did not see you coming."

"Don't apologize, my good Martin," replied Gabriel (for it was he); "I did not come to disturb your peace of mind, but on the other hand to assure myself of it."

"Oh, Monseigneur has only to look at me, then!" said Martin.

"That's what I was doing, Martin," observed Gabriel. "So you are happy, are you?"

"Happier, Monseigneur, than the birds of the air or the fish in the sea."

"That is easily explained," returned Gabriel, "for you have found rest and plenty in your own home."

"Yes," said Martin-Guerre, "without doubt that is one of the reasons of my contentment. It may be that I have travelled sufficiently, seen enough battles, watched and fasted and suffered in a hundred ways sufficiently, to have earned the right, Monseigneur, to take pleasure in refreshing myself with a few days' rest. As for the plenty," he continued, in more serious fashion, "I have found the house well supplied,—too well supplied, in fact. The money does not belong to me, and I don't want to touch it. Arnauld du Thill brought it here, and I propose to restore it to its rightful owners. Much the greater part of it belongs to you, Monseigneur, for it was the money intended for your ransom which he stole. That sum is put aside all ready to be handed to you. As for the balance, it makes little difference how or where Arnauld obtained it; the gold would soil my fingers. Master Carbon Barreau thinks as I do, honest man, and having enough to live on, he declines to accept the unworthy heritage of his nephew. When the expenses of the trial are paid, the rest will go to the poor of the province."

"But in that case your property will not amount to much, my poor Martin," said Gabriel.

"I ask your pardon, Monseigneur. One does not serve a master so generous and open-handed as yourself for a long while without having something laid by. I brought a very respectable sum in my wallet from Paris. Besides, Bertrande's family were comfortably situated, and have left her some property. In short, we shall still be the magnates of the neighborhood when I have paid our debts and made all proper restitution."

"Touching this matter of restitution, Martin, I hope you will not refuse from my hand that which you scorned as a legacy from Arnauld. I beg you, my faithful servant, to keep, as a remembrance and a slight recompense, the sum which you say belongs to me."

"What, Monseigneur?" cried Martin,—"a gift of such magnificence to me!"

"Go to!" replied Gabriel; "do you imagine that I can pretend to pay you for your devotion? Shall I not always be your debtor? Have no scruples of pride with me, Martin, and let us say no more about it. It is understood that you will accept the trifle that I offer you—less to you than to me, in truth; for you tell me that you do not need this sum to live in comfort and to be highly considered in your province, consequently this will not add much to your happiness. Now as to this happiness of yours; you have not spoken very fully to me about it, but it ought to consist principally in your return to the loved spots which your infancy and your youth knew. Am I not right?"

"Yes, Monseigneur, that is quite true," said Martin-Guerre. "I have felt very contented and happy since I returned, just because I am at home. I gaze with emotion upon the houses and trees and roads, which no stranger would ever look at a second time. In fact, it seems that one never breathes so freely as in the air which he breathed the first day of his life."

"And your friends, Martin?" asked Gabriel. "I told you that I came to set my mind at rest on all matters touching your welfare. Have you found all your old friends again?"

"Alas! Monseigneur, some have died; but I have found a goodly number of the companions of my early days, and they all seem as fond of me as ever. They, too, are glad to acknowledge my frankness, my faithful friendship, and my devotion. My word! but they are ashamed that they could ever have mistaken Arnauld du Thill for me, for he seems to have given them some specimens of a nature very different from mine. There were two or three of them who quarrelled with the false Martin-Guerre because of his evil actions. You should see how proud and contented they are now! In short, they all vie with one another in overwhelming me with tokens of esteem and affection,—in order to make up for lost time, I fancy. Since we are talking about the causes of my happiness, Monseigneur, that is a very potent one, I assure you."

"I believe it, good Martin, I can well believe it. Ah, but in speaking of all the affection which sweetens your life you do not mention your wife."

"Ah, my wife," replied Martin, scratching his ear with an embarrassed air.

"To be sure, your wife," said Gabriel, anxiously. "What! it can't be that Bertrande still torments you as before? Has not her disposition changed for the better? Is she still ungrateful for the kindness of heart and the relenting fate which have given her such a loyal and affectionate husband? Is she still trying, Martin, with her shrewish and quarrelsome ways, to force you to leave your home and your dear old haunts a second time?"

"Oh, no, quite the contrary, Monseigneur," said Martin-Guerre; "she makes me too fond of my haunts and my native province. She waits upon me, coddles me, and kisses me. No more whims or domestic rebellions. Ah, indeed she is so sweet and equable as I never remember to have seen her before. I can't open my mouth that she doesn't come running to me; and she never waits for me to express my wishes, but seems to divine them. It is wonderful! and as I am naturally easy-going and good-natured myself, rather than despotic and domineering, our life is all honey, and our household the most united and happy one in the world."

"I am glad to hear it," said Gabriel; "but you almost frightened me at first."

"The reason for that, Monseigneur, was that I feel a little embarrassment and confusion, if I may say so, when this subject is under discussion. The sentiment I find in my heart when I examine myself on that subject is a very singular one, and makes me a little ashamed. But with you, Monseigneur, I may speak in all frankness and sincerity, may I not?"

"To be sure," said Gabriel.

Martin-Guerre looked carefully around to see that no one was listening, and especially that no one was within hearing. Then he said in a low voice, —

"Well, Monseigneur, I not only forgive poor Arnauld du Thill, at this moment I bless him. What a service he rendered me! He made a lamb out of a tigress, an angel out of a devil. I welcome the fortunate results of his brutal manners, without having to reproach myself for them. For all tormented and harassed husbands, and they say the number of them is enormous, I can wish nothing better than a double, — a double as — persuasive as mine. In short, Monseigneur, although Arnauld du Thill did most certainly cause me much annoyance and suffering, still do you not think that those troubles are more than atoned for, if he did but know it, by his energetic system, whereby he assured my domestic happiness and tranquillity for the rest of my days?"

"There's no doubt of that," said the young count, smiling.

"I am right, then," said Martin, joyfully, "in blessing Arnauld, even though I do it in secret, since I am reaping every hour the happy fruits of his involuntary collaboration. I am somewhat of a philosopher, as you know, Monseigneur, and I always look on the bright side. Therefore I am bound to say that Arnauld has done me more good than harm at every point. He has been my wife's husband in the interim; but he has given her back to me sweeter than a day in June. He stole my property and my friends from me temporarily; but thanks to him, my property returns to my possession in increased amount, and my friends even more closely bound to me. In fact, he was the means of subjecting me to some very rough experiences, notably at Noyon and at Calais; but my life to-day seems only more agreeable for his meddling with it. Wherefore I have every reason to be, and I am, well satisfied with this good Arnauld."

"You have a grateful heart," said Gabriel.

"Oh, but he whom, before all and above all, my grateful heart ought to thank and to reverence," continued Martin, becoming serious again, "is not Arnauld du Thill, my involuntary benefactor, but you, Monseigneur, you, to whom I really owe all these benefits,—my country, fortune, friends, and wife!"

"Again I repeat, enough of that, Martin," said Gabriel. "I ask only that you should have all these good things. And you have them, haven't you? Tell me again if you are happy."

"I repeat, Monseigneur, I am happier than I have ever been."

"That is all I desire to know," remarked Gabriel. "And now I must go."

"What, go?" cried Martin. "Are you really thinking of going so soon, Monseigneur?"

"Yes, Martin, there is nothing to keep me here."

"Pardon me, of course there is nothing. When do you mean to leave?"

"This very evening."

"And you never told me!" cried Martin-Guerre. "And I, sluggard! was dreaming away in utter forgetfulness. But wait, wait, Monseigneur, it will not be long!"

"Wait for what?" asked Gabriel.

"Why, for me to make my preparations for departure, to be sure!"

He rose nimbly and hastily, and ran to the door of the house.

"Bertrande, Bertrande!" he called.

"Why do you call your wife, Martin?" asked Gabriel.

"To get my things ready, and to say adieu, Monseigneur."

"But that's useless, my good Martin; for you are not going with me."

"What! You are not going to take me, Monseigneur!"

"No, I must go alone."

"Never to return?"

"Not for a long while, surely."

"What fault have you to find with me, Monseigneur, I pray you tell me?" asked Martin, sadly.

"None at all, my good Martin; you are the most devoted and faithful of servants."

"Yet you do not take me with you," returned Martin, "although it is natural that the servant should follow his master, that the squire should attend upon his lord."

"I have the best of reasons for it, Martin."

"May I venture to ask what they are, Monseigneur?"

"In the first place," replied Gabriel, "it would be downright cruelty for me to tear you away from this happy life which has come to you so lately, and from the repose you have so well earned."

"Oh, as for that, it is my duty to accompany you, Monseigneur, and to serve you to my last hour; and I would give up Paradise, I believe, for the sake of being at your side."

"Yes, but it is my duty not to abuse your zeal, for which I am grateful with all my heart," said Gabriel. "In the second place, the sad casualty which befell you at Calais will not allow you hereafter to render me such active service as you have done formerly."

"It is true, alas! Monseigneur, that I can no longer light by your side, or attend you in the saddle. But at Paris, at Montgommery, or in the field even, there are many confidential commissions with which you can still intrust the poor cripple, I hope, and which he will execute to the best of his ability."

"I know it, Martin; and I might perhaps be selfish enough to accept your sacrifice were it not for a third reason."

"May I know that, Monseigneur?"

"Yes," Gabriel replied with melancholy gravity; "but only on condition that you will not seek to go to the bottom of it, and that you will be content with it, and not persist any further in following me."

"It must be a very serious and very imperious reason, then, Monseigneur?"

"It is a sorrowful and unanswerable one, Martin," said Gabriel, in a hollow voice. "Until now my life has been an honorable one; and if I had chosen to allow my name to be uttered more freely it would have been a glorious one. In fact, I believe that I may claim, without boasting, to have rendered France and her king great and valuable services; for to speak only of St. Quentin and Calais, I think I may say that at those two places I discharged my debt to my country to the full."

"Who knows it better than I?" said Martin-Guerre.

"Very true, Martin; but in the same degree as this first part of my life has been loyal and unselfish and open to the broad light of day, the balance of my days will be passed in gloom and fear, always seeking to hide itself in the darkness. Doubtless, I shall have the same vigor at my command; but it will be exerted for a cause which I cannot avow, and to attain an end which I must conceal. Thus far, in the open field, before God and man, it has been my pleasure to strive manfully and joyously for the reward of gallantry. Hereafter it is my duty, in darkness and suffering, to avenge a crime. Hitherto I have fought; now I must punish. From being a soldier of France I have become the executor of the will of God."

"Holy Jesus!" cried Martin-Guerre, with hands clasped as if in supplication.

"Therefore," continued Gabriel, "I must needs undertake alone this ill-omened task,—in which I pray Heaven to employ my arm only, not my will, and in which I desire to be merely the blind instrument, not the guiding and directing brain. Since I ask, since I hope and trust, that my fearful duty will employ only half of my own being, how can you think that I would dream of associating you with it?"

"That is very true, and I understand, Monseigneur," said the faithful squire, with lowered head. "I thank you for having condescended to give me this explanation, much as it grieves me; and I accept it, as I promised to do."

"I thank you, too, for your submissiveness," replied Gabriel; "for I assure you that your devotion helps to lighten the heavy burden which is almost too much for me even now."

"But, Monseigneur, is there absolutely nothing that I can do to serve you at this crisis?"

"You can pray God, Martin, to spare me the necessity of taking the initiative in this struggle, which I contemplate with such bitter pain. You have a devout heart, and have led an honest and pure life, my friend, and your prayers may be of more help to me now than your arm."

"I will pray, Monseigneur, I will pray,—how ardently I need not tell you!"

"And now, adieu, Martin," said Gabriel; "I must leave you and return to Paris, to be prepared and on the spot whenever it pleases God to give the signal. All my life I have defended the right, fighting on the side of justice; may God remember that in my favor at the supreme hour of which I speak! May He mete out justice to His servant, even as I have done to mine!"

With his eyes upturned to heaven, the noble youth repeated,—

"Justice! justice!"

For six months past, whenever Gabriel's eyes had been open, they were generally intently fixed upon that Heaven at whose hands he asked for justice; when they were closed, he seemed always to see once more the gloomy Châtelet, in his gloomier reflections, which would at such times make him cry aloud, "Vengeance!"

Ten minutes later he tore himself away with great difficulty from the tearful farewells of Martin-Guerre and Bertrande de Rolles, who had come at her husband's summons.

"Adieu, adieu, good Martin, my faithful friend!" he said, releasing his hands almost by force from the fervent grasp of his squire, who was kissing and sobbing over them. "I must go now. Adieu! We shall meet again."

"Adieu, Monseigneur! God preserve you!—oh, I pray that He will preserve you!"

Poor Martin, choked with grief, could say no more than that.

Through his tears he saw his master and benefactor remount his horse in the fast-gathering darkness, which soon hid from his eyes the sombre figure of the horseman, as it had hidden his life from him for a long time past.

CHAPTER IV
TWO LETTERS

After the happy ending of the complicated trial between the two Martin-Guerres, Gabriel de Montgommery disappeared again for several months, and resumed his wandering, mysterious, and apparently purposeless existence. Again he was seen and recognized in twenty different places; nevertheless, he was never far away from the neighborhood of Paris and the court, always standing back in shadow, so that he might see everything without being seen.

He awaited events; but events arranged themselves very little to his liking. The soul of the young man, entirely absorbed by one idea, did not yet see its way clear to the issue which his righteous vengeance awaited.

The only important occurrence in the world of politics during these months was the conclusion of peace by the treaty of Cateau-Cambrésis.

The Constable de Montmorency, jealous of the exploits of the Duc de Guise, and of the new claims to the gratitude of the nation and to his master's favor which his rival was acquiring every day, had finally extorted Henri's consent to that treaty through the all-powerful influence of Diane de Poitiers.

The treaty was signed April 3, 1559. Although concluded in the full tide of victory, it was hardly advantageous to France.

She retained the three bishoprics Metz, Toul, and Verdun, with their dependencies; she was to keep Calais for eight years only, and to pay eight hundred thousand crowns to Great Britain if the place was not restored within that period (but it never was restored, and the eight hundred thousand crowns were never paid). France regained possession of St. Quentin and Ham, and retained Turin and Pignerol in Piedmont.

But Philip II. obtained unconditional cession of the strong posts of Thionville, Marienbourg, and Hesdin. The walls of Thérouanne and Yvoy were razed. He caused the restitution of Bouillon to the bishopric of Liège, the Isle of Corsica to Genoa, and to Philibert of Savoy the greater part of Savoy and Piedmont, which had been conquered under François I.; finally, he insisted upon his own marriage with the king's daughter Élisabeth, and that the Duke of Savoy should be united to the Princess Marguerite. These terms were very advantageous for him, and he could have demanded none more favorable even after the battle of St. Laurent.

The Duc de Guise, coming back in hot haste and furious with rage from the army, warmly and not unjustly accused Montmorency of treason, and the king of fatal weakness in having thus surrendered by a stroke of the pen what the Spanish forces had failed to wrest from France after thirty years of successful fighting.

But the harm was done, and the ominous discontent of Le Balafré was of no avail to repair it.

Gabriel found no satisfaction in this state of things. His vengeance pursued the man in the person of the king, not the king to the detriment of the nation. He would have been glad to avenge himself with his country behind him, but not against her.

However, he made a note in his mind of the natural resentment of the Duc de Guise at seeing the sublime efforts of his genius paralyzed and rendered of no account by underhand intriguing.

The wrath of a Coriolanus might well, if occasion offered, serve to aid Gabriel's projects. Besides, François de Lorraine was not the only malcontent in the kingdom,—far from it.

One day Gabriel encountered near the Pré-aux-Clercs Baron de la Renaudie, whom he had not seen since the morning conference in the Rue St. Jacques.

Instead of avoiding a familiar face whenever he saw it approaching, as he had been in the habit of doing, Gabriel accosted the baron.

The two men seemed made to appreciate each other; they were much alike in more than one respect,—notably in steadfastness and energy of character. Both were born for action, and were passionately devoted to every just cause.

After exchanging salutations, La Renaudie said confidently,—

"Well, I have seen Master Ambroise Paré. You are one of us, are you not?"

"In heart, yes; but in appearance, no," Gabriel replied.

"And when may we expect that you will give yourself to our cause absolutely and without concealment?"

"I will no longer hold with you the selfish language which perhaps angered you against me," Gabriel replied. "On the other hand, I answer thus: I will be at your service when you need me, and when I no longer need you."

"That is generous, indeed!" was La Renaudie's response. "As a gentleman I admire, but as a party man I cannot hope to imitate you. However, if you but await the moment when we need the help of all our friends, know that moment has arrived."

"Pray, what has happened?" asked Gabriel.

"A secret blow is in preparation against those of the Religion. They propose to get rid of all the Protestants at once."

"What leads you to think so?"

"Why, they scarcely take pains to hide it," replied the baron. "Antoine Minard, President of the Parliament, said boldly at a council meeting at St. Germain that it was necessary to strike a decisive blow, if they did not wish to become a sort of republic like the Swiss States."

"What! he uttered the word 'republic'?" cried Gabriel, in surprise. "Doubtless he exaggerated the danger so that an exaggerated remedy might be applied."

"Not so much," rejoined La Renaudie, in a lower tone. "He did not exaggerate very much, in truth; for we, too, have changed our views somewhat since our meeting in Calvin's chamber, and Ambroise Paré's ideas do not seem so bold to us to-day; and then, you see, they are driving us to extreme measures."

"In that case," said Gabriel, eagerly, "I may be one of you sooner than I thought."

"That is pleasant to hear," cried La Renaudie.

"In what direction must I keep my eyes?" asked Gabriel.

"Upon the parliament," said the baron, "for there the issue will be joined. The Evangelical party has a strong minority there,—Anne Dubourg, Henri Dufaur, Nicolas Duval, Eustache de la Porte, and twenty others. To the harangues which call for the vigorous prosecution of heretics, the adherents of Calvinism reply by demanding the convocation of a general council to deal with religious affairs in accordance with the terms of the decrees of Constance and Bâle. They have right on their side; therefore it will be necessary to use violence against them. But we are watching, and do you watch with us."

"Very well," said Gabriel.

"Remain at your house in Paris until you are notified that we have need of you," continued La Renaudie.

"That will be painful for me," observed Gabriel; "but I will do it, provided that you do not leave me to pine in idleness too long. You have written and talked enough, I should think, and now you ought to lay aside words for deeds."

"That is my opinion," rejoined La Renaudie. "Hold yourself in readiness, and be tranquil."

They parted, and Gabriel walked thoughtfully away.

In his thirst for vengeance, was he not allowing his conscience to go astray somewhat? Already it seemed to be driving him on toward civil war; but since events would not come to him, he must go to them.

That same day he returned to his house in the Rue des Jardins St. Paul, where he found his faithful Aloyse alone. Martin-Guerre was no longer there; André had remained with Madame de Castro; Jean and Babette Peuquoy had returned to Calais with the intention of going thence to St. Quentin, whose gates had been opened to the loyal weaver by the treaty of Cateau-Cambrésis.

Thus the master's return to his lonesome abode was more melancholy even than usual. Ah, but did not the motherly old nurse love him enough for all? We despair of picturing the worthy creature's joy when Gabriel informed her that he had come to stay with her for some time in all probability. He lived in most absolute secrecy and solitude, to be sure; but he was there by her side, and very rarely left the house. Aloyse could feast her eyes on him, and wait upon him. It was a long time since she had been so happy.

Gabriel, smiling sadly upon her, envied her loving heart its happiness. Alas! he could not share it with her. His life henceforth was even to himself a terrible enigma, of which he both dreaded and longed to know the solution.

Thus his days passed in impatience and apprehension, anxious and bored for more than a month.

As he had promised his nurse, he hardly ever left the house; but sometimes in the evening he would go and prowl around the Châtelet, and on his return would shut himself up for hours at a time in the funeral vault, whither the unknown bearers had secretly brought his father's body.

Gabriel seemed to take a gloomy pleasure in going back thus to the day when the outrage had been put upon him, that he might keep up his courage with his wrath.

When he looked upon the forbidding walls of the Châtelet, but above all when he contemplated the marble tomb where the sufferings of that noble life had finally found rest, the terrible morning when he had closed the eyes of his murdered father came back to him in all its horror.

Then his hands would move convulsively, his hair stand on end, and his chest heave with passion; and he would emerge from that terrible communion with the dead with his hatred renewed and more bitter than ever.

During such moments of anguish, Gabriel regretted having allowed his vengeance to follow in the wake of circumstances, for it seemed insupportable to him to have to wait for it.

His blood boiled to think that while he was waiting so patiently his murderous enemies were triumphant and joyous. The king sat peaceably on his throne at the Louvre. The constable was growing rich on the miseries of the people, and Diane de Poitiers rioting in infamous debauchery.

This state of things could not last. Since God's vengeance was sleeping, and the sufferings of the oppressed were growing daily greater, Gabriel determined that he would do without the help of God or man, or rather that he would constitute himself the instrument of divine justice and of human wrath.

Thereupon, carried away by an irresistible impulse, he would place his hand on the hilt of his sword, and make a motion as if to go and seek his revenge.

But then his conscience would awake and remind him of Diane de Castro's letter, written at Calais, in which his beloved had implored him not to undertake to chastise with his own hand, and not to strike even the guilty unless he were to do it involuntarily, and by the will of God.

Then he would read again that affecting missive, and involuntarily let his sword fall back into its scabbard. Stricken with remorse, he would resign himself once more to wait.

Gabriel was one of those men who are born for action, but have not executive ability. His vigor and energy were marvellous when supported by an army, or a small party, or even one great man; but he was not fitted by nature to carry out extraordinary achievements alone, even for a good object, and still less when they were to end in a crime. He was neither a powerful prince nor a startling genius by birth, and the power and the will to take the initiative were equally lacking in him.

When beside Coligny, and again when with the Duc de Guise, he had accomplished marvellous exploits. But now, as he had given Martin-Guerre to understand, his task was a very different one; instead of having enemies to fight in the open field, he had to chastise a king, and there was no one to assist him in that fearful work.

Nevertheless he still relied upon the same men who had formerly lent him their powerful aid,—Coligny the Protestant, and the ambitious Duc de Guise.

A civil war for the defence of religious truth, a revolution to assist in the triumph of a great genius,—such were the objects of Gabriel's secret hopes. The death or deposition of Henri II., or at all events his punishment, would be the result of either of the uprisings. Gabriel would show himself in the second rank, but as one worthy to be in the first. He would faithfully keep the oath he had sworn to the king himself; he would visit his perjury upon his children and his children's children.

If these two chances failed him, then he would have no other resource but to leave everything to God.

But it seemed at first as if these two chances were not likely to fail him. One day, it was the 13th of June, 1559, Gabriel received two letters almost at the same time.

The first was handed to him about five o'clock in the afternoon by a mysterious individual, who refused to deliver it except to himself in person, and would not deliver it to him until he had compared his features with the details of an exact description.

This letter read as follows:—

> FRIEND AND BROTHER,—The hour has come; the persecutors have thrown away their masks. Let us thank God! Martyrdom leads to victory.
>
> This evening at nine o'clock call at the house with a brown door, Number 11 Place Maubert.
>
> You must strike three blows upon the door at regular intervals. A man will open it and will say to you, "Do not enter, for you cannot see clearly." You will reply, "I have my light with me." He will then lead you to a stairway with seventeen steps, which you must ascend in darkness. At the top another acolyte will thus accost you, "What do you seek?" Reply, "What is right." You will then be shown into an unfurnished room where some one will whisper in your

ear the password, "Genève," to which you will reply with the counter-sign, "Gloire." Thereupon you will be at once conducted to those who have need of you to-day.

Till this evening, friend and brother, prudence and courage. Burn this letter.

L. R.

Gabriel called for a lighted lamp, burned the letter in the messenger's presence, and replied simply, —

"I will be there."

The man bowed and withdrew.

"Well," said Gabriel, "at last the Reformers are losing their patience."

About eight o'clock, as he was still deep in thought concerning La Renaudie's summons, Aloyse entered his room with a page in the Lorraine livery.

He brought a letter which read thus: —

MONSIEUR AND DEAR FRIEND, — I have been six weeks at Paris, having taken my leave of the army, where there was nothing more for me to do. I am assured that you also nave been at home for some time. Why have I not seen you? Have you forgotten me in these days of short memories and ingratitude? No, I know you too well; it is impossible.

Come to me, pray. I will expect you, if you please, to-morrow morning at ten in my apartments at the Tournelles.

Come, if only that we may condole with each other on the profit that has been made of our success.

Your very affectionate friend,
François de Lorraine.

"I will be there," said Gabriel to the page.

When the boy had withdrawn, —

"Well, well," he thought, "the ambitious man too is awake."

Thus encouraged by a twofold hope, he set out a quarter of an hour later for the Place Maubert.

CHAPTER V
A PROTESTANT CONVENTICLE

The house Number 11 Place Maubert, where La Renaudie had appointed a rendezvous with Gabriel, belonged to an advocate named Trouillard. It was already vaguely pointed at among the people as a place of resort for heretics; and the fact that psalms were sometimes heard sung there in the evening gave some credibility to these dangerous rumors. But after all they were only rumors, and it had never occurred to the police to investigate them.

Gabriel had no difficulty in finding the brown door, and following his instructions, he knocked three times at regular intervals.

The door opened as if of itself, but a hand seized Gabriel's in the darkness within, and a voice said,—

"Do not enter, for you cannot see clearly."

"I have my light with me," replied Gabriel, following the formula prescribed by the letter.

"Enter, then," said the voice, "and follow the hand that guides you."

Gabriel obeyed, and took a few steps in that way; then the hand released its hold, and the voice said,—

"Go on by yourself now."

Gabriel felt with his foot the first step of a staircase; he ascended, counting seventeen steps, then stopped.

"What do you seek?" said a different voice.

"What is right," was his reply.

A door opened at once in front of him, and he entered a room very dimly lighted.

A man was there alone; he approached Gabriel and said in a low tone,—

"Genève."

"Gloire," returned the young count at once.

The man then struck a bell, and La Renaudie himself entered by a concealed door.

He came directly to Gabriel and pressed his hand affectionately.

"Do you know what took place in parliament to-day?" he asked.

"I have not left my house until now," replied Gabriel.

"You will learn all about it here, then," said La Renaudie. "You have not yet bound yourself to us, but no matter; we will bind ourselves to you. You shall know our plans, and our strength; there shall be nothing concealed from you henceforth in the affairs of our party, while you may remain free to act alone or with us as you choose. You have told me that you were one of us in spirit, and that is sufficient. I do not even ask your word as a gentleman not to disclose anything that you may see or hear. With you it is a needless precaution."

"Thanks for your confidence," said Gabriel, much affected. "I will give you no cause to repent it."

"Come in with me," continued La Renaudie, "and stay by my side; I will tell you the names of those of our brethren whom you do not know. You can judge for yourself of everything else. Come."

He took Gabriel's hand, pressed the secret spring of the concealed door, and together they entered a large oblong hall, where about two hundred persons were gathered.

A few torches scattered here and there cast only a dim light upon the moving groups. Otherwise there was no furniture, nor hangings, nor seats; a common wooden pulpit for the preacher or orator, — that was all.

The presence of a score or so of women explained, but did not justify (let us hasten to say), the scandalous reports which were spread among the Catholics as to these secret nocturnal meetings of the Reformers.

No one noticed the entrance of Gabriel and his guide. All eyes and all thoughts were fixed upon him who stood on the rostrum at that moment, a sectary of sad mien and grave speech.

La Renaudie told Gabriel his name.

"It is Nicolas Duval, a councillor of parliament," he said beneath his breath. "He is just beginning to describe what took place to-day at the Augustins. Listen."

And Gabriel listened.

"Our regular place of meeting at the palace," the orator continued, "being occupied by the preparations for the celebration of Princess Élisabeth's marriage, we sat temporarily for the first time at the Augustins; and in some mysterious way the appearance of that unaccustomed apartment made us from the very first feel a vague presentiment that something out of the usual course would occur.

"However, Giles Lemaître, the president, opened the sitting in the customary form; and there seemed to be nothing to justify the apprehensions by which some of us had been disturbed.

"The question that had been discussed the Wednesday preceding was reopened. It related to the regulation of religious opinion. Antoine Fumée, Paul de Foix, and Eustache de la Porte spoke successively in favor of toleration, and their eloquent and vigorous language seemed to have made a marked impression on the majority.

"Eustache de la Porte resumed his seat amid loud applause, and Henri Dufaur was just opening his mouth to complete the conquest of those who were still hesitating, when suddenly the great door opened, and the usher of parliament announced in a loud voice, 'The king!'

"The president did not seem in the least surprised, but descended hastily from his chair to meet the king. All the members arose in confusion, some altogether amazed, others very calm, as if they quite anticipated the event.

"The king entered, accompanied by the Cardinal de Lorraine and the constable.

"'I do not come to disturb your labors, Messieurs of the parliament,' he said in the first place, 'but to assist them.'

"After a few meaningless compliments, he concluded his remarks thus:—

"'Peace has been concluded with Spain; but the fomenters of scandalous heresies have taken advantage of the wars in which we have been engaged to gain a foothold in the kingdom; and they must be stamped out, now that the war is over. Why have you not ratified the edict against the Lutherans which I caused to be submitted to you? However, I repeat, go on freely in my presence with the deliberations you have already begun.'

"Henri Dufaur, who had the floor, boldly resumed his speech at the king's command, pleaded earnestly for liberty of conscience, and even ventured to add to his outspoken discourse some sorrowful but severe strictures upon the measures adopted by the king's government.

"'Do you complain of disturbances?' he cried. 'Very well, we know their author.' I might reply as Elias replied to Ahab, "It is thou who tormentest Israel!"'

"Henri II. bit his lips and turned pale, but said nothing.

"Then Dubourg rose, and gave utterance to still more direct and weighty remonstrances.

"'I consider, Sire,' said he, 'that there are certain crimes which should be pitilessly punished, such as adultery, blasphemy, and perjury, but which are condoned every day amid the prevailing licentiousness of the time. But of what are the men accused who are thus to be delivered over to the hand of the executioner? Is it of *lèse-majesté*? They never omit the name of the prince in their prayers. They have never preached revolution or treason. What! Because they have discovered the great vices and the shameful shortcomings of the Roman hierarchy, by the light of the Holy Scriptures, and because they have demanded that they should be reformed, have they assumed a license which makes them worthy of the stake?'

"Still the king never moved; but we could see that he was with difficulty restraining an outburst of indignation.

"Giles Lemaître, the president, basely essayed to foment his mute wrath.

"'Talk about heretics!' cried he, with feigned indignation. 'Let us deal with them as with the Albigenses; Philippe Auguste burned six hundred of them in one day.'

"This violent language perhaps served our cause better than the more moderate steadfastness of our friends. It became evident that the final result would be at least evenly balanced.

"Henri II. understood that, and determined to carry everything with a sudden *coup d'état*.

"'Monsieur le Président is right,' said he; 'we must put an end to these heretics, or they will escape us. To begin with, Monsieur le Connétable, let those two rebels be arrested on the spot.'

"With his finger he pointed out Henri Dufaur and Anne Dubourg, and then hurriedly left the hall, as if he could no longer contain himself.

"I need not tell you, friends and brothers, that Monsieur de Montmorency obeyed the king's orders. Dubourg and Dufaur were seized and carried away while occupying their seats as councillors of parliament, and we were left in utter consternation.

"Giles Lemaître alone found courage to speak:—

"'It is just,' said he. 'So may all those be punished who dare to fail of respect to the majesty of royalty!'

"But as if to give the lie to his words, the guards at that moment entered the hall, and proceeded to execute orders which they produced, by arresting De Foix, Fumée, and De la Porte, all of whom had spoken before the king appeared at all, and had confined themselves to defending the principle of toleration in matters of religion, without suggesting the least reproach against the sovereign.

"Thus it became evident that it was not for their remonstrances uttered in the king's presence, but simply for their religious opinions, that five members of parliament, inviolable by law, had been charged with a capital crime, by means of a shameful subterfuge."

Nicolas Duval ceased to speak. Mutterings of grief and anger had interrupted him twenty times, only to follow more closely than ever his description of that momentous and stormy session, which to us at this distance in time seems as if it must have been told of another assembly, and bears a startling resemblance to scenes that were enacted two hundred and thirty years later.

But there was this important difference,—that at the later epoch it was liberty and not royalty which had the last word to say!

The minister David followed Nicolas Duval upon the rostrum.

"Brothers," said he, "before we take counsel together, let us lift up our voices and our hearts to God with a psalm, that He may quicken the spirit of truth in us."

"Psalm forty!" cried several voices in the assemblage, and they all began to sing the stirring words of that psalm.

It was an extraordinary selection to calm excited imaginations. It was much more like a strain of menace, it must be confessed, than like a prayer for guidance.

But wrath was uppermost at that moment in those sturdy souls, and it was with marvellous impressiveness that all present joined in singing these verses, in which the lack of poetic talent was replaced by the emotion which animated them:—

> "Gens insensés, où avez-vous les cœurs
> De faire guerre à Jésus-Christ?
> Pour soutenir cet Ante-Christ,
> Jusques à quand serez persécuteurs?
> Traîtres abominables!

> Le service des diables,
> Vous allez soutenant:
> Et de Dieu les édits
> Par vous sont interdits
> À tout homme vivant." [1]

The last stanza was especially significant:—

> "N'empêchez plus la predication,
> De la parole et vive voix
> De notre Dieu, le roi des rois!
> Où vous verrez sa malédiction,
> Sur vous, prompte s'étendre,
> Qui vous fera descendre
> Aux enfers ténébreux,
> Où vous serez punis
> Des maux qu'avez commis
> Par tourmens douloureux." [2]

The psalm at an end, it was as if this appeal to God had relieved the oppressed heart at once; silence was restored, and the assemblage was in readiness to deliberate.

La Renaudie was the first to speak, in order to state concisely the condition of affairs and its import.

"Brothers," said he, from where he stood on the floor, "being thus brought face to face with an unprecedented proceeding which overturns all preconceived notions of right and justice, we have now to decide what course of conduct should be adopted by the adherents of the Reformed religion. Shall we still suffer our burdens patiently, or shall we act? Such are the questions which each one of us must propound to his own conscience and answer according to its dictates. You see that our oppressors propose nothing less than a general massacre, and propose to strike us out from the list of the living, as one erases a badly written word from a manuscript. Shall we wait like sheep for the fatal blow; or shall we rather (since law and justice are thus violated by those very persons whose sacred duty it is to protect them) try to do justice with our own hands, and to that end temporarily substitute force for law? It is for you to reply, friends and brothers."

La Renaudie made a short pause, as if to afford time for all their intellects to digest the momentous question; then he resumed, desirous at once to facilitate and hasten the conclusion:—

"Those whom the cause of religion and of truth should hand together are unfortunately, as we all know, divided into two factions,—that of

Geneva, and that of the nobility; but when face to face with danger and a common foe, it is fitting, it seems to me, that we should have only one heart and one will. The members of both factions are alike invited to state their opinions and suggest the remedies that occur to them. The advice which offers the best chance of success should be unanimously adopted, from whatever quarter it comes; and now, my friends and brothers, speak freely and confidently."

La Renaudie's speech was followed by a considerable period of hesitation.

Those who listened to him were lacking in just those two qualities, courage and confidence; and in the first instance, notwithstanding the bitter indignation which really filled all their hearts, the power of royalty then enjoyed such great prestige that the Reformers, who were novices at conspiring, did not dare to express at once and without reserve their ideas on the subject of armed rebellion. They were devoted to their opinions, and determined as a body; but each individual recoiled before the responsibility of striking the first blow. They were all ready to follow, but no one dared to lead.

Then, too, as La Renaudie had said, they were suspicious of one another; neither of the two parties knew whither the other would lead it; and their objects were, in truth, too dissimilar to make the choice of roads and guides a matter of indifference to them.

The Geneva faction were really aiming at the foundation of a republic, while that of the nobility simply desired to bring about a change of dynasty.

The elective forms of Calvinism, the principle of equality which was everywhere inculcated by the new church, tended directly toward the republican system as it was in vogue in the Swiss cantons; but the nobility did not wish to go so far, and would have been content, in accordance with the advice of Élisabeth of England, to depose Henri II., and replace him with a Calvinist king. The Prince de Condé's name was whispered about as a suitable selection.

It would be difficult to imagine two more diametrically opposed elements co-operating in a common cause.

Therefore, Gabriel saw regretfully that after La Renaudie's address the two almost hostile camps eyed each other askance, without appearing to think of drawing conclusions from the premises he had so boldly laid down.

A moment or two passed in this unfortunate indecision, amid a confused murmuring of many voices. La Renaudie could but ask himself whether he had not, by being too blunt and outspoken, unwittingly done away with all the effect of Nicolas Duval's recital; but having started on that course, he determined to put everything to the touch, to win or lose all, and so he thus addressed a thin, puny little man with bristling eyebrows and bilious appearance, who made one of a group near him:—

"Well, Lignières, are you not going to speak to our brothers, and tell them what you have at heart?"

"So be it!" replied the little man, and his gloomy countenance lighted up. "I will speak; but I will not yield an inch, or extenuate anything."

"Go on,—you are among friends," said La Renaudie. While Lignières was on his way to the rostrum the baron whispered to Gabriel,—

"That is a dangerous instrument to make use of Lignières is a fanatic,— whether in good or bad faith I know not,—who urges everything to extremes, and is always more repellent than attractive. But no matter! We must know at any price what we have to rely upon, must we not?"

"Yes," said Gabriel, "so that all these closed hearts may open to emit the truth."

"Lignières and his doctrines hot from Geneva will wake them up, never fear," rejoined La Renaudie.

The orator plunged at once *in médias res.*

"The law has brought about its own condemnation," said he. "What resource remains? An appeal to force, and nothing else. You ask what we ought to do! If I do not reply to that question, here is something which will reply for me."

He held up a silver medal.

"This medal," he continued, "is far more eloquent than any words of mine. For the benefit of those who are too far away to see it I will say what it represents. It bears the image of a flaming sword cutting off the blossom of a lily, whose stalk bends and falls near by; the sceptre and the crown are rolling in the dust."

Then he added, as if he feared that he might be misunderstood,—

"Medals ordinarily serve to commemorate accomplished facts; may this one serve as prophetic of something yet to occur! I will say no more."

Indeed, he had said enough. He came down from the pulpit amid the plaudits of an inconsiderable portion of the assembly, and the in mutterings of a much larger number.

But the general attitude was of stupefied silence.

"Well," said La Renaudie, in a low voice, to Gabriel, "that is clearly not the right chord to strike. We must try another."

"Monsieur le Baron de Castelnau," he continued aloud, addressing a young man of thoughtful appearance and handsomely clad, who was leaning against the wall ten feet from him,—"Monsieur de Castelnau, have you not a word to say to us?"

"I might perhaps have had nothing to say independently; but I should like to say a word or two in reply," the young man responded.

"We are all attention," said La Renaudie.

"This young man," he added, speaking in Gabriel's ear again, "belongs to the party of the nobility; and you should have seen him at the Louvre the day you brought the news of the capture of Calais. Castelnau is frank, loyal, and brave. He will set up his flag as boldly as Lignières, and we shall see if he will be received any more warmly."

Castelnau mounted one of the steps of the rostrum, and spoke from that slight elevation.

"I will begin," he said, "like the orators who have preceded me. We have been iniquitously attacked; let us use like weapons to defend ourselves. Let us do in the open field, amid the panoply of war, what they have done in parliament among the red robes! But I differ in opinion from Monsieur de Lignières as to the rest. I, too, have a medal to show you. Here it is; it is not his. From a distance it seems to you to resemble the crowns from the royal mint which we carry in our purses, and in fact, like them, it does bear the stamp of a crowned head; but in lieu of 'Henricus II, rex Galliæ,' its legend reads, 'Ludovicus XIII., rex Galliæ.' [3] I have done."

The Baron de Castelnau left his place with his head proudly erect. His allusion to the Prince de Condé was flagrant. Those who had applauded Lignières muttered at his words, and vice versa.

But the large majority of those present were still motionless and speechless between the two minorities.

"What do they want, pray?" Gabriel softly asked La Renaudie.

"I am afraid that they don't want anything," was the baron's reply.

At that moment the advocate Des Avenelles asked a hearing.

"This is their man, I fancy," La Renaudie remarked. "Des Avenelles is my host when I am in Paris,—an honest and sagacious fellow, but too cautious, almost to timidity even. His word will be law with them."

Des Avenelles from the beginning justified La Renaudie's prediction.

Said he: "We have listened to many bold and even audacious words; but has the moment really arrived to utter them? Are we not going a little too fast? We are shown a very worthy and lofty purpose, but not a word is said as to the means of attaining it. They must needs be criminal. My heart is more oppressed by the severities to which we are subjected than that of any other member of this assemblage. But when we have so many prejudices to overcome, should we add to the burden by casting upon the cause of our religion the odium of an assassination?—yes, of an assassination; for you cannot obtain by any other means the result which you dare to propose."

Des Avenelles was interrupted by almost unanimous applause.

"What did I say?" whispered La Renaudie. "This advocate is the real expositor of their views."

Des Avenelles continued,—

"The king is in the very bloom and flower of his vigor. To wrest the throne from him, he must be hurled headlong from it. What living man would take upon himself that act of violence? Kings are divine, and God only has the right to govern them. Ah, suppose that some accident, some unforeseen ill, some blow struck by a private hand, should take away the king's life at this moment, and leave the guardianship of an infant monarch in the hands of those arrogant subjects who are our veritable oppressors!— then it would be this guardianship, and not royalty itself, the Guises and not François II., against whom our attacks would be directed. Civil war would be not only justifiable but laudable, and revolution a sacred duty, and I would be the first to cry, 'To arms!'"

This energetic moderation moved the assembly to admiration; and fresh tokens of approbation were showered upon Des Avenelles as a recompense for his prudent courage.

"Ah!" muttered La Renaudie to Gabriel, "I regret now having asked you to come, for you will begin to compassionate us."

But Gabriel, lost in thought, was saying to himself,—

"No, I have no right to reproach them for their weakness, for it is much like my own. While I was secretly relying upon them, they seem to have been relying upon me."

"What do you mean to do, pray?" cried La Renaudie to his triumphant host.

"To maintain a legal attitude and wait!" replied the advocate, firmly. "Anne Dubourg, Henri Dufaur, and three others of our friends in parliament have been arrested; but who says that they will dare to convict them, or even to accuse them? My opinion is that any overt act of violence on our part would result simply in provoking reprisals on the part of those in authority. And who knows that our moderation may not be the salvation of the victims? Let us have the tranquillity of conscious strength, and the dignity which befits a righteous cause. Let us leave all the wrong-doing to our persecutors. Let us wait. When they see that we are moderate in our demands, but resolute, they will think twice before declaring war upon us,—just as I implore you, friends and brothers, to think twice before you give them the signal for reprisals."

Des Avenelles ceased, and the applause was renewed.

The advocate, vain of his success, desired to confirm his victory.

"Let all who agree with me raise their hand," he added.

Almost every hand was raised to assure Des Avenelles that he had spoken the mind of the gathering.

"Let us see, then," said he: "our decision is—"

"To decide nothing at all," interposed Castelnau.

"To postpone until a more favorable moment any extreme measures," Des Avenelles concluded, casting an angry glance at the interrupter.

The minister David suggested singing another psalm to beseech God to deliver the poor prisoners.

"Come, let us be going," said La Renaudie to Gabriel; "all this annoys and angers me. These people only know how to sing. They have nothing seditious but their psalms."

When they were on the street they walked along in silence, both deeply absorbed in their reflections.

At the Pont Notre Dame they parted, La Renaudie returning to the Faubourg St. Germain, and Gabriel going toward the Arsenal.

"Adieu, Monsieur d'Exmès," said the former. "I am sorry to have caused you to waste your time thus. But believe me, I pray, when I assure you that this is not our last word. The prince, Coligny, and some of our most reliable heads were absent this evening."

"My time with you has not been wasted," replied Gabriel. "You will be convinced of that very shortly."

"So much the better, so much the better," rejoined La Renaudie. "Nevertheless, doubt—"

"Have no doubt at all," said Gabriel. "It was necessary for me to know if the Protestants were really beginning to lose patience. It is of more use to me than you can imagine to have learned that they are not tired out yet."

[1] "Ye men of wrath, why thus conspire ye
To wage mad war against your Saviour Christ,
By showing favor to this Anti-Christ,
Till ye yourselves shall persecutors be?
Ye doers of evil,
The works of the Devil,
You thus are upholding:
And with impious hands
From the Lord's high commands
Are the people withholding."

[2] "No longer now, with loud unseemly noise,
Seek to delay the utterance of the word
Of the great King of Kings, our God the Lord!
Else shall His malediction from the skies,
Upon ye descending,
To woe never-ending
In hell's darkest recess
Consign ye, to languish
In torment and anguish
Your sins to redress."

[3] These two rare and curious medals are to be seen to-day in the "Cabinet des Médailles."

CHAPTER VI
ANOTHER TRIAL

The disaffection of the Protestants having failed him, there remained still one more hope of assistance for Gabriel in his thirst for vengeance; namely, that furnished by the ambition of the Duc de Guise.

Consequently he was very prompt the next morning at ten o'clock in keeping the appointment François de Lorraine had made with him at the Tournelles.

It was evident that the young Comte de Montgommery was expected; for as soon as his name was announced he was shown into the presence of him who was now called the conqueror of Calais, thanks to Gabriel's daring scheme.

Le Balafré came eagerly forward to meet him, and grasped both his hands affectionately.

"Ah, here you are at last, my forgetful friend," said he. "I have been obliged to send for you, to follow you into your retirement, and if I had not done so God only knows when I should have seen you! Why is it? Why have you not been to visit me since my return?"

"Monseigneur," said Gabriel, in a low tone, "much distressing anxiety—"

"Ah! There it is! I was sure of it!" the duke interrupted him. "So they were false, were they, to the promises they made you h They deceived you, and insulted and tormented you. Oh, I was very suspicious that there was some infamy at the bottom of it all! My brother, the Cardinal de Lorraine, who was present when you arrived at the Louvre from Calais, and heard you spoken of as the Comte de Montgommery, imagined, with his priestly keenness, that you were destined to be the dupe or the victim of those people. Why did you not apply to him? He might have been of some assistance to you in my absence."

"I thank you, Monseigneur," replied Gabriel, gravely, "but you are mistaken, I assure you. All their promises to me were redeemed with the utmost exactitude."

"Oho, but you have such a way of saying it, my friend!"

"I speak as I feel, Monseigneur; but I will repeat that I make no complaints, and that the promises upon which I relied have been fulfilled — to the letter. So let us talk no more of my affairs, I beg, for you know that subject of conversation was never agreeable to me, and it is to-day more painful than ever. I ask you, Monseigneur, in pity not to insist upon your kindly meant inquiries."

The duke was struck with Gabriel's dolorous tone.

"Very well, my friend," said he; "I shall be afraid now of touching unintentionally upon some one of your scarcely healed scars, and I will question you no further about yourself."

"Thanks, Monseigneur," was Gabriel's reply, in a dignified tone, by no means free from emotion.

"But I wish you to be sure of this," continued Le Balafré, "that at all times and places, and for any purpose whatsoever, my influence, my fortune, and my life are at your service, Gabriel; and that if I am ever to be so fortunate as that you should need my help, you have but to hold out your hand to grasp mine."

"Thanks, Monseigneur," Gabriel said again.

"That being agreed between us," said the duke, "on what subject is it your pleasure that we should converse?"

"Why, of yourself, Monseigneur," replied the young count, — "of your glory and of your future plans; those are the subjects which interest rue. In them you will find the magnet which has drawn me to you in all haste at your first call."

"My glory? my plans for the future?" retorted François de Lorraine, with a shake of the head. "Alas! those are gloomy subjects of conversation for me as well."

"What mean you, Monseigneur?" Gabriel exclaimed.

"What I say, my friend. Yes, I confess that I did think I had won some renown; it seemed to me that my name deserved to be pronounced with some respect in France to-day, and with a certain degree of awe throughout Europe. And since my not unworthy past made it my duty to think of the future, I was forming plans based upon my reputation, and dreaming of great achievements, — great for my country, and for myself as well. I would have accomplished them, I have faith to believe — "

"Well, Monseigneur?" said Gabriel, inquiringly.

"Well, Gabriel, since my return to this court six months since, I have ceased to believe in my glory, and have abandoned all my plans."

"Why so, in God's name?"

"Why, in the first place, don't you know of the shameful treaty with which they have crowned our victories? If we had been forced to raise the siege of Calais, if the English still had the gateways of France in their hands,—in short, if defeat at all points had demonstrated the insufficiency or incompetency of our forces, and the impossibility of continuing an unequal conflict, we could not have been asked to sign a more unfavorable and dishonorable treaty than that of Cateau-Cambrésis."

"That is true, Monseigneur," Gabriel remarked; "and every one grieves to think that such a magnificent harvest yielded so little fruit."

"Oh, well," rejoined the duke; "how can you expect me to sow for people who know so little about reaping? And then, too, have they not forced me to remain ingloriously idle by this glorious peace of theirs? There is my sword, doomed for a long time to rust in its scabbard. War everywhere at an end, at whatever cost, puts an end at the same time to my fair dreams of glory; and between ourselves that was one of the main objects sought to be accomplished."

"But you are no less mighty even in this forced inaction, Monseigneur," said Gabriel. "You are respected at court, worshipped by the people, and dreaded by foreign nations."

"Yes, I believe I am beloved at home, and feared abroad," Le Balafré replied; "but do not tell me, my friend, that I am respected at the Louvre. While they are thus publicly reducing to nought the certain results of our success, they are threatening my private influence as well. When I returned from the North, whom did I find in greater favor than ever? That insolent, beaten hound of St. Laurent fame,—that Montmorency, whom I detest!"

"Oh, no more than I do, surely!" muttered Gabriel.

"It was by his influence and for his own purposes that this peace for which we are all blushing was concluded. Not content with thus making my efforts appear of less account, he was very careful to look after his own interests in the treaty, and to have the amount of his ransom after being taken prisoner at St. Laurent repaid to him,—for the second or third time, I believe! To such a degree does he speculate upon his defeat and disgrace."

"And does the Duc de Guise enter upon a rivalry with such as he?" asked Gabriel, with a disdainful smile.

"He shudders at the thought, my friend; but you can see that it is forced upon him! You can see that Monsieur le Connétable is protected by something stronger than glory or renown,—by some person more powerful than the king himself! You can see that my services can never equal those of Madame Diane de Poitiers, whom may the lightning wither!"

"Oh, that God might listen to you!" muttered Gabriel.

"What has that woman done to the king, in Heaven's name?" continued the duke. "Are the people really in the right when they speak of philters and charms? For my part, I believe that they are bound together by some stronger tie than love. It cannot be passion alone which thus indissolubly connects them; it must be fellowship in crime. I would swear that remorse has a place among their souvenirs of the past, and that they are more than lovers,—they are accomplices!"

The Comte de Montgommery shivered from head to foot.

"Do you not agree with me, Gabriel?" Le Balafré asked him.

"I do, indeed, Monseigneur," replied Gabriel, in a hollow voice.

"And to put the finishing touch to my humiliation," the duke went on, "do you know, my friend, what reward I found awaiting me here at Paris, over and above the monstrous treaty of Cateau-Cambrésis? The immediate revocation of my appointment as lieutenant-general of the kingdom. These extraordinary functions became unnecessary in time of peace, so I was told; and without a word of warning, without even a word of thanks, they erased that title, just as one throws upon the dust-heap a piece of drapery which is of no further use."

"Is it possible that no more consideration than that was shown you?" cried Gabriel, desirous to add fuel to the fire which was burning in that incensed heart.

"Why should they show more consideration to a superfluous servant?" said the duke, with clinched teeth. "As for Monsieur de Montmorency, that is another affair altogether. He was and he remains constable. That, mind you, is an honor of which they do not think of depriving him, and which he has earned by forty years of defeat and failure! Oh, by the cross of Lorraine, if the war-wind blows again, they may come and go on their knees to me and implore me, and call me the savior of my country! I will send them to their constable then; let him save them if he can. That is his business, and the duty that devolves upon the office he holds. But for myself, since they condemn me to idleness, I accept the sentence, and will take my ease until the dawn of better days."

Gabriel, after a pause, replied with much gravity of manner,—

"This determination on your part is a grievous one, Monseigneur, and I greatly deplore it; for I was just about to make a proposition to you—"

"Useless, my friend, useless!" exclaimed Le Balafré. "My mind is made up. And then, too, I repeat, and you know it as well as I, the peace has taken from us every hope of renown."

"Pardon, Monseigneur," rejoined Gabriel, "but the peace is the one thing that makes my plan feasible."

"Really?" said François de Lorraine, tempted in spite of himself. "Pray, is it some bold stroke like the siege of Calais?"

"Something still bolder, Monseigneur."

"How can that be?" exclaimed the duke. "Upon my word, you have succeeded in arousing my curiosity thoroughly."

"May I tell you about it, then?"

"To be sure you may; in fact, I beg you to do so."

"Are we quite alone?"

"Entirely; not a living soul is within the sound of our voices."

"Well, then, Monseigneur," Gabriel began resolutely, "this is what I have to say to you: This king and this constable choose to dispense with your services; why do not you dispense with them? They have ejected you from the office of lieutenant-general of the kingdom; assume it once more on your own responsibility."

"How do you mean? Explain yourself!" said the duke.

"Monseigneur, foreign princes fear you, the people adore you, and the army is at your command to a man; you are already more of a king in France than the king himself. You are king by right of genius, he only because the crown is on his head. Dare to speak with the voice of a master, and the nation will listen to you like obedient subjects. Will Henri II. be any stronger in the Louvre than you in your camp? He who now speaks to you will be proud and happy to be the first to address you as 'your Majesty.'"

"Well, this is an audacious and daring scheme of yours, Gabriel," commented the Duc de Guise.

But he did not give the least sign of irritation; on the contrary, his features wore a smile under their simulated expression of surprise.

"If it is an audacious scheme, it is a heart of extraordinary daring to which I propose it," replied Gabriel, firmly. "I speak for the good of France.

We need a great man for king. Is it not calamitous that all your ideas of grandeur and of conquest should be thus disgracefully impeded by the caprice of a wanton and the jealousy of a favorite? If you were once at the helm with unfettered hands, where would your genius stop? You would renew the glory of Charlemagne."

"You know the house of Lorraine can trace its descent from him!" said Le Balafré, eagerly.

"Who could doubt it after seeing you in action?" replied Gabriel. "Be in your turn another Hugh Capet for the Valois."

"Yes, but suppose I should be only a Constable de Bourbon?"

"You slander yourself, Monseigneur. The Constable de Bourbon called foreigners to his assistance,—foes they were too. You need make use of none but your own country's forces."

"But where are these forces, which, according to you, are at my disposal?" asked Le Balafré.

"Two parties are offered to you," was Gabriel's reply.

"Who are they, pray?—for you see I allow you to go on, as if all this were something more than a mere figment of your imagination. Who are these two parties?"

"The army and the Protestants, Monseigneur," Gabriel answered. "You have it in your power to assume the position of a military chieftain at once."

"A usurper!" exclaimed Le Balafré.

"Say a conqueror! But if you would prefer, Monseigneur, be the king of the Huguenots."

"How about the Prince de Condé?" said the duke, smiling.

"He is fascinating and clever, but you are great and brilliant. Do you suppose that Calvin would hesitate between you?—and there is no doubt that the son of the cooper of Noyon is the dictator of his party. Say one word, and to-morrow you have at your command thirty thousand Reformers."

"But I am a Catholic prince, Gabriel."

"Glory is the true religion of heroes like yourself, Monseigneur."

"I should involve myself in trouble at Rome."

"That will be an excuse for making yourself her master."

"Ah, my friend, my friend!" rejoined the duke, looking keenly at Gabriel, "you hate Henri II. bitterly!"

"As much as I love you, I confess," said the youth, with noble frankness.

"I prize your sincerity, Gabriel," said Le Balafré, with a more serious manner; "and to prove it to you, I will lay bare my heart to you."

"And my heart will close its door forever upon what you may confide to it."

"Listen, then," continued the duke. "I will confess that I have before now sometimes dreamed of this end which you suggest to me to-day. But I think you will agree with me, my friend, in this, that when one sets out with such a goal in view, he should at least be reasonably sure of reaching it, and that to hazard such a step prematurely is to invite destruction."

"True," replied Gabriel.

"Very well," the duke went on, "do you really consider that the time is ripe for the fulfilment of my ambition? Preparations for so momentous a stroke should be made long beforehand, and men's minds must be made up and ready to second them. Now, do you believe that the people have accustomed themselves in advance, so to speak, to the idea of a change of dynasty?"

"They are accustomed to it," said Gabriel.

"I doubt it," returned the duke. "I have commanded armies, have defended Metz and taken Calais, and have twice been lieutenant-general of the kingdom; but all that is not sufficient. I have not yet come near enough to royal power. Doubtless there are discontents, but factions are not a people. Henri II. is young, clever, and brave, and he is the son of François I. There is no such danger in delay as to make one dream of dispossessing him."

"And so you hesitate, Monseigneur?" asked Gabriel.

"I do more than that, my friend, I refuse," replied Le Balafré. "Ah, if Henri II. should die suddenly to-morrow, by accident or disease—"

"So he thinks of that as well!" said Gabriel to himself. "Well, Monseigneur, if that unexpected blow should fall, what would you do?" he continued aloud.

"Then," rejoined the duke, "with a young and inexperienced king, altogether under my influence, I would become in some sort the regent of the kingdom. And if the queen-mother or Monsieur le Connétable undertook to act in opposition to me; if the Protestants raised a revolution,—if, in short, the State should be in danger and needed a firm hand at the helm, opportunities would arise of themselves, and I should become almost necessary. In such a case your scheme might be very welcome, my friend, and I would gladly hearken to you."

"But until then," said Gabriel,—"until this very improbable death of the king?"

"I will resign myself to wait, my friend, and will content myself with preparations for the future. And if the seeds sown in my mind bear fruit only for my son, it will be because God so willed it."

"Is this your last word, Monseigneur?"

"It is my last word," replied the duke. "But I am no less grateful to you, Gabriel, for having had this confidence in my destiny."

"And I, Monseigneur, am grateful to you for having had so much confidence in my discretion."

"Yes," rejoined the duke; "it is understood that all that has passed between us is as if it had never been said."

"Now I will take my leave," said Gabriel, rising.

"What, already!" exclaimed the duke.

"Yes, Monseigneur, I have learned what I desired to know. I will remember your words; they are safely buried in my heart, yet I will remember them. Excuse me, but it was essential for me to ascertain whether the royal ambition of the Duc de Guise was still slumbering. Adieu, Monseigneur."

"*Au revoir*, my friend."

Gabriel left the Tournelles even more gloomy and anxious than when he had entered there.

"So," said he to himself, "both the human auxiliaries upon whom I thought I could rely have failed me. I have none but God to look to now!"

CHAPTER VII
A PERILOUS STEP

Diane de Castro in her apartments in the royal palace was meanwhile leading a miserable existence of grief and mortal terror.

Yet every tie was not broken that bound her to him who had loved her so dearly. Almost every week André the page was sent to the Rue des Jardins St. Paul, to make inquiries of Aloyse concerning Gabriel's welfare.

The information which he brought back to Diane was far from reassuring. The young Comte de Montgommery was always the same,— moody and anxious and gloomy. The good nurse could not speak of him that her eyes did not fill with tears, and her cheeks lose their color.

Diane hesitated fora long while. Finally, one morning during this same month of June she took a decided step in order to put an end to her dread.

She wrapped herself in a very modest cloak, hid her face under a veil, and left the Louvre at an hour when people were scarcely stirring there, accompanied by André alone, with the purpose of visiting Gabriel at his house.

Since he avoided her and made no sign, she would go to him.

Surely a sister might visit her brother! Indeed, was it not her duty to warn him or console him?

Unfortunately, all the courage which it had cost Diane to resolve upon that step was to be in vain.

Gabriel also selected the lonely hours of the early morning for his wanderings, which he had by no means abandoned; and when Diane knocked with trembling hand at the door of his house, he had already been gone more than half an hour.

Should she await his return? It was always uncertain, and a too long absence from the Louvre might expose Diane to slander.

But no matter; she determined to wait at least until the expiration of the time she had set aside for the visit.

She inquired for Aloyse, for she also desired to see her, and question her with her own lips.

André escorted his mistress into an unoccupied room, and went to inform the nurse.

Not for many years, not since the happy days of Montgommery and Vimoutiers, had Aloyse and Diane met,—the woman of the people and the daughter of the king.

Yet both their lives had been engrossed by the same thought, and anxiety upon the same subject still filled their days with dread, and robbed their nights of sleep.

So when Aloyse, coming hurriedly into the room, would have bowed low before Madame de Castro, Diane threw herself into the good woman's arms, and warmly embraced her, saying as she used to say in the old days,—

"Dear nurse!"

"What, Madame!" exclaimed Aloyse, moved to tears, "do you really remember me? Do you recognize me?"

"Do I remember you! do I recognize you!" returned Diane; "you might as well ask me if I remember Enguerrand's house, or if I would recognize the Château de Montgommery!"

Meanwhile Aloyse with clasped hands was looking at Diane more attentively.

"How beautiful you are!" she cried, sighing and smiling at once.

She smiled, for she had dearly loved the young girl who had developed into the beautiful lady before her. She sighed, for as she dwelt upon her lovely features she could better estimate Gabriel's wretchedness.

Diane understood this look, which was both melancholy and enraptured, and hastened to say, with a slight blush,—

"I have not come to talk of myself, nurse."

"Is it of him, then?" said Aloyse.

"Of whom else, pray? for to you I can lay bare my heart. How unfortunate that I did not find him! I came to console him and myself at the same time. How is he? Always dejected and despairing, is he not? Why has he not been once to the Louvre to see me? What does he say? What is he doing? Tell me, oh, pray tell me, nurse!"

"Alas! Madame," replied Aloyse, "you are quite right in thinking that he is dejected and despairing. Imagine—"

Diane interrupted her.

"Wait a moment, good Aloyse," said she; "before you begin I have a word to say. I could stay here till to-morrow listening to you, you know, without growing weary, or without noticing the flight of time. But I must return to the Louvre before my absence is noticed. So promise me one thing: when I have been here an hour, whether he has returned or not, tell me so, and send me away."

"But, Madame," said Aloyse, "I am quite capable of forgetting the hour myself, and I should not grow weary of talking to you any sooner than you would of listening to me, you see."

"What can we do, then?" asked Diane. "I dread the effect of our combined weakness."

"Let us intrust the difficult duty to some third person," said Aloyse.

"The very thing! André."

The page, who had remained in an adjoining room, undertook to rap at the door when an hour had passed.

"And now," said Diane, taking her seat by the nurse's side, "we can talk at our ease, and tranquilly, if not joyfully."

But this interview, though of the deepest interest to these two afflicted creatures, was nevertheless full of difficulty and bitterness.

In the first place, neither of them knew how far the other was cognizant of the terrible secrets of the Montgommery family.

Then, too, in what Aloyse did know of her young master's later life there were many troublesome matters which she was afraid to mention. In what way could she explain his long absences, his sudden returns, his preoccupation, and his silence?

At last, however, the good nurse did tell Diane all that she knew, — that is to say, all that she had seen; and Diane while listening to her doubtless experienced a delicious pleasure in hearing Gabriel spoken of, mingled though it was with deep grief at learning such sad news of him.

In truth, Aloyse's revelations were not of a nature calculated to calm Madame de Castro's apprehensions, but rather to rekindle them; for this earnest and impassioned witness of the young count's anguish and suffering brought vividly before Diane's mind all the torments by which his life was harassed.

Diane became more and more fully persuaded that if she wished to save those whom she loved it was high time for her to intervene.

An hour is quickly gone, no matter how painful the subject of conversation. Diane and Aloyse were startled and amazed when Andre's rap was heard at the door.

"What! already?" they cried in one breath.

"Well, be it so!" said Diane. "I am going to stay just a quarter of an hour longer."

"Be careful, Madame!" said the nurse.

"You are right, nurse; I must and will go now. But one word: in all that you have told me of Gabriel you have omitted—I mean, does he never speak of me?"

"Never, Madame, I must agree."

"Oh, it is better so!" sighed Diane.

"And he would do better still never even to think of you any more."

"Do you believe, nurse, that he does think of me, then?" asked Madame de Castro, eagerly.

"I am only too sure of it, Madame," said Aloyse.

"Nevertheless, he carefully avoids me; he even shuns the Louvre."

"If he does avoid the Louvre, Madame," said Aloyse, shaking her head, "it is not because of her whom he loves."

"I understand," thought Diane, shuddering; "it is because of him whom he hates.

"Oh!" she said aloud, "I must see him,—absolutely I must."

"Do you wish me, Madame, to tell him from you to go to the Louvre to seek you?"

"No, no,—not to the Louvre!" exclaimed Diane, in alarm. "Don't let him come to the Louvre! I will see—I will be on the lookout for another opportunity like this morning. I will come here again myself."

"But suppose that he has gone out again?" observed Aloyse. "What day will you come, what week,—can you tell at all? He will wait for you; have no fear of that."

"Alas!" said Diane, "poor king's child that I am, how can I say that at such a day or such an hour I shall be free? However, if it is possible, I will send André on before to warn him."

At this moment the page rapped a second time, fearful that he had not been heard before.

"Madame," he cried, "the streets and squares about the Louvre are beginning to be thronged."

"I am coming," replied Madame de Castro; "I am coming.

"Well, we must part, my good nurse," she continued. "Embrace me as you used to do when I was a child, you know, in the old, old happy days."

While Aloyse, unable to utter a word, held Diane close to her breast, —

"Oh, watch over him! take good care of him!" she said in the nurse's ear.

"As I did when he was a child, in the old, old happy days," said Aloyse.

"Oh, better, even better, Aloyse! In that time he was not in such sore need."

Diane left the house without having met Gabriel, and half an hour later she was safely in her apartments at the Louvre. But if she had no reason to feel disturbed at the result of the hazardous step she had taken, her anguish and dread on the subject of Gabriel's unknown designs were even greater than before.

The forebodings of a woman's loving heart are apt to be only too accurate forecasts of the future.

Gabriel did not return home until the day was well advanced. The heat was intense, and he was wearied in body and mind.

But when Aloyse uttered Diane's name and told of her visit, he stood erect with new life, his chest heaving and his heart throbbing.

"What did she want? What did she say? What did she do? Oh, why was I not here? Come, tell me everything, Aloyse, — every word, every movement."

He took his turn at questioning the nurse, hardly giving her time to reply.

"She wants to see me?" he cried. "She has something to say to me? And she doesn't know when she may be able to come again? Oh, Aloyse, Aloyse, I cannot wait in such uncertainty! surely you can see that. I shall go to the Louvre at once."

"To the Louvre! Oh, Heaven preserve us!" ejaculated Aloyse, in terror.

"Yes, to be sure," replied Gabriel, calmly. "I am not banished from the Louvre, so far as I know; and the man who had the honor of restoring Madame de Castro to liberty at Calais surely has the right to pay his respects to her in Paris."

"Of course," said Aloyse, trembling like a leaf; "but Madame de Castro was very particular to say that you were not to come to the Louvre to see her."

"Have I anything to fear there?" said Gabriel, proudly. "That would be one reason more for me to go."

"No," replied the nurse; "it was probably on her own account that Madame de Castro feared your coming."

"Her reputation would suffer much more from a secret and surreptitious action, if discovered, than from a public visit in broad daylight, such as I propose to pay,—such as I will pay her to-day, at this moment."

He called for a servant to bring him a change of clothes.

"But, Monseigneur," said poor Aloyse, at the end of her arguments, "Madame de Castro herself has remarked that you have shunned the Louvre hitherto. You have not thought best to go there once since your return."

"I have not been to see Madame de Castro because she has not summoned me," said Gabriel. "I have avoided the Louvre because I had no reason to go there; but to-day a feeling that I cannot resist urges me to go (although my action may result in nothing), for Madame de Castro wishes to see me. I have sworn, Aloyse, to allow my own will to slumber, and to leave everything to God and my destiny, and I am going to the Louvre at once."

Thus Diane's step bade fair to produce the opposite effect from that contemplated by her.

CHAPTER VIII
THE IMPRUDENCE OF PRECAUTION

Gabriel met with no opposition to his entrance to the Louvre. Since the taking of Calais the name of the young Comte de Montgommery had been heard too often for any one to think of refusing him leave to enter the suite of apartments occupied by Madame de Castro.

Diane, with one of her women, was engaged at the moment on some fancy-work. Very frequently she involuntarily let her hands fall in her lap, and would sit and dream about her interview with Aloyse that morning.

Suddenly André entered in great bewilderment.

"Madame, Monsieur le Vicomte d'Exmès!" he announced. (The boy had not ceased to call his old master by that name.)

"Who? Monsieur d'Exmès! here!" Diane repeated, overwhelmed.

"Yes, Madame, he is close behind me," said the page. "Here he is."

Gabriel appeared at the door, doing his best to control his emotion. He bowed low to Madame de Castro, who, in her confusion, did not at first return his salute.

However, she dismissed the page and her maid with a gesture, and they were left alone. Then they approached, and their hands met in a cordial grasp.

For some seconds they remained with hands joined, gazing at each other in silence.

"You thought best to come to my house, Diane," said Gabriel at last, in a deep voice. "You wished to see me, to speak with me; so I have hastened to you."

"Did it need that action on my part, Gabriel, to apprise you that I wanted to see you? Did you not know it well enough without that?"

"Diane," Gabriel replied with his sad smile, "I have given sufficient proofs of courage heretofore, so I may venture to confess that in coming to the Louvre, I am afraid."

"Afraid of whom?" asked Diane, who was herself afraid of the effect of her own question.

"Afraid of you!—of myself!" replied Gabriel.

"And that is why you chose rather to forget our former affection?—I speak of the legitimate and sanctified side of it," she hastened to add.

"I should have preferred to forget everything, I confess, Diane, rather than put foot inside the Louvre. But alas! I could not. And the proof—"

"The proof?"

"The proof is that I seek you always and everywhere; that though dreading your presence I would have given anything in the world to see you a moment in the distance. The proof is, too, that while prowling about Fontainebleau, or Paris, or St. Germain, around the royal châteaux, instead of desiring what I was supposed to be on the lookout for, it has been you, your sweet and lovely face, a sight of your dress among the trees, or on some terrace, that I have longed for and invoked and coveted! Last of all the proof lies in this fact: that you had only to take one step toward me to make me forget prudence, duty, terror, everything! And here I am in the Louvre, which I ought to shun. I reply to all your questions. I feel that all this is hazardous and insane, nevertheless I do it. Have I given you proof enough now, Diane?"

"Oh, yes, Gabriel, yes," said Diane, hastily, trembling with excitement and emotion.

"Ah, would to Heaven that I had been wiser," continued Gabriel, "and had adhered to my former resolution to see you no more, to flee from you if you summoned me, and to keep silence if you questioned me! That would have been much better for both of us, Diane, believe me. I knew what I was doing. I preferred to cause you anxiety rather than real grief. Oh, my God! why am I without power to withstand your voice and your look?"

Diane began to understand that she had really been wrong in her desire to be relieved from her mortal uncertainty. Every subject of conversation was painful for them, every question concealed a danger. Between these two beings whom God had created for happiness perhaps, there was no possibility of aught but doubt and peril and misery, thanks to the machinations of man.

But since Diane had thus challenged fate, she had no desire to avoid it; quite the contrary. She would go to the bottom of the abyss to which her anxiety had exposed her, though she were to find there nought but despair and death.

After a thoughtful silence, she began thus:—

"I was desirous to see you, Gabriel, for two reasons;

"I had an explanation to make to you in the first instance, as well as one to ask at your hands."

"Speak, Diane," replied Gabriel. "Lay bare my heart, and rend it at your will. It is yours."

"In the first place, Gabriel, I felt that I must let you know why, after I received your message, I did not at once assume the veil you sent back to me, and enter some convent immediately, as I expressed my intention of doing in our last sad interview at Calais."

"Have I reproached you in the least as to that, Diane?" returned Gabriel. "I told André to say to you that I gave you back your promise, and those were no mere empty words on my part; I meant what I said."

"I also mean to become a nun, Gabriel, and be sure that I have simply postponed carrying out my resolve."

"But why, Diane,—why renounce the world in which you were made to shine?"

"Set your mind at rest upon that point, dear friend; it is not altogether to remain faithful to the oath I took, but to satisfy the secret longing of my soul as well, that I intend to leave this world where I have suffered so bitterly. I must have peace and rest, and I know not now where to find either except with God. Do not envy me this last refuge."

"Oh, but I do envy you!" said Gabriel.

"But you see," continued Diane, "I have had a good reason for not at once carrying out my unalterable purpose; I wished to be sure that you gratified the request I made in my last letter,—that you forbore to make yourself judge and executioner; that you did not attempt to anticipate God's will."

"If one only could anticipate it!" muttered Gabriel.

"In short, I hoped," Diane went on, "that I might be able, in case of need, to throw myself between the two men whom I love, but who abhor each other; and who can say that I might not thus prevent a disaster, or a crime? Surely you do not blame me for such a thought as that, Gabriel?"

"I cannot blame an angel for doing what the angelic nature prompts, Diane. You have been very generous, but it is easy to understand it of you."

"Ah!" cried Madame de Castro, "how can I know that I have been generous, or to what extent I am generous now? I am wandering in darkness and at hazard! Besides, it is upon that very point that I wish to question you, Gabriel; for I desire to know my destiny in all its horror."

"Diane, Diane, it is a fatal curiosity!" said Gabriel.

"No matter!" replied Diane, "I will not live in this fearful perplexity and anxiety another day. Tell me, Gabriel, have you become convinced that I am really your sister, or have you absolutely lost all hope of ever learning the truth as to that strange secret? Tell me, I ask,—nay, I implore you!"

"I will tell you," said Gabriel, mournfully. "Diane, there is an old Spanish proverb which says that we must always be prepared for the worst. I have, therefore, accustomed myself, since our parting, to look upon you in my thoughts as my sister. But the truth is that I have obtained no new proof; only, as you say, I have no more hope, no more means of acquiring proof."

"God in Heaven!" cried Diane. "The—he who might furnish these proofs, was he no longer alive when you returned from Calais?"

"He was, Diane."

"Ah, I see, then, that the sacred promise made to you was not redeemed? Who, then, told me that the king had received you with wonderful favor?"

"All that was promised, Diane, was strictly performed."

"Oh, Gabriel, with what an ominous expression you say that! What fearful puzzle still underlies all this, Holy Mother of God!"

"You have asked me, Diane, and you shall know the whole," said Gabriel. "You shall share equally with me in my awful secret. And, indeed, I shall be glad to know what you think of what I am about to disclose to you,— whether, after you have heard it you will still persist in your clemency, and whether your tone and your features and your movements will not in any event belie the words of forgiveness which may come to your lips.—Listen."

"I listen in fear and trembling, Gabriel."

Thereupon, Gabriel, in a breathless, quivering voice, told Madame de Castro the whole sombre story: of the king's reception of him, and how Henri had again reaffirmed his promise; the remonstrances which Madame de Poitiers and the constable had seemed to be making to him; of the night of feverish anguish that he had passed; of his second visit to the Châtelet, his descent into the bowels of the pestilence-laden prison, and the lugubrious narrative of Monsieur de Sazerac,—in short, everything.

Diane listened without interrupting him, without an exclamation or a movement, as mute and rigid as a statue, her eyes fixed in their sockets, and her very hair fairly standing on end.

There was a long pause when Gabriel had finished his gloomy story. Then Diane tried to speak, but could not, for her tongue refused to perform its office. Gabriel seemed to feel a dreadful species of pleasure as he observed her anguish and her terror. At last, she succeeded in ejaculating,—

"Mercy for the king!"

"Ah!" cried Gabriel, "do you ask for mercy for him? Then you, too, must judge him guilty! Mercy? Ah, your very appeal is a condemnation! Mercy? He deserves death, does he not?"

"Oh, I did not say that," replied Diane, in dismay.

"Indeed you did say it, in effect! I see that you agree with me, Diane. You think and feel as I do. But we come to different conclusions in accordance with the difference in our natures. The woman pleads for mercy, and the man demands justice!"

"Ah!" cried Diane, "rash, insane creature that I am! Why did I tempt you to come to the Louvre?"

As she said these words some one rapped softly at the door.

"Who is there? What is wanted? *Mon Dieu!*" exclaimed Madame de Castro.

André partially opened the door.

"Excuse me, Madame," said he, "a message from the king."

"From the king!" echoed Gabriel, whose face lighted up.

"Why do you bring me this letter now, André?"

"Madame, they told me it was urgent."

"Very well, give it me. What does the king want of me? You may go, André. If there is any reply, I will call you."

André left the room. Diane broke the seal of the king's letter, and read in a low tone, and with increasing terror, what follows:—

> MY DEAR DIANE,—I am told that you are at the Louvre; do not go out, I beg you, until I have visited you in your apartments. I am at a sitting of the council which is likely to end at any moment. When I leave the council-chamber I will come immediately to you. Expect me very soon.
>
> It is a long while since I have seen you alone! I am in low spirits, and feel that I must have a few moments' talk with my beloved daughter. Farewell for the moment.

HENRI.

Diane, with colorless cheeks, crumpled the letter in her hands when she had read it.

What should she do?

Dismiss Gabriel at once? But suppose on his way out he should meet the king, who might arrive at any moment!

Should she keep the youth with her? The king would find him there when he came in.

To warn the king would excite his suspicion, while on the other hand to warn Gabriel would simply arouse his anger by seeming to dread it.

A meeting between these two men, each of whom was so threatening to the other, now appeared inevitable, and it was she herself, Diane, who would gladly shed her own blood to save them, who had brought about the fatal encounter!

"What does the king write to you, Diane?" asked Gabriel, with an assumed tranquillity which was belied by the trembling of his voice.

"Nothing, nothing, really," replied Diane. "A reminder of the reception this evening."

"Perhaps I discommode you, Diane," Gabriel remarked. "If so, I will go."

"No, no, don't go!" cried Diane, hastily. "But then," she continued, "if you have any business which demands your immediate attention elsewhere, I should not like to detain you."

"That letter has troubled you, Diane. I fear that I have wearied you, and will take my leave."

"You weary me, my friend! Can you believe it?" said Madame de Castro. "Was it not I who went in search of you, in some measure? Alas! I fear, very imprudently. I will see you again, but not here—at your own house. The first opportunity that presents itself for me to get away, I will come to see you, and resume this sweet though painful interview. I promise you. Rely upon me. At the moment, you are right, I confess; I am somewhat preoccupied and in pain. I feel as if I were in a burning fever—"

"I see, Diane, and I will leave you," replied Gabriel, sadly.

"We shall meet again soon, my friend," said she. "Now go, go!"

She accompanied him as far as the door.

"If I keep him here," she thought, "it is certain that he will see the king; if he goes away at once, there is at least a chance that they may not meet."

Yet she hesitated still, and was anxious and tremulous.

"Pardon me, Gabriel," said she, quite beside herself, as they stood on the threshold; "just a word more. *Mon Dieu*! Your narrative has upset me so that it is hard for me to collect my thoughts. What was I about to ask you? Ah, I know! Just one word, but one of much importance. You have not yet told me what you intend to do. I begged for mercy, and you cried, 'Justice!' Pray tell me how you hope to obtain justice!"

"I do not know yet," said Gabriel, gloomily; "I trust in God for the event and the opportunity."

"For the opportunity!" repeated Diane, with a shudder. "For the opportunity,—what do you mean by that? Oh, come back, come back! I cannot let you go, Gabriel, until you have explained to me that word 'opportunity;' stay, I implore you!"

Taking his hand, she led him back into the room.

"If he meets the king elsewhere," thought poor Diane, "they will be quite alone,—the king without attendants, and Gabriel with his sword at his side; whereas if I am present, I can at least throw myself between them, and implore Gabriel to withhold his hand, or intercept his blow. Yes, he must remain.

"I feel better now," said she, aloud. "Remain, Gabriel, and let us renew our conversation, and do you give me the explanation I ask. I am much better."

"No, Diane; you are even more excited than you were," replied Gabriel. "Do you know what has come into my mind as an explanation of your alarm?"

"No, indeed, Gabriel. How should I know?"

"Well," said Gabriel, "just as your cry for mercy was an avowal that the crime was patent in your eyes, so your present apprehensions show that you believe the chastisement would be legitimate. You dread my vengeance for the culprit; and since you appreciate the justice of it, you are keeping me here to warn him of possible reprisals on my part, which, though they might terrify and afflict you, would not astonish you,—which would, on the other hand, seem quite natural to you. Am I not right?"

Diane was startled, so truly had the blow struck home. Nevertheless, collecting all her force, she said,—

"Oh, Gabriel, how can you believe that I could conceive such thoughts of you? You, my own Gabriel, a murderer! you deal a blow from behind at one who could not defend himself! Impossible! It would be worse than a crime; it would be dastardly. Do you imagine that I am trying to keep you? Oh, no, far from it; go whenever you please, and I will open the door for you. I am perfectly calm; *mon Dieu*, yes!—perfectly calm upon this point at least. If anything worries me, it is no such idea as that, I assure you. Leave me, leave the Louvre, with your mind at rest. I will come again to your house to finish our conversation. Go, my friend, go! You see how anxious I am to keep you!"

As she spoke she had led him into the anteroom, where the page was in attendance. Diane thought of ordering him to stay with Gabriel until he had left the Louvre; but that precaution would have betrayed her suspicion.

However, she could not resist the impulse to call André to her side by a sign, and whisper in his ear,—

"Do you know if the council is at an end?"

"Not yet, Madame," replied André, beneath his breath. "I have not yet seen the councillors leave the hall."

"Adieu, Gabriel," resumed Diane, aloud, with much animation. "Adieu, my friend. You almost force me to send you away, to prove that I have no such object as you allege in keeping you here. Adieu!—but for only a short time."

"For only a short time," said the youth, with a melancholy smile, as he pressed her hand.

He left her: but she stood looking after him until the last door had closed behind him.

Then returning to her room, she fell upon her knees before her *prie-Dieu*, weeping bitterly, and with palpitating heart.

"O *mon Dieu, mon Dieu!*" she prayed, "in Jesus' name, watch over him who is perhaps my brother, as well as over him who is perhaps my father! Preserve the two beings whom I love, O my God! Thou alone canst do it now."

CHAPTER IX
OPPORTUNITY

In spite of her earnest efforts to prevent it, or rather because of those very efforts, events occurred as Madame de Castro had foreseen and dreaded.

Gabriel had gone from her presence sorrowful and agitated. Diane's fever had communicated itself to him in some measure, and clouded his eyes and confused his thoughts.

He passed mechanically down the stairways and along the familiar corridors of the Louvre, without paying much attention to exterior objects.

Nevertheless, as he was on the point of opening the door of the great gallery, he did remember that on his return from St. Quentin it was there that he had met Mary Stuart, and through the intervention of the young queen-dauphine had succeeded in reaching the king's presence, where the first fraud and humiliation had been practised upon him.

For he had not been deceived and outraged on one occasion only; several times had his enemies trampled upon his hope before its life was finally extinct. After he had first been made their dupe, he would have done well to expect similar treatment, and to have anticipated such exaggerated and cowardly interpretations of the letter of a sacred agreement.

While these irritating reminiscences were coursing through his brain, he opened the door and entered the gallery.

At the other end of the gallery, the corresponding door opened at the same moment.

A man entered.

It was Henri II., — Henri, the author of, or at least the principal accessory in, the foul and dastardly deception which had forever withered Gabriel's heart and poisoned his life.

The king came forward alone, unarmed and unattended.

The offender and the offended, for the first time since the perpetration of the outrage, found themselves face to face, alone, and scarcely one hundred feet apart,—a distance which could be traversed in twenty seconds with twenty steps.

We have said that Gabriel had stopped short, motionless and rigid as a statue,—like a statue of Vengeance or of Hatred.

The king halted, as he suddenly espied the man whom for nearly a year he had seen only in his dreams.

The two stood thus for a moment without moving, as if mutually fascinated by each other.

In the whirl of sensations and thoughts which filled Gabriel's brain, the poor fellow in his distraction could fix upon no course to adopt, and form no resolution. He waited.

As for Henri, despite his proved courage, the sensation that he experienced was beyond question fear; but at the humiliating thought he held his head erect, banished his first cowardly impulse, and made up his mind what to do.

To call fur help would have been to show fear; to retire as he had come would have been to flee.

He pursued his way toward the door, where Gabriel remained as if nailed to the spot.

Moreover, a superior force, a sort of irresistible and fatal fascination, urged him on toward the pale phantom who seemed to be waiting for him.

The perplexities of his destiny began to unfold themselves around him.

Gabriel experienced a species of blind, instinctive satisfaction as he saw him approach; but still he could not succeed in evolving any distinct thought from the clouds that obscured his intellect. He simply laid his hand upon the hilt of his sword.

When the king was within a few steps of Gabriel, the personal dread which he had previously thrust away seized him anew, and held his heart fast, as it were in a vice.

He said to himself in a vague way that his last hour had come, and that it was just.

However, his step did not falter. His feet seemed to carry him along of their own accord, and independently of his own dazed will. It is thus that somnambulists go about.

When he was directly in front of Gabriel, so that he could hear his quick breathing, and might touch him with his hand, he mechanically raised his hand to his velvet cap, and saluted the young count.

Gabriel did not acknowledge the salute. He maintained his marble-like attitude; and his hand, like that of a graven image, never left his sword.

In the king's eyes Gabriel was no longer a subject, but a messenger of God, before whom he must bow; while to Gabriel Henri was no longer a king, but a man, who had slain his father, and to whom he owed nothing but bitter hatred.

However, he allowed him to pass without doing aught, and without a word.

The king, on his part, did not move aside nor turn around nor express any feeling at such lack of respect.

When the door had closed between the two men, and the charm was broken, each of them awoke, as it were, rubbed his eyes, and asked himself, —

"Was it not a dream?"

Gabriel slowly left the Louvre. He did not regret the lost opportunity, nor did he repent that he had allowed it to escape him.

He felt a sort of confused joy.

"My prey is coming to me," he thought; "already he is fluttering around my nets, and getting within reach of my spear."

He slept that night more soundly than he had done for a long while.

The king, however, was not so tranquil. He went on to Diane's apartments, where she was expecting him, and welcomed him with such transports of delight as we can imagine.

But Henri was absorbed and restless. He did not venture to speak of the Comte de Montgommery, although he fancied that Gabriel was doubtless coming from his daughter's apartments when they met. However, he did not choose to touch that chord; therefore, while he had set out to pay Diane this visit in a spirit of effusive affection and confidence, he maintained from beginning to end an air of suspicion and constraint.

He then returned to his own apartments, sad and gloomy. He felt displeased with himself and others, and his sleep that night was very troubled and broken.

It seemed to him that he was becoming involved in a labyrinth from which he should never come out alive.

"However," he said to himself, "I offered myself to that man's sword to-day in a measure; so it is evident that he does not wish to kill me."

The king, in order to distract his thoughts and seek forgetfulness for his troubles, determined to leave Paris for a time. During the days immediately following his encounter with the Comte de Montgommery, he went successively to St. Germain, Chambord, and Madame de Poitiers's Château d'Anet.

Toward the close of the month of June he was at Fontainebleau.

He was constantly moving about, and had the appearance of a man wishing to drown his trouble in motion and noise and excitement.

The approaching fêtes in connection with his daughter Élisabeth's marriage with Philip II. afforded an excuse as well as opportunity for this feverish need of continual action.

At Fontainebleau he desired to entertain the Spanish ambassador with the spectacle of a great hunt in the forest, and it was appointed to take place on the 23d of June.

The day broke hot and threatening, and the weather became very tempestuous.

Nevertheless Henri did not countermand the orders he had given, for the excitement would surely be no less in a storm.

He selected the fleetest and highest-mettled horse in his stables, and followed the hunt with a sort of fury; and it happened at one time that carried away by his own ardor and the temper of his horse, he outstripped all his companions, lost sight of the hunt completely, and missed his way in the forest.

Clouds were piling up in the sky, and ominous rumblings were heard in the distance. The storm was about to break.

Henri, leaning forward upon his foaming steed, whose headlong pace he made no attempt to slacken, but on the contrary, urging him on with voice and spur, rode on and on, more swiftly than the wind, among the trees and rocks; the dizzy gallop seemed to suit his humor, for he laughed loud and long.

For a few moments he had forgotten his troubles.

Suddenly his horse reared in terror; a dazzling flash lighted up the sky, and the sudden apparition of one of those huge white rocks which abound in the forest of Fontainebleau, towering aloft at a corner of the path, had startled him.

A loud peal of thunder increased twofold the fear of the skittish animal. He bounded forward, and the sudden movement broke the rein close to the bit, so that Henri entirely lost control.

Then began a furious, fearful mad race.

The horse, with mane erect, foaming flanks, and rigid legs, shot through the air like an arrow.

The king, clinging to the animal's neck to save himself from falling, his hair on end, and his clothes blowing about in the wind, vainly tried to seize the rein, which would have been of no use in his hands.

Any one seeing the horse and his rider pass thus in the tempest would have infallibly taken them for a vision from the infernal regions, and would have thought only of exorcising the evil spirit with the sign of the cross.

But no one was at hand; not a living soul, not an inhabited dwelling. That last chance of safety which the presence of a fellow-man affords to one in peril was lacking to this anointed horseman.

Not a woodcutter, not a beggar, not a poacher, not even a thief, to save this crowned king!

The pouring rain, and the more and more frequent peals of thunder, ever nearer at hand, drove the maddened steed to an even more headlong and terrific pace.

Henri, with staring eyes, tried in vain to recognize the path along which the fatal race was being run. At last he did succeed in fixing his position at a certain cleared space among the trees, and then he fairly shook with terror, for the path led straight to the summit of a steep rock, whose perpendicular wall overhung a deep chasm, a veritable abyss!

The king did his utmost to stop the horse with his hand and voice, but to no purpose.

To throw himself from the saddle was to break his neck against some tree-trunk or granite bowlder, and it was better not to resort to that desperate measure until the last moment.

In any event Henri felt that he was lost, and full of remorse and dread, was already commending his soul to God.

He did not know at just what part of the path he was, or whether the precipice was close at hand or at some distance; but he must be ready, and he was just about to let himself to the ground, at all hazards.

At this moment, as he cast a last look about him in all directions, he saw a man at the end of the path, mounted like himself, but standing beneath the shelter of an oak.

At that distance he could not recognize the man, whose features and form, in addition, were hidden by a long cloak and a broad-rimmed hat. But it was doubtless some gentleman who had lost his way in the forest, as he himself had done.

At last Henri felt that his safety was assured. The path was narrow, and the stranger had only to move his horse forward a step or two to block the king's passage; or by simply reaching out his hand he might stop him in his headlong course.

Nothing could be easier; and even though there were some risk attending it, the unknown, on recognizing the king, ought not to think twice about incurring the risk to save his master.

In less than one twentieth of the time it has taken to read these words, the three or four hundred paces which separated Henri from his rescuer had been traversed.

Henri, to attract attention, uttered a cry of distress and waved his hand. The stranger saw him, and made a movement; he was doubtless making ready.

But oh, in terror's name! although the maddened horse passed directly before the unknown horseman, he failed to make the slightest attempt to stop him.

Indeed, it seemed as if he fell back somewhat, to avoid any possible contact.

The king uttered a second cry, no longer appealing and imploring, but of rage and despair.

However, he thought that the iron feet of his horse seemed to be now striking on stone, and not on the sod. He had arrived at the fatal precipice.

He whispered the name of God, released his foot from the stirrup, and let himself fall to the ground, at every risk.

The rebound carried him some fifteen paces away; but miraculously, as it appeared, he fell upon a little mound of moss and grass, and sustained no injury. It was full time! Less than twenty feet away was the sheer precipice.

The poor horse, amazed at being thus relieved of his burden, gradually lessened his pace, so that when he reached the edge of the chasm, he had time to measure its width, and instinctively threw himself upon his haunches, with flaming eyes and disordered mane, and foam flying from his distended nostrils.

But if the king had been still upon his back, the shock of his sudden stop would surely have thrown him into the abyss.

Having offered a fervent prayer of thanksgiving to God, who had so evidently protected him, and having soothed and remounted his horse, his first thought was to hasten back and vent his anger upon the wretch who would so basely have left him to die, except for the intervention of God.

The stranger had remained in the same spot, still motionless beneath the folds of his black cloak.

"Wretch!" cried the king, when he had approached within ear-shot. "Did you not see the danger I was in? Did you not recognize me, regicide? And even though it were not your king, ought you not to rescue any man in such peril of his life, when you have only to stretch out your arm to do it, miscreant?"

The stranger did not move, nor did he reply; he simply raised his head slightly, which was shaded from Henri's eyes by his broad felt hat.

The king recoiled as he recognized the pale and dejected features of Gabriel. He said no more, but muttered to himself, lowering his head, —

"The Comte de Montgommery! Then I have nothing more to say."

And without another word, he put spurs to his horse and galloped off into the forest.

"He would not kill me," he said to himself, seized with a death-like tremor; "but it seems that he would let me die."

Gabriel, once more alone, repeated with a gloomy smile, —

"I feel that my prey is coming nearer, and the hour is approaching."

CHAPTER X
BETWEEN TWO DUTIES

The marriage contracts of Élisabeth and Marguerite de France were to be signed at the Louvre on the 28th of June, and the king returned to Paris on the 25th, more cast down and preoccupied than ever.

Especially since Gabriel's last appearance, his life had become a torment to him. He avoided being left alone, and constantly sought means of banishing temporarily the sombre thought by which he was possessed, so to speak.

But he had not mentioned that second encounter to a single soul; he was at once anxious and afraid to unbosom himself on the subject to some devoted and faithful heart; for he himself no longer knew what to think or what course to adopt, and the fearful thought which haunted him had thrown his mind into utter confusion.

Finally he determined to open his heart to Diane de Castro.

Diane had surely seen Gabriel again, he said to himself; there was no question that the young count had just left her when he encountered him the first time, so that Diane might possibly know his plans. In that case, she could and she ought either to set her father's mind at rest or to warn him; and Henri, despite the bitter doubts with which he was ceaselessly assailed, did not believe his beloved daughter capable of treachery toward him, or of conniving at it.

A mysterious instinct seemed to whisper to him that Diane was no less anxious than he. In fact, Diane de Castro, although she knew nothing of the two strange meetings which had taken place between the king and Gabriel, was equally ignorant as to what had become of the latter during the last few days. André, whom she had despatched several times to the house in the Rue des Jardins St. Paul to learn something of Gabriel's movements, had brought her no information. He had disappeared from Paris again. We have seen him haunting the king at Fontainebleau.

In the afternoon of June 26 Diane was sitting pensively in her apartments, quite alone, when one of her women came hurriedly in to announce the king.

Henri's face wore its ordinary grave expression. After the first greetings, he plunged at once into the matter in hand, as if to throw off his troublesome anxiety at the first opportunity.

"Dear Diane," said he, gazing intently into his daughter's eyes, "it is a long time since we have spoken together of Monsieur d'Exmès, who has now taken the title of Comte de Montgommery. It is a long time also since you have seen him, is it not? Tell me."

Diane at Gabriel's name turned pale and shuddered.

"Sire," she replied, "I have seen Monsieur d'Exmès once only since my return from Calais."

"Where did you see him, Diane?" asked the king.

"At the Louvre, Sire, in this very room."

"About a fortnight ago, was it not?"

"I should think it was about that time, Sire," replied Madame de Castro.

"I suspected as much," returned the king.

He paused a moment, as if to rearrange his ideas.

Diane observed him attentively and fearfully, trying to divine the purpose of his unexpected question.

But Henri's serious expression seemed impenetrable.

"Excuse me, Sire," she said, mustering all her courage. "May I venture to ask your Majesty why, after your long silence as to him who saved me from disgrace at Calais, you have done me the honor to pay me this visit to-day, and at this hour, expressly, I should judge, to interrogate me about him?"

"Do you wish to know, Diane?" asked the king.

"Sire, I am so bold," she replied.

"Very well, then, you shall know all," said Henri; "and I pray that my confidence may invite and induce yours. You have often told me that you loved me, my child."

"I have said it, and I say it again, Sire," cried Diane: "I love you as my sovereign, my benefactor, and my father."

"Therefore I may reveal everything to my loyal and loving daughter," said the king; "so listen, Diane."

"I listen with all my soul, Sire."

Henri then described his two encounters with Gabriel,—the first in the gallery of the Louvre, and the other in the forest of Fontainebleau. He told Diane of the strange demeanor, as of mute rebellion, which the young man had adopted, and how on the first occasion he had declined to raise his hand to salute his king, and the second time had declined to raise his hand to save his life.

Diane at this recital could not conceal her grief and her alarm. The conflict which she so dreaded between Gabriel and the king had already manifested itself on two occasions, and might soon appear again in a still more dangerous and terrible form.

Henri, affecting not to notice his daughter's emotion, ended with these words:—

"These are serious offences, are they not, Diane? They almost amount to *lèse-majesté*! And yet I have concealed these insults from everybody, and dissembled my indignation, because this young man has really suffered at my hands in the past, notwithstanding the glorious service he has rendered my kingdom, which ought doubtless to have been rewarded much more generously." Fixing a piercing glance upon Diane, the king continued,—

"I do not know, Diane, nor do I wish to know, whether you have been made acquainted with the wrong I have done Monsieur d'Exmès; I only wish you to feel that my silence has been due to my appreciation of that wrong and my regret for it. But is it not imprudent for me to maintain silence? Do not these outrages give warning of others more flagrant still? Ought I not to have an eye to Monsieur d'Exmès? Upon these points I have come, Diane, to ask for your friendly advice."

"I am grateful for your confidence in me, Sire," replied Diane, sorrowfully, being thus forced to choose between the duty which she owed respectively to the two men who were dearest to her on earth.

"It is a very natural confidence, Diane," the king returned. "Well?" he added, observing that his daughter seemed to be at a loss.

"Well, Sire," replied Diane, with an effort, "I think that your Majesty is right, and that for you to take some notice of Monsieur d'Exmès's movements will perhaps be the wisest course you can adopt."

"Do you think, then, Diane, that my life is in danger from him?" asked Henri.

"Oh, I did not say that, Sire!" cried Diane, warmly. "But Monsieur d'Exmès seems to have been wounded to the quick, and there may be danger perhaps—"

Poor Diane stopped abruptly, quivering with the torture she was undergoing, the perspiration standing on her forehead in great beads. This species of denunciation, which her moral sense had almost torn from her, was very repugnant to her noble heart.

But Henri put a wholly different construction upon her very evident distress.

"I understand you, Diane," said he, rising and pacing heavily to and fro. "Yes, I foresaw it clearly. You see I must be suspicious of this young man; but to live with this Damocles's sword forever hanging over my head is impossible. The obligations of kings are not the same as those by which other gentlemen are governed. I propose to take effective measures to protect myself against Monsieur d'Exmès."

He walked toward the door as if to leave the room, but Diane threw herself in his path.

What, Gabriel to be accused and perhaps imprisoned! And it was she, Diane, who had betrayed him! She could not abide the thought. After all, Gabriel's words had not been so full of menace.

"Sire, one moment, pray!" she cried. "You are mistaken; I swear that you are mistaken! I have not said a word to imply that your doubly sacred head is in danger. Nothing in Monsieur d'Exmès's confidences could ever make me suspect him capable of crime. Otherwise, great God! would I not have told you everything?"

"Very true," said Henri, stopping once more; "but what did you mean to say, then, Diane?"

"I meant to say simply that I thought it would be well for your Majesty to avoid as far as possible these vexatious encounters where an offended subject is enabled to show his forgetfulness of the respect due to his king. But a regicide's failure to show respect is a very different matter. Sire, would it be worthy of you to try to remedy one unjust act by another equally iniquitous?"

"No, surely not; I had no such intention," said the king; "and I have proved it by keeping these occurrences to myself. Since you have dissipated my suspicions, Diane; since you will answer for my bodily safety to your own conscience and before God; and since in your opinion I may be perfectly tranquil—"

"Tranquil!" Diane interrupted with a shudder. "Ah, I didn't go so far as that, Sire. With what a terrible load of responsibility you overwhelm me! On the contrary, your Majesty ought to be careful and on your guard—"

"No," said the king, "I cannot live in a condition of never-ending dread and apprehension. For two weeks I have entirely ceased to enjoy life. This state of affairs must come to an end. One of two things must happen: either trusting in your word, Diane, I shall go tranquilly on with my life, thinking of the welfare of my realm, and not of my enemy,—in short, without troubling myself further about Vicomte d'Exmès; or I shall see that this man who bears me ill-will is put where he can no longer injure me, by giving information of his outrages; and since I occupy too proud and lofty a position to defend myself, I shall leave that task to those whose duty it is to safeguard my person."

"And who are they, Sire?" asked Diane.

"Why, Monsieur de Montmorency, first of all, as constable and commander-in-chief of the army."

"Monsieur de Montmorency!" echoed Diane, with an accent of horror.

That detested name at once recalled to her mind all the misfortunes of Gabriel's father, his long and harsh captivity, and his death. If Gabriel in turn should fall into the constable's hands, a like fate was in store for him, and his destruction was certain.

In her imagination Diane saw him whom she had loved so dearly immured in a dungeon without light or air, and dying there in one night, or, more fearful still, lingering on for twenty years, and dying at the last cursing God and man, but more than all Diane the traitress, who with her equivocal and hesitating words had basely betrayed him.

There was no proof that Gabriel wished to slay the king, or would be able to do it, while there was no room for doubt that the bitter enmity of Monsieur de Montmorency would have no mercy on Gabriel.

Diane went over all this in her mind in a few seconds, and when the king finally propounded the direct question to her,—

"Well, Diane, what advice do you give me? Since you are better able than I to form an opinion as to the perils which beset my path, your word shall be my law. Ought I to think no more about Monsieur d'Exmès, or ought I, on the other hand, to busy myself with him exclusively?"

She replied in an agony of terror at his last words, "I have no other counsel to offer your Majesty than that of your own conscience. If any other than a man whom you had offended, Sire, had failed to show proper respect to you, or had basely abandoned you when in danger of your life, you would not, I fancy, have come to ask my advice as to the fit punishment to be meted out to the culprit. Therefore some very weighty motive must have constrained your Majesty to adopt a policy of silence which seems to imply forgiveness. Now I confess that I can see no reason why you should not continue to act as you have begun; for it seems to me that if Monsieur d'Exmès had been capable of meditating a crime against you, he could hardly have expected two fairer opportunities than those which were offered him in a lonely gallery in the Louvre, and in the forest of Fontainebleau on the edge of a precipice—"

"You need say no more, Diane," said Henri; "and I will not ask you another question. You have banished a serious anxiety from my heart, and I thank you sincerely for it, my dear child. Let us say no more about this. Now I shall be able to devote my thoughts freely to our approaching marriage festivities. I desire that they shall be magnificent, and that you shall be as magnificent as they. Diane, do you hear?"

"I beg your Majesty to excuse me," said Diane; "but I was just about to ask leave to absent myself from these festivities. I should much prefer, if I must confess it, to remain here by myself."

"What!" exclaimed the king; "but do you know, Diane, that this will be truly a royal display? There will be games and tournaments, all on the most splendid scale, and I myself shall be one of those who hold the lists against all comers. What pressing affairs can you have to keep you away from such superb spectacles, my darling daughter?"

"Sire," replied Diane, in a tone of the utmost gravity, "I have to pray."

A few minutes later the king quitted Madame de Castro, with his heart relieved of part of its anguish.

But alas! he left poor Diane with so much the more anguish at her heart.

CHAPTER XI
OMENS

The king, thenceforth almost free from the anxiety which had weighed upon him, urged on most energetically the preparations for the magnificent fêtes which he proposed to provide for his fair city of Paris, on the occasion of the happy marriages of his daughter Élisabeth with Philip II., and his sister Marguerite with the Duke of Savoy.

Very happy marriages, in sooth, and which surely deserved to be celebrated with such rejoicing and splendor. The author of Don Carlos has told us so well that we need not repeat it, what was the result of the first. We shall see to what the preliminaries of the other led.

The contract of marriage between Philibert Emmanuel and Marguerite de France was to be signed on the 28th of June.

Henri caused the announcement to be made that on that and the two following days there would be lists open at the Tournelles for tilting and other knightly sports.

And upon the pretext of paying a higher compliment to the bride and groom, but really to gratify his own intense passion for sport of that nature, the king declared that he would himself be among the challengers.

But on the morning of the 28th the queen, Catherine de Médicis, who at that time scarcely ever showed herself in public, sent an urgent request to the king for an interview with him.

Henri, we need not say, acquiesced at once in his wife's desire.

Catherine thereupon entered his apartment in much emotion.

"Ah, dear Sire," she exclaimed as soon as she saw him, "in Jesus' name, I implore you not to leave the Louvre until the end of this month of June."

"Why so, Madame, pray?" asked Henri, amazed at this unexpected request.

"Sire, because you are threatened by great peril during these last few days."

"Who has told you that?" demanded the king.

"Your star, Sire, which appeared last night in an observation made by myself and my Italian astrologer, with most threatening indications of danger,—of mortal danger!"

We must know that Catherine de Médicis about this time began to devote herself to those magical and astrological practices which very rarely deceived her in the whole course of her life, if we may trust the memoirs of the time.

But Henri was a confirmed scoffer in this matter of reading the stars, and he smilingly replied to the queen,—

"Well, Madame, if my star portends danger, it may come to me here as well as elsewhere."

"No, Sire," Catherine replied; "it is beneath the vault of heaven and in the open air that peril awaits you."

"Really!—a tempest perhaps?" said Henri.

"Sire, do not joke about such things!" retorted the queen. "The stars are the written word of God."

"Well, then, we must agree," said Henri, "that the divine handwriting is generally very obscure and confused."

"How so, Sire?"

"The erasures seem to me to make the text unintelligible, so that each one may decipher it almost to suit himself. You have read, Madame, in the celestial conjuring book, as you say, that my life is threatened if I quit the Louvre?"

"Yes, Sire."

"Very well. Now, Forcatel only last month saw something very different there. You think highly of Forcatel, Madame, I believe?"

"Yes," said the queen; "he is a learned man, who has already learned to read in the book where we are just beginning to spell."

"Know, then, Madame," rejoined the king, "that Forcatel read for me in these stars of yours this beautiful verse, which has no other fault except that it is utterly unintelligible:—"

"'If this is not Mars, dread his image.'"

"In what does that prediction weaken the one I have told you of?" asked Catherine.

"Just wait, Madame!" said Henri: "I have somewhere the nativity which was cast for me last year. Do you remember what destiny it foretold for me?"

"Very indistinctly, Sire."

"According to that horoscope, Madame, it is written in the stars that I shall die in a duel! Surely, that would be a rare and novel experience for a king. But a duel, in my humble opinion, is not the image of Mars, but the god himself."

"What is your conclusion from that, Sire?"

"Why, this, Madame: that since all these prophecies are contradictory and inconsistent, the surest way is to have no faith in any of them. The deceitful things give one another the lie, you can see yourself."

"So your Majesty will persist in leaving the Louvre during the next few days?"

"Under any other circumstances I should be most happy, Madame, to gratify you by remaining with you; but I have promised and publicly announced that I would be present at these festivities; so I must attend them."

"At all events, Sire, you will not enter the lists, will you?"

"There, again, my pledged word requires me, to my great regret, to refuse you, Madame. But what possible danger can there be for me in these sports? I am grateful to you from the bottom of my heart for your solicitude; yet let me assure you that your fears are altogether imaginary, and that to yield to them would be to imply a false belief that danger could possibly attend this courtly, good-natured jousting, which I by no means propose to have done away with on my account."

"Sire," rejoined Catherine, "I am accustomed to give way to your will, and to-day again I resign myself, but with grief and alarm at my heart."

"You will come to the Tournelles, Madame, will you not?" said the king, kissing Catherine's hand, — "were it for no other object than to applaud my prowess with the lance and convince yourself of the absurdity of your fears."

"I will obey you to the end," replied the queen, as she withdrew.

Along with all the court, except Diane de Castro, Catherine was present at the first day's tilting, where throughout the day the king crossed lances with all comers.

"Well, Madame, the stars seem to have been mistaken," he said jokingly to the queen in the evening.

Catherine sadly shook her head.

"Alas!" said she, "the month of June is not yet at an end."

The second day, the 29th, likewise passed off equally uneventfully. Henri did not leave the lists; and his good fortune was in proportion to his daring.

"You see, Madame, that the stars proved deceptive as to this day also," he again observed to Catherine, when they returned to the Louvre.

"Ah, Sire, now I only dread the third day!" cried the queen.

The last day of the tournament, June 30, was Friday, and was intended to be the most brilliant and splendid of the three, and to bring the festivities to a fitting close.

The four challengers were—

The king, who wore a white and black favor,—the colors of Madame de Poitiers;

The Duc de Guise, who wore white and pink;

Alphonse d'Este, Duc de Ferrare, who wore yellow and red; and

Jacques de Savoie, Duc de Nemours, whose colors were black and yellow.

Says Brantôme:—

> "These four princes were the most skilful knights who could be found at that time, not in France alone, but in all countries. Thus on that day they performed prodigies of valor; and it was impossible to know to whom the palm should be awarded, although the king was one of the best and most expert horsemen in his realm."

Fortune seemed to divide her favors with impartial hand among these four dexterous and renowned challengers; and as course succeeded course, and the day drew to its close, it was hard to say to which of them the honor of the tournament belonged.

Henri was throughout in an almost feverish state of excitement. He was in his element in all such sports and passages-at-arms; and he was quite as eager to be victorious on such occasions as on a real battle-field.

However, the evening came on apace, and the trumpets and clarions sounded the signal for the last course.

It was Monsieur le Duc de Guise's turn to hold the lists, and he did it in such knightly fashion as to win hearty applause from the ladies and the assembled multitude.

Then the queen, who began to breathe freely once more, rose from her seat.

It was the signal for departure.

"What! is everything over?" cried the excited and jealous king. "Wait, Mesdames, wait a moment! Is it not my turn to run a course?"

Monsieur de Vieilleville reminded the king that he had opened the lists; that the four challengers had all run the same number of courses: that they had all met with equal success, to be sure, and no one could be declared victor, but that the lists were closed and the day at an end.

"What!" retorted Henri, impatiently; "if the king is the first to enter the lists, he should be the last to leave them. I do not choose that the day should end in this way. See, there are still two unbroken lances."

"But there are no more assailants, Sire," replied Monsieur de Vieilleville.

"I beg your pardon," said the king; "do you not see that man who has kept his visor down all the time, and has not yet run? Who is it, Vieilleville?"

"Sire, I don't know,—I had not noticed him."

"Monsieur," said Henri, approaching the unknown, "you will, if you please, break this last lance with me."

The individual addressed did not reply for a moment, but at last in a deep and solemn voice, which he struggled to control, he said,—

"I beg your Majesty to allow me to decline this honor."

The tone of his voice caused Henri, without knowing why, to feel a strange uneasiness mingled with his feverish excitement.

"Allow you to decline! no, I cannot allow that, Monsieur," said he, with a gesture of nervous anger.

Then the stranger silently raised his visor.

For the third time within a fortnight, the king saw the pale and dejected countenance of Gabriel de Montgommery.

CHAPTER XII
THE FATAL JOUST

At sight of the solemn and ominous features of the young count, the king felt an involuntary tremor of surprise, perhaps of terror, which set every nerve quivering.

But he would not confess to himself, still less let others observe that first shudder, which he at once repressed. His heart reacted against his instinct; and just because he had been afraid for one second, he afterward exhibited a degree of courage which amounted to recklessness.

Gabriel said again in his slow, grave tones, —

"I implore your Majesty not to persist in your desire!"

"Nevertheless I do persist in it, Monsieur de Montgommery," the king replied.

His perception being obscured by so many contending emotions, Henri imagined that he could detect a sort of challenge in Gabriel's words, and the tone in which they were uttered. Alarmed by the sudden return of that anxious feeling which Diane de Castro had relieved temporarily, he bore up vigorously against his weakness, and determined to have done with this dastardly terror, which he deemed unworthy of himself, — Henri II., a son of France, and a king!

Therefore he said to Gabriel with a firmness that was almost overdone, —

"Make your preparations, Monsieur, to run a course against me."

Gabriel, whose whole being was in as confused and overwrought a state as that of the king, bowed without replying.

At that moment, Monsieur de Boisy, the grand equerry, approached the king and said to him that the queen had sent him to implore his Majesty to tilt no more that day for love of her.

"Say to the queen," replied Henri, "that it is just for love of her that I am going to run this one course."

Turning to Monsieur de Vieilleville, he said, —

"Come, Monsieur de Vieilleville, put on my armor at once."

In his preoccupation, he demanded from Monsieur de Vieilleville a service which was an attribute of the office of Monsieur de Boisy, the grand equerry, and Monsieur de Vieilleville in his surprise respectfully reminded him of that fact.

"To be sure!" said the king, putting his hand to his forehead. "What has become of my brains, I wonder?"

He met Gabriel's cold and statue-like glance, and continued impatiently, —

"But no, I was right. Was it not Monsieur de Boisy's place to finish his commission from the queen, by reporting my words to her? I knew perfectly well what I was doing and what I said! Give me my armor, Monsieur de Vieilleville."

"That being so, Sire," said Monsieur de Vieilleville, "and since your Majesty is absolutely determined to break one lance more, I beg to remind you that it is my turn to run against you, and I claim my right. In fact, Monsieur de Montgommery did not present himself at the opening of the lists, and only entered when he believed them closed."

"You are right, Monsieur," said Gabriel, earnestly; "and I will gladly withdraw, and give place to you."

But in the count's eagerness to shun the combat with him, the king persisted in fancying that he detected the insulting reflections of an enemy upon his courage.

"No, no!" he replied, stamping his foot on the ground. "It is against Monsieur de Montgommery and no other that I propose to run this course, and there has been enough delay! Give me my armor."

He met the count's fixed, stern gaze with a proud and haughty glance, and without more words he put his head forward that Monsieur de Vieilleville might adjust his casque.

Clearly his destiny had blinded him.

Monsieur de Savoie came to renew Catherine de Médicis's entreaties that the king would leave the field.

As Henri did not trouble himself to reply to these urgent representations, the duke added in a low tone, —

"Madame Diane de Poitiers, Sire, also asked me to warn you secretly to be on your guard against him with whom you are to dispute this bout."

At Diane's name, Henri started in spite of himself, but again he repressed his emotion.

"Shall I show myself a craven, then, before my beloved?" he asked himself.

And he maintained the dignified silence of one who is importuned to depart from an unalterable resolution.

Meanwhile, Monsieur de Vieilleville, while adjusting his armor, took occasion to say to him beneath his breath, —

"Sire, I swear by the living God that for three nights I have dreamed of nothing but that some mishap would befall you to-day, and that this last day of June would be a fatal one for you." [4]

But the king did not appear to have heard him; he was already armed, and he seized his lance.

Gabriel was handed his, and also entered the lists.

The two combatants mounted their horses and took the field.

A deep, awful silence pervaded the entire assemblage; all eyes were so intent upon the spectacle before them that breathing seemed almost to be suspended.

However, the constable and Diane de Castro being absent, every one in that vast throng, except Madame de Poitiers, was in ignorance of the fact that there were between the king and the Comte de Montgommery any causes of enmity or any wrongs to be avenged. No one clearly foreboded a bloody issue to a mock combat. The king, accustomed to these sports unattended with danger, had shown himself in the arena a hundred times within three days, under conditions which apparently differed in no respect from those existing at this moment.

And yet there was a vague sensation of something awe-inspiring and out of the common course in this adversary who had remained shrouded in mystery until the very end, in his significant reluctance to enter the lists, — likewise in the king's stubborn obstinacy; and in the face of this unknown danger, every one waited in breathless silence. Why? No one could have told. But a stranger arriving at that moment, and observing the expression on every face, would have said, —

"Some critical event is about to take place."

There was terror in the very air.

One extraordinary circumstance demonstrated clearly the sinister complexion of the thoughts of the throng.

In ordinary combats, and as long as they lasted, the clarions and trumpets never ceased their deafening flourishes. They were the very incarnation of the spirit of enjoyment that pervaded the tournament.

But when the king and Gabriel entered the lists, the trumpets suddenly, as if by common consent, were still; not a sound was to be heard from one of them, and the pervading horrified expectancy became doubly painful in that unwonted silence.

The two champions felt even more than the spectators the influence of these extraordinary tokens of disquiet which seemed to fill the air, so to speak.

Gabriel no longer thought or saw,—in fact, he hardly breathed. He went on mechanically and as if in a dream, doing by instinct what he had formerly done under similar circumstances, but guided in some measure by a secret and potent will, which surely was not his own.

The king was even more passive and lost in abstraction than he. He also seemed to have a sort of cloud before his eyes, and had the appearance of acting and moving in a mental phantasmagoria, which was neither reality nor a dream.

Every now and then a ray of light shone in upon his brain, so that he reviewed clearly and all at once the predictions which the queen had made two days before, as well as those of his horoscope, and those of Forcatel. Suddenly, by the help of some awe-inspiring gleam of intelligence, he understood the meaning and the correlation of all those ominous auguries. A cold sweat bathed him from head to foot. For an instant he felt an almost irresistible impulse to give up the combat and leave the lists; but the thousands of eyes that were gazing eagerly upon him nailed him to his place.

Moreover, Monsieur de Vieilleville was just giving the signal for the onset.

The die was cast. Forward! and God's will be done!

The two horses set off at a gallop, at that moment being more intelligent and less blinded perhaps than their riders, heavily barbed and armored.

Gabriel and the king met in the centre of the arena. Their lances came together and were shattered upon their shields, and they passed on without any other mishap.

So the presentiments of evil had been false! There was a great murmur of satisfaction uttered with one accord by all those lightened hearts. The queen cast a grateful glance toward heaven.

But their rejoicing was premature.

The horsemen were still within the lists. After having galloped each to the opposite end from that at which he had entered, they must return to their respective points of departure, and thus meet a second time.

But what danger was to be apprehended now? They would pass without coming in contact.

But whether because of his anxiety, whether it was by intention or by accident (for who besides God can tell the reason?), Gabriel, when he rode back, did not throw away, as the custom was, the broken shaft of the lance, which had been left in his hand. He carried it lowered in front of him.

As he rode along at a gallop, the shaft came in contact with Henri's head.

The visor of the casque was broken by the force of the blow, and the lance pierced the king's eye and came out at his ear.

Not more than half of the spectators, who were already rising to leave the lists, witnessed that fearful blow; but those who did gave utterance to a loud cry, which told the others.

Meanwhile Henri had let his reins drop from his hands, and clinging to his horse's neck, had reached the end of the arena, where Messieurs de Vieilleville and de Boisy were waiting to receive him.

"Ah, I am killed!" were the king's first words.

Then he muttered, —

"Let no one molest Monsieur de Montgommery! It was no more than just — I forgive him."

And with that he lost consciousness.

We will not try to depict the confusion that ensued. Catherine de Médicis was carried from the spot, half dead with grief and terror. The king was at once borne to his own apartment at the Tournelles, without regaining consciousness for an instant.

Gabriel dismounted and stood leaning against the barrier as motionless as if turned to stone, and seemingly overcome with horror at the blow he had struck.

The king's last words had been understood and repeated, and no one ventured to molest Gabriel; but every one around was whispering, and looking askance at him in awe.

Admiral de Coligny, who had been a spectator of the tournament, alone had courage to approach the young count; and as he passed by at his left side, he said to him in a low voice, —

"A terrible accident, my friend! I know well that it was all chance; our ideas and the speeches you heard, as La Renaudie has informed me, at the meeting in the Place Maubert, surely had no connection with this fatality. No matter! although you cannot be punished for what was but an accident, be on your guard. I advise you to disappear for a time, and to get away from Paris, if not from France. Rely always upon me; *au revoir*."

"Thanks," Gabriel replied without moving,

A mournful and feeble smile flickered about his colorless lips while the Protestant leader was speaking to him.

Coligny nodded to him, and went on.

Some moments later, the Duc de Guise, who had superintended the king's removal, also came toward Gabriel, as he was giving certain orders to the attendants.

He passed very near the young count, on the right side, and as he passed, whispered in his ear, —

"An unfortunate blow, Gabriel! But no one can blame you for it; you are only to be pitied. But just think! if any one had overheard our conversation at the Tournelles, what fearful conjectures the evil-disposed might draw from this very easily explained but very distressing accident! But it makes no difference, for I am powerful now; and I am always your friend, as you know. However, do not show yourself for a few days; but do not leave Paris, — that would be useless. If any one should dare to make a criminal accusation against you, remember what I say to you: rely upon me everywhere and always, and in any emergency."

"Thanks, Monseigneur," said Gabriel again, in the same tone, and with the same melancholy smile.

It was very clear that both the Duc de Guise and Coligny had, not an absolute conviction, but a vague suspicion, that the accident which they pretended to deplore had not been altogether unintentional. In their hearts, the religious zealot and the ambitious noble, without wishing to do violence to their respective consciences, were satisfied, — the latter that Gabriel had seized at any risk the opportunity to make himself useful to the fortune of a patron whom he adored, and the former that the fanaticism of the young Huguenot had attained sufficient strength to urge him on to deliver his oppressed brethren from their persecutor.

Therefore both felt in duty bound to say a few words to their discreet and devoted auxiliary: and that explains why they had, one after the other, approached him as we have related, and Gabriel's appreciation of their motives had made him receive their double error with that sad smile.

Meanwhile the Duc de Guise had returned to the anxious groups who were standing around. Gabriel cast a glance about him, saw the alarmed curiosity with which he was regarded, and with a deep sigh determined to leave the fatal spot.

He returned to his house in the Rue des Jardins St. Paul without molestation or question.

At the Tournelles the king's apartment was closed to everybody except the queen and their children and the surgeons who had come to the relief of the royal patient.

But Fernel and all the other doctors very soon recognized the fact that there was no hope, and that Henri II. must die.

Ambroise Paré was at Peronne, and it did not occur to the Duc de Guise to send for him.

The king lay in an unconscious state for four days.

On the fifth day he came to himself sufficiently to give some orders,— notably to command that his sister's marriage should be celebrated at once.

He saw the queen also, and made certain suggestions to her concerning his children and the affairs of the kingdom.

Then fever seized him; he became delirious, and suffered torments.

At last, on the 10th of July, 1559, on the day following that on which, in accordance with his last wish, his weeping sister Marguerite had married the Duke of Savoy, Henri II. breathed his last, after eleven long days of agony.

The same day Madame Diane de Castro took her departure, or rather her flight, for her old home,—the Benedictine convent at St. Quentin, which had been reopened after the peace of Cateau-Cambrésis.

[4] "Mémoires de Vincent Carloix," secretary to Monsieur de Vieilleville.

CHAPTER XIII
A NEW ORDER OF AFFAIRS

For the mistress, as well as for the favorite male dependant of a king, true death comes, not with death itself, but with disgrace.

Consequently the son of the Comte de Montgommery might feel that he had taken ample vengeance for his father's horrible entombment and death upon both the constable and Diane de Poitiers, if through his instrumentality those two guilty ones should fall from power to exile, and from lofty and brilliant position to obscurity.

It was this result that Gabriel was still awaiting in the gloomy and anxious solitude of his dwelling, where he had buried himself after the fatal blow of June 30. It was not his own punishment that he dreaded, if Montmorency and his accomplice should remain in power, but he loathed the thought of their chastisement being remitted. He therefore waited.

During the eleven days that elapsed before Henri's agony was relieved by death, the Constable de Montmorency had put forth every effort to retain his share of influence in the government. He had written to all the princes of the blood, urging them to take their seats in the council of the young king. Above all, he had impressed the consequence of this proceeding upon Antoine de Bourbon, King of Navarre, the next heir to the throne after the king's brothers. He had written him to make all haste, inasmuch as the least delay would enable strangers to assume a supremacy from which they could not afterward be easily dislodged. In fact, he had sent couriers here and there in all directions, urging some and imploring others, and had omitted nothing in his vigorous attempts to form a party capable of making head against that of the Guises.

Diane de Poitiers, despite her deep affliction, had done her best to second his efforts, for her fate now was indissolubly connected with that of her old lover.

With him in power she might still reign, to good effect at all events, although not openly.

When, on the 10th of July, 1559, the eldest son of Henri II. was proclaimed king by the herald-at-arms, under the name of François II., the young prince was only sixteen; and although he had in the eyes of the law attained his majority, his youth and inexperience, as well as his feeble health, would compel him, for several years at least, to relinquish the conduct of affairs to a minister who in his name would be far more powerful than himself.

Now who should be that minister,—say rather, that tutor,—the Duc de Guise or the constable; Catherine de Médicis or Antoine de Bourbon?

That was the question of absorbing interest on the day following the death of Henri II.

On that day François II. was to receive the deputies of parliament at three o'clock. The person whose name he should present to them as that of his minister might well be saluted by them as their real sovereign.

All energies were therefore bent in that direction; and on the morning of the 12th of July Catherine de Médicis and François de Lorraine both waited upon the young king, upon the pretext that they had come to offer him their condolence, but really to whisper their advice into his ear.

The widow of Henri II., with such an important end in view, had even broken through the etiquette which required that she should remain in seclusion for forty days.

Catherine de Médicis, although slighted and cast aside by her husband, had felt for the last twelve years the first symptoms of that vast and far-reaching ambition which governed the rest of her life.

But since she could not be regent over a king who had attained his majority, her only chance was to reign by the hand of a minister who was devoted to her interests.

The Constable de Montmorency would not meet the occasion; for he had under the late reign contributed in no slight degree to the substitution of the influence of Diane de Poitiers for that which Catherine might legitimately have exercised. The queen-mother had not forgiven his actions in that regard, and thought much more seriously about chastising him for his always harsh and often cruel treatment of her.

Antoine de Bourbon would have been a more docile instrument in her hands; but he was of the Reformed religion, and his wife, Jeanne d'Albret, had her own ambition to satisfy; and then, too, his title as a prince of the blood might arouse dangerous desires in him if conjoined with the real power of a minister.

The Duc de Guise remained; but would François de Lorraine acknowledge with good grace the queen-mother's right to exercise a sort of moral authority, or would he refuse to admit anybody to a share in his power?

The last point was one on which Catherine was very anxious to be enlightened; and so she welcomed with joy the prospect of an interview in the king's presence which chance had brought about between her and the duke on the morning in question.

She determined to find or to invent opportunities to test Le Balafré, and to ascertain his disposition toward her.

But the Duc de Guise was no less expert in politics than in war, and maintained a careful watch upon himself.

This prologue to the drama took place at the Louvre, in the royal apartment where François II. had been installed the day before; and the only *dramatis personæ* were the queen-mother, Le Balafré, the young king, and Mary Stuart.

François and his youthful queen contrasted with the cold and selfish ambitions of Catherine and the Duc de Guise were like two fascinating children, frankly and ingenuously in love with each other, and ready to bestow their confidence upon the first passer-by who should be adroit enough to win their hearts.

They were in sincere affliction for the death of the king their father; and Catherine found them very sad and cast down.

"My son," said she to François, "it is well for you to shed these tears to the memory of him whom you, above all others, should regret. You know that I share your bitter grief. However, you must remember that you have other duties than those of a son to fulfil. You are also a father,—the father of your people. After you have paid this fitting tribute of sorrow to the past, turn your face to the future. Remember that you are king, my son,—I should say your Majesty, to use a form of address which will remind you of your duties and your rights at the same time."

"Alas!" said François, shaking his head, "it is a very heavy burden, Madame, this sceptre of France, for the hands of sixteen years to carry; and nothing warned me to expect that my inexperienced and light-minded youth would so soon be overwhelmed with such a weighty responsibility."

"Sire," Catherine replied, "accept with resignation and gratitude the office which God lays upon you; it will be for those who surround and love you to lighten your burden to the best of their ability, and to add their efforts to your own to assist you to bear it worthily."

"Madame, I thank you," murmured the young king, much embarrassed to know what reply to make to these advances.

Mechanically he glanced toward the Duc de Guise, as if to ask the advice of his wife's uncle.

At his very first step as king, even in his mother's presence, the poor youth, with the crown on his head, seemed instinctively to appreciate the pitfalls which lay in his path.

But the Duc de Guise said, with no sign of hesitation, —

"Yes, Sire; your Majesty is right, — thank the queen, thank her with all your heart, for her kind and encouraging words. But be not content with being grateful to her; tell her boldly that among those who love you and whom you love she occupies the foremost place, and that for that reason you ought to and do rely upon her invaluable maternal co-operation in the difficult task which you have been called upon so young to undertake."

"My uncle De Guise is a faithful interpreter of my thoughts, Madame," said the delighted young king to his mother; "and even if I do not repeat his words for fear that I may weaken their force, consider them, I pray, Madame and beloved mother, as if I had myself uttered them, and vouchsafe to promise me your priceless help in my weakness."

The queen-mother had already favored the Duc de Guise with a grateful and approving glance.

"Sire," she said to her son, "the little talent that I can boast of is at your service, and I shall be proud and happy every time that you care to consult me. But I am only a woman; and you need beside your throne a defender who knows how to wield a sword. The strong arm and manly vigor that are requisite your Majesty will doubtless discover among those whose alliance and relationship make you look naturally to them for support."

Thus Catherine lost no time in paying her debt to the Duc de Guise for his fair words.

A tacit bargain was thus made between them by a single glance; but let us say at once that it was not sincerely entered into on either side, and was not destined, as we shall see, to be of long duration.

The young king understood his mother, and encouraged by a glance from Mary, held out his hand timidly to Le Balafré.

With that grasp of the hand he conferred upon him the government of France.

However, Catherine de Médicis did not choose to allow her son to bind himself prematurely, nor until the Duc de Guise had given to herself certain pledges of his goodwill.

So she anticipated the king, who would probably have gone on to confirm his confidential impulse by some formal promise, and was the first to speak.

"In any event, Sire, before you have a minister, your mother has, not a favor to ask at your hands, but a demand to make."

"Say, then, a command, Madame," replied François. "Speak, I beg you."

"Well, then, my son," Catherine continued, "I refer to a woman who has done me much harm, but has injured France even more. It is not for us to censure the failings of one who is more than ever sacred in our eyes now. But unfortunately your father is no more, Sire; his will is no longer supreme in this château; and yet this woman, whom I will not call by name, dares still to remain here, and to inflict upon me the outrage of her presence even to the end. During the king's protracted unconsciousness, it was suggested to her that it was not decent for her to remain at the Louvre. 'Is the king dead?' she asked. 'No, he still breathes.' 'Very well! none but he has the right to give orders to me.' And she had the brazen impudence to remain."

The Duc de Guise interrupted the queen-mother at this point, and hastened to say,—

"Pardon me, Madame, but I think that I know his Majesty's intentions with regard to her of whom you are speaking."

Without other preamble, he struck a bell, and a valet appeared.

"Let Madame de Poitiers be informed," said he, "that the king wishes to speak with her at once."

The valet bowed, and withdrew to carry out the order. The young monarch gave no sign whatever of surprise or dissatisfaction at seeing his authority thus taken from his hands without a word from him. The fact is that he was overjoyed at anything that tended to lessen his responsibility, and release him from the necessity of giving orders or acting as king.

However, Le Balafré thought best to give to his proceeding the sanction of royal approbation.

"I trust I do not presume too far, Sire," he continued, "in feeling confident of your Majesty's wishes touching this matter?"

"No, surely not, my dear uncle," François replied eagerly. "Go on, pray. I know beforehand that whatever you do will be well done."

"And what you say is well said, darling," whispered Mary Stuart, softly, in her husband's ear.

François blushed with pride and pleasure. For a word or a glance of approbation from his adored Mary he would, in very truth, have bartered and abandoned all the kingdoms on earth.

The queen-mother awaited with impatient curiosity the course which the Duc de Guise proposed to adopt.

She thought best, however, to add, as much to break the silence as to better signify her own purpose,—

"She whom you have sent for, Sire, may well, in my opinion, leave the Louvre in the possession of the only legitimate queen of the late king, as well as the charming queen of the present one;" here she bowed graciously to Mary Stuart. "Has not this beautiful and wealthy lady her superb royal Château d'Anet, where she can seek shelter and consolation?—a much more royal and superb establishment, certainly, than my modest dwelling of Chaumont-sur-Loire."

The Duc de Guise said nothing, but did not fail to note down that hint in his mind.

We must avow that he hated Diane de Poitiers no less bitterly than Catherine de Médicis did. For it was Madame de Valentinois who up to that time, to please the constable, had used all her influence to hinder and frustrate Le Balafré's fortune and his schemes; and she doubtless would have succeeded in relegating him forever into obscurity if Gabriel's lance had not shattered the enchantress's power when it struck down Henri II. in the prime of life.

But François de Lorraine's day of vengeance had come at last, and he knew how to hate as well as to love.

At this moment the usher announced in a loud voice,—

"Madame le Duchesse de Valentinois."

Diane de Poitiers entered, evidently in much anxiety, but with her head still erect as of yore.

CHAPTER XIV
RESULTS OF GABRIEL'S VENGEANCE

Madame de Valentinois made a slight reverence to the young king, a still slighter one to Catherine de Médicis and Mary Stuart, but seemed not to see the Duc de Guise.

"Sire," said she, "your Majesty has sent me your commands to appear before you—"

She checked herself. François II., at once indignant and embarrassed by the insolent bearing of the ex-favorite, hesitated, blushed, and finally said,—

"Our uncle De Guise has consented to take it upon himself to make known our intentions with regard to you, Madame."

Diane turned slowly toward Le Balafré, and seeing the bitter, mocking smile which was playing about his lips, tried to wither him with the most imperious of her Juno-like glances.

But Le Balafré was much less easily frightened than his royal nephew.

"Madame," said he to Diane, after bestowing a profound salute upon her, "the king has noticed your sincere grief, caused by the terrible calamity which has overwhelmed us all. He is grateful to you for it. His Majesty trusts that he anticipates your dearest wish by permitting you to leave the court for a more retired spot. You are at liberty to go as soon as you find it convenient; this evening, for instance."

A tear of rage appeared in Diane's flaming eye.

"His Majesty has gratified my most earnest desire," said she. "What is there here for me to do now? I have nothing so much at heart as to withdraw to my place of exile, Monsieur, at the earliest possible moment, never fear!"

"Everything turns out for the best, then," replied the Duc de Guise, carelessly playing with the knots of his velvet cloak. "But, Madame," he added more gravely, and imparting to his words the significant accent of an order, "your Château d'Anet, which you owe to the benevolence of the late king, is something too worldly, too exposed, and too frivolous a retreat for a desolate recluse like yourself. Therefore Queen Catherine offers you in exchange for it her Château de Chaumont-sur-Loire, which is farther from Paris, and proportionately better suited to your present tastes and needs, I presume. It will be at your disposal as soon as you desire."

Madame de Poitiers very well understood that this pretended exchange was simply a mask to cover an arbitrary confiscation. But what could she do? How resist? She no longer possessed either influence or power. All her friends of the day before were her enemies of to-day. She must needs bow to fate, and she did so.

"I shall be only too happy," said she, in a hollow voice, "to offer to the queen the magnificent domain which I owe to the generosity of her royal spouse."

"I accept the reparation, Madame," said Catherine de Médicis, dryly, casting a disdainful glance at Diane, and one full of gratitude to the Duc de Guise.

In truth, it was he who presented Anet to her.

"The Château de Chaumont-sur-Loire is at your disposal, Madame," she added, "and shall be put in condition to receive its new proprietress worthily."

"And there," resumed the Duc de Guise, meeting the withering glances with which Diane was favoring him by a little harmless raillery, — "there, in peace, Madame, you may employ your leisure in resting from the weariness which has, I am informed, been caused during the last few days by your frequent correspondence and interviews with Monsieur de Montmorency."

"I did not think that I was doing a disservice to him who was then king," Diane retorted, "by conferring with the great statesman and great warrior of his reign as to whatever concerned the welfare of the kingdom."

In her eagerness to repay sharp words in kind, Madame de Poitiers did not reflect that she was thus furnishing arms against herself, and reminding Catherine de Médicis of her other enemy, the constable.

"It is true," said the relentless queen-mother: "Monsieur de Montmorency has shed the light of his glory and his good works upon two entire reigns; and it is full time, my son," she added, addressing the young king, "that you should consider how you may assure him also the honorable retirement he has so laboriously earned."

"Monsieur de Montmorency," Diane retorted bitterly, "agreed with me in anticipating such an acknowledgment and recompense of his long and arduous services. He was with me when your Majesty commanded my presence. He is probably still in my apartments, and I will seek him there, and notify him of the generous consideration that is in store for him; he should come at once to offer his gratitude to the king with his leave-taking. And he is a man, remember; he is constable, and one of the powerful noblemen of the realm! Rest assured that sooner or later he will find an opportunity to demonstrate more forcibly than by words his profound gratitude to a king so filled with pious regard for the past, and to the new advisers who show themselves such valuable assistants in the work of justice and of public interest which he has at heart."

"A threat!" said Le Balafré to himself. "The viper squirms under the heel. Oh, well, so much the better! I prefer it so!"

"The king is always ready to receive Monsieur le Connétable," observed the queen-mother, pale with rage. "And if Monsieur le Connétable has any demands to present to his Majesty's consideration, or any observations to address to him, he has but to come forward. He will be listened to, and, as you say, Madame, justice will be done!"

"I will send him hither at once," was Madame de Poitiers's defiant reply.

She again bestowed a superb bow upon the king and the two queens, and left the room, with head still erect, but wounded to her very soul, — with pride on her features, but death at her heart.

If Gabriel could have seen her, he would have felt sufficiently revenged upon her.

Even Catherine de Médicis, at the price of that humiliation, consented to forego any further reprisals against Diane!

But the queen-mother had noticed with some uneasiness that at the name of the constable the Duc de Guise had remained silent, and had paid no further attention to Madame de Poitiers's irritating insolence.

Could it be that Le Balafré feared Monsieur de Montmorency, and wished to spare him? Would he, in case of need, form an alliance with Catherine's old foe?

It was essential that the Florentine should know what to expect in that direction before she allowed the power to fall without resistance into the hands of François de Lorraine.

Therefore, in order to ascertain his views and those of the king as well, she remarked, after Diane had gone:

"Madame de Poitiers is very impudent, and seems very strong in her reliance upon her constable. Be sure, my son, that if you allow Monsieur de Montmorency to retain any authority, be it much or little, he will share it with Madame Diane."

Still the Duc de Guise said nothing.

"As for me," continued Catherine, "if I were to offer my opinion to your Majesty, it would be that you should not divide your confidence among several persons, but that you should select for your sole minister either Monsieur de Montmorency or your uncle De Guise or your uncle De Bourbon, as you choose. But let it be one or the other, and not all. Let there be only one will in the State,—that of the king, advised by the small number of persons who have no other interest than in its welfare and glory. Is not that your opinion, Monsieur de Lorraine?"

"Yes, Madame, if it is yours," replied the duke, condescendingly.

"Aha!" said Catherine to herself, "I guessed aright: he was thinking of allying himself with the constable. But he must decide between him and me, and I think he cannot hesitate long.

"It seems to me, Monsieur de Guise," she continued aloud, "that you ought to share my opinion so much the more fully, because it will be to your advantage; for the king knows my thought, and that it is neither the Constable de Montmorency nor Antoine de Navarre whom I would like to have him select for his adviser; and when I thus declare my sentiments in favor of the exclusion of a multiplicity of advisers, I do not aim my remarks against you."

"Madame," said the Duc de Guise, "accept with my heartfelt gratitude my no less entire devotion."

The subtle politician emphasized the last words, as if he had made up his mind and had definitely sacrificed the constable to Catherine.

"That is very well," said the queen-mother. "When these gentlemen of the parliament arrive, it is fitting that they should find among us this rare and affecting unanimity of views and feelings."

"I, above all others, am overjoyed at this cordial agreement," cried the young king, clapping his hands. "With my mother to advise me and my uncle for minister, I begin to feel on better terms with this royalty which terrified me so at first."

"We will reign *en famille*," added Mary Stuart, gayly.

Catherine de Médicis and François de Lorraine smiled pityingly at these hopes—illusions, rather—of the young king and queen. Each of them had for the moment what they most desired,—he the certainty that the queen-mother would not object to allowing the supreme power to be intrusted to him, and she the belief that the minister would share his supreme power with her.

Meanwhile Monsieur de Montmorency was announced. The constable, it must be said, was at first more dignified and calm than Madame de Valentinois. Doubtless he had been forewarned by her, and had determined at least to fall with colors flying.

He bowed respectfully before François II., and began at once to speak.

"Sire," said he, "I anticipated that the old servant of your father and grandfather would meet with little favor from you. I have no complaint to make of this sudden change of fortune which I foresaw; I will go into retirement without a murmur. If the king or France ever have need of me, I shall be found at Chantilly, Sire; and my property, my children, and my own life,—all that I possess will always be at your Majesty's service."

This moderation seemed to move the young king, who, more embarrassed than ever, turned in his distress to his mother.

But the Duc de Guise, feeling that no intervention could so surely turn the old constable's reserve to anger as his own, interposed with the most courteous formality of manner,—

"Since Monsieur de Montmorency is about to quit the court, he would do well, I think, before his departure, to hand to his Majesty the royal seal, which the late king intrusted to him, and which we need from this time."

Le Balafré was not mistaken. These apparently simple words excited the jealous constable's wrath to the highest pitch.

"Here is the seal," he said bitterly, as he produced it from beneath his doublet. "I intended to hand it to his Majesty without requiring him to ask it of me; but I see that his Majesty is surrounded by persons disposed to advise him to heap insults upon those who deserve nothing but gratitude."

"To whom does Monsieur de Montmorency mean to refer?" asked Catherine, haughtily.

"What? I spoke of those by whom his Majesty is surrounded, Madame," snarled the constable, giving the rein to his natural testiness and brutality.

But he had chosen his time ill; and Catherine was only awaiting an opportunity to burst out.

She rose, and casting all decorum to the winds, began to reproach the constable for the harsh and disdainful manner he had always adopted toward her, his hostility for everything Florentine, the preference which he had openly shown to the mistress over the lawful wife. She was not ignorant of the fact that it was to him that all the humiliation suffered by her countrymen who had followed her to France was to be attributed. She knew, too, that during the early years of her married life Montmorency had had the hardihood to suggest to Henri that he should cast her off as being barren, and that since then he had basely slandered her.

To this the constable, who was little accustomed to reproof, replied with a sneer, which was in itself a fresh affront.

Meanwhile the Duc de Guise had had time to take François II.'s orders, or rather to dictate those orders to him in a low tone; and now, calmly raising his voice, he proceeded to crush his rival, to the unbounded delight of Catherine de Médicis.

"Monsieur le Connétable," said he, with his jeering courtesy, "your friends and creatures who sit with you at the council-board—Bochetel, L'Aubespine, and the rest, notably his Eminence the Keeper of the Seals, Jean Bertrandi—may probably prefer to imitate you in your longing for retirement. The king desires you to express his gratitude to them. Tomorrow they will be quite at liberty, and their places will have been filled."

"'T is well," muttered Monsieur de Montmorency between his clinched teeth.

"As for your nephew, Monsieur de Coligny, who is at once governor of Picardy and of the Île de France," continued Le Balafré, "the king considers that the double task is altogether too heavy for one man, and desires to relieve him of one of his governments at his choice. You will have the kindness to notify Monsieur l'Amiral to that effect, will you not?"

"To be sure," rejoined the constable, with a bitter sneer.

"As for yourself, Monsieur le Connétable—" the duke continued quietly.

"Am I to be deprived of my constable's bâton?" interrupted Monsieur de Montmorency, sharply.

"Oh," replied François de Lorraine, "you know that it is impossible, and that the office of constable is not like that of lieutenant-general of the kingdom, but that the former is conferred for life. However, is it not incompatible with that of grand master, which you also hold? It seems to be so to his Majesty, who asks for your resignation of the last-named charge, Monsieur, and deigns to confer it upon me, since I have no other."

"It is for the best," retorted Montmorency, grinding his teeth. "Is that all, Monsieur?"

"Why, yes; I think so," said the Duc de Guise, resuming his seat.

The constable felt that it would be difficult for him to restrain his rage any longer,—that he should perhaps make a scene, and by failing in respect for the king become a rebellious subject instead of a disgraced one. He did not wish to afford his triumphant foe that satisfaction; so he saluted the king abruptly, and made ready to take his leave.

However, before departing, and as if thinking better of his determination,—

"Sire," said he, "allow me one word more, to fulfil my last duty to the memory of your glorious father. He who struck the fatal blow, the author of all our grief, was not perhaps simply careless, Sire,—at least I have reason to think so. In this melancholy catastrophe there may have been—in my opinion, there was—an element of criminal intent. The man whom I accuse did, I know, consider himself wronged by the late king. Your Majesty will without doubt order a strict inquiry into this matter."

The Duc de Guise was alarmed at this formal and dangerous charge against Gabriel; but Catherine de Médicis took it upon herself to reply.

"Be assured, Monsieur," said she to the constable, "that your intervention was not needed to remind us of such a deed as that; for the necessity of dealing promptly with the offender is not forgotten by those to whom the kingly existence so cruelly terminated was quite as precious as to you. I, the widow of Henri II., cannot yield to any other person in the world the initiative in such a matter. Therefore be quite easy, Monsieur; your solicitude is premature. You may withdraw with your mind at rest on that point."

"I have nothing further to say, then," said the constable.

He was not even to be allowed to gratify in person his implacable resentment to the Comte de Montgommery, and to pose as the denouncer of the culprit and the avenger of his master.

Suffocated with shame and anger, he went from the royal presence in despair.

He departed the same evening for his estate at Chantilly.

That day Madame de Valentinois also quitted the Louvre, where she had been more of a queen than the queen herself, for her gloomy and distant exile at Chaumont-sur-Loire, whence she never returned while she lived.

Thus Gabriel's vengeance upon Madame de Poitiers was complete.

It is true that the ex-favorite had in store a terrible vengeance for him who had thus hurled her from her lofty position.

As for the constable, Gabriel had not done with him, but would be on the watch for the day when he should regain his influence.

However, we will not anticipate events, but return in haste to the Louvre, where the deputies of parliament are just being announced to François II.

CHAPTER XV
CHANGE OF TEMPERATURE

In accordance with Catherine de Médicis's wish, the deputies found the most perfect unanimity of sentiment prevailing at the Louvre. François II., his wife at his right hand, and his mother at his left, presented the Duc de Guise to them as lieutenant-general of the kingdom, the Cardinal of Lorraine as superintendent of the finances, and François Olivier as keeper of the seals. Le Balafré was triumphant, the queen-mother smiled upon his triumph, and everything went off as smoothly as possible; and no suspicion of a misunderstanding appeared to cast a shadow upon the fortunate auspices which inaugurated this reign, which bade fair to be as long as its opening was happy.

One of the councillors of the parliament apparently thought that a suggestion of clemency would not be ill-timed amid so much happiness, and as he passed before the king with a group of others he cried, —

"Mercy for Anne Dubourg!"

But the good councillor forgot how zealous a Catholic the new minister was. Le Balafré, as his habit was, pretended to have misunderstood; and without going through the formality of consulting the king or the queen-mother, so sure was he of their approbation, he replied in a loud, firm voice, —

"Yes, Messieurs, yes; the prosecution of Anne Dubourg and those accused with him will be at once taken up and carried to its close, never fear!"

With this assurance, the members of parliament left the Louvre, sad or joyous according to their respective opinions, but all convinced that never were the governing powers more united in sentiment and better pleased with one another than those to whom they had just paid their respects.

After their departure, the Duc de Guise still noticed upon Catherine's lips the smile which every time that she glanced at him seemed to be stereotyped there.

François II. rose from his seat, tired out with the formalities he had gone through.

"At last we are done for to-day, I trust, with business and ceremony," said he. "Mother, uncle, may we not one of these days leave Paris for a while, and pass the balance of our period of mourning at Blois, for instance, on the banks of the Loire, that Mary loves so dearly? Oh, can we not, tell me?"

"Oh, do try to make it possible!" said Mary Stuart. "In these lovely summer days Paris is so wearisome and the country so charming!"

"Monsieur de Guise will attend to that," said Catherine. "But your labors are not yet quite at an end for to-day, my son; before I leave you to yourself I must ask for half an hour more of your time, for you have a sacred duty yet to perform."

"What is it, Mother?" asked François.

"A duty which devolves upon you as the guardian of public justice, Sire," said Catherine,—"the same one in which Monsieur le Connétable flattered himself that he would anticipate me; but a wife's justice is keener than a friend's."

"What does she mean?" the Duc de Guise asked himself, in alarm.

"Sire, your august father died a violent death. The man who dealt the blow either is simply an unfortunate wretch or a culprit. For my own part, I incline to the latter supposition; but in any event the question is worth the trouble of solving. If we treat such an attack with indifference, without even taking pains to ascertain whether it was involuntary or not, what risks do not all kings run,—you, above all, Sire? Therefore an inquiry into what is called the 'accident' of the 30th of June is essential."

"But in that case," said Le Balafré, "it would be necessary to order Monsieur de Montgommery's arrest at once, Madame, as a regicide."

"Monsieur de Montgommery has been under arrest since morning," said Catherine.

"Under arrest! And upon whose order, pray!" cried the Duc de Guise.

"Upon mine," replied the queen-mother. "There was no regularly constituted authority at that time, and I took it upon myself to issue that order. Monsieur de Montgommery might take flight at any moment, and it was of the utmost importance to prevent it. He has been brought to the Louvre without disturbance or excitement. I ask you, my son, to question him."

Without waiting for permission, she touched a bell, as the Duc de Guise had done two hours earlier. But this time Le Balafré scowled heavily; a storm was brewing.

"Order the prisoner to be brought hither," said Catherine to the usher who appeared.

There was an embarrassing silence when the usher had left the room. The king seemed undecided, Mary Stuart anxious, and the Duc de Guise very much displeased. The queen-mother alone affected an air of dignity and assurance.

The Duc de Guise alone broke the silence with these words, —

"It seems to me that if Monsieur de Montgommery had desired to make his escape, nothing would have been easier during the last fortnight."

Catherine had no time to reply, for Gabriel was led in at that moment.

He was pale but composed. That morning very early four armed domestics had come to seek him at his house, to the great dismay of Aloyse. He had accompanied them without any attempt at resistance, and since then had awaited events without apparent anxiety.

When Gabriel entered the apartment with a firm step and tranquil bearing, the young king changed color, whether from emotion at sight of him who had stricken his father to death, or from alarm at having for the first time to perform the functions of dispenser of justice of which his mother had spoken, — in very truth the most awe-inspiring duty which the Lord has imposed upon the kings of the earth.

Consequently, it was with a scarcely audible voice that he said to Catherine, turning toward her, —

"Speak, Madame; it is for you to speak."

Catherine de Médicis made haste to avail herself of this permission. She now believed herself to be certain of her omnipotence with François and his minister. She addressed Gabriel in a haughty, magisterial tone.

"Monsieur," said she, "we have thought fit, before any other steps were taken, to cause you to appear before his Majesty in person, and to question you with our own lips, so that there may be no necessity of offering you any reparation if we find you innocent, and that justice may be the more prompt and effective if we find you guilty. Extraordinary crimes demand extraordinary tribunals. Are you ready to reply to our questions, Monsieur?"

"I am ready to listen to you, Madame," was Gabriel's reply.

Catherine was rather irritated than convinced by the calm demeanor of the man whom she had bitterly hated even before he had made her a widow,—whom she hated the more for all the love which for one moment she had felt for him. She continued with an offensive bitterness in her tone,—

"Several curious circumstances conspire to throw suspicion on you, Monsieur, and to accuse you,—your long absences from Paris, your voluntary exile from court for nearly two years, your presence and your mysterious demeanor at the fatal tournament, your very refusal to enter the lists against the king. How did it happen that you, who are accustomed to these sports and passages-at-arms, omitted the ordinary and necessary precaution of throwing away the shaft of your lance as you were riding back? How do you explain such strange forgetfulness? Answer! What have you to say to all this?"

"Nothing, Madame," said Gabriel.

"Nothing?" said the queen-mother, completely taken aback.

"Absolutely nothing."

"What!" rejoined Catherine; "you confess, then? You avow that—"

"I neither avow nor confess anything, Madame."

"Oho! then you deny?"

"Nor do I deny anything. I simply say nothing."

Mary Stuart could not restrain a movement of approbation. François II. listened and looked on with eager curiosity; and the Duc de Guise remained mute and motionless.

Catherine began again in a tone which became momentarily more and more biting,—

"Monsieur, be careful! You would do better, perhaps, to try to defend or justify your action. Understand one thing: Monsieur de Montmorency, who can, in case of need, be heard as a witness, declares that to his certain knowledge you might well have certain grievances against the king, some grounds for personal enmity."

"What were they, Madame? Did Monsieur de Montmorency say what they were?"

"Not yet, but doubtless he will tell."

"Very well! let him tell them, if he dares!" retorted Gabriel, with a proud but quiet smile.

"So you refuse altogether to speak, do you?" Catherine persisted.

"I refuse."

"Do you know that the torture may bring your disdainful silence to terms?"

"I do not think it, Madame."

"By proceeding in this way, you risk your life, I warn you."

"I will not defend it, Madame. It is no longer worth the trouble."

"You are fully determined, then, Monsieur? Not a word?"

"Not one single word, Madame," said Gabriel, shaking his head.

"And quite right, too!" cried Mary Stuart, as if carried away by an irresistible impulse. "Noble and grand this silence is! It is the course of a gentleman who does not even choose to repel suspicion for fear that suspicion may fall upon him. I say, for my part, that this very refusal to speak is the most eloquent and convincing of justifications!"

During this outburst the old queen was gazing at the younger one with a stern and angry expression.

"Yes, I may be wrong to speak thus," continued Mary; "but I care not! I speak as I feel and as I think. My heart will never allow my lips to remain closed. My impressions and my emotions must find vent. My instinct is the only policy that I recognize, and it cries out to me now that Monsieur d'Exmès never conceived and executed such a crime in cold blood, but that he was only the blind instrument of fate, and believes himself to be above any other supposition, and therefore scorns to justify himself. My instinct tells me this, and I give it voice. Why not?"

The young king gazed joyfully and affectionately at his *mignonne*, as he called her, while she expressed herself with an eloquence and animation which made her twenty times more fascinating than usual.

Gabriel cried in a touched and penetrating voice, —

"Oh, thanks, Madame! I thank you! And you have done well; not on my account, but your own, you have done well to act thus."

"Indeed, I know it," replied Mary, with the most gracious accent that one could dream of.

"Well, have we reached the end of this sentimental childishness!" cried Catherine, indignantly.

"No, Madame," said Mary Stuart, wounded in her self-respect as a young wife and a young queen, "no; if you have made an end of your childishness, we, who are young, thank God! are only just beginning. Am I not right, my gentle Sire?" she added, turning prettily toward her youthful spouse.

The king did not reply in words, but touched with his lips the ends of the lovely fingers Mary held out to him.

Catherine's wrath, which she had restrained up to that time, now burst forth; she had not yet succeeded in accustoming to treat as king a son who was still almost a child; moreover, she believed herself to be secure in the support of the Duc de Guise, who had not declared himself thus far, and whom she did not know to be the devoted patron, and, we might almost say, a tacit accomplice of the Comte de Montgommery. Thus she dared to give free vent to her ire.

"Ah, this is the way matters stand!" she said in reply to Mary Stuart's last words, which were slightly contemptuous. "I claim a right, and I am laughed at. I ask, in all moderation, that the murderer of Henri II. may at least be interrogated: and when he declines to justify his act, his silence is approved,—nay, more, it is even applauded. Very well! since things have come to such a pass, away with cowardly reserve and half-measures! I proclaim myself aloud as the accuser of the Comte de Montgommery. Will the king refuse justice to his mother because she is his mother? We will examine the constable, and Madame de Poitiers, too, if necessary! The truth shall be brought to light; and if secrets of State are involved in this affair, we will have the judgment and sentence kept secret. But the death of a king treacherously murdered before the eyes of all his subjects shall, at any price, be avenged."

During this harangue of the queen-mother, a sad and resigned smile played about Gabriel's lips.

He recalled, in his own mind, the last two lines of Nostradamus's prediction,—

"Enfin, l'aimera, puis las! le tuera,
Dame du roy."

And so the prophecy, thus far so faithfully fulfilled, was to be accomplished to the end! Catherine would cause the condemnation and death of him whom she had loved! Gabriel expected it, and was ready for it.

However, the Florentine, thinking perhaps that she might have gone too far, checked herself a moment; and turning with her most gracious manner to the Duc de Guise, who was still silent, she said,—

"But you say nothing, Monsieur de Guise. You are of my opinion, are you not?"

"No, Madame," replied Le Balafré, slowly; "no, I confess that I am not of your opinion, and that is why I said nothing."

"Ah, you too turn against me!" rejoined Catherine, in a hollow, threatening voice.

"I am so unfortunate as to disagree with you in this matter, Madame," said the duke. "However, you see that until now I have been heartily with you, and that in everything concerning the constable and Madame de Valentinois I entirely agreed with your plans."

"Yes, because they served your own," muttered Catherine. "I see it now when it is too late."

"But as for Monsieur de Montgommery," continued Le Balafré, calmly, "I cannot conscientiously share in your feeling, Madame. It seems to me impossible to hold a brave and loyal gentleman answerable for a pure accident. Prosecution would result in a triumph for him, and his accusers would be confounded. And concerning the risks to which, in your opinion, Madame, the lives of our kings would be exposed by an indulgent mode of dealing which prefers to believe in misfortune rather than in crime, why, I am convinced, on the other hand, that the real danger would lie in making the people too familiar with the idea that royal lives are not held in such sacred reverence as they have supposed."

"Doubtless these are very exalted political maxims," retorted Catherine, bitterly.

"I consider them true and in good sense, at all events, Madame," added Le Balafré; "and for all these reasons, and others besides, I am of opinion that what we ought now to do is to apologize to Monsieur de Montgommery for this arbitrary arrest, which happily has been kept secret,—more happily for us than for him; and when our apologies have been accepted, we have only to restore him to the world, free and honorable and honored as he was yesterday, and as he will be to-morrow and forever after. I have spoken."

"Superb!" sneered Catherine.

Turning sharply to the young king, she asked,—

"And does this fine opinion that we have just listened to happen to coincide with yours, my son?"

The demeanor of Mary Stuart, who was bestowing a grateful glance and smile upon the Duc de Guise, left François II. no room for hesitation.

"Yes, Mother," he replied, "I confess that my uncle's opinion is mine."

"And so you betray your father's memory, do you?" retorted Catherine, in a deep voice which she struggled to render unmoved.

"On the other hand, Madame, I respect it," said François. "My father's first words after his wound were to request that Monsieur de Montgommery should not be molested, were they not? And did he not, in one of his rare intervals of consciousness while he lay dying, repeat that request, or rather command? Allow his son, Madame, to obey him."

"Very well! and you thrust aside at the very beginning your mother's devout will—"

"Madame," interrupted the Duc de Guise, "allow me to remind you of your own words, 'only one will in the kingdom.'"

"But I also said, Monsieur, that of the minister should always be subordinate to that of the king," cried Catherine.

"Yes, Madame," observed Mary Stuart, "but you added, the king's will should be enlightened by those persons who are interested only in his glory and his welfare. Now, no one is more interested than I, his wife, in either of those subjects, I fancy; and I advise him, as my uncle De Guise does, to believe rather in the loyalty than in the perfidy of a tried and valiant subject, and not to begin his reign with an iniquitous act."

"Do you yield to such suggestions as these, my son?" Catherine asked once more.

"I yield to the voice of my conscience, Mother," replied the young king, with more firmness than could have been expected of him.

"Is this your last word, François?" continued Catherine. "Be careful! If you refuse your mother the first request that she makes of you; if you thus assume the attitude of an independent master toward her, and act like the docile instrument of others,—you may reign alone, with or without your faithful ministers. I will have nothing more to do with anything that concerns king or kingdom, but I will deprive you of the benefit of my experience and devotion. I will return to my retirement, and abandon you, my son. Consider, consider well!"

"We should deplore her retirement, but would resign ourselves to bear it," murmured Mary Stuart, in a low voice which none but François heard.

But the amorous, imprudent youth, like a faithful echo, repeated aloud,—

"We should deplore your retirement, but would resign ourselves to bear it, Madame."

"Ah, very good!" was all Catherine said.

Then she continued in a voice of suppressed rage, pointing at Gabriel,—

"As for that villain, I shall meet with him again, sooner or later."

"I know it, Madame," replied the young man, whose mind was still dwelling on the horoscope.

But Catherine heard him not.

In a perfect fury of wrath, she included the charming young king and queen and the Duc de Guise in a baleful glance, viperish and awful,—a fatal glance, wherein one might have read the promise of all the crimes dictated by Catherine's ambition and the whole sombre history of the last kings of the Valois line.

Without another word she left the room.

CHAPTER XVI
GUISE AND COLIGNY

After Catherine de Médicis's departure, there was a moment of silence. The young king seemed amazed at his own hardihood; while Mary, with the keen intuition of affection, could not avoid a shudder at the thought of the queen-mother's last threatening glance. The Duc de Guise was secretly delighted to find himself thus freed from an ambitious and dangerous associate before his first hour of authority was at an end.

Gabriel, who was the occasion of all this trouble, was the first to speak.

"Sire," said he, "and you, Madame, and you also, Monseigneur, I thank you with all my heart for your kind and generous treatment of a poor wretch whom Heaven itself has abandoned. But notwithstanding my profound gratitude, with which my heart is overflowing, I ask you of what use is it to turn aside danger and death from so mournful and hopeless an existence as mine? My life is of no value for any purpose, or to any person, not even myself. For that reason I would not have disputed Madame Catherine's right to take it, because henceforth it is useless to me."

He added sorrowfully in his own mind, "And because it may yet become a nuisance."

"Gabriel," the Duc de Guise rejoined, "your life has been gloriously and worthily lived in the past, and contains equal possibilities for the future. You are a man of vigor and energy, such as are in great request by those who govern empires, and are seldom available."

"Then, too," the sweet and soothing voice of Mary Stuart chimed in, "yours is a great and noble heart, Monsieur de Montgommery. I have known you for a long while, and Madame de Castro and myself have very often talked together about you."

"In short," observed François II., "your past services, Monsieur, justify me in relying upon you for like services in the future. The embers of war, which are now smouldering, may burst into a blaze at any moment, and I do not wish that a momentary despair, whatever be its cause, should deprive the country forever of a defender who is, I am sure, as loyal as he is gallant."

Gabriel listened with a grave and wondering sadness to these kind words of hope and encouragement. He gazed in turn at each of the exalted personages who had addressed them to him, and appeared to be in very deep thought.

"Well," he at last replied, "this unexpected good-will which all of you, who ought perhaps to hate me, thus demonstrate, has changed my heart and my destiny. At your service, Sire, at yours, Madame and Monseigneur, so long as you live, I place the existence of which you have made me a gift, so to speak. I was not born a villain, and your kindness touches me deeply. I was born to be devoted to somebody, to sacrifice myself, and to serve as the instrument of noble ideas and great men,—sometimes a happy, but at others a fatal instrument, alas! as God, in His wrath, knows only too well! But let us speak no more of the gloomy past, since you are good enough to believe in the possibility of a future for me. That future, however, belongs not to me, but to you; and henceforth I cherish what you admire, and think as you think. I abdicate my will. Let the beings and the objects in whom I believe, do with me as they please. My sword, my blood, my life,—all that I am, is theirs. I give my arm unreservedly and irrevocably to assist your genius, Monseigneur, as I devote my soul to religion."

He did not say which religion; but those who heard him were such devoted Catholics that no thought of the Reformed religion entered their minds.

The eloquent abnegation of the young count deeply touched them all. Mary had tears in her eyes; and the king congratulated himself on having been firm enough to rescue such a grateful heart. As for the Duc de Guise, he believed that he knew better than any one how far Gabriel's ardent self-sacrifice might go.

"Yes, my friend," said he, "I have need of you. I shall call upon you some day, in the name of France and the king, to draw the sword you promise us."

"It shall be ready, Monseigneur,—to-morrow, to-day, always!"

"Keep it in its scabbard for the present," said the duke. "As his Majesty has said, peace prevails at the moment,—there is a truce to war and faction. So rest on your sword awhile, Gabriel, and give this unfortunate notoriety which your name has attained of late time to die away. Surely, not a soul of those who are entitled to the name and possess the heart of a gentleman will ever dream of accusing you for your misfortune. But your real glory demands that this undesirable renown should sink into oblivion. Hereafter, say in a year or two, I will ask the king to bestow upon you again the office of captain of the Guards, of which you have never ceased to be worthy."

"Ah," said Gabriel, "it is not honors that I covet, but opportunities to be useful to my king and country, opportunities to fight. I dare not say opportunities to die, for fear that I may seem ungrateful."

"Do not talk so, Gabriel," replied Le Balafré. "Just say that when the king shall call upon you for assistance against his foes, you will respond to the summons without delay."

"I will, Monseigneur, wherever I am, or may be required to go."

"It is well," said the Duc de Guise; "I ask no more than that of you."

"For my part," said François II., "I thank you for your promise, and you may rely upon me to see that you do not repent having redeemed it."

"While I," added Mary Stuart, "assure you that your devotion always will meet with equal confidence on our part, and that you shall be one of those friends from whom we have no secrets, and to whom we will refuse nothing."

The young count, more deeply touched than he chose to confess to himself, bowed, and touched respectfully with his lips the hand which the queen held out to him.

He then pressed the hand of the Duc de Guise, and receiving his dismissal by a kindly gesture from the king, withdrew, being thenceforth bound, by force of a generous action, to the son of the man upon whom he had sworn to be revenged even in the persons of his children.

Gabriel found Admiral de Coligny awaiting him when he reached home.

Aloyse had informed the admiral, who had come to pay a friendly visit to his companion-in-arms at St. Quentin, that her master had been summoned to the Louvre that morning; she had imparted her anxiety to him, and Coligny had determined to remain until the count's return should reassure them both.

He received Gabriel with much cordiality, and questioned him as to what had taken place.

Without going into details, Gabriel merely told him that upon his offering a simple explanation of his connection with the deplorable death of Henri II. he had been dismissed unharmed personally and with his honor unsullied.

"It could not have been otherwise," exclaimed the admiral; "for the whole nobility of France would have protested as one man against any suspicion which would have cast a blot upon the fame of one of its worthiest members."

"Let us drop the subject," said Gabriel, with sorrowful constraint. "I am very glad to see you, Monsieur l'Amiral. You know that I am already at heart a member of your sect, for I have told you and written you to that effect. Since you think that I would not bring discredit upon the faith in which I believe, I not only wish to, but I do now abjure the faith in which I was brought up; your discourse and Master Paré's, the books I have read and my own reflections, have completely convinced me, and I am with you heart and soul."

"Welcome news! and it comes very opportunely," said the admiral.

"I think, however," said Gabriel, "that even in the interest of the Religion itself, it might perhaps be better to keep my conversion secret for a time. As Monsieur de Guise just observed, any sort of notoriety is best avoided for the present. Besides, this delay will conform better with the new duties I have to perform."

"We shall always be proud to announce your name publicly as one of us," said the admiral.

"But my proper course is to decline, or at all events postpone, this priceless token of your esteem," Gabriel replied. "But I do wish to give you this pledge of my utter, immovable faith, and to be able to call myself in my own mind one of your brethren, both in purpose and in fact."

"This is glorious, indeed!" exclaimed Monsieur de Coligny. "All that I ask is your permission to inform the leaders of our party of the notable conquest which our ideas have definitively made."

"Oh, I consent to that with all my heart," said Gabriel. "The Prince de Condé," continued the admiral, "La Renaudie, and Baron de Castelnau, already know you, and appreciate your merit fully."

"Alas! I much fear that they overestimate it; for, viewed in the most favorable light, my merit is very slight."

"No, no!" returned Coligny; "they do well to rely upon it. I know you well also. Besides," continued he, in a lower tone, "we may perhaps have an opportunity to put your new zeal to the proof very soon."

"Indeed!" said Gabriel, in surprise. "You know, Monsieur l'Amiral, that you can rely upon me,—nevertheless, with certain reservations, which I must make known to you."

"Who has not his reservations to make!" rejoined the admiral. "But listen, Gabriel: It was not only as a friend, but as a partisan as well, that I came to visit you to-day. We have spoken of you with the prince and La Renaudie. Even before your definite adhesion to our principles we looked upon you as an auxiliary of peculiar merit, and of impregnable honesty; in fact, we all agreed in regarding you as a man capable of serving us if you chose, but incapable of betraying us, whatever might happen."

"Indeed, I do possess that last qualification, in default of the former," Gabriel replied. "You may always rely upon my word, if not upon my assistance."

"Then we resolved to have no secrets from you," said the admiral. "You will be, like one of our leaders, made acquainted with all our plans, and you will be held to no responsibility except silence. You are not like other men; and exceptional measures must be taken with exceptional men. You will remain quite free, and we only shall be bound."

"Such confidence!" exclaimed Gabriel.

"Your engagement is left entirely to your own discretion, I repeat," said the admiral. "To begin with, let me tell you one fact: the schemes which were revealed to you in the Place Maubert, and which were then postponed, are practicable to-day. The weakness of the young king, the domineering arrogance of the Guises, the purpose of persecuting us which is no longer hidden,—all urge us to action; and we are about to act."

"Pardon me," Gabriel interrupted him; "I have already told you, Monsieur l'Amiral, that I can only give myself to your cause with certain limitations. Before you go any further with your confidences, I ought to tell you definitely that I do not mean to concern myself with the political aspects of the Reformation,—at least during the continuance of the present reign. I freely offer my fortune, my time, and my life to assist in the propagation of our principles and in extending our moral influence; but I have no right to view the movement except in its religious bearing, and in no sense as a party question. François II., Mary Stuart, as well as the Duc de Guise himself, have treated me very generously,—yes, nobly. I will not betray their confidence any more than yours. Allow me to refrain from action, and occupy myself only with the principle for which we strive. Demand my testimony whenever you please; but I reserve the independence of my sword."

Monsieur de Coligny replied, after a moment's reflection,—

"My words, Gabriel, were not mere empty sounds. You are and shall still be quite free. Go on alone in your own path if you please; act independently of us or not at all. We shall never call you to account. We know," he added, with a significant expression, "that it is sometimes your way to prefer to dispense with associates or advisers."

"What do you mean?" asked Gabriel, in surprise.

"I know what I mean," replied the admiral. "For the present you ask that you may take no part in our conspiracies against the royal authority. So be it! Our duty will be done when we have given you notice of our movements and purposes. Then you may follow us or stand apart; that is your affair, and yours only. You will always know, either by letter or messenger, when and where we have need of you, and then you will act as seems good to you. If you come to us, you will always be welcome; if you stay away, no one will have any fault to find. Such is the agreement to which the leaders of the party have come concerning you, even before you had told me where you stood. You can accept such conditions, I should think."

"Indeed, I do accept them; and I thank you heartily," said Gabriel.

During the night which followed that eventful day, Gabriel, kneeling before his father's tomb in the mortuary vault of the counts of Montgommery, communed with his dead in these words:—

"Yes, my Father, I did indeed take oath not only to punish your murderer in his own lifetime, but also to visit his sins upon his children after him. There is no doubt of it, O my Father, no doubt! But I did not anticipate what has happened. Are there not obligations even more sacred than the fulfilment of an oath? What duty can compel one to strike down an enemy who puts the sword in one's hand, and presents his bare breast to receive the blow? If you were living, my Father, I am sure you would advise me to postpone my wrath, and not to meet confidence with treachery. Forgive me, then, from the grave, for doing what if you were living you would require me to do. Moreover, something seems to tell me that my vengeance is merely suspended, and that but for a short time. You know on high what we can only feel a presentiment of here below. But the pallor of this sickly king, and the frightful glance with which his mother threatened him, and the predictions (which have thus far proved accurate, and which decree that my own life must fall a prey to that woman's rancorous hatred), and the conspiracies already set on foot against the reign which began only yesterday,—all combine to lead me to think it probable that the boy of sixteen will occupy the throne for a much less time even than the man of forty, and that I shall very soon be able to resume my task and my oath of expiation, my Father, under the reign of another of the sons of Henri II."

CHAPTER XVII
REPORTS AND DENUNCIATIONS

Seven or eight months passed by, unmarked by any important occurrences either for the personages of this story, or for the actors upon the stage of history.

Nevertheless, during that time events of considerable importance were preparing.

To understand what they were, and learn all about them, we have only to pay a visit, on the 25th of February, 1560, to the place of all others where news is supposed to be most plentiful; that is to say, the cabinet of Monsieur le Lieutenant de Police, who was at that time one Monsieur de Braguelonne.

On the evening of the 25th of February, Monsieur de Braguelonne, lounging carelessly on his Cordova leather couch, was listening to the report of Master Arpion, one of his secretaries.

Master Arpion was reading aloud as follows, —

> "To-day the notorious thief, Gilles Rose, was arrested in the great hall of the palace, in the act of cutting off the end of a golden girdle, on the person of a canon of Ste. Chapelle."

"A canon of Ste. Chapelle! Well, upon my word!" exclaimed Monsieur de Braguelonne.

"It was a very sacrilegious performance," observed Master Arpion.

"And very clever, too," replied the lieutenant of police, "very clever! for your canon is a suspicious mortal. I will tell you presently, Master Arpion, what must be done with this cunning thief. Go on."

> "The demoiselles of the hovels in the Rue du Grand-Heuleu," continued Arpion, "are in a state of open revolt."

"For what cause, in God's name?"

"They claim to have addressed a petition directly to our lord the king, asking to be allowed to retain their establishments, and meanwhile they have had an encounter with the watch and put them to rout."

"That is very amusing!" laughed Monsieur de Braguelonne. "We can easily set that to rights. Poor girls! Is there anything else?"

Master Arpion continued,—

"Messieurs les Deputés de la Sorbonne having presented themselves at Madame la Princesse de Condé's house at Paris, to insist that she should not eat flesh during Lent, were received with jeers and derision by Monsieur de Sechelles, who said to them, among other insulting things, that he liked them less than a boil on his nose, and that such calves as they made strange ambassadors."

"Ah, that is a serious matter!" said the lieutenant, rising. "Refusing to abstain from meat, and poking fun at Messieurs de la Sorbonne! This tends to swell your account, Madame de Condé; and when we present you with the total—Arpion, is that all?"

"*Mon Dieu*, yes! for to-day. Monseigneur has not told me what to do with this Gilles Rose."

"In the first place," said Monsieur de Braguelonne, "you will take him, together with the most adroit pickpockets and burglars you can find in the prison, and send the whole lot of fine fellows to Blois, where they can have an opportunity to exhibit their tricks and cleverness for the king's entertainment during the fêtes which are being arranged for his Majesty."

"But, Monseigneur, suppose they retain the articles they have stolen in fun?"

"Then they shall be hung."

At this moment an usher entered and announced,—

"Monsieur le Inquisiteur de la Foi!"

Master Arpion did not need to be told to withdraw, He bowed respectfully and left the room.

The man who was ushered in was, in fact, a notable and formidable personage.

To his every-day titles of Doctor of the Sorbonne and Canon of Noyon, he added the extraordinary and high-sounding appellation of 'Grand Inquisitor of the Faith in France.' And in order that he might bear a name as sonorous as his title, he called himself Démocharès, although he was really plain Antoine de Mouchy. The people had christened his subordinates *mouchards*,—police spies.

"Good-evening, Monsieur le Lieutenant de Police," said the grand inquisitor.

"The same to you, Monsieur le Grand Inquisiteur," responded the lieutenant.

"Any news in Paris?"

"I was just about to ask you that very question."

"That means that there is none," observed Démocharès, with a profound sigh. "Ah, these are hard times! There is nothing going on,—no conspiracies, and no crime at all! What cowardly wretches these Huguenots are! Our profession has a decided grievance against them, Monsieur de Braguelonne!"

"No, no!" replied Monsieur de Braguelonne, emphatically. "No, governments change, but the police remains."

"Nevertheless," retorted Monsieur de Mouchy, bitterly, "see what the result has been of our descent upon the main army of the Reformers in the Rue des Marais. By surprising them at table in the midst of their dinner, we hoped to take them in the act of eating pork in the guise of the paschal lamb, as you had told us; but the only result of that magnificent expedition was one poor little larded chicken. Can such exploits as that reflect much credit upon your organization, Monsieur le Lieutenant de Police?"

"One can't always succeed," said Monsieur de Braguelonne. "Were you any more fortunate yourself, in the matter of the advocate of Place Maubert,—Trouillard, was it not? Yet you expected great things of it."

"I admit it," said Démocharès, piteously.

"You expected to prove as clearly as the day," continued Monsieur de Braguelonne, "that this Trouillard had abandoned his two daughters to the tender mercies of his fellow-enthusiasts after a frightful orgy; but, behold! the witnesses whom you had bought at such a high price suddenly retracted everything and gave you the lie."

"The traitors!" muttered De Mouchy.

"More than that," said the lieutenant, pitilessly pursuing his advantage, "I received reports from various sources, all of which went to show that the virtue of the two young girls was without a stain."

"It was infamous," grumbled Démocharès.

"A bad failure, Monsieur le Grand Inquisiteur de la Foi, a bad failure!" repeated Monsieur de Braguelonne, with much complacency.

"Well," cried Démocharès, impatiently, "if the affair did miscarry, it was all your fault!"

"What, my fault!" ejaculated the amazed lieutenant.

"To be sure. You content yourself with reports and retractations, and such nonsense. Of what consequence are these repulses and contradictions? We must go ahead all the same, and boldly accuse the villains as if we had met no rebuff at all."

"What! without proofs?"

"Yes, and convict them."

"When they have committed no crime?"

"Yes, and hang them."

"Without judges?"

"Yes, a hundred times yes! Without judge or crime or proof! There's no great merit in hanging only those who are really guilty."

"But what an outcry of rage there will be against us then!" said Monsieur de Braguelonne.

"Ah! that is what I expected you would say," rejoined Démocharès, triumphantly. "That is the very corner-stone of my whole system, Monsieur. For what does this rage of which you speak lead to? Conspiracy. What is the outcome of conspiracy? Revolution. And what is the principal result of revolution? Why, to make your office and mine of very great importance and utility."

"To be sure, from that point of view!" said Monsieur de Braguelonne, laughing.

"Ah, Monsieur," observed Démocharès, with the air of a master, "remember this principle, 'In order to reap crimes we must first sow them.' Persecution is a very great force."

"Well, I must say," rejoined the lieutenant, "that it seems to me we have not been behindhand in that direction since the beginning of this reign. It would be difficult to stir up and provoke the discontented of all sorts more than we have done."

"Pshaw! what have we done?" asked the grand inquisitor, scornfully.

"Well, in the first place, do you consider the daily domiciliary visits and despoiling of all the Huguenots, innocent or guilty, of no account?"

"My faith! yes, I consider them of absolutely no account," was Démocharès's reply; "for you see with what tranquil patience they bear these annoyances, which are altogether too trifling."

"And the punishment of Anne Dubourg, nephew of a chancellor of France, who was burned two months since in the Place de Grève,—was that nothing?"

"It was a very small thing," said the fastidious De Mouchy. "What was the result of it? The murder of President Minard, one of his judges, and an apocryphal conspiracy of which we never, succeeded in finding any traces. So that was nothing to make a very great amount of talk about."

"Well, what do you say to the last edict?" asked Monsieur de Braguelonne,—"the last edict, which strikes, not at the Huguenots alone, but at the whole nobility of the kingdom. For my own part, I said frankly to Monsieur le Cardinal de Lorraine that I thought it went a little too far."

"Are you speaking of the ordinance suppressing pensions?" said Démocharès.

"No, indeed, but of the one which requires all suitors, whether of high or low birth, to quit the court within twenty-four hours, under pain of being hanged. You must agree that to decree the halter for gentlemen and clowns alike is rather severe, and likely to lead to trouble."

"Yes, the order does not lack audacity," said Démocharès, with a smile of satisfaction. "Fifty years ago such an edict would, I confess, have excited the whole nobility to revolt. But now you see they only complain, and do nothing overt. Not one of them has raised a hand."

"That's where you are mistaken, Monsieur le Grand Inquisiteur," said Braguelonne, lowering his voice; "and though they may not be stirring at Paris, there is trouble brewing in the Provinces."

"Aha!" cried De Mouchy, eagerly, "you have some intelligence of that sort?"

"Not yet, but I expect it every moment."

"From what quarter?"

"From the Loire."

"Have you agents there?"

"Only one, but he is a good one."

"Only one? that's very risky," remarked Démocharès, with a very knowing air.

"I much prefer, myself," replied Monsieur de Braguelonne, "to pay a single trustworthy man, who is at once intelligent and reliable, the price of twenty stupid rascals. That is my way; what do you think?"

"Oh, that's all very well; but who is responsible to you for this man?"

"Well, his head in the first place; and then his past services, too, for he has been put to the proof."

"Never mind; it's very risky," persisted Démocharès. Master Arpion came softly in while Monsieur de Mouchy was speaking, and whispered in his master's ear.

"Aha!" cried the lieutenant, triumphantly. "Very well! Arpion, introduce Lignières at once. Yes, while Monsieur le Grand Inquisiteur is here; for is he not one of us?"

Arpion saluted and withdrew.

"This Lignières is the very man of whom I was speaking to you," continued Monsieur de Braguelonne, rubbing his hands. "You shall hear what he says. He has just arrived from Nantes. We have no secrets from each other, have we?—and I am very glad to have an opportunity to prove to you that my way is as good as another."

At this point Master Arpion opened the door to Lignières.

It was the selfsame little fellow, lean and hungry-looking, whose acquaintance we have already made at the Protestant meeting in the Place Maubert,—the same who had so boldly exhibited the republican medal, and prated about decapitated lilies and crowns trodden under foot.

Thus we may see that even if the name of instigating agent (*agent provocateur*) had not come into use at that time, the article itself was in a flourishing condition.

CHAPTER XVIII
A SPY

Lignières, as he entered the room, cast a look of cold distrust upon Démocharès, and after he had saluted Monsieur de Braguelonne, remained cautiously silent and motionless, waiting to be questioned.

"I am delighted to see you, Monsieur Lignières," was Monsieur de Braguelonne's greeting. "You may speak with perfect freedom before Monsieur le Grand Inquisiteur de la Foi en France."

"Oh, to be sure!" Lignières made haste to exclaim; "and if I had had any idea that I was in the presence of the illustrious Démocharès, pray believe, Monseigneur, that I should not have hesitated as I have."

"Very well!" said De Mouchy, nodding his head approvingly, and evidently much flattered by the spy's respectful deference.

"Come, speak, Monsieur Lignières!—waste no time," said the lieutenant of police.

"But it may be," suggested Lignières, "that Monsieur is not thoroughly conversant with what took place at the last meeting but one held by the Protestants at La Ferté?"

"In fact, I know very little about it," replied Démocharès.

"Then if I may," added Lignières, "I will briefly recount the serious facts which I have gathered recently; that course will be better, and make what comes after more readily understood."

Monsieur de Braguelonne gave the signal of assent, for which Lignières was waiting. This little delay was doubtless annoying to the impatient lieutenant; but it also flattered his pride by affording an opportunity of showing off to the grand inquisitor the superior capacity and extraordinary eloquence of the agent he had chosen.

It is certain that Démocharès was not only surprised, but that he felt the delight of a skilful connoisseur who recognizes a more unexceptionable and perfect instrument than he has himself previously possessed.

Lignières, much excited by this appreciation in such a high quarter, tried to show himself worthy of it, and his performance was really very fine.

"That first assemblage at La Ferté was really not of very much importance," he began. "There was nothing done or said that was not very insipid; and it was to no purpose that I proposed overthrowing his Majesty, and establishing in France a constitution like that in vogue among the Swiss cantons; my suggestions found no echo but insulting remarks. It was only provisionally determined to present a petition to the king, praying that there might be an end to the persecutions of the Reformers, and that the Guises should be dismissed, a ministry formed, headed by the princes of the blood, and the States-General be convoked forthwith. Simply a petition!—a very meagre result that. However, they made an accurate computation of their numbers and effected an organization; that is something tangible. Then the matter of choosing leaders came up. So long as it was only a question of the subordinate leaders in the different districts there was no trouble; but the commander-in-chief, the head and front of the conspiracy,—that is where the difficulty began. Monsieur de Coligny and the Prince de Condé declined through their respective mouthpieces the dangerous honor which it was proposed to confer upon one or the other of them. It would be much better, so we were told in their behalf, to select some Huguenot who occupied a less lofty position, so that the movement might bear a more unmistakable stamp of its popular character,—a fine excuse for the simpletons! However, they were content with it; and after much debate they finally elected Godefroid de Barry, Seigneur de la Renaudie."

"La Renaudie!" Démocharès repeated the name. "Yes, he is in fact one of the ardent ringleaders of these scoundrels. I know him to be an energetic and resolute man."

"You will soon know him for a Catiline!" said Lignières.

"Oh, ho!" said the lieutenant of police; "I think that is going a little too far."

"You will see," returned the spy,—"you will see if I am going too far! I come now to our second convocation, which met at Nantes the 5th of this month of February."

"Aha!" cried Démocharès and Braguelonne together.

Both moved closer to Master Lignières, with eager curiosity.

"That was the time," said Lignières, bursting with importance, "when they no longer confined themselves to mere talk. Listen! Shall I give your

Lordships at length all the details and the proofs, or shall I hasten at once to the results?" added the villain, as if he wished to continue to hold their two hearts dependent on his words as long as possible.

"Give us the facts—the facts!" cried the lieutenant, impatiently.

"Very well, then, and you will shudder when you hear them. After some unimportant preliminary speechmaking, La Renaudie took the floor; and this, in substance, is what he said: 'Last year, when the Queen of Scotland desired to try the ministers at Stirling, all their parishioners determined to follow them to that place; and although they were unarmed, this extensive movement was quite sufficient to frighten the regent and induce her to forego the violent measures she had meditated. I propose that here in France we begin in like manner,—that a great multitude of those of our belief should make their way to Blois, where the king is living for the moment, and should present themselves without arms before his Majesty, and hand him a petition wherein he will be implored to recall the edicts of persecution, and allow the Reformers the free exercise of their religion; and since their secret meetings in the night-time have been falsely slandered, he will be asked to permit them to assemble in their places of worship under the eyes of the constituted authorities.'"

"Well, well, always the same thing!" Démocharès interrupted, in a tone of disappointment. "Peaceful and respectful demonstrations, which amount to nothing! Petitions! protests! supplications! Is this the awe-inspiring news you had to give us, Master Lignières?"

"Oh, wait,—just wait!" replied Lignières. "You can understand that I cried down this innocent proposition of La Renaudie's just as you do,—nay, even more than you. To what, I asked, had such purposeless steps led before, or to what could they be expected to lead? Others of the Protestants spoke in the same strain. Thereupon La Renaudie, with much satisfaction, disclosed the true inwardness of his heart, and betrayed the audacious scheme which lay hidden beneath his innocent words."

"Let us hear this audacious scheme," said Démocharès, with the air of a man not easily to be astonished.

"It is well worth the trouble of frustrating, I think," continued Lignières. "While men's minds are occupied with the mob of timid, unarmed petitioners, who approach the throne as suppliants, five hundred horsemen and a thousand foot,—you understand, Messieurs, fifteen hundred men,—selected from among the noblemen who are most determined and most devoted to the Reformation and to the princes, are to come together from the various provinces, under thirty chosen leaders, to advance quietly upon Blois by different roads, enter the town, with or without force, — with or without force, I say, — carry off the king, the queen-mother, and Monsieur de Guise, and bring them to trial, and fill their places with the princes of the blood, leaving it for the States-General to decide upon the form of government which shall finally be adopted. There, Messieurs, is the plot. What do you say to it? Is it a childish one? Should it be passed by without being noticed? In short, am I good for nothing, or am I useful to some extent?"

He came to an end with an expression of triumph. The grand inquisitor and the lieutenant exchanged glances of surprise, not unmixed with alarm. There was a long pause, during which their minds were busy with reflections of various descriptions.

"By the Mass, but this is admirable, I declare!" cried Démocharès, at last.

"Say rather that it is terrible," observed Monsieur de Braguelonne.

"We shall see; we shall see!" continued the grand inquisitor, shaking his head very knowingly.

"Why," said Monsieur de Braguelonne, "we only know the schemes which this La Renaudie avows; but it is very easy to guess that nothing will come of them; that Messieurs de Guise will be on their guard; that they will all be cut in pieces; and that if his Majesty intrusts the power to the Prince de Condé, it will only be by force."

"But we are forewarned!" returned Démocharès. "All that these poor fools mean to do against us will turn against themselves, and they will fall into their own trap. I promise you that Monsieur le Cardinal will be delighted, and would have paid a high price for such an opportunity of making an end of his enemies."

"God grant that he may continue to be delighted to the end!" said Monsieur de Braguelonne.

Addressing Lignières, who had now become a man to be treated well, an invaluable ally, and of great consequence, he said, —

"As for you, Monsieur le Marquis," (the rascal was really a marquis) "you have rendered a most valuable service to his Majesty and to the State. You shall be worthily rewarded for it, never fear!"

"Yes, my word for it!" added Démocharès; "you deserve a handsome reward, Monsieur, and you possess all my esteem! To you, also, Monsieur de Braguelonne, my sincere congratulations upon your choice of agents. Ah, Monsieur de Lignières has a claim to my highest consideration, in truth!"

"That is a very generous recompense for what little I have been able to do," said Lignières, bowing modestly.

"You know that we are not ungrateful, Monsieur de Lignières," continued the lieutenant. "But come, you have not told us everything, have you? Did they fix a time, or a place of rendezvous?"

"They are to meet in the neighborhood of Blois on the 15th of March," replied Lignières.

"The 15th of March! Well, well!" exclaimed Monsieur de Braguelonne. "We have only twenty days before us, and Monsieur le Cardinal de Lorraine is at Blois! It will take about two days to notify him and receive his orders. What a responsibility!"

"But what a triumph at the end!" said Démocharès.

"Have you the names of the leaders, dear Monsieur de Lignières?" asked the lieutenant.

"Yes, I have them written down," was the reply.

"What a jewel of a man!" exclaimed Démocharès, admiringly. "He helps to reconcile me to human nature."

Lignières unbuttoned an inner pocket in his doublet, and drew from it a scrap of paper, and having unfolded it, he read aloud as follows:—

"List of the leaders, with the names of the provinces which they respectively command:—

"Castelnau de Chalosses,—Gascogne.

"Mazères,—Béarn.

"Du Mesnil,—Périgord.

"Maillé de Brézé,—Poitou.

"La Chesnaye,—Maine.

"Sainte-Marie,—Normandie.

"Cocqueville,—Picardie.

"De Ferrières-Maligny,—Île de France and Champagne.

"Châteauvieux,—Provence, etc.

"You can read that list and make your comments upon it at your leisure, Monsieur," said Lignières, handing the treacherous paper to the lieutenant.

"This is nought but organized civil war!" exclaimed Monsieur de Braguelonne.

"Take notice too," added Lignières, "that while these detachments are making their way toward Blois, other leaders in each province are to hold themselves in readiness to put down any movement that may be attempted in behalf of Messieurs de Guise."

"Good! We will have them all as in a great net!" said Démocharès, rubbing his hands. "Why, you seem overwhelmed, Monsieur de Braguelonne! After the first feeling of surprise, I declare that, for my own part, I should be very sorry if all this had not taken place."

"But just see how little time we have left!" observed the lieutenant. "In truth, my good Lignières, while I would not for the world reproach, I must say that since the 5th of February you have had time enough to notify me."

"How could I?" asked Lignières. "I was intrusted by La Renaudie with more than twenty commissions between Nantes and Paris. And not only have I succeeded in gleaning some valuable information, but to have neglected or postponed his commissions would have been to arouse suspicion, while to write you a letter or send a messenger would have been to compromise our secrets."

"Very true," said Monsieur de Braguelonne, "you are always right. Let us say no more about what is done, but consider what there remains to do. You have told us nothing of the Prince de Condé. Was he not with you at Nantes?"

"He was there," Lignières replied. "But before taking any decided step he wished to consult Chaudieu and the English ambassador, and so he said that he would accompany La Renaudie to Paris for that purpose."

"Is he coming to Paris, then? And is La Renaudie also coming?"

"Better than that; they ought both to be here ere this." said Lignières.

"And where do they lodge?" asked Monsieur de Braguelonne, eagerly.

"That I can't tell you. I took pains to ask, in a careless way, where I might find our leader if I had any communication to make; but they only gave me an indirect channel of correspondence. La Renaudie probably does not wish to compromise the prince."

"That is a great pity, I must admit," reflected the lieutenant. "We shall have difficulty in finding traces of them."

At this moment Master Arpion entered once more with his soft and mysterious tread.

"Well, what is it, Arpion?" asked Monsieur de Braguelonne, sharply. "You knew very well that we were engaged with important business, and why the devil do you interrupt us?"

"I should not have ventured to enter unless for something of equal importance," replied Arpion.

"Well, what is it? Tell me quickly, and aloud; for we are all friends here."

"A man named Pierre des Avenelles—" began Arpion.

De Braguelonne, Démocharès, and Lignières exclaimed simultaneously,—

"Pierre des Avenelles!"

"That's the advocate of the Rue des Marmousets, who ordinarily entertains the Protestants at Paris," said Démocharès.

"And upon whose house I have long had my eye," added De Braguelonne. "But the good man is very sly and careful, and has always eluded my surveillance. What does he want, Arpion?"

"To speak with Monseigneur at once," replied the secretary. "He seems to me to be in a state of great alarm."

"He cannot know anything," said Lignières, quickly and jealously. "Besides," he added, with lofty scorn, "he is an honest man."

"We shall see; we shall see!" observed the grand inquisitor. (That was his favorite expression.)

"Arpion," Monsieur de Braguelonne said to the secretary, "show this man in immediately."

"I will, Monseigneur," said Arpion, leaving the room.

"Pardon me, my dear Marquis," continued De Braguelonne, addressing Lignières, "this Des Avenelles knows you, and the unexpected sight of you might disturb him. And then, too, neither you nor I would care to have him know you were one of us. Be good enough to step into Arpion's closet while this interview is in progress; it is there at the end of the passage. I will recall you as soon as we have done with him. You might remain, if you will,

Monsieur le Grand Inquisiteur, for your imposing presence cannot fail to be useful."

"Very well; I will remain to please you," said Démocharès, well content.

"And I will withdraw," said Lignières; "but remember what I say, Monsieur le Lieutenant. You will not learn anything of importance from this fellow Des Avenelles. A poor fool! A timid but upright soul! But of no particular account, — of no account at all."

"We will do the best we can. But go, go, my dear Lignières! here is our man."

In fact, Lignières had but just time to make his escape when a man entered, pale and trembling with nervous excitement, escorted, indeed, almost carried, by Master Arpion.

It was Pierre des Avenelles, the advocate, whom we first-met with Sieur Lignières, at the meeting in the Place Maubert, where he made the success of the evening, if our readers remember, with his courageously timid speech.

CHAPTER XIX
AN INFORMER

On the occasion of this, our second meeting with Pierre des Avenelles, he was all timidity, and had lost his courage.

After bowing to the floor before Démocharès and De Braguelonne, he began in a faltering voice,—

"I am, I presume, in the presence of Monsieur le Lieutenant de Police?"

"And of Monsieur le Grand Inquisiteur de la Foi," added De Braguelonne, waving his hand toward De Mouchy.

"Oh, Holy Virgin!" cried poor Des Avenelles, turning still paler if that were possible. "Messeigneurs, you see, being a very great culprit,—alas! one who has been too guilty,—may I hope for mercy? I know not. Can my sincere wish to atone for my sins help me to lighten their punishment? It is for your clemency to reply."

Monsieur de Braguelonne saw at once with what manner of man he had to do.

"To confess is not sufficient," he said harshly; "there must be reparation as well."

"Oh, there shall be, Monseigneur, if I can accomplish it!" returned Des Avenelles.

"Very well; but in order to accomplish it," continued the lieutenant, "you must have it in your power to be of some service to us, or to give us some valuable information."

"I will try to do so," said the advocate, almost choked with terror.

"It will be very difficult," retorted De Braguelonne, carelessly, "for we already know all there is to know."

"What! you know—"

"Everything, I tell you; and in this pass to which you have brought yourself your tardy repentance will hardly avail to save your head, I promise you."

"My head! Oh, Heaven! My head in danger? Yet I have come—"

"Too late," said the inflexible De Braguelonne. "You cannot now be of any use to us, and we know in advance everything that you can tell us."

"Perhaps not," said Des Avenelles. "Excuse my question, but what do you know?"

"In the first place, that you are one of these damned heretics," interposed Démocharès, in a voice of thunder.

"Alas, alas! that is only too true!" replied Des Avenelles. "Yes, I am of the Religion,—why, I'm sure I have no idea; but I will abjure it, Monseigneur, if you will only spare my life. The meeting-house is surrounded by too many perils, and I will go back to Mass."

"That is not all," said Démocharès; "you are in the habit of entertaining Huguenots at your house."

"No one has ever been able to find one in any of their visitations," returned the advocate, eagerly.

"Very true," said Monsieur de Braguelonne; "for you probably have some secret exit from your house,—some hidden passage, some as yet unknown means of communication with the outer world. But one of these days we will not leave one stone of your house standing on another, and it will be forced to yield us its secret."

"I will give it up to you myself," said the advocate; "for I admit, Monseigneur, that I have at times furnished board and lodging to those of the Religion. They pay well; and my profession is so unremunerative! One must live! But it shall never happen again; and if my abjuration is accepted, no Huguenot will ever dare to knock at my door again."

"You have also spoken frequently at the Protestant meetings," continued Démocharès.

"I am an advocate," whined Des Avenelles. "Besides, I have always spoken in favor of moderate measures. You ought to know that, since you know everything."

Summoning courage to raise his eyes to these two forbidding personages, Des Avenelles went on,—

"But, asking your pardon, it seems to me that you do not know everything; for you speak only about me, and have nothing to say about the affairs of the party in general, which are in truth of vast moment. Therefore I am glad to see that there are many things of which you still know nothing."

"That is just where you are mistaken," retorted the lieutenant; "and we will prove it to you."

Démocharès motioned him to be careful.

"I understand you, Monsieur le Grand Inquisiteur," said he; "but there can be no imprudence in showing our hand to Monsieur, for Monsieur will not leave this place for a long time to come."

"What! not leave here for a long time?" cried Pierre des Avenelles, in affright.

"No, certainly not," coolly remarked Monsieur de Braguelonne. "Do you imagine, pray, that under color of coming here to make revelations, you will be allowed at your ease to observe our position, and assure yourself as to the extent of our information, and then go and report everything to your accomplices? That won't do, my dear Monsieur; and you are our prisoner from this moment."

"Prisoner!" Des Avenelles repeated the word as if overwhelmed at the thought; but upon reflection he adopted a different tone. Our man, we remember, had the courage of cowardice in the highest degree.

"Oh, well,—in fact, I much prefer it so!" he cried. "I am much safer here with you than I should be at home, in the midst of all their plot-hatching. And since you have determined to keep me here, Monsieur le Lieutenant, you will have no scruples now about consenting to reply to some of my respectful questions. In my humble opinion, you are not so thoroughly well informed as you believe, and I think I may find some way of proving my good faith and my loyalty by some valuable revelation."

"Hum! I much doubt it," replied Monsieur de Braguelonne.

"In the first place, what do you know about the latest meetings of the Huguenots, Monseigneur?" asked the advocate.

"Do you mean the one held at Nantes?" said the lieutenant.

"Ah! do you know that? Very well! Yes, the one held at Nantes. What took place there?"

"Do you refer to the conspiracy that was formed there?" rejoined Monsieur de Braguelonne, slyly.

"Alas, yes! I see that I can tell you nothing of consequence on that subject," replied Des Avenelles. "That conspiracy—"

"Has for its object to carry off the king from Blois, substitute the princes for Messieurs de Guise by force, convoke the States-General, etc. All this is ancient history, my dear Monsieur des Avenelles, for it happened way back on the 5th of February."

"And the conspirators who feel so sure of their secret!" exclaimed the advocate. "They are lost, and myself with them; for doubtless you know the leaders of the conspiracy?"

"The secret leaders as well as the avowed ones. The former are the Prince de Condé and the admiral; while the avowed leaders are La Renaudie, Castelnau, Mazères—But it would take too long to enumerate them all. See, here is a list of their names, and of the provinces as well which they are respectively expected to incite to rebellion."

"Great God of mercy! How skilful are the police, and what fools the conspirators!" cried Des Avenelles. "Is there not, then, the least little word which I can tell you, which you do not already know? The Prince de Condé and La Renaudie, for instance,—do you know where they are?"

"Together in Paris."

"Why, this is frightful! And there is nothing left for me to do but to commend my soul to God! Yet, stay!—one word more, in pity's name! Whereabouts in Paris are they?"

Monsieur de Braguelonne did not immediately reply, but with his clear and piercing glance seemed to be reading Des Avenelles's soul and his eyes to their lowest depths.

The latter, with labored breath, repeated his question,—"Do you know in what part of Paris the Prince de Condé and La Renaudie now are, Monseigneur?"

"We shall have no difficulty in finding them," replied Monsieur de Braguelonne.

"But you haven't found them yet!" cried Des Avenelles, with delight. "Ah! God be praised! I may still win my pardon. *I* know where they are, Monseigneur."

Démocharès's eye glistened; but the lieutenant of police concealed his satisfaction.

"Pray, where are they?" he said in the most indifferent tone imaginable.

"At my house, Messieurs, at my house!" said the advocate, proudly.

"I knew it," calmly replied Monsieur de Braguelonne. "What do you say,—you knew that, too?" ejaculated Des Avenelles, whose cheeks lost their color again.

"To be sure I did; but I wished to test your good faith. Come, it is all right, and I am content with you! Your case was a very serious one, to say the least. To think of having sheltered such great villains!"

"You made yourself quite as guilty as they," said Démocharès, sententiously.

"Oh, don't say so, Monseigneur!" rejoined Des Avenelles. "I feared I was incurring great risks, and I have hardly dared to breathe since I have known the horrible plans of my two guests. But I have known them only three days,—only three days, I solemnly swear! You should know that I was not present at the Nantes gathering. When the Prince de Condé and the Seigneur de la Renaudie arrived at my house in the early part of this week, I believed myself to be harboring adherents of the Reformed religion, but not conspirators. I have a holy horror of conspirators and conspiracies! They said nothing to me on the subject at first; and it is that for which I am angry with them. Thus to expose to deadly peril, without his knowledge, a poor fellow who had never done them aught but good turns,—that was very wrong. But these great personages never do otherwise."

"What's that?" was Monsieur de Braguelonne's sharp retort,—for he considered himself a very great man indeed.

"I refer to the great personages of the Reformed religion," the advocate made haste to explain. "However, they began by keeping everything from me; but they were whispering together all day long, and writing day and night; visits they received every minute. I watched and listened; in short, I guessed at the beginning of the plot, so that they were obliged to tell me everything,—their meeting at Nantes, their great conspiracy; in fact, all this that you know, and which they thought so carefully concealed. But since that revelation I have not been able to sleep or eat; I have just existed. Every time that anybody came to my house—and God knows how often people have come there!—I would imagine that they had come to carry me before the judges. During the night, in my rare moments of feverish sleep, I dreamed of nothing but courts and scaffolds and executioners, and I would awake bathed in a cold perspiration, to begin again my unceasing attempts to foresee and estimate the risk I was running."

"The risk you were running, did you say?" said Monsieur de Braguelonne. "Why, prison in the first place—"

"And torture in the second," added Démocharès.

"To be followed probably by hanging," said the lieutenant.

"Or the stake, possibly," continued the grand inquisitor.

"The wheel has been known to be used in such cases," the lieutenant put in, as a suitably effective end to the list.

"Imprisoned! tortured! hanged! burned alive! broken on the wheel!" Poor Des Avenelles repeated every word as if he had actually undergone each of the punishments they enumerated.

"*Dame*! You are an advocate, and should know the law," retorted Monsieur de Braguelonne.

"Indeed, I know it only too well!" cried Des Avenelles. "Therefore, after three days of mortal anguish, I could restrain myself no longer: I felt that such a secret was too heavy a burden for my responsibility, and I came to deposit it in your hands, Monsieur le Lieutenant de Police."

"That was the safest course to pursue," replied Monsieur de Braguelonne; "and although, as you see, your revelation is of no great service to us, still we will take your good intentions into consideration."

He talked for some moments in a low tone with De Mouchy, who seemed to be urging him, not without much resistance, to adopt a certain course of action.

"Before everything, I beg you, for mercy's sake," said Des Avenelles, imploringly, "not to betray my defection to my former—accomplices; for, alas! they who murdered President Minard might well do me an ill turn also."

"We will keep your secret," replied the lieutenant of police.

"But you propose to keep me a prisoner, do you not?" said Des Avenelles, with a very humbled and frightened air.

"No; you may return freely to your own house at any moment," replied De Braguelonne.

"Do you mean it?" said the advocate. "Ah! I see you propose to arrest my guests?"

"Not your guests, either. They will remain as free as yourself."

"How is that?" asked Des Avenelles, in amazement.

"Just listen to me a moment," replied Monsieur de Braguelonne, in an authoritative tone, "and pay good heed to my words. You will return at once to your own house, lest a too long absence should arouse suspicion. You will say not a word more to your guests, either as to your own fears or their secrets. You will act, and leave them to act, as if you had not been in this room to-day. Do you understand me? Hinder nothing, and express surprise at nothing. Let things take their course."

"That is easily done," said Des Avenelles.

"However," added Monsieur de Braguelonne, "if we need any information, we will either send to you for it or summon you hither, and you will hold yourself always in readiness to serve us in either way. If a descent upon your house is judged necessary, you will lend a hand in making it effective."

"Since I have done so much merely to make a beginning, I will go through with it," said Des Avenelles, with a sigh.

"Very well. One word in conclusion. If matters progress in a way to prove that you have obeyed these very simple instructions, you shall have your pardon; but if we have reason to suspect that you have been in the least degree indiscreet, you will be the first to be punished, and will suffer worse than all the others."

"You shall be burned alive, by our Lady!" chimed in Démocharès, in his deep and gloomy voice.

"However—" began the trembling advocate.

"That is sufficient," said De Braguelonne. "You have heard; see that you remember. *Au revoir*."

He made an imperious motion with his hand. The too prudent advocate left the room, relieved and anxious at the same time.

After his departure, for a moment nothing was said by the two others.

"You wished it so, and I yielded," said the lieutenant, finally; "but I confess that I have serious doubts as to the wisdom of that mode of procedure."

"No, everything is as well as can be," replied Démocharès. "This business must be allowed to take its own course, and with that in view, the important point was not to give the alarm to the conspirators. Let them think themselves sure of their secret, and go ahead in their false security. They fancy that they are marching in darkness, while we are following all their movements in the broad daylight. It is superb! Such another occasion to strike a deadly blow at the root of the heresy will not present itself in twenty years. Besides, I know the ideas of his Eminence the Cardinal de Lorraine upon this matter."

"Better than I do, to be sure," said De Braguelonne. "What are we to do now?"

"You will remain at Paris," said Démocharès, "and with the assistance of Lignières and Des Avenelles, keep a strict watch upon the two leading conspirators. I shall set out in an hour for Blois, to warn Messieurs de Guise. The cardinal will be somewhat alarmed at first, but Le Balafré is with him to encourage him; and when he comes to think it over, he will be in an ecstasy of delight. It is for those two to assemble in a fortnight around the king, without disturbance, all the forces they have available. Meanwhile, our Huguenots will have nothing to startle them; they will fall in a body, or one by one, into the trap we have laid, the blind fools, and they will be at our mercy. We shall have them, and then,—'General slaughter!'"

The grand inquisitor stalked up and down the room rubbing his hands for joy.

"May God grant," said Monsieur de Braguelonne, "that no unforeseen event shall reduce this splendid scheme to nought!"

"Impossible!" Démocharès made haste to say. "General slaughter! We have them on the hip! Call Lignières back, if you will, so that he may finish with the information he has for us, which I am to report to the Cardinal de Lorraine. But I look upon the heresy as already extinct. General slaughter!"

CHAPTER XX
A CHILD KING AND QUEEN

If in imagination we go forward two days, and traverse forty leagues of space, we may fancy ourselves on the 27th of February at the splendid Château de Blois, where the court was temporarily established.

There had been a great celebration at the château the day before, with jousting and ballets and allegorical representations, all under the direction of Monsieur Antoine de Baïf the poet.

So that on the morning in question the young king and his queen, for whose entertainment the fête had been given, had risen rather later than usual, and not fully rested from the fatigue of their holiday-making.

Fortunately no reception was appointed for that day, so that they were at liberty to amuse themselves by chatting over at their leisure the things that had pleased their fancy.

"For my own part," said Mary Stuart, "I thought all the entertainments the finest and rarest things imaginable."

"Yes," replied François, "especially the ballets and the scenes that were acted. But I must confess that the sonnets and madrigals seemed to me a trifle tiresome."

"What!" cried Mary; "why, they were very bright and clever, I assure you."

"But too everlastingly eulogistic, you must agree, *mignonne*. You see, it's not especially amusing to hear one's self praised thus by the hour; and I could not help fancying last evening that the good God Himself must sometimes have His moments of being bored in His Paradise. Then you must remember, too, that these gentlemen, especially Messieurs de Baïf and de Maisonfleur, have a way of interlarding their discourse with numbers of Latin words, which I do not always understand."

"But that has a very learned air," said Mary, "and it is a fashion which makes me feel very literary and of very correct taste."

"Ah, Mary, you know so much yourself!" replied the young king, smiling. "You can make verses, and you understand Latin, too, while I have never succeeded in making any headway in it."

"But study is our lot, and the only amusement we women have, just as you men and princes are born to action and command."

"Nevertheless," rejoined François, "just for the sake of equalling you in one thing, I would like to know as much as my brother Charles."

"Apropos of our brother Charles," Mary interrupted, "did you notice him yesterday in the part he assumed in the allegory of 'Religion defended by the Three Divine Virtues'?"

"Yes," said the king; "he was one of the horsemen who represented the virtues,—Charity, I think."

"The very same," replied Mary. "Well, did you see, Sire, with what fury he belabored the head of poor Heresy?"

"Yes, indeed, when she came forward in the midst of the flames with the body of a serpent. Charles seemed to be quite beside himself, really."

"And, tell me, gentle Sire," continued the queen, "did not that head of Heresy seem to you to resemble some one?"

"Why, yes," said François, "I thought I must be mistaken; but it assuredly wore the expression of Monsieur de Coligny, did it not?"

"Say, rather, that it was Monsieur l'Amiral, feature for feature."

"And all those devils who carried him off!" said the king.

"And the joy of our uncle the cardinal!"

"And my mother's smile."

"It was almost frightful!" said the young queen. "And yet, François, your mother was very beautiful last evening with her dress of shimmering gold and her tan-colored veil,—a magnificent costume!"

"Yes, it was," replied the king; "and so, my *mignonne*, I have ordered a similar dress for you at Constantinople, through Monsieur de Grandchamp, and you shall also have a veil of Roman gauze like my mother's."

"Oh, thanks, my gallant spouse! Thanks! I certainly do not envy the fate of our sister Élisabeth of Spain, who, they say, never wears the same dress twice. And yet I should not like to have any woman in France, even your mother, seem to be more finely dressed than I, especially in your eyes."

"Ah, what difference does it make, after all?" said the king; "for will you not always be the loveliest of them all?"

"It hardly seemed so yesterday," pouted Mary; "for after the torch-dance that I danced, you never said a single word to me. I must needs think that you did not like it."

"Indeed I did!" cried François; "but what could I say, in God's name, beside all those clever wits of the court who were pouring compliments upon you in prose and verse? Dubellay claimed that you had no need of a torch like the other ladies, but that the light that shone from your eyes was sufficient. Maisonfleur was appalled at the danger from the vivid sparks from your eyes which were never extinguished and might destroy the entire hall. Whereupon Ronsard added that the stars which shone in your head might serve to lighten the darkness of the night, and to put the sun to shame by day. Was there any need, pray, after all those poetic flights for me to come and add my poor testimony that I thought you and your dance fascinating?"

"Why not?" was Mary's playful retort. "That little word from you would have rejoiced my heart more than all their tasteless flattery."

"Well, then, I say it this morning, *mignonne*, with all my heart; for the dance was perfect, and almost made me forget the Spanish *pavane* which I used to like so much, and the Italian *pazzemeni*, which you and poor Élisabeth danced together so divinely. In fact, dear, whatever you do is always done better than what others do; for you are the fairest of the fair, and the prettiest women look like chambermaids beside you! Yes, in your royal attire or in this simple dishabille, you are always the same, my queen and my love. I see only you, and I love none but you!"

"Dear *mignon*!"

"My adored darling!"

"My life!"

"My supreme and only good! See! Though you had but a peasant's hood, I would love you better than all the queens of the earth!"

"For my own part," replied Mary, "though you were but a simple page, you and none other would reign in my heart."

"Oh, *mon Dieu*!" added François, "how I love to pass my fingers through your soft silky, fair hair, and to play with it and tangle it! I can well imagine that your women might often ask leave to kiss that round white neck, and those arms, so beautifully turned and so plump. But don't you let them any more, Mary!"

"Why not, pray?"

"Because I am jealous!" said the king.

"Foolish child!" laughed Mary, with an adorable childish gesture.

"Ah!" cried François, passionately, "if I had to choose between renouncing my crown and my Mary, the choice would soon be made."

"What madness!" exclaimed Mary. "How could any one give up the crown of France, which is the fairest of all after the heavenly crown?"

"Because of the mark it makes upon my brow!" said François, with a smile that was half playful and half sad.

"What!" said Mary. "Oh, but I forgot that we have one matter to settle — and a matter of the most supreme importance — which my uncle De Lorraine has thrust upon us."

"Oh, ho!" cried the king; "that does not often happen."

"He leaves it for us," said Mary, very seriously, "to decide upon the color of the uniform of our Swiss Guards."

"That is a mark of confidence which does us great honor. Let us consult upon it. What is your Majesty's opinion upon this difficult question, Madame?"

"Oh, I must only speak after you, Sire."

"Well, then, I think that the style of the coat should remain the same, — a broad doublet with full sleeves, with slashings in three colors. Am I not right?"

"Yes, Sire; but what shall the colors be? That is the question?"

"It is not an easy one; but that is because you do not help me, my fair adviser. The first color?"

"It ought to be white," said Mary, — "the color of France."

"Then the second," declared François, "shall be that of Scotland, — blue."

"Very well; but the third?"

"How would yellow do?"

"Oh, no; that is the color of Spain. Green would be better."

"That is the color of the Guises," said the king.

"Very well, Monsieur; is that a reason for excluding it?"

"No, indeed; but will these three colors harmonize well?"

"Well thought of!" cried Mary Stuart. "Let us take red, the color of Switzerland; it will be in a measure a reminder of their country to the poor fellows."

"An idea as kind as your heart, Mary," the king responded. "There! that momentous affair has come to a glorious conclusion. Ouf! we have had enough trouble with it; fortunately, more serious matters do not give us so much. And your dear uncles, Mary, are so willing to relieve me of all the burden of government! it is delightful! They do the writing, and I have only to sign my name, sometimes without even reading; so that my crown placed upon my royal couch would serve quite as well as I, if the whim should seize me to take a journey."

"Do you not feel sure, Sire," asked Mary, "that my uncles will never have aught at heart save your interest and that of France?"

"How can I help knowing it?" was the reply. "They tell me of it too often to give me any hope of forgetting it. For instance, it is the day for a meeting of the council to-day: and we shall see Monsieur le Cardinal de Lorraine come in with his deep humility and his overdone respect,—which do not always amuse me, I confess,—and shall hear him say in his soft voice, bowing at every word, 'Sire, the suggestion I have the honor to make to your Majesty is aimed only at maintaining the honor of your crown. Your Majesty cannot doubt the zeal for the glory of your reign and the welfare of your people by which we are animated. Sire, the splendor of the throne and of the Church is the only end,' etc."

"How perfectly you imitate him!" cried Mary, laughing and clapping her hands.

But in a more serious tone she continued,—

"We must be indulgent and generous, François. Pray, do you suppose that your lady-mother, Catherine de Médicis, gives me much pleasure when, with her pale face sternly set, she reads me endless sermons upon my dress and my servants and my establishment? Can you not hear her now saying to me, with her lips pursed up, 'My daughter, you are the queen. I am to-day only the second woman in the kingdom; but if I were in your place, I should require my women to attend Mass no less regularly than vespers and the sermon; if I were in your place, I would never wear carnation velvet, because it is too gaudy a color; if I were in your place, I would have my silver-gray dress made over, because it is too *décollettée*; if I were in your place, I would never dance myself, but would be content to watch others; if I were in your place—'"

"Oh, oh!" cried the king, shrieking with laughter; "it is my mother herself! But then, you see, *mignonne*, she is my mother, after all; and I have already offended her grievously by leaving no share for her in the affairs of

State, which are entirely administered by your uncles; so we must put up with some things we don't like, and respectfully bear with her scolding. I, too, will resign myself to the gentle tutelage of the Cardinal de Lorraine, just because you are his niece, do you hear?"

"Thanks, dear Sire!—thanks for the sacrifice!" and Mary emphasized her words with a kiss.

"But, joking apart," continued François, "there are times when I am tempted to renounce the title of king, as I have already abandoned the power."

"Oh, why do you say that?" cried Mary.

"Because I feel it, Mary. Ah, if only it were not necessary to be King of France in order to be your husband! Just consider a moment! I have nought but the weariness and restraints of royalty. The humblest of our subjects is freer than I. Why, if I had not been downright angry at the suggestion, we should have had to occupy separate apartments! Why, do you suppose? Because they alleged that it was the custom of kings and queens of France!"

"How ridiculous they are with their customs!" exclaimed Mary. "Oh, well, we have changed all that, and established a new custom,—which, thank God, is much better than the other."

"To be sure it is, Mary. But, tell me, do you know the secret desire I have been cherishing for a long time?"

"No,—indeed I do not."

"Well, it is to break loose for a while,—to fly or steal away, and leave the throne to take care of itself; to turn our backs upon Paris, Blois, yes, even upon France itself, and go—where? I don't know nor care, so long as it is far away from here, where we can breathe at our ease for a little while like other people. Mary, would not such a journey, say for six months or a year, please you?"

"Oh, I should be perfectly delighted, my beloved Sire," replied Mary, "especially for your sake; for I am sometimes unquiet about your health, and you suffer too frequently with these distressing headaches. The change of air and of scene would distract your thoughts, and be a most excellent thing for you. Yes, let us go, let us go! But, oh! the cardinal and the queen-mother,—will they listen to such a plan?"

"Well, after I am king and I am master," said François. "The kingdom is quiet and peaceable; and since they get along very well without my will in the government, they can do quite as well without my presence. We will take our flight in advance of the winter, Mary, like the swallows. Let us see. Where would you like to go? Suppose we were to visit your Scottish States?"

"What! cross the seal," said Mary. "Expose your delicate chest, my *mignon*, to those dangerous fogs? No! I should prefer our smiling Touraine and this fair Château de Blois. But why should we not pay a visit to our sister Élisabeth in Spain?"

"The air of Madrid is not wholesome for kings of France, Mary."

"Oh, well! Italy, then!" suggested Mary. "It is always lovely there, and always warm,—blue sky and blue water; orange-trees in flower, and music, and continual holiday-making!"

"Italy accepted!" cried the king, joyously. "We will see the Holy Catholic Religion in all its glory,—the magnificent churches and the relics of the saints."

"And Raphael's paintings," added Mary, "and St. Peter's, and the Vatican."

"We will ask the Holy Father for his blessing, and will bring back our hands full of indulgences."

"Oh, it will be delightful," said the queen, "to realize this lovely dream together, side by side, beloved and loving, with heaven in our hearts, and on our heads—"

"Paradise!" cried François, enthusiastically.

But even as he spoke, carried away by the fascinating thought, the door opened suddenly, and the Cardinal de Lorraine, pushing aside the usher in attendance, who had no time to announce him, burst into the royal apartment, pale and breathless.

The Duc de Guise, less excited but quite as serious, followed his brother at a short distance, and his measured step could be heard in the antechamber through the door, which remained open.

CHAPTER XXI
END OF THE ITALIAN JOURNEY

"Well, Monsieur le Cardinal," said the young king, warmly, "am I not to be allowed a moment of leisure and freedom even in this place?"

"Sire," replied Charles de Lorraine, "I am very sorry to disobey your Majesty's orders; but the affair which has led my brother and myself hither is of too great moment to admit of delay."

As he spoke, the Duc de Guise came gravely in, saluted the king and queen silently, and remained standing behind his brother, mute, immovable, and very serious.

"Very well! I am listening, Monsieur; therefore speak," said François to the cardinal.

"Sire," continued the latter, "a conspiracy against your Majesty has been discovered, and your life is no longer safe in this Château de Blois; you should depart hence immediately."

"A conspiracy! Depart from Blois!" exclaimed the king. "Pray, what does all this mean?"

"It means, Sire, that evil-minded men are conspiring against the life and the crown of your Majesty."

"What!" said François, "can they have any ill-will against me, so young as I am, and only seated on the throne yesterday! against me, who have never injured a single soul,—that is to say, knowingly or wilfully! Who are these evil-minded men, Monsieur le Cardinal?"

"Why, who should they be," rejoined Charles de Lorraine, "if not these cursed Huguenot heretics?"

"Heretics again!" cried the king. "Are you sure, Monsieur, that you are not allowing yourself to be led astray by suspicions which have no foundation in fact?"

"Alas!" said the cardinal, "there is, unhappily, no room for doubt now."

The young king, whose delightful dreams were thus interrupted by this unpleasant reality, seemed greatly annoyed; Mary was much disturbed by his ill-humor, and the cardinal very anxious over the news he had brought. Le Balafré, alone calm and self-controlled, awaited the result of all this talk in an attitude of utter impassibility.

"In God's name, what have I done to my people that they love me no longer!" continued François, bitterly.

"I think I told your Majesty that it is only the Huguenots who are rebellious," said the Cardinal de Lorraine.

"Well, they are Frenchmen!" rejoined the king. "In fact, Monsieur le Cardinal, I have intrusted all my power to your hands in the hope that you would cause it to be blessed, and yet I am continually encompassed by anxiety and complaints and discontent."

"Oh, Sire, Sire!" exclaimed Mary Stuart, reproachfully.

The Cardinal de Lorraine retorted dryly,—

"It would be hardly fair, Sire, to hold us responsible for ills which are due entirely to the troublous condition of the time."

"Nevertheless, Monsieur," continued the youthful king, "I should like for once to know the real condition of affairs, and to be without you at my side for a while, so that I might ascertain whether the disaffection is directed against myself or you."

"Oh, your Majesty!" cried Mary Stuart, in great alarm.

François said no more, for he already reproached himself for having gone too far. The Duc de Guise did not manifest the least disturbance. Charles de Lorraine, after an embarrassing silence, replied, with the dignified and constrained air of a man unjustly offended,—

"Sire, since we are unfortunate enough to see that our efforts are misunderstood or not appreciated, and are therefore useless, it only remains for us, as your loyal subjects and devoted kinsmen, to give place to others more worthy or more fortunate—"

The king, in his confusion, said nothing; and the cardinal continued, after a pause,—

"Your Majesty has only to tell us in whose hands to place our seals of office. So far as I am concerned, nothing will be easier than to fill my place. Your Majesty will simply have to choose between Monsieur le Chancelier Olivier, Monsieur le Cardinal de Tournon, and Monsieur de l'Hôpital."

Mary Stuart hid her face in her hands in despair; while poor repentant François would have asked for nothing better than to recall his childish indignation, but the haughty silence of Le Balafré frightened him.

Charles de Lorraine continued: "The office of grand master, however, and the management of affairs in case of war, demand such extraordinary talents and such lofty renown that, after my brother, I can think of only two men who could venture to pretend to fill his place,—Monsieur de Brissac, perhaps—"

"Oh, Brissac is always scolding, and always in a passion!" exclaimed the king; "he is not to be thought of!"

"Well, the other one," continued the cardinal, "is Monsieur de Montmorency, who surely has the renown even though he lacks the necessary talents."

"Oh, no!" François objected again; "Monsieur le Connétable is too old for me, and he formerly treated the dauphin too slightingly to make it probable that he would serve the king with due respect to-day. But, Monsieur le Cardinal, why do you omit to mention my other kinsmen, the princes of the blood,—the Prince de Condé, for example?"

"Sire," said the cardinal, "it is with deep regret that I inform your Majesty of the fact, but among the names of the secret leaders of the conspiracy that has been unearthed, that of the Prince de Condé stands first."

"Is it possible?" asked the young king, almost stupefied.

"Sire, there is no doubt about it."

"Then this must be really a serious conspiracy against the State?" said François.

"It is almost a rebellion, Sire," replied the cardinal; "and since your Majesty relieves my brother and myself from the most awful responsibility that has ever been laid upon us, my duty compels me to implore you to name our successors as soon as possible,—for the Huguenots will be under the walls of Blois in a few days."

"What do you say, my uncle?" cried Mary, in dismay.

"The truth, Madame."

"Are the rebels numerous?" asked the king.

"Sire, they are said to be two thousand strong," replied the cardinal. "There were rumors that their advance-guard was already near La Carrelière, but I could hardly believe them until Monsieur de Mouchy brought me intelligence of the conspiracy from Paris. We will withdraw now, Sire, Monsieur de Guise and myself—"

"What's that?" exclaimed François. "Do you both select such a time of danger as this to desert me?"

"But I thought I understood, Sire," returned Charles de Lorraine, "that such was your Majesty's intention."

"What do you wish?" said the king. "I cannot help being sad when I see how many enemies you have made—I mean how many enemies I have! But come, let us say no more about it, good uncle; give me more details as to the insolent attempt of these rebels."

"Pardon, Sire!" retorted the cardinal, still standing on his dignity; "after what your Majesty has said, it seems to me that others than ourselves—"

"Oh, dear uncle, I implore you to say no more about my hasty words, which I am sorry for," said François II. "What more can I say? Must I apologize, pray, and ask your pardon?"

"Oh, Sire!" said Charles de Lorraine, "at the moment that your Majesty restores his precious confidence to us—"

"Entirely, and with all my heart," added the king, offering his hand to the cardinal.

"Just so much valuable time lost!" said the Duc de Guise, gravely.

It was the first word he had uttered since the beginning of the interview.

He came forward now, as if all that had gone before had been simply unimportant preliminaries a wearisome prologue, in which he had allowed the Cardinal de Lorraine to sustain the principal part; but these puerile discussions being at an end, he haughtily took the floor and assumed the initiative.

"Sire," said he to the king, "this, in brief, is the condition of affairs: two thousand rebels, commanded by Baron de la Renaudie, and encouraged underhand by the Prince de Condé, are preparing a descent at this time from Poitou, Béarn, and other provinces, with the view of surprising Blois and carrying off your Majesty."

François made a gesture of indignation and surprise.

"Carry off the king!" cried Mary Stuart.

"And you with him, Madame," continued Le Balafré. "But never fear; we will take good care of your Majesties."

"What measures do you propose to take?" asked the king.

"We received warning of this only an hour since," said the Duc de Guise. "But the first thing to do, Sire, is to assure the safety of your sacred person. For that purpose, it is necessary that you should leave this unfortified town of Blois and its unprotected château this very day, to withdraw to Amboise, where there is a fortified château which will protect you against a sudden blow."

"What!" said the queen; "imprison ourselves in that vile Château d'Amboise, perched up on top of a rock, and so gloomy and sad!"

"Child!" was what Le Balafré's harsh look said to his niece, though he did not put it in words.

He said simply, —

"Madame, it must be done!"

"But that will be flying from these rebels!" said the young king, trembling with rage.

"Sire," rejoined the duke, "you cannot fly from an enemy who has not yet attacked you, nor even declared war against you. We are supposed to be in ignorance of the guilty designs of these factionists."

"However, we do know them," said François.

"I beg your Majesty to rely upon me as regards these questions of honor," replied François de Lorraine. "We do not shun the combat simply by changing the field of battle; and I sincerely hope that the rebels will take the trouble of following us to Amboise."

"Why do you say that you hope so, Monsieur?" asked the king.

"Why?" said Le Balafré, with his superb smile. "Because it will be a good opportunity to put an end once for all to heretics and heresy; because it is high time to strike at them in some other way than in fiction and allegory; because I would have given two fingers of my hand—my left hand—to bring about without difficulty the decisive struggle which these reckless fools are inviting, for our triumph."

"Alas!" sighed the king, "is this struggle anything less than civil war?"

"Let us accept it for the sake of having done with it," replied the Duc de Guise. "This, in a word, is my plan,—your Majesty must remember that we have only these rebels to deal with: Saving this retreat from Blois, which will not arouse their suspicions, I hope, we will affect the most complete security and most utter ignorance in regard to their plans. And when they advance upon us, like the traitors that they are, to surprise us, we shall be the ones to surprise them, and catch them in their own trap. Therefore let no sign of alarm escape you, or any appearance of flight; this advice is meant especially for you, Madame," he said, turning to Mary. "My orders will be given, and your people notified to be ready, but it will be done secretly. Let there be no suspicion outside of our preparations or our apprehensions, and I will answer for everything."

"What hour is fixed for our departure?" asked François, with a dejected air of resignation.

"Sire, three in the afternoon," said the duke; "I have taken all needful steps."

"What! before coming to me?"

"Even so, Sire," replied Le Balafré, firmly; "for before I came to you, I was perfectly sure that your Majesty would listen to the voice of reason and honor."

"Very well!" said the young king, with a feeble smile, completely conquered, "we will be ready at three o'clock, Monsieur; we have every confidence in you."

"Sire," said the duke, "I thank you for your confidence, and will strive to merit it. But I beg your Majesty to excuse me, for at such times minutes are precious, and I have twenty letters to write, and a hundred commissions to give out. Therefore my brother and myself will humbly take leave of your Majesty."

He saluted the king and queen quite abruptly, and went out with the cardinal.

François and Mary gazed at each other ruefully for a moment without speaking.

"Well, my darling," said the king at last, "how about our fair vision of a journey to Rome?"

"It seems to have resolved itself into a flight to Amboise," sighed Mary.

At this moment Madame Dayelle, the queen's first lady-in-waiting, appeared.

"Pray, Madame, is this true that I have heard?" said she, after the ordinary salutation. "Must we break up our establishment here at once, and quit Bloise for Amboise?"

"It is only too true, my poor Dayelle," replied Mary.

"Do you know, Madame, that there is nothing, absolutely nothing, in that château?—not even a decent mirror!"

"Then we must carry everything from here, Dayelle," said the queen. "Write out at once a list of the things we must have; I will dictate to you. In the first place, my new dress of crimson damask with gold lace trimming—"

Turning to the king, who was still standing in the window recess, thoughtful and sad,—

"Just fancy, Sire," said she, "the audacity of these Reformers! But, pardon me, you ought also to be thinking about what things you will need at Amboise, so that you will not be unprovided."

"No," said François; "I will leave all that to Aubert, my *valet de chambre*. I myself can think of nothing but my disappointment."

"Do you think mine is any less bitter?" said Mary. "Madame Dayelle, put down my violet farthingale covered with gold camblet, and my white damask dress with silver trimming. But we must make the best of it," she continued, addressing the king, "and not run the risk of being without articles of the first importance. Madame Dayelle, don't forget my bedgown of plain cloth-of-gold trimmed with lynx. Not for ages, Sire, has the old Château d'Amboise been inhabited by the court, has it?"

"Since the days of Charles VIII.," said François, "I do not think that a king of France has ever lived there for more than two or three days."

"And we may have to stay there a whole month!" exclaimed Mary. "Oh, those wretched Huguenots! Don't you think, Madame Dayelle, that the bedchamber at all events will be partly furnished?"

"The surest way, Madame," said the lady-in-waiting, shaking her head, "will be to go prepared to find nothing at all there."

"Then put down the gold-framed mirror," said the queen, "the violet velvet jewel-case, and the shaggy carpet to put around the bed. But have subjects ever before been known, Sire," she continued in a low tone, returning to the king's side, "to march against their master thus, and drive him from his own house, so to speak?"

"Never, I think, Mary," was François's melancholy reply. "Sometimes scoundrels have been known to resist the execution of the king's commands, as was the case fifteen years since at Mérindol and La Cabrière; but to attack the king in the first place,—I could never have imagined such a thing, I declare!"

"Oh, my uncle Guise is right, then! We cannot take too many precautions against these hot-headed rebels. Madame Dayelle, add a dozen or so pairs of shoes, and twelve pillows and sheets. Is that all? Really, I believe I am losing my mind! Wait a moment, my dear! Here, put in this velvet pincushion and this gold candlestick and bodkin and gilt needle-case. There, I see nothing else."

"Will not Madame carry her two jewel-cases?"

"Yes, indeed, I will carry them!" cried Mary, eagerly. "Leave them here! Why, they might fall into the hands of these miscreants, might they not, Sire? I am quite sure I will carry them."

"It will be a wise precaution," said François, with a slight smile.

"I think I have omitted nothing else of consequence, my dear Dayelle?" continued Mary, looking around the room.

"Madame will remember her 'Book of Hours,' I trust," said the maid-of-honor, rather affectedly.

"Ah, I should have forgotten them," said Mary, ingenuously. "Let me have the finest ones,—the one which my uncle the cardinal gave me and the scarlet velvet one with the gold ornaments. Madame Dayelle, I leave you to look after all this. You see how preoccupied the king and myself are by the disagreeable necessity for this sudden departure."

"Madame has no need to quicken my zeal," said the duenna. "How many chests and trunks must I order to carry everything! Five will suffice, I should think."

"Order six, and go now!" replied the queen. "We must not fall short in this deplorable extremity,—six, without counting those of my women, remember! But let them make their own arrangements, for I haven't the heart to attend to all these details. Yes, François, I am like you; I can think of nothing but these Huguenots, alas! You may go now, Dayelle."

"Any orders for the footmen and coachmen, Madame?"

"Let them wear simply their cloth coats," said the queen. "Go, dear Dayelle, without further loss of time."

Dayelle bowed and had taken three or four steps toward the door, when Mary called her back.

"Dayelle," said she, "when I said that our people should wear only their cloth coats, you understand that I meant for the journey. Let them not fail to take with them their capes of violet velvet and their violet cloaks lined with yellow velvet. Do you understand?"

"Yes, Madame. Has Madame any other orders to give?"

"No, nothing more," said Mary. "But see that everything is done promptly; we have only about three hours. Don't forget the footmen's cloaks."

Dayelle left the room without further hindrance.

Mary then turned to the king.

"You approve of these cloaks for our people, Sire, do you not?" she asked. "The Reformers will surely allow us to dress our household as we think fitting. We must not humiliate royalty too much before the rebels. I even venture to hope, Sire, that we may find it possible to give a little fête in their faces at Amboise, though it be such a detestable place."

François shook his head rather gloomily.

"Oh, don't you sneer at the idea!" said Mary. "That would intimidate them more than you think, by letting them see that, after all, we are not much afraid of them. A ball under such circumstances would be most excellent politics, I am not afraid to say; and even your mother, capable woman that she is, could suggest nothing better. But no matter! For all that I say, my heart is none the less torn, my poor, dear Sire. Ah, the villanous Huguenots!"

CHAPTER XXII
TWO APPEALS

Since the fatal tournament Gabriel had led a calm and retired but gloomy life. This man of energetic movement and action, whose days had formerly been so filled with life and excitement, now seemed to take delight only in solitude and forgetfulness.

He never appeared at court, never saw a friend, and scarcely ever left his house, where he passed the long, sad, and dreamy hours with his faithful old nurse Aloyse and the page André, who had come back to him when Diane de Castro had taken her sudden flight to the Benedictine convent at St. Quentin.

Gabriel, still a young man in years, had grown old from grief. He brooded over the past, and had no longer any hope.

How many times during those months, each of which was years long, had he regretted that he was still alive! How many times did he wonder why the Duc de Guise and Mary Stuart had placed themselves between him and the anger of Catherine de Médicis, and had laid upon him the bitter burden of life! What had he to do on earth? What was he good for? Could the tomb be any more barren of result than this existence in which he was languishing,—if, indeed, it could be called an existence!

There were moments, however, when his youthful vigor rose in protest in spite of himself.

Then he would stretch his arms and raise his head and gaze at his sword. At such times he would have a vague feeling that his life was not ended, but that there was still a future for him, and that hours of hot fighting, and perhaps of victory, might sooner or later enter again into his destiny.

In view of everything, however, he could see only two chances of returning to the life of action for which he was best fitted,—a foreign war or religious persecution.

If France, if the king, should find themselves involved in some new war, undertaken for conquest, or to repel invasion, the Comte de Montgommery told himself that his youthful ardor would at once return, and that it would be pleasant for him to die as he had lived,—fighting.

And then how glad he would be to pay the involuntary debt he owed the Duc de Guise and young King François!

Again Gabriel would reflect that it would be a glorious thing to die in defence of the new truths which had shed their light upon his soul during the later days. The cause of the Reformation—in his eyes the cause of justice and liberty—was also a noble and saintly cause to serve.

The young count read assiduously the controversial books and sermons which then abounded. He burned with excitement over the great principles revealed in lofty and soul-stirring words by Luther, Melanchton, Calvin, Theodore de Bèze, and so many others. The books of all these untrammelled thinkers had fascinated and convinced him, and drawn him on to adopt their principles. He would have been proud and happy to sign the attestation of his faith with his blood.

It was always the noble instinct of this noble heart to devote his life to some person or some cause.

Not long since he had risked his life a hundred times to save or to avenge, it might be his father or his beloved Diane,—oh, memories forever bleeding in that wounded heart!—and now, in default of those cherished beings, he would have been glad to struggle in defence of sacred ideas,—

His country in his father's place; his religion in place of his love.

Alas, alas! it is in vain to talk, for it is not the same thing; and enthusiasm for abstract principles can never equal, either in its suffering or its delight, the enthusiasm of fondness for our fellow-creatures.

But yet for one or the other of these two causes, the Reformation or France, Gabriel would have been content to sacrifice his life; and he relied upon one of them to bring about the desired termination of his career.

On the morning of the 6th of March Gabriel was leaning back in his chair in the corner of his fireplace, brooding over the thoughts which had become his very life, when Aloyse brought in to him a messenger, booted and spurred and covered with mud, as if he had just travelled a long way.

It was a rainy morning.

The courier had just arrived from Amboise, under a strong escort, the bearer of several letters from Monsieur le Duc de Guise, lieutenant-general of the kingdom.

One of the letters was addressed to Gabriel, and its contents were as follows:—

> MY DEAR COMPANION,—I am writing this to you in great haste, with neither leisure nor possibility of explaining myself. You told the king and myself that you were devoted to us, and that if ever we were in need of your devoted service, we had only to call upon you.
>
> We do call upon you to-day.
>
> Set out at once for Amboise, where the king and queen are now installed for some weeks. I will tell you on your arrival in what way you can be of use.
>
> It is always understood that you are quite at liberty to act or to hold aloof. Your zeal is too valuable for me to wish to make a bad use of it, or compromise you. But whether you are with us or prefer to remain neutral, I should think I was neglecting a duty if I failed to have confidence in you.
>
> Come, therefore, in all haste, and you will be, as always, most welcome.
>
> Your affectionate friend,
FRANÇOIS DE LORRAINE.
>
> Amboise, the 4th March, 1560.
>
> P.S. Herewith is a safe-conduct, for use in case you should be questioned *en route* by some royal troop.

The messenger from the Duc de Guise had already departed to execute his other commissions when Gabriel finished the letter.

The eager youth rose at once, and said without hesitation to the nurse,—

"Good Aloyse, call André, please, and tell him to have the dapple-gray saddled and to prepare my travelling wallet."

"Are you going away, Monseigneur?" the good woman asked.

"Yes, nurse, to Amboise, within two hours."

There was nothing more to be said; and Aloyse, without a word, went sadly from the room to see that her young master's orders were carried out.

But while his preparations were being made, behold, another messenger appeared, and demanded to speak with the Comte de Montgommery alone.

He made no commotion, and, unlike his predecessor, had no escort. He came in silently and very modestly, and without uttering a sound, handed Gabriel a letter which he had in charge.

Gabriel started as he thought that he recognized him as the same who had formerly brought him La Renaudie's invitation to attend the Protestant meeting in the Place Maubert.

It was in fact the same man; and the letter bore the same signature. It said:—

> FRIEND AND BROTHER,—I did not wish to leave Paris without having seen you; but I had no time, for events came thick and fast, and hurried me on. I must go now, and have not even pressed your hand, nor have I told you our plans and our hopes.
>
> But we know that you are with us, and I know what manner of man you are.
>
> With such as you there is no need of preparation, of meetings, and speech-making,—a word is sufficient.
>
> This is the word: We need you. Come.
>
> Be at Noizai near Amboise by the 10th or 12th of this month of March. You will find there your brave and noble friend De Castelnau. He will tell you what is going on, for I dare not trust it to paper.
>
> It is agreed that you are in no wise bound; that you have a perfect right to stand apart; and that you may always abstain from acting with us without incurring the least suspicion or receiving the slightest reproach.
>
> But in any event come to Noizai, I will meet you there, and we will seek your advice, if we cannot have your assistance.
>
> Then, too, can anything be accomplished by our party unless you are informed with regard to it?
>
> So adieu till we meet at Noizai. We rely upon your presence, at all events.
>
> L. R.

P.S. If any troop of our friends should fall in with you *en route*, our password is, once more, *Genève*, and our countersign, *Gloire de Dieu*!

"In an hour I set out," said Gabriel to the silent messenger, who bowed and took his leave.

"What does all this signify?" Gabriel asked himself when he was alone; "and what is the meaning of these two appeals coming from parties so hostile, and appointing a rendezvous at almost the same place? But it makes no difference at all! My obligations toward the omnipotent duke and toward the oppressed Reformers are equally certain. My duty is to set out at once. Then come what come may! However difficult my position may become, my conscience knows well that I shall never turn traitor."

An hour later Gabriel began his journey, accompanied only by André.

But he hardly foresaw the extraordinary and terrible alternative by which his loyal soul was to be confronted.

CHAPTER XXIII
A PERILOUS CONFIDENCE

In the Duc de Guise's apartments at the Château d'Amboise, Le Balafré himself was interrogating a tall, vigorous, nervous individual, with strongly marked features and proud and fearless bearing, who wore the uniform of a captain of arquebusiers.

"Maréchal de Brissac," said the duke, "has assured me, Captain Richelieu, that I may have the fullest confidence in you."

"Monsieur le Maréchal is very kind," said Richelieu.

"It seems that you are ambitious, Monsieur," continued Le Balafré.

"Monseigneur, I am at least ambitious not to remain captain of arquebusiers all my life. Although I come of very good stock (for there were lords of Plessis on the field at Bovines), I am the fifth of six brothers, and consequently I have to do my best to eke out my little fortune, and not depend too much upon my patrimony."

"Good!" said the Duc de Guise, with an air of satisfaction. "You have the opportunity now, Monsieur, to do us good service, and you shall not repent it."

"Behold me, Monseigneur, ready to undertake whatever you please to intrust to me."

"To begin with," said Le Balafré, "I have ordered that you command the guard at the principal entrance of the château."

"Where I promise to give a good account of myself, Monseigneur."

"In my opinion," continued the duke, "it is not likely that the Protestants will be sufficiently ill-advised to make their assault on a side where they will be obliged to carry seven doors one after the other; but as nobody is to be allowed to enter or leave the place by any other entrance, the post will be of the greatest importance. Therefore let nobody pass, either from within or without, without a special order signed by me."

"It shall be done, Monseigneur. By the way, a young gentleman, called the Comte de Montgommery, has just arrived, with no special order, but with a safe-conduct bearing your signature. He comes from Paris, he says. Shall I allow him to come in, as he asks, Monseigneur?"

"Yes, yes, at once!" said the Duc de Guise, eagerly. "But wait a moment; I have not completed my instructions to you. To-day, about noon, the Prince de Condé will present himself at the gate where you are to be on guard: we have sent for him that we might have at our hand the reputed chief of the rebels, who, I'll wager, will not dare to furnish food for our suspicions by failing to neglect our summons. You will open to him, Captain Richelieu, but to no other — not even to such as come with him. You will be careful to have all the recesses and casemates which there are in the arch well filled with men; and as soon as he arrives, you will parade them all, arquebuse in hand, and matches lighted, under pretence of receiving him with the proper honors."

"It shall be done as you say, Monseigneur," said Richelieu.

"When the Huguenots attack," continued the duke, "and the action begins, you must personally keep your eye upon our man, Captain; and, mark my words well, if he stirs one step, or gives the least sign of an inclination to join the assailants, or if he even hesitates to draw his sword against them, as his duty calls upon him to do, do not hesitate with your own hands to strike him down."

"I can see no difficulty about this, Monseigneur," said Captain Richelieu, simply, "except that my rank as a simple captain of arquebusiers will make it rather hard, perhaps, for me to be always as near him as I ought to be."

Le Balafré reflected a minute, and said, —

"Monsieur le Grand Prieur and the Duc d'Aumale, who will never quit the supposed traitor's side for a moment, will give you the signal, and you will obey them."

"I will obey them, Monseigneur," replied Richelieu.

"Good!" said the Duc de Guise; "I have no other orders to give you, Captain. You may go. If the glory of your house began with Philippe Auguste, you may well begin it anew with the Duc de Guise. I rely upon you, and you may rely upon me. Go. Introduce Monsieur de Montgommery at once, if you please."

Captain Richelieu bowed deeply and withdrew.

A few minutes later Gabriel was announced. He was sad and pale; and the cordial welcome which the Duc de Guise extended to him did not smooth the trouble from his brow.

In fact, after putting together his own conjectures and a few words which the guards had not scrupled to let fall in the presence of a gentleman bearing the duke's safe-conduct, the young enthusiast had almost arrived at the truth.

The king who had pardoned him and the party to which he was devoted, body and soul, were openly at war, and his loyalty was likely to be compromised in the struggle.

"Well, Gabriel," began the duke, "you ought to know by this time why I have sent for you."

"I suspect the reason, but am not altogether sure of it, Monseigneur," Gabriel replied.

"The Protestants are in open rebellion," said Le Balafré, "and are in arms, and on their way to attack the Château d'Amboise,—that is our latest intelligence."

"It is a grievous and appalling state of things," observed Gabriel, reflecting on his own situation.

"Why, my friend, it is a magnificent opportunity," retorted the duke.

"What do you mean, Monseigneur?" said Gabriel, in amazement.

"I mean that the Huguenots expect to surprise us, whereas we are all ready for them. I mean that their plans are discovered and betrayed. It is fair warfare, since they have been the first to draw the sword; but our enemies are about to deliver themselves into our hands. They are lost, I tell you."

"Is it possible?" exclaimed the Comte de Montgommery, completely crushed.

"Judge for yourself," continued Le Balafré, "to what extent all the details of their insane enterprise are known to us. On the 16th of March, at noon, they are to assemble before the town and attack us. They have friends in the king's guard; therefore the guard was changed. Their friends were to open the western gate to them; but that gate is walled up. Lastly, their different bands were to proceed secretly hither through certain paths in the forest of Château-Begnault. The royal troops will fall upon these detached parties unexpectedly as fast as they appear, and will not allow half of their forces to reach Amboise. We are accurately informed, and thoroughly upon our guard, I should say!"

"Thoroughly!" replied Gabriel, in great alarm. "But who has been able to furnish you with such complete information?" he added in his perplexity, and without realizing what he said.

"Ah," rejoined Le Balafré, "there are two who have betrayed all their plans,—one for money, the other from fear. Two traitors they are, I admit,—one a paid spy, the other a faint-hearted alarmist. The spy—whom you know perhaps, as many of our friends do, and whom you should distrust—is the Marquis de — —."

"No, do not tell me!" cried Gabriel, quickly; "do not give me their names! I asked you for them thoughtlessly. You have already told me quite enough; but there is nothing more difficult for a man of honor than not to betray traitors."

"Oh," said the Duc de Guise, with some surprise, "we all have perfect confidence in you, Gabriel. We were speaking of you only yesterday with the queen; I told her that I had written you, and she was very much pleased."

"Why did you write to me, Monseigneur? You have not yet informed me."

"Why?" rejoined Le Balafré. "Because the king has but a few devoted and reliable servants. You are among them, and you are to command a party against the rebels."

"Against the rebels? Impossible!" said Gabriel.

"Impossible! And why impossible, pray?" returned Le Balafré. "I am not in the habit of hearing that word from your lips, Gabriel."

"Monseigneur," said Gabriel, "I also am of the Religion."

The Duc de Guise leaped to his feet, and gazed at the count with an expression of wonder which amounted almost to terror.

"Matters are in this condition," Gabriel continued, smiling sadly: "if it be your pleasure, Monseigneur, to put me face to face with the English or Spaniards, you know that I will not draw back, but that I will offer my life for my country with joy, as well as with devotion; but in a civil, a religious, war against my fellow-countrymen, my brothers, I am compelled, Monseigneur, to reserve the freedom of action which you were good enough to insure me."

"You a Huguenot!" the duke finally succeeded in ejaculating.

"And a most devoted one, Monseigneur," said Gabriel; "it is my crime, and my excuse therefor as well. I believe utterly in the new ideas, and have given my heart to them."

"And your sword too, without doubt?" was the duke's biting rejoinder.

"No, Monseigneur," said Gabriel, gravely.

"Come, come!" retorted Le Balafré; "do you expect to make me believe that you know nothing of this plot which has been concocted against the king by your brothers, as you call them, and that these same brothers cheerfully renounce so gallant an ally as you?"

"You must believe just that," said the young count, more seriously than ever.

"Then you must be the one to desert them," rejoined the duke; "for your new faith compels you to choose between two breaches of faith,—that's all."

"Oh, Monsieur!" cried Gabriel, reproachfully,

"Well, how can you arrange matters otherwise?" asked Le Balafré, throwing his cap with an angry movement upon the chair he had just quitted.

"How can I arrange matters otherwise?" repeated Gabriel, with a cold and almost stern demeanor. "Why, it's very simple. In my opinion, the falser the position in which a man is placed the more sincere and outspoken he should be. When I became a Protestant I steadfastly and loyally declared to the leaders of the sect that my sacred obligations to the king and queen and the Duc de Guise would absolutely prevent me from bearing arms in their ranks during this reign, if indeed the occasion should arise. They know that in my eyes the Reformation is a matter of religious belief, and not of party feeling. With them as with you, Monseigneur, I stipulated for absolute freedom of action; and I have the right to refuse my aid to them, as I refuse it to you. In this desperate conflict between my gratitude and my faith my heart will bleed with every blow that is struck; but my arm will not strike one. That, Monseigneur, is wherein you have failed to understand me; and in this way, I trust, by remaining neutral, to continue to be honorable and honored."

Gabriel spoke proudly and with much animation. Le Balafré, gradually regaining his tranquillity, could but admire the frankness and the nobleness of heart of his former comrade-in-arms.

"You are a strange man, Gabriel," he pensively remarked.

"Why strange, Monseigneur? Is it because I speak as I act and act as I speak? I knew nothing of this conspiracy of the Protestants, I swear.

However, I admit that when I was at Paris I received, on the same day that your letter arrived, a letter from one of them; but this letter was as barren of explanation as yours, and said simply, 'Come.' I had a foreboding of the dread dilemma in which I should be involved; but I have, nevertheless, responded to this twofold appeal. Monseigneur, I have come so that I might prove recreant to neither of my duties; I have come to say to you, 'I cannot fight against those whose faith I share,' and to say to them, 'I cannot fight against those who have spared my life.'"

The Duc de Guise held out his hand to the count.

"I was wrong," said he, cordially. "Pray, attribute my angry impulse to my chagrin at finding you, upon whom I have relied so confidently, among my enemies."

"Your enemy!" exclaimed Gabriel. "Ah, no!—I am not and never can be that, Monseigneur. Because I have declared myself more openly than they, am I any more your enemy than the Prince de Condé and Monsieur de Coligny, who are, as I am, Protestants, and not under arms?"

"Under arms! I beg your pardon, but they are," returned Le Balafré. "I know it,—I know all! But their arms are hidden. Nevertheless, if we should meet, it is certain that I should dissimulate even as they do, should call them my friends, and in case of need officially bear witness to their entire innocence,—a comedy, it is true, but a necessary one."

"Well, then, Monseigneur," said Gabriel, "since you are so kind as sometimes to lay aside conventionalities in dealing with me, tell me, I beg you, that when politics are not in question, you can still believe in my devotion to you, and my honor, Huguenot though I be; above all things, assure me that if a foreign war should break out some day, you would do me the favor to remind me of my word, and give me an opportunity to die for my king and country."

"Yes, Gabriel," said the duke, "while I deplore the difference in faith which now separates us, I trust you and shall always trust you the same; and in order to prove it to you and to redeem the momentary suspicion which I so deeply regret, take this and make such use of it as you please."

He sat down at a table and wrote a line which he signed and handed to the young count.

"It is an order allowing you to leave Amboise, wherever you may wish to go," said he. "With this paper you are entirely at liberty. And you may be sure that I would not give any such mark of esteem and confidence to the

Prince de Condé, whom you just mentioned, and that the moment he sets foot in this château he will be watched from a distance like an enemy, and guarded unknowingly as closely as a prisoner."

"In that case, I refuse this mark of your confidence and esteem, Monseigneur," said Gabriel.

"What! Why so?" asked the amazed duke.

"Monseigneur, do you know whither I shall go at once, if you allow me to leave Amboise?"

"That is your affair, and I do not even ask to know," rejoined Le Balafré.

"But I propose to tell you," said Gabriel. "When I leave you, Monseigneur, I shall go to fulfil my other duty: I shall go at once among the rebels, and shall seek for one of them at Noizai."

"At Noizai? Castelnau is in command there," remarked the duke.

"Yes, he is; you are indeed well informed in every detail, Monseigneur."

"What do you propose to do at Noizai, my unfortunate friend?" Le Balafré asked him.

"Ah, what shall I do indeed? Say to them, 'You summoned me, and I am here; but I can do nothing for you;' and if they question me as to what I have heard and noticed on the road, I must keep silent and not warn them of the trap that you have laid for them, for your confidence in me takes away my right to do that. Therefore, Monseigneur, I ask a favor at your hands—"

"What is it?"

"Retain me in custody here, and thus save me from cruel perplexity,— for if you allow me to go, I must make my appearance among those who are bent on their own destruction; and if I do go to them, I shall not be at liberty to save them."

"Gabriel," returned the Duc de Guise, "upon due reflection I neither can nor will exhibit such suspicion. I have unfolded to you my whole plan of campaign, and you are going among your friends, who are vitally interested in knowing that plan,—yet here is your passport."

"Then, Monseigneur," replied Gabriel, overwhelmed, "at least grant me this last favor in the name of what little I was able to do to enhance your renown at Metz and in Italy and at Calais, and in the name of what I have suffered since,—and indeed, I have suffered bitterly."

"To what do you refer?" said the duke. "If I can, I will grant it, my friend."

"You can, Monseigneur, and I think that you ought, because those who are in arms against you are Frenchmen. I ask you, then, to allow me to divert them from their fatal project, not by revealing to them its inevitable issue, but by advising them, and beseeching and imploring them."

"Gabriel, be careful!" said the duke, solemnly; "if one word as to our preparations falls from your lips, the rebels will persist in their design, simply modifying their mode of execution; and in that event the king and Mary Stuart and myself will be the ones to be destroyed. Weigh this well. Will you bind yourself upon your honor as a gentleman that you will not let them divine or even suspect, by a word or an allusion or a gesture, anything of what is going on here?"

"Upon my honor as a gentleman, I swear it!"

"Go, then," said the Duc de Guise, "and do your best to induce them to abandon their criminal purpose, and I will gladly renounce my easy victory, thinking how much French blood is spared. But if, as I believe, our last reports are well-founded, they have such blind and obstinate confidence in the success of their enterprise that you will fail, Gabriel. But no matter! go and make a last effort. For their sakes, and still more for yours, I have no disposition to refuse."

"In their names and my own I thank you, Monseigneur."

A quarter of an hour later he was on his way to Noizai.

CHAPTER XXIV
THE DISLOYALTY OF LOYALTY

Baron Castelnau de Chalosses was a gallant, noble-minded youth to whom the Protestants had assigned by no means the least difficult task when they sent him to forestall the royal troops at the Château de Noizai, which was the place appointed for the general rendezvous of the different sections of the disaffected on the 16th of March. It was essential that he should be visible to the Huguenots, but should conceal himself from the Catholics; and his delicate position called for the display of as much caution and presence of mind as courage.

Thanks to the password contained in La Renaudie's letter, Gabriel met with no hindrance in making his way to Baron de Castelnau's quarters.

It was already afternoon of the 15th.

Within eighteen hours the Protestants were to assemble at Noizai, and to attack Amboise before twenty-four hours had elapsed; so that it is clear there was no time to lose if they were to be dissuaded from their design.

Baron de Castelnau knew Comte de Montgommery well, for he had often met him at the Louvre, and besides, the chief men of the party had often spoken of him in his presence.

He came forward to meet him, and received him as a friend and an ally.

"So you have come, Monsieur de Montgommery," he remarked when they were alone. "To tell the truth, I hoped that you would be here, but hardly dared to expect you. La Renaudie was much blamed by the admiral for writing you as he did. 'It was essential,' he said, 'to advise the Comte de Montgommery of our plans, but not to summon him to join us. He might have been left to do as he chose. Has the count not given us fair warning that so long as François II. reigned, his sword did not belong to us; in fact, that it did not even belong to himself?' La Renaudie's reply to all this was that his letter bound you to nothing, but left you in possession of absolute independence of action."

"That is quite true," replied Gabriel.

"Nevertheless, we thought that you would come," continued Castelnau, "for the letter of that hot-headed baron gave you no information as to what was going on, and I am intrusted with the duty of informing you of our plan and our hopes."

"I am listening," said the Comte de Montgommery.

Castelnau then repeated to Gabriel everything that the Duc de Guise had previously told him in detail.

Gabriel saw with horror how exact Le Balafré's information was. Not one single point in the report of his spies and informers was inaccurate, nor had they omitted to apprise him of one single detail of the plot.

The conspirators were really lost beyond recall.

"Now you know everything," said Castelnau, as he brought his narration to a close, leaving his listener a prey to most cruel perplexity. "I have now only to put to you a question to which I can easily forecast your reply. I am right, am I not, in thinking that you cannot join us?"

"I cannot," replied Gabriel, sadly shaking his head.

"Very good!" added Castelnau; "we shall be none the less good friends for that. I know that you stipulated in advance for the privilege of holding aloof from the combat; and you are doubly entitled to exercise it, since we are sure of victory."

"Are you then indeed so sure?" asked Gabriel, significantly.

"Perfectly so," rejoined the baron; "for the enemy have no suspicion of our movements, and will be taken unawares. We were afraid for a moment, when the king and court transferred their quarters from the unfortified town of Blois to the strong Château d'Amboise, for they clearly had a suspicion that something was wrong."

"That embarrassed you, no doubt," observed Gabriel.

"Yes, but our hesitation soon came to an end," continued Castelnau; "for we found that this unexpected change of residence, far from injuring our prospects, on the contrary, served marvellously well to make them brighter. The Duc de Guise is now sleeping in false security; and you must know, dear Count, that we are in correspondence with some who are within the town, and the western gate will be put into our hands as soon as we present ourselves before it. Oh, success is beyond doubt, I assure you; and you may, without scruple, hold aloof from the battle."

"The most magnificent expectations are sometimes deceived by the event," was Gabriel's grave comment.

"But in this instance we have not a single chance against us,—not one!" Castelnau repeated, rubbing his hands with delight. "To-morrow will behold the triumph of our party and the fall of the Guises."

"And—how about treachery?" said Gabriel, struggling with his emotion, and with his heart torn to see such youthful gallantry rushing headlong into the abyss with eyes closed.

"Treachery is impossible," was Castelnau's imperturbable response to that suggestion. "Only the leaders are in the secret, and not one of them is capable of it. Upon my word, Monsieur de Montgommery," he exclaimed, interrupting himself, "I believe that you are jealous of us; and it seems to me as if you were trying with all your might to throw cold water on our undertaking, because of your chagrin at having no share in it. Fie, my envious friend!"

"Yes, indeed, I do envy you!" returned Gabriel, gloomily.

"There! I was sure of it," laughingly exclaimed the young baron.

"But stay a moment; you have some confidence in me, have you not?"

"Blind confidence, if we are to speak soberly."

"Very well; are you willing to listen to good advice, coming from a true friend?"

"To what purpose?"

"Abandon your design of taking Amboise to-morrow. Send trusty messengers at once to all of our brethren who are to join you here to-night or in the morning, to let them know that the plan has miscarried, or has at least been postponed."

"Why so, pray? Why?" demanded Castelnau, beginning to take alarm. "You must surely have some weighty reason for speaking thus to me." "Mon Dieu, no!" replied Gabriel, with a constraint that cost him dear.

"It cannot be," said Castelnau, "that you advise me for no reason whatever to abandon, and cause my brethren to abandon likewise, a project which seems to progress so favorably?"

"No, there is a reason; you are quite right, but I cannot explain to you. Can you not, will you not, believe my word? I have already gone further in this matter than I should have done. Do me the honor to trust my word, dear friend."

"Consider," rejoined Castelnau, very seriously, "that if I take upon myself this extraordinary course of turning back at the last moment, I shall have to answer for it to La Renaudie and the other leaders. May I refer them to you?"

"Yes," replied Gabriel.

"Will you tell them," continued Castelnau, "the motives which dictate your advice?"

"Alas! I have not the right to do it."

"How can you expect me to yield to your representations, then? Should I not be bitterly reproached for having thus, for a single word, destroyed our hopes, which were almost certainty? Howsoever vast and well-deserved is the confidence we all have in you, Monsieur de Montgommery, still a man is but a man, and may be deceived, no matter how good his intentions. If no one is allowed to consider and pass judgment upon your reasons, we shall certainly be obliged to neglect your counsel."

"Then beware!" rejoined Gabriel, harshly; "on your head alone be the responsibility for all the calamities that may ensue!"

Castelnau was struck with the accent with which the count uttered these words.

"Monsieur de Montgommery," said he, "light has suddenly come to me, and I think I can descry the true state of affairs. You have either been intrusted with or have surmised some secret which you are not permitted to disclose. You have some important information as to the probable result of our enterprise,—that we have been betrayed, for instance. Am I not right?"

"I did not say that!" cried Gabriel, eagerly.

"Or else," continued Castelnau, "you saw your friend, the Duc de Guise, on your way here, and he, in ignorance of your fellowship with us, has given you an insight into the real state of things."

"Nothing I have said can have given rise to any such supposition!" cried Gabriel.

"Or again," Castelnau went on, "you have, as you passed through Amboise, noticed preparations being made, overheard conversations, or induced confidences,—in short, our plot is discovered!"

"Do you mean to say," said Gabriel, horror-stricken, "that I have given you any reason to believe anything of the sort?"

"No, Monsieur le Comte; no, indeed, for you were bound to secrecy, I can see. Therefore I do not even ask you for a positive assurance that I am right, not even a word, if you prefer not. But if I am mistaken, a gesture, a glance of the eye, or your silence, even, will be sufficient to enlighten me."

Gabriel, meanwhile, sorely perplexed, was recalling the last part of the obligation he had given the Duc de Guise.

Upon his honor as a gentleman he had bound himself not to allow any person to divine or even to suspect, from any word or allusion or gesture on his part, what was taking place at Amboise.

As he kept silence for a long while, the Baron de Castelnau, whose eyes were riveted upon Gabriel's face, spoke again.

"Do you mean to say nothing more?" said he. "You are silent; I understand you, and shall act accordingly."

"What do you propose to do?" asked Gabriel, hastily.

"To warn La Renaudie and the other leaders, as you advised me to do in the first place, that they must cease their preparations, and to announce to our friends when they reach here that some one in whom we have perfect confidence has made known to me—has made known to me probable treachery—"

"But there is nothing of the sort!" Gabriel hurriedly interrupted. "I have given you no information at all, Monsieur de Castelnau!"

"Count," rejoined Castelnau, seizing Gabriel's hand in a grasp that spoke louder than his words, "may not your reticence itself be a warning, and our salvation? And once put on our guard, then—"

"Well, what then?" echoed Gabriel.

"Everything will go well for us, and ill for them," said Castelnau. "We will postpone our enterprise to a more propitious time; discover at any cost the informers, if there be any among us; redouble our precautions and our mystery; and one fine day, when everything is thoroughly prepared, certain then of our aim, we will renew our attempt, and, thanks to you, will not fail, but achieve a triumphant success."

"That is precisely what I wish to avoid!" cried Gabriel, who was horrified to find himself upon the verge of involuntary betrayal of confidence. "There, Monsieur de Castelnau, is the real reason of my warning and my advice. In my mind, your enterprise is absolutely a culpable one, to say nothing of its danger. By attacking the Catholics you put yourselves entirely in the wrong, and justify any reprisals they may resort to. From being unjustly oppressed subjects, you become rebels. If you have complaints to make of the ministers, must you avenge yourselves upon our young king? Ah, I feel sad even unto death as I reflect upon all this misery! For the good of the cause you ought forever to renounce this unholy strife. Rather let your principles do battle for you! No bloodshed for the truth! That is all that I wished to say to you;

that is why I conjure you and all our brethren to hold your hand from these grievous civil wars, which can only retard the spread of our principles."

"Is that really the only motive of all your talk?" asked Castelnau.

"The only one," Gabriel replied in a hollow voice.

"Then I must thank you for your good intentions, Monsieur le Comte," retorted Castelnau, coldly; "but I must no less continue to act on the lines laid down for me by the leaders of the Reformed party. I can readily conceive that it must be very painful for a gentleman like yourself, being debarred from the combat, to see others fighting without you; but you alone cannot be allowed to fetter and paralyze a whole army."

"You propose, then," said Gabriel, pale and dejected, "to allow the others to go on with this fatal design, and to go on with it yourself?"

"Yes, Monsieur le Comte," responded Castelnau, whose words had a firmness in them that admitted no argument; "and with your permission, I will now go to issue the necessary orders for to-morrow's assault."

He saluted Gabriel, and left the room without awaiting his reply.

CHAPTER XXV
THE BEGINNING OF THE END

Gabriel did not leave the Château de Noizai, however, but determined to pass the night there. His presence would afford the Reformers a pledge of his good faith, in case they were attacked; and beyond that, he still retained some slight hope that in the morning he might prevail, if not upon Castelnau, upon some other leader who was less blindly obstinate. If La Renaudie would only come!

Castelnau left him entirely free, and seemed inclined to be rather disdainful in his avoidance of him.

Gabriel encountered him several times during the evening in the halls and corridors of the château, going hither and thither, giving orders for reconnoitring parties and the forwarding of supplies.

But not a single word was exchanged between the two youths, each as proud and as noble as the other.

During the long hours of that night of anguish the Comte de Montgommery, too restless and anxious to sleep, remained upon the ramparts, listening, meditating, and praying.

With the first glimmer of dawn, the Protestant troops began to arrive in small detached parties.

At eight o'clock they had already assembled in large numbers; and at eleven Castelnau could count all whom he expected.

But not one of the leaders was known to Gabriel. La Renaudie had sent word that he and his forces would make their way to Amboise by way of the forest of Château-Regnault.

Everything was ready for departure. Captains Mazères and Raunay, who were to lead the advance-guard, had already gone down to the terrace in front of the château to form their detachments in marching order. Castelnau was triumphant.

"Well," he remarked to Gabriel as he encountered him,—he had, in his satisfaction, forgiven the conversation of the night before,—"well, you see, Monsieur le Comte, that you were wrong; and everything is going on as well as possible!"

"Wait!" said Gabriel, shaking his head.

"Indeed, we must wait, if we are to believe you, doubter!" said Castelnau, smiling. "Not one of our people has failed to keep his engagement; they have all arrived at the time appointed, with more men than they had promised. They have all marched through their respective provinces without being disturbed, and—what is perhaps even better—without having created any disturbance. Is it not, in truth, almost too good fortune?"

The baron was interrupted by the sound of trumpets and the clangor of arms and a great noise outside; but in the intoxication of his confidence he was in no degree alarmed, and thought of nothing but some fortunate event.

"See!" said he to Gabriel; "I will engage that those are more unexpected reinforcements,—Lamothe, doubtless, and Deschamps, with the conspirators of Picardy. They were not due to arrive until to-morrow; but they must have made forced marches, the brave fellows, in order to bear their part of the conflict and share in the victory. Those are friends."

"Ah, but are they?" asked Gabriel, whose face changed color when he heard the trumpets.

"Who else can they be?" rejoined Castelnau. "Come into this gallery, Monsieur le Comte; through the embrasures we can look down upon the terrace whence the noise comes."

He drew Gabriel after him; but when they had reached the edge of the wall he uttered a loud cry, raised his arms, and stood as if turned to stone.

The confusion had been occasioned not by Protestant troops, but by a body of Royalists. The new-comers were not commanded by Lamothe, but by Jacques de Savoie, Duc de Nemours.

Under cover of the woods which surrounded the Château de Noizai, the royal troops had succeeded before they were discovered in getting within close range of the open terrace, where the advance-guard of the rebels was being drawn up in order of battle.

There was no show of resistance whatever, for the Duc de Nemours had made it his first care to seize the stacks of arms.

Mazères and Raunay had been obliged to surrender without striking a blow; and just at the moment when Castelnau looked down from the battlements, his troops, conquered without a struggle, were handing their swords to the enemy. On the spot where he had thought he should see his soldiers, he saw nought but a band of prisoners.

He could scarcely believe his eyes. For a moment he stood motionless, stupefied, bewildered, and speechless. Such an event was so entirely at variance with his thoughts that at first he found it difficult to understand it.

Gabriel, who was less surprised at this sudden blew, was no less overwhelmed.

As they stood gazing at each other, equally pale and dejected, an ensign entered hastily in search of Castelnau.

"What is the condition of affairs?" the latter asked him, recovering his voice, by force of his anxiety.

"Monsieur le Baron," the ensign replied, "they have gained possession of the drawbridge and the first gate. We only had time to close the second one; but we shall not be able to hold it, and in less than a quarter of an hour they will be in the courtyard. Shall we, nevertheless, try to resist, or send them a flag of truce? We await your orders."

"Give me but time to put on my armor, and I will come down," said Castelnau.

He hastened into one of the apartments of the château to buckle on his sword and cuirass, and Gabriel followed him.

"What do you propose to do?" he asked him, sadly.

"I know not; I know not!" replied Castelnau, excitedly; "but I can at least die."

"Alas!" sighed Gabriel; "why did you not hearken to me yesterday?"

"Yes, you were right, I can see now," returned the baron. "You anticipated what has happened; perhaps you knew of it beforehand."

"Perhaps," observed Gabriel; "and therein lies my greatest suffering. But remember, Castelnau, that life is full of strange and awful caprices of fate! Suppose that I was not at liberty to dissuade you by divulging the real reasons, which were struggling for utterance? Suppose that I had given my word of honor as a gentleman not to give you any occasion, directly or indirectly, to suspect the truth?"

"In such case you would have done quite right to say nothing," said Castelnau; "and in your place I should have done just as you did. It was I, madman, who should have understood you; I who should have known that a valiant heart like yours would not try to dissuade me from battle except for most potent reasons. But I will expiate my mistake by death."

"Then I will die with you," said Gabriel, calmly.

"You! and why?" cried Castelnau. "The one thing that you say you are absolutely compelled to do is to refrain from fighting."

"True, I shall not fight," said Gabriel; "I cannot. But life has become a grievous burden to me; the apparently two-faced part I am playing is intolerable. I shall go into the fray unarmed. I will slay no one, but will allow myself to be slain. I may be able to intercept the blow aimed at you. If I cannot wear a sword, I may still be a buckler."

"No," rejoined Castelnau, "remain here. I ought not to involve you in my destruction, nor will I do it."

"Ah, but think!" exclaimed Gabriel, earnestly; "you are about to involve in it, uselessly and hopelessly, all of our brethren who are confined in this château with you. My life is much less useful than theirs."

"Can I do otherwise for the glory of our faith than ask them to make this sacrifice?" said Castelnau. "Martyrs often bring more renown to their cause, and are more useful to it, than victors."

"Very true," replied Gabriel; "but is it not your first duty as leader to do your utmost to save the forces which have been intrusted to you; to die finally at their head, if their salvation is not to be reconciled with honor?"

"So you advise me—" said Castelnau.

"To try every peaceable means of accommodation. If you resist, you have no possible chance of escaping defeat and massacre. If you yield to necessity, they will not have the right, in my opinion, to punish the instigators of a plan that has been left unexecuted. Mere projects cannot be punished, since they can only be conjectured. By laying down your arms, you will disarm your enemies."

"I so bitterly repent not having followed your previous advice," said Castelnau, "that I prefer to follow it now; and yet I confess that I hesitate, for it is very distasteful to me to draw back."

"In order to draw back, you must first have taken a step forward," said Gabriel. "Now what is there up to this point to prove your rebellion? You do not declare yourself culpable until you actually draw your sword. Hold! My presence may even yet, thank God! be of some advantage to you. I was unable to save you yesterday, but do you wish that I should try to save you to-day?"

"What will you do?" asked Castelnau, completely unmanned.

"Nothing unworthy of you, be assured! I will go to the Duc de Nemours, who commands the royal soldiery. I will inform him that no resistance will be offered, that the gates will be opened, and you will surrender, but upon certain conditions: he must engage his ducal word that no harm shall befall you or your comrades, and that after he has escorted you to the king, in order to submit to him your grievances and requests, he will cause you to be set at liberty."

"And if he refuses?" asked Castelnau.

"If he refuses, the fault will be on his side; he will have declined a perfectly frank and honorable adjustment of the affair, and all the responsibility for the bloodshed will fall upon his head. If he refuses, Castelnau, I will return to you, to die at your side."

"Do you believe," said Castelnau, "that La Renaudie, were he placed as I am, would agree to what you propose?"

"Upon my soul! I believe that any reasonable man would agree to it."

"Go on, then!" exclaimed Castelnau; "our despair will be so much the more to be dreaded if your mission to the duke fails, as I fear it will."

"Thanks!" said Gabriel. "I have strong hopes myself that I shall succeed, and thus, with God's help, preserve all these gallant and noble lives."

He went quickly down, and caused the door leading to the courtyard to be opened; and with a flag of truce in his hand, he walked toward the Duc de Nemours, who, sitting on his horse in the midst of his troops, was awaiting the issue.

"I do not know whether Monseigneur recognizes me," said Gabriel to the duke; "but I am the Comte de Montgommery."

"Yes, Monsieur de Montgommery, I do recognize you," replied Jacques de Savoie. "Monsieur de Guise advised me that I should find you here, but said that you had his permission, and charged me to treat you as a friend."

"A precaution which may be of ill service to me with other less fortunate friends," observed Gabriel, with a sorrowful shake of the head. "However, Monseigneur, may I venture to beg a moment's conversation with you?"

"I am at your service," said Monsieur de Nemours. Castelnau, who was following distractedly all the movements of the duke and Gabriel from a grated window of the château, saw them draw aside from the rest, and converse for some moments with much animation. Then Jacques de Savoie called for writing materials, and using a drumhead for a table, wrote a few rapid lines, which he handed to Gabriel, who seemed to be profuse in his thanks.

"There must be some hope for us," thought Castelnau. Gabriel rushed headlong back into the château, and a moment later, breathless and without a word, placed the following document in Castelnau's hands:—

> Monsieur de Castelnau and his companions now within the Château de Noizai having agreed upon my arrival to lay down their arms and surrender to me, I, the undersigned, Jacques de Savoie, have sworn upon my princely faith, upon my honor, and as I hope for the salvation of my soul, that they shall not be molested, but shall be set at liberty entirely unharmed, fifteen of them only, including Monsieur de Castelnau, to go with me to Amboise, to present their grievances to the king in a peaceable manner.
>
> Given at the Château de Noizai this 16th of March, 1560.
>
> JACQUES DE SAVOIE.

"Thanks, my friend," Castelnau said to Gabriel, after he had read the foregoing; "you have saved our lives, and our honor, which is dearer than life. On these conditions I am ready to follow Monsieur de Nemours to Amboise; for we shall not appear there as prisoners before their conqueror, but as oppressed subjects before their king. Once more I thank you."

But as he warmly clasped the hand of his preserver, Castelnau remarked that Gabriel had relapsed into his former state of melancholy.

"What troubles you now, pray?" he asked.

"I am thinking now about La Renaudie and the other Protestants who were to attack Amboise to-night," replied Gabriel. "Alas! I fear it is too late to save them; but I will at least make the attempt. La Renaudie was to advance by the forest of Château-Regnault, was he not?"

"Yes," said Castelnau, earnestly; "and there is yet time for you to find him there, and save him as you have saved us."

"At all events, I will do my best," said Gabriel. "The Duc de Nemours will leave me at liberty, I think. Adieu, then, dear friend; I go to continue, if possible, my work of conciliation. *Au revoir!*—at Amboise."

"*Au revoir!*" Castelnau replied.

As Gabriel had anticipated, the Duc de Nemours made no opposition to his leaving Noizai and its detachment of royal troops.

The zealous, devoted youth was free to urge his horse in the direction of the forest of Château-Regnault.

Castelnau and those who remained with him followed Jacques de Savoie to Amboise, trusting and tranquil.

But upon their arrival they were at once lodged in prison. There they were to remain, so they were informed, until the affray was at an end, and there was no longer any danger to be apprehended in allowing them access to the king.

CHAPTER XXVI
THE FOREST OF CHÂTEAU-REGNAULT

The forest of Château-Régnault was fortunately only about a league and a half distant from Noizai. Gabriel urged his horse thither at a gallop; but after he had reached the spot, he rode about in every direction for more than an hour without falling in with any party, either of friends or foes.

At last he thought he distinguished the regular gallop of cavalry beyond a bend in the path he was pursuing; but they could not be Huguenots, for they were laughing and talking, while the Huguenots were too vitally concerned to conceal their movements not to preserve most complete silence.

"No matter!" thought Gabriel; and he hurried on, and soon came upon the red scarfs of the king's troops.

As he made his way toward their leader he recognized him, and was recognized by him.

It was Baron de Pardaillan,—a gallant young officer who had made the Italian campaign with him under Monsieur de Guise.

"Ah, it is the Comte de Montgommery!" cried Pardaillan. "I thought you were at Noizai, Count."

"I have just come from there," said Gabriel.

"Well, what has occurred there?—ride by my side awhile and tell me."

Gabriel told the story of the sudden arrival of the Duc de Nemours, of his carrying the terrace and the drawbridge, of his own mediation between the parties, and the peaceful submission which had been its happy result.

"*Pardieu!*" exclaimed Pardaillan; "Monsieur de Nemours was in luck, and I should be glad to be equally fortunate myself. Do you know, Monsieur de Montgommery, against whom my own movements are directed at this moment?"

"La Renaudie, doubtless."

"Precisely. And do you know what La Renaudie is to me?"

"Why, your cousin, I believe,—yes, I remember."

"Yes, he is my cousin," Pardaillan said; "and more than that, he is my friend and my comrade-in-arms. Ah, do you know how bitter a thing it is to fight against one who has so often fought at one's side?"

"Yes, indeed," replied Gabriel; "but you are not sure of meeting him, are you?"

"Alas! I am only too sure!" returned Pardaillan. "My instructions are exact; and the reports of those who have betrayed him are only too accurate. See! after marching another fifteen minutes I shall find myself face to face with La Renaudie in the second path to the left."

"But suppose you were to avoid that path?" whispered Gabriel.

"I should be false to my honor and to my duty as a soldier," was Pardaillan's reply. "Besides, it is better that I should not be able to do it. My two lieutenants received Monsieur de Guise's orders as well as myself, and they would interfere to prevent my running counter to them. No; my only hope is that La Renaudie will consent to surrender, and a faint hope it is; for he is as proud as Lucifer, and as brave as a lion. Moreover, he has an opportunity to fight, and will not be taken by surprise, as Castelnau was; and again, we are not very superior to him in point of numbers. However, you will assist me, will you not, Monsieur de Montgommery, in urging him to yield?"

"Alas!" said Gabriel, with a sigh, "I will do my best."

"The Devil take these civil wars!" cried Pardaillan, in conclusion.

They rode along in silence for almost ten minutes.

When they had taken the second path to the left, Pardaillan said,—

"Now we should be approaching them. How my heart beats! For the first time in my life, I believe, as God hears me, that I am afraid."

The royal troops were no longer laughing and talking, but advanced slowly and cautiously.

They had not gone two hundred paces, when they thought they could see through a thicket of trees the glistening of weapons upon a path, which ran parallel with the main road.

Their uncertainty was not of long duration, for almost immediately a firm voice cried out,—

"Halt! Who goes there?"

"It is La Renaudie's voice," Pardaillan said to Gabriel.

Then he replied to the challenge, —

"Valois and Lorraine!"

Instantly, La Renaudie on horseback, followed by his little band, debouched from the bypath.

However, he ordered his troops to halt, and rode forward a few steps alone.

Pardaillan imitated him by crying to his people, "Halt!" and riding toward him accompanied only by Gabriel.

One would have said they were two friends in haste to meet after a long separation, rather than two foes ready to meet in deadly conflict.

"I should have already replied to you as I ought," said La Renaudie, as he approached, "if I had not thought that I recognized the voice of a friend. Unless I am greatly mistaken, that visor conceals the features of my dear Pardaillan."

"Yes, it is I, my poor La Renaudie," replied Pardaillan; "and if I may give you a brother's advice, it is to abandon your enterprise, dear friend, and lay down your arms at once."

"Oh, yes! that is indeed brotherly advice!" retorted La Renaudie, ironically.

"Yes, Monsieur de la Renaudie," interposed Gabriel, coming forward, "it is the advice of a loyal friend, I bear you witness. Castelnau surrendered to the Duc de Nemours this morning; and if you do not follow his example, you are lost."

"Aha, Monsieur de Montgommery!" exclaimed La Renaudie, "are you with these fellows?"

"I am neither with them nor with yourself," said Gabriel, in a grave and melancholy tone. "I stand between you."

"Oh, forgive me, Monsieur le Comte," added La Renaudie, deeply moved by the noble and dignified bearing of Gabriel. "I had no wish to wound you, and I think I would doubt my own loyalty rather than yours." "Pray believe me, then," said Gabriel, "and do not hazard a useless and disastrous conflict. Surrender."

"Impossible!" replied La Renaudie.

"But reflect, I beg you," said Pardaillan, "that we are no more than a feeble advance-guard."

"For Heaven's sake," retorted the Protestant leader, "do you suppose that my whole force consists of this handful of gallant fellows whom you see?"

"I warn you," said Pardaillan, "that you have traitors in your ranks."

"Well, they are in yours now," returned La Renaudie. "I will undertake to obtain your pardon from Monsieur de Guise," cried Pardaillan, who knew not which way to turn.

"My pardon!" exclaimed La Renaudie; "I hope to be more concerned with granting than receiving pardons!"

"Oh, La Renaudie! La Renaudie! Surely you do not wish to compel me to draw my sword against you,—Godefroy, my old comrade, my playfellow?"

"We must be prepared even for that, Pardaillan; for you know me too well to believe that I am inclined to yield the field to you."

"Monsieur de la Renaudie," cried Gabriel, "once more I tell you that you are wrong."

But he was rudely interrupted.

The horsemen on both sides, Remaining apart, but in full view of one another, could not understand the meaning of all this parleying between their chiefs, and were burning with eagerness to come to closer quarters.

"In God's name, what do they find to talk about at such length?" muttered the troopers of Pardaillan.

"Ah!" said the Huguenots, "do they think that we came here to watch them while they talk over their private business?"

"Wait a moment! wait!" said one of La Renaudie's band, in which every soldier was a leader, "I know a way to cut short their conversation;" and just as Gabriel began to speak, he fired a pistol-shot at the king's troops.

"You see," cried Pardaillan, sorrowfully, "your people have struck the first blow!"

"But without any order from me!" retorted La Renaudie, warmly. "However, the die is cast, and it makes no difference now. Forward, my friends, forward!"

He turned toward his men as he spoke, and Pardaillan, not to be taken by surprise, did the same, and also shouted, "Forward!"

The firing began.

Gabriel, however, remained motionless between the red and the white, the Royalists and the rebels. He scarcely even drew his horse aside, but sustained the fire of both parties.

At the first volley the plume of his helmet was cut through by a ball, and his horse killed under him.

He extricated his feet from the stirrups and stood in the same spot without a tremor, and like one dreaming in the midst of that terrible affray.

The supply of powder was soon exhausted; and the two little bands rushed forward, and continued the combat with their swords.

Gabriel, amid all the clashing and clanging, never stirred from his place, nor did he once lay his hand upon his sword; he simply stood gazing at the mad blows which were raining about him, as if he had been the image of France among her foes.

The Protestants, inferior in numbers and in discipline, began to falter.

La Renaudie in the tumult found himself face to face with Pardaillan once more.

"Engage with me!" he cried; "let me at least die by your hand."

"Ah!" said Pardaillan, "the one of us two who slays the other will be the more generous."

They crossed swords with much vigor. The blows they dealt resounded upon their coats-of-mail like hammer-strokes upon the anvil. La Renaudie circled about Pardaillan, who, sitting firmly on his saddle, parried and thrust without token of weariness. Two rivals thirsting for vengeance could not have seemed more implacable.

At last La Renaudie buried his sword in the breast of Pardaillan, who fell headlong from his horse.

But the cry which followed the fatal blow came from the lips of La Renaudie.

Happily for the victor, he had not even the time to look upon his disastrous victory, for Montigny, Pardaillan's page, levelled his arquebuse at him and fired, and he fell from his horse mortally wounded.

Nevertheless, before he expired La Renaudie yet retained strength sufficient to strike dead upon the spot, with a backward stroke of his sword, the page who had shot him.

Around these three bodies the battle waged more furiously than ever.

But the Huguenots were clearly worsted; and in a short time, being deprived of their leader, they were utterly routed.

The greater number of them were killed; but a few were taken prisoners, and some escaped.

This horrible bloody affray lasted less than ten minutes.

The royal troopers prepared to return to Amboise, and the bodies of La Renaudie and Pardaillan were placed upon the same horse.

The Forest of Château-Regnault.

Gabriel, who, despite his eager longing, and spared without doubt by both sides, had not received a scratch, gazed mournfully at the two lifeless bodies in which, but a few moments before, had beat the two noblest hearts he had ever known.

"Which of the two was the braver?" he asked himself. "Which better loved the other? Which is the greater loss to his unhappy country?"

CHAPTER XXVII
A GLIMPSE AT THE POLITICS OF THE SIXTEENTH CENTURY

Even after the surrender of the Château de Noizai, and the skirmish in the forest of Château-Regnault, the whole affair was not at an end.

The majority of the conspirators of Nantes had not been notified of these two repulses which their party had met with, and were still on their way to Amboise, prepared to assault the place that night.

But we know that thanks to the precise information furnished by Lignières, they were expected.

The youthful king had no inclination to retire, but walked anxiously, with feverish tread, up and down the vast unfurnished hall which had been set apart for his accommodation.

Mary Stuart, the Duc de Guise, and the Cardinal de Lorraine were also watching and waiting with him.

"What an everlasting night!" ejaculated François. "I am in agony; my head is on fire; and those intolerable pains in my ear are beginning to torment me again. What a night! Oh, what a night!"

"Poor dear Sire!" said Mary, soothingly, "do not excite yourself so, I pray; you only increase your bodily and mental anguish as well. Take a few moments' rest, in pity's name!"

"What! how can I rest, Mary?" said the king,—"how can I keep calm when my people are rebelling, and are in arms against me? Ah, all this trouble will surely shorten the small portion of life God has granted me!"

Mary replied only by the tears which streamed down her lovely face.

"Your Majesty ought not to be so deeply affected," said Le Balafré. "I have already had the honor to assure you that our measures were taken, and that victory is beyond peradventure. I give you my personal guaranty of it, Sire."

"Have we not begun well, Sire?" added the Cardinal de Lorraine. "Castelnau a prisoner, and La Renaudie slain,—are these not happy omens for the issue of this affair?"

"Happy omens indeed!" said François, bitterly.

"To-morrow everything will be at an end," continued the cardinal; "the other leaders of the rebels will be in our power, and we can terrify, by force of a frightful example, those who might venture to try to emulate them. It must be done, Sire," said he, replying to the king's involuntary movement of horror. "A solemn 'Act of Faith,' as they say in Spain, is essential for the outraged glory of the Catholic religion, and the threatened security of the throne. To begin with, Castelnau must die. Monsieur de Nemours took it upon himself to swear that he should be spared; but that is not our affair, and we have promised nothing ourselves. La Renaudie has escaped punishment by death; but I have already given orders that at daybreak to-morrow his head be exposed upon the bridge of Amboise with this inscription: 'Leader of the rebels.'"

"Leader of the rebels!" echoed the king; "why, you yourself say that he was not the leader, and that the confessions and the correspondence of the conspirators point to the Prince de Condé alone as the real prime mover of the undertaking."

"In Heaven's name, speak not so loud, Sire, I implore you!" the cardinal exclaimed. "Yes, it is true, the prince has led and directed the whole affair, but from afar. These rascals call him the 'Silent Captain;' and he was to unmask himself after their first success. But failing that first success, he has not unmasked himself, nor will he do so. Therefore let us not drive him to that perilous extremity. Let us not seem to recognize in him the mighty head and front of the rebellion. Let us pretend not to see it, so that we may incur no risk of showing our feeling."

"Nevertheless, Monsieur de Condé is the real arch-rebel!" said François, whose youthful impatience was little in sympathy with all these "governmental fictions," as they came to be called at a later day.

"Very true, Sire," said Le Balafré; "but the prince, far from avowing his schemes, denies them. Let us pretend to believe his word. He came to-day to shut himself up here in Amboise, where he has been kept in sight, just as he has conspired, from a safe distance. Let us feign to accept him as an ally, which will be less hazardous than to have him for an avowed enemy. The prince, in fact, will assist us, if need be, to repel his own accomplices to-night, and be present at their execution to-morrow. Does he not thereby undergo a penalty a thousand times more grievous than any which is imposed upon us?"

"Yes, indeed he does," replied the king; "but will he do that; and if he does, can it be possible that he is guilty?"

"Sire," said the cardinal, "we have in our hands, and will deliver to your Majesty, if you desire, irrefragable proof of Monsieur de Condé's secret complicity. But the more flagrant and undeniable these proofs are, the more necessary is it for us to dissimulate; and, for my part, I deeply regret certain words which I have let fall, and which, if reported to the prince, might offend him."

"What, you fear to *offend* a culprit such as you say he is!" cried François. "But what is all this uproar without, in God's name? Can it be the rebels already?"

"I will go and see," said the Duc de Guise.

But before he had crossed the threshold, Richelieu, the captain of arquebusiers, entered, and said hastily to the king, —

"Pardon, Sire, but Monsieur de Condé thinks he overheard certain words reflecting upon his honor, and he urgently demands the privilege of clearing himself from these insulting suspicions in your Majesty's presence, once for all."

The king might have refused to see the prince; but the Duc de Guise had already made a sign. Captain Richelieu's arquebusiers stepped aside, and Monsieur de Condé entered, with head erect and cheeks flushed.

He was followed by a few nobles, and a number of canons of St. Florentin, regular attaches of the Château d'Amboise, whom the cardinal had transformed into soldiers that night to assist in the defence, and who, as was frequently the case in those days, carried the arquebuse with the rosary, and wore the helmet under their cowl.

"Sire, I trust you will pardon my boldness," said the prince, after saluting the king; "but it is perhaps justified in advance by the insolence of certain charges, which are made, it seems, in the dark by my foes against my loyalty, and which I feel called upon to bring forth into the light that I may confound and chastise them."

"To what do you refer, my cousin?" asked the king, gravely.

"Sire," replied Condé, "they dare to say that I am the real leader of the rebels, whose foolhardy and impious undertaking is at this moment throwing the realm into confusion, and filling your Majesty's heart with dismay."

"Ah, they say that, do they?" returned François. "Who says it, pray?"

"I succeeded just now in surprising these hateful slanders, Sire, upon the lips of these reverend brothers of St. Florentin, who, believing doubtless that they were among friends, did not scruple to repeat aloud what had been whispered in their ears."

"Do you mean to accuse those who repeated the offensive words, or those who whispered them in the first place?" asked François.

"Both, Sire," replied Condé, "but especially the instigators of these foul and cowardly calumnies."

As he said these words, he turned his gaze full upon the face of the Cardinal de Lorraine, who did his best to hide his embarrassed countenance behind his brother.

"Very well, my good cousin," replied the king, "you have our permission to disprove the slander, and to accuse the slanderers. Proceed."

"To disprove the slander, Sire?" repeated the prince. "Ah, will not my actions do that better than any words of mine! Did I not come at the first summons to this château, to take my place among your Majesty's defenders? Is that the act of a guilty man, Sire?—I put the question to yourself, Sire?"

"Then proceed to accuse the slanderers," said François, who chose to make no more direct reply.

"I will do so, not in words, but by deeds, Sire," said Monsieur de Condé. "They must, if they have the courage, themselves accuse me in the light of day. I here cast down my glove to them before God and the king. Let the man, of whatever rank or quality he may be, who dares to affirm that I am the author of this conspiracy come forward! I offer to do battle with him when and where he chooses; and if in any point he be not upon a level with me, I agree to make myself his equal in every way for this combat."

The Prince de Condé, as he ceased to speak, threw his glove at his feet. His glance had not ceased to form an eloquent commentary upon his challenge, and had fixed itself proudly upon the Duc de Guise, who did not move a muscle.

There was a moment of silence,—every one reflecting, no doubt, upon this extraordinary spectacle of the lie given by a prince of the blood to the whole court, where there was not a page who did not know him to be guilty twenty times over of that offence from which he defended himself with such well-simulated indignation.

And, in truth, the youthful king was probably the only one who was innocent enough to be astonished; and no one thought any the worse of the prince's valor or virtue.

The political theories of the Italian courts, brought into France by Catherine de Médicis and her Florentines, were then fashionable in France. He who was most skilful in deceit was considered the most clever; and to conceal one's thoughts and disguise one's purpose was the acme of political skill. Frankness would have been looked upon as folly.

The noblest and purest characters of the time—Coligny, Condé, the Chancellor Olivier—had not succeeded in keeping clear of the contagion.

Therefore the Duc de Guise did not despise the Prince de Condé; he rather admired him. But he said to himself, smiling, that he was at least as good an actor as the other. Taking a step forward, he slowly removed his glove, and cast it beside that of the prince.

There was a murmur of surprise; and the first impression was that he proposed to answer Monsieur de Condé's defiant challenge.

But in that case he would not have been the subtle politician he prided himself on being.

In a loud, firm voice, and as if really convinced by the prince's demeanor, he said,—

"I approve Monsieur le Prince de Condé's words, and support him in them; and I am so devotedly his humble servant, having the honor to be his kinsman, that I here offer myself as his second, and will assist him in his just defence against all comers."

Le Balafré, with these words, let his inquiring glance rove boldly upon all those who stood around.

The Prince de Condé could only lower his own. He felt himself more thoroughly worsted than if he had been overthrown in the lists.

"Will no one," continued the Duc de Guise, "take up either the Prince de Condé's glove or mine?"

No one stirred, of course.

"My cousin," observed François II., with a melancholy smile, "you are, as you desired, thoroughly cleared of all suspicion of felony, in my opinion."

"Yes, Sire," said the "Silent Captain," with ingenuous impudence; "and I thank your Majesty for having assisted me."

He turned with an effort to Le Balafré, and added,—

"I also am grateful to my good ally and kinsman, Monsieur de Guise. I hope to prove afresh to him, and to all others, by my behavior to-night against the rebels, if there be an attack, that he was not wrong in taking my part."

Thereupon the Prince de Condé and the Duc de Guise exchanged most profoundly courteous salutations.

Then the prince, being well and duly justified, and having no further business there, bowed to the king, and left the room, followed by those who had come in with him.

None were left in the royal apartment but the four personages whose dreary waiting had been enlivened and their apprehension distracted for a moment by this singular comedy.

It was a chivalrous scene, peculiar to the politics of the sixteenth century.

CHAPTER XXVIII
THE TUMULT OF AMBOISE

After the departure of the Prince de Condé, neither the king nor Mary Stuart nor the brothers De Lorraine referred to what had just taken place. They seemed to avoid the dangerous subject by tacit understanding.

Minutes and hours passed away in the gloomy and restless silence of expectation.

François II. often passed his hand across his burning brow; while Mary, seated apart, gazed sorrowfully at the pale, thin face of her young spouse, and furtively brushed away a tear from time to time. The Cardinal de Lorraine was wholly intent upon the sounds to be heard without; while Le Balafré, whose dispositions were all made, and whose rank, as well as his office, obliged him to stay by the king's side, seemed to chafe bitterly at his forced inaction, and every now and then quivered with impatience and stamped upon the floor, as a fiery war-horse chafes at the rein which restrains him.

However, the night drew to a close; the bell of the château, followed by that on St. Florentin, struck six, then half after six. The day began to break; and there had been no sign of an assault, no alarm given by the sentinels.

"Well," said the king, with a sigh of relief, "I begin to believe, Monsieur le Cardinal, that Lignières has misled your Eminence, or else that the Huguenots have changed their minds."

"So much the worse if they have," replied Charles de Lorraine, "for we are sure to put down the rebellion."

"Oh, no! so much the better!" exclaimed François; "for the contest of itself would be a humiliation for royalty—"

But his sentence was yet unfinished when two shots of an arquebuse, the signal which had been agreed upon as an alarm, were fired, and the shout was heard, repeated from post to post along the ramparts,—

"To arms! to arms! to arms!"

"There can be no doubt that the enemy are upon us!" cried the cardinal, turning pale in spite of himself.

The Duc de Guise rose, apparently well content, and said simply as he saluted the king, "Sire, I shall soon be with you again," and went hurriedly from the room.

His powerful voice could be plainly heard, giving orders in the antechamber, when there was a second volley of arquebuses.

"You see, Sire," said the cardinal, perhaps to put his fear to shame with the sound of his voice, — "you see that Lignières was well informed, and only made an error of a few hours."

But the king heard him not; angrily biting his colorless lips, he had ears only for the ever-growing noise of artillery and arquebuses.

"Even yet I can hardly believe in the possibility of such audacity!" he muttered. "Such an outrage upon the crown—"

"Can only result in shame and abasement for the wretches, Sire," rejoined the cardinal.

"Alas!" returned the king, "if we may judge by the noise they make, the Protestants are present in large force, and are scarcely afraid."

"This disturbance will be quenched at once like a fire of straw," said Charles de Lorraine.

"It doesn't seem so, for the noise is coming nearer," replied François; "and the fire instead of being quenched is blazing brighter, I think."

"Holy Virgin!" cried Mary Stuart, in terror; "do you hear the bullets ringing against the walls?"

"Yet it seems to me, Madame—" stammered the cardinal. "I think, your Majesty—As for me, I cannot see that the uproar increases any."

But his words were drowned by a fearful explosion.

"There is your answer," retorted the king, smiling bitterly, "even if your pale and terrified face were not enough to contradict you."

"I can detect the odor of powder," cried Mary. "And oh, just hear those piercing shrieks!"

"Better and better!" exclaimed François. "Come, come! The Reformers have carried the walls of the town by this time, doubtless, and propose to besiege us in the château in regular form."

"But, Sire," the cardinal stammered, shaking like a leaf, "in this conjuncture would it not be better for your Majesty to withdraw to the donjon? We may be sure that they will not carry that at all events."

"Who,—I?" cried the king; "hide myself from my own subjects! from heretics! Let them come even as far as this, my good uncle,—I shall be very glad to know to what point they will carry their insolence. You will hear them beg us to sing a psalm or two with them in French, and to turn our chapel of St. Florentin into a meeting-house."

"Sire, for Heaven's sake, think a little of what is prudent," said Mary.

"No," replied the king, "I propose to see this matter through to the bitter end. I will await these faithful subjects on this spot; and by my royal name! let one of them but fail to show me the respect that is my due, and he shall learn whether this dagger hangs at my side for show only!"

The minutes rolled on, and the arquebuse-firing grew more and more brisk. The poor cardinal could no longer utter a word, and the king was wringing his hands in helpless wrath.

"In God's name," exclaimed Mary, "will no one come to give us news? Is the danger so pressing that no one can leave his place for an instant?"

"Ah!" said the king, quite beside himself with excitement, "this waiting is intolerable, and anything else would be preferable to it, I think! I know one way of ascertaining what is going on, and that is to go to the scene of the affray myself. Monsieur le Lieutenant-General cannot refuse to receive me as a volunteer."

François took two or three, steps toward the door, but Mary threw herself in front of him.

"Sire," she cried, "consider! Ill as you are!"

"I no longer feel my pain," said the king. "Indignation has taken the place of suffering."

"Wait yet a moment, Sire!" urged the cardinal. "I am sure that the uproar is really growing fainter now. Yes, the reports are much less frequent. Ah! here is a page, with news, no doubt."

"Sire," said the page, "I am instructed by Monsieur le Duc de Guise to say to your Majesty that the Protestants have given way and are in full retreat."

"At last! That is happy news!" cried the king.

"As soon as Monsieur le Lieutenant-General thinks that he can safely leave the walls," continued the page, "he will hasten to make his report to the king."

The page thereupon left the room.

"Well, Sire," observed the Cardinal de Lorraine, triumphantly, "was I not right in predicting that it would be mere child's play, and that Monsieur my illustrious and gallant brother would soon give a good account of these singers of hymns?"

"Oh, my dear uncle," François retorted ironically, "how suddenly your courage has returned!"

As he spoke, a second explosion was heard, much louder and more awful than the first.

"What can that noise mean?" said the king.

"In truth, it is strange," the cardinal replied, beginning to tremble afresh.

Fortunately his alarm did not last long. Richelieu, the captain of arquebusiers, came in almost immediately with his face begrimed with powder, and a bloody sword in his hand.

"Sire," Richelieu thus addressed the king, "the rebels are utterly routed. They scarcely had time to explode a quantity of powder which they had deposited near one of the gates, and which inflicted no damage on us. Those who were not taken or slain recrossed the bridge and have barricaded themselves in one of the houses in the Faubourg du Vendômois, where we shall have an easy prey. Your Majesty may see from this window how we will treat them."

The king ran quickly to the window, followed by the cardinal, and more slowly by the queen.

"Yes, indeed," said he, "there they are, having their turn at being besieged. But what is this I see? What is all the smoke pouring from the house?"

"Sire, it has been set on fire," said the captain.

"Very good! marvellously well done!" ejaculated the cardinal. "Look, Sire, see them leaping from the window! Two, three, four,—more, more! Do you hear their shrieks?"

"Oh, God! the poor wretches!" cried Mary Stuart, clasping her hands.

"It seems to me," observed the king, "that I can distinguish at the head of our troops the plume and scarf of our cousin De Condé. Is it really he, Captain?"

"Yes, your Majesty," replied Richelieu. "He has been among us all the time, sword in hand, fighting beside Monsieur de Guise."

"Well, Monsieur le Cardinal," said François, "you see that he did not wait to be asked."

"He could not have afforded to, Sire!" replied Charles de Lorraine. "Monsieur le Prince would have risked too much if he had acted otherwise than he has."

"Oh, see!" cried Mary, repelled and fascinated at once by the horrible spectacle without; "the flames are much more intense! the house will fall in upon the poor wretches!"

"It has fallen!" said the king.

"Thank God, it is all over!" cried the cardinal.

"Ah, let us leave the place, Sire; it makes me ill," said Mary, drawing the king away from the window.

"Yes," said François, "I can feel nought but pity now."

He left the cardinal standing alone at the window in great exultation; but he soon turned away too, as he heard the voice of the Duc de Guise.

Le Balafré entered, proud and unmoved, accompanied by the Prince de Condé, who, for his part, had much ado to hide his grief and shame.

"Sire, it is all over," said the Duc de Guise to the king; "and the rebels have paid the penalty of their crime. I render thanks to God, who has delivered your Majesty from this peril; for from what I have seen, I conclude it was greater than I supposed. We have traitors among us."

"Can it be?" cried the cardinal.

"Yes," replied Le Balafré; "when they made their first assault, they were seconded by the men-at-arms who came hither with Lamothe. They attacked us in flank, and for a moment were masters of the town."

"That is terrible!" said Mary, pressing close to the king.

"It would have been much more so, Madame," continued the duke, "if the rebels had also been seconded, as they hoped to be, by an attack which Chaudieu, brother of the minister, was to make upon the Porte des Bons Hommes."

"Did the attack fail?" asked the king.

"It did not take place, Sire. Captain Chaudieu, thank Heaven! was delayed, and will arrive only to find his friends annihilated. Now let him come at his leisure! he will find everything ready for him both within and without the walls. And, to give him food for reflection, I have ordered that twenty or thirty of his accomplices should be hanged on top of the battlements of Amboise. The spectacle will prove a sufficient warning to him, I fancy."

"That was well thought of!" said the cardinal.

"I thank you, my cousin," said the king to Le Balafré; "but I see that God's merciful protection has been most bountifully shown in this affair, since to Him alone we must attribute the confusion that prevailed in the counsels of our enemies. Let us in the first place, then, repair to the chapel to return thanks to Him."

"After that," said the cardinal, "we will issue orders for the punishment of the surviving culprits. Sire, you will be present at their execution with the queen and queen-mother, will you not?"

"Why, will that be necessary, pray?" asked the youthful king, walking toward the door, much annoyed.

"Sire, it is indispensable," urged the cardinal, following him. "The glorious King François I. and your father, of illustrious memory, Sire, never failed to be present at the burning of heretics. As for the King of Spain, Sire—"

"Other kings may do as they please," said François, still going toward the door, "and I, too, propose to have my own way."

"I ought to inform your Majesty that the nuncio from his Holiness absolutely relies upon your presence at the first 'Act of Faith' of your reign," added the pitiless cardinal. "When everybody else is present,—even the Prince de Condé, I venture to say,—is it fitting that your Majesty should be absent?"

"Alas, *mon Dieu*! we will talk of this matter again presently," rejoined François. "The guilty men are not yet condemned."

"Oh, I beg your Majesty's pardon, but they are!" said the cardinal, earnestly.

"So be it! Thus you impose this terrible necessity upon me in my feebleness," replied the king. "But now, Monsieur le Cardinal, let us go, as I said, to kneel before the altar and thank God, who has deigned to turn aside from us the peril of this conspiracy."

"Sire," said the Duc de Guise, "we must not exaggerate these things, and give them more importance than they deserve, therefore I trust that your Majesty will not speak of this movement as a conspiracy; it was, in truth, nought but a *tumult*."

CHAPTER XXIX
AN ACT OF FAITH

Although the conspirators had inserted in a manifesto, seized among La Renaudie's papers, a declaration that they would "attempt nothing against the king's majesty, nor the princes of the blood, nor the good of the kingdom," they had, nevertheless, been taken in open rebellion, and might well expect to meet the fate of those who are vanquished in civil wars.

The mode of treatment that had been adopted with regard to those who professed the principles of the Reformation, while they were conducting themselves as peaceful and submissive subjects, left little room for hope of pardon now.

In fact, the Cardinal de Lorraine hurried on their condemnation with a passionate zeal that was quite characteristic of the ecclesiastic of those days, though it was hardly Christlike.

He intrusted the proceedings against the nobles who were implicated in the deplorable affair to the parliament of Paris and the Chancellor Olivier. Thus matters progressed finely. The interrogations were quickly gone through, and the sentences pronounced still more quickly.

They dispensed with even these empty formalities in the cases of the less highly placed abettors of the rebellion, people of small importance, who were being broken on the wheel or hanged every day at Amboise without wearying parliament with their cases. The honor and expense of a trial were only accorded to persons of some quality or note.

At last, thanks to the pious ardor of Charles de Lorraine, everything was concluded in their cases as well in less than three weeks.

The 15th of April was fixed for the public execution at Amboise of twenty-seven barons, eleven counts, and seven marquises; in all, fifty gentlemen, leaders of the Protestants, were to meet their death that day.

Nothing was neglected which could assist in imparting to that extraordinary religious function all desirable pomp and splendor. Extensive preparations were made. From Paris to Nantes public curiosity was inflamed by all the expedients in vogue at that time; that is to say, the execution was announced by all preachers and curés from their pulpits.

On the appointed day, three superb galleries, the central and most sumptuous of which was reserved for the royal family, were erected on the platform of the château at the foot of which the bloody drama was to be enacted.

Around the square were wooden benches filled with all the faithful from the neighborhood who could be got together, willingly or on compulsion. The bourgeoisie and peasants, who might have had some distaste for such a grewsome spectacle, were induced to go either by threats or bribes; some had their taxes remitted; others were threatened with the loss of their offices or their privileges as freemen. All these divers motives, added to the morbid curiosity of some and the fanaticism of others, caused such a concourse of people at Amboise that more than ten thousand were encamped in the fields the night before the fatal day.

Early in the morning of the 15th the roofs of all the houses in the town were covered with a moving mass; and windows looking upon the square were let for ten crowns,—which was an enormous price for the time.

A vast scaffold, draped in black cloth, was erected in the middle of the enclosure. On it was to be seen the *chouquet*,—a block upon which each of the condemned had to rest his head while he knelt to receive the blow. Near by a chair draped in black was reserved for the clerk, whose duty it was to call the names of the gentlemen one by one, and read aloud the sentence of each in succession.

The square was guarded by the Scotch company and the gendarmes of the royal household.

After solemn Mass in the chapel of St. Florentin, the condemned men were led to the foot of the scaffold. Several of them had already been subjected to the torture. They were surrounded by monks, who tried to make them renounce their heretical principles; but not one of the Huguenots consented thus to apostatize before death, and they steadfastly refused to reply to the monks, whom they suspected of being spies of the Cardinal de Lorraine.

Meanwhile the galleries reserved for the court were filled, except the one in the centre. The king and queen, whose consent to be present at the execution had almost to be torn from them by force, had at last succeeded in obtaining leave to postpone their attendance till toward the end, when only the principal chiefs remained to be punished. If they would but come at some time, that was all the cardinal asked. Poor royal children! Poor crowned slaves! They, as well as the peasants, had been prevailed upon by arousing their fear for their offices and privileges.

At noon the execution began.

When the first of the condemned men mounted the steps of the scaffold, his companions thundered out a French psalm, translated by Clément Marot, as much to afford him on whom the punishment was about to fall some last consolation as to mark their own constancy in the face of their enemies and their doom.

Therefore they sang at the foot of the scaffold, —

> "Dieu nous soit doux et favorable,
> Nous bénissant par sa bonté,
> Et de son visage adorable
> Nous fasse luire sa clarté." [5]

A verse was sung for every head as it fell; but every head that fell made one voice less in the chorus.

In an hour but twelve gentlemen remained, and they the most prominent leaders of the conspiracy.

Then there was a pause. The two executioners were weary, and the king was arriving.

François II. was more than pale; he was absolutely livid. Mary Stuart took her place at his right, and Catherine de Médicis at his left.

The Cardinal de Lorraine took his place beside the queen-mother; and the Prince de Condé was shown to a seat beside the young queen.

When the prince appeared upon the platform, almost as pale as the young king himself, the twelve condemned men saluted him.

He gravely responded to their salutation.

"I always bow in the presence of death," he remarked aloud.

The king was received, however, with less respect than the Prince de Condé. No acclamation welcomed him upon his arrival. He noticed the omission, and turning to the cardinal, he said, with an angry frown, —

"Ah, Monsieur le Cardinal, I will never forgive you for forcing us to come hither!"

Charles de Lorraine, however, had raised his hand as a signal for the marks of devotion to be manifested, and a few voices scattered through the crowd cried, —

"*Vive le roi!*"

"You hear, Sire?" rejoined the cardinal.

"Yes," said the king, sadly; "I hear a few awkward fellows, who but serve to make the general silence more noticeable."

Meanwhile the remainder of the royal gallery had been occupied. The king's brothers, the papal nuncio, the Duchesse de Guise, had taken their places there one after another.

Then came the Duc de Nemours, also very pale, and looking as if he were the prey of bitter remorse.

Last of all two men took their stations there, behind the others, whose presence in that place and at that time was perhaps not less remarkable than that of the Prince de Condé.

They were Ambroise Paré and Gabriel de Montgommery.

They had been led thither by very different motives.

Ambroise Paré had been summoned to Amboise some days before by the Duc de Guise, who was decidedly alarmed concerning the health of his royal nephew; and Mary Stuart, no less alarmed than her uncle, and seeing how dejected François was at the mere thought of the *auto-da-fè* implored the surgeon to be at hand to assist the king in case he should faint.

Gabriel, however, had come to make one last supreme effort to save at least one of the condemned,—the one who was to suffer last, and whom he reproached himself for having involuntarily, by his well-meant advice, led into this fatal extremity,—the young and gallant Castelnau de Chalosses.

Castelnau, we must remember, had surrendered only upon the written and subscribed assurance of the Duc de Nemours, who had guaranteed his life and liberty; whereas, immediately upon reaching Amboise he had been cast into prison, and to-day was to be beheaded,—last of all, as being the most guilty of all.

We must, however, be just to the Duc de Nemours. When he saw his word and honor as a gentleman thus compromised, he was in despair, and indignant to the highest degree; and for three weeks he went ceaselessly from the Cardinal de Lorraine to the Duc de Guise, and from Mary Stuart to, the king, begging and demanding and imploring the release of him to whom he owed this debt of honor. But the Chancellor Olivier, to whom they referred the question, declared, according to Monsieur de Vieilleville, that "a king is in nowise bound by his word to a rebellious subject, nor by any promise whatsoever made to him on his [the king's] behalf." This almost broke the heart of the Duc de Nemours, "who," the chronicler naïvely adds, "was worried only about his signature; for as to his word, he would always have given the lie to any one without exception who dared to upbraid him for it, save his Majesty alone, so valiant and noble-hearted a prince was he!"

Like Gabriel, the Duc de Nemours had been drawn to the place of execution—which was more terrible to him than to any other—by a secret hope of still saving Castelnau at the last moment.

Meanwhile the Duc de Guise, on horseback, with his captains beneath the gallery, had given a signal to the executioners; and the punishments and singing of psalms began again after the brief interruption.

In less than a quarter of an hour eight heads fell. The fair young queen was almost fainting.

Only four conspirators remained at the foot of the scaffold.

The clerk read in a loud voice,—

"Albert Edmond Roger, Comte de Mazères, guilty of heresy, of the crime of *lèse-majesté*, and of attacking with arms in his hand the person of the king."

"'T is false!" cried the Comte de Mazères from the scaffold.

Then, showing to the people his blackened arms and his breast all bruised by the torture, he continued: "See the condition to which I have been reduced in the king's name! But I know that he knows nothing of it; and so I still cry, *Vive le roi!*"

His head fell. The last three Protestants who were awaiting their turns at the foot of the scaffold sang again the first verse of the psalm,—

> "Dieu nous soit doux et favorable,
> Nous bénissant par sa bonté,
> Et de son visage adorable
> Nous fasse luire sa clarté." [6]

The clerk's voice was heard once more,—

"Jean Louis Alberic, Baron de Raunay, guilty of heresy, of the crime of *lèse-majesté*, and of attacking with arms in his hand the person of the king."

"You lie like two clowns, you and your cardinal," said De Raunay; "it is only against him and his brother that we took up arms. I hope they may both meet death as peacefully and as pure in heart as I."

Thereupon he laid his head upon the block.

The last two condemned men sang on,—

> "Dieu tu nous as mis à l'épreuve,
> Et tu nous as examinés;
> Comme l'argent que l'on épreuve,
> Par feu tu nous as affinés." [7]

Again the clerk resumed his deadly summons, —

"Robert Jean René Briquemaut, Comte de Villemongis, guilty of heresy, of the crime of *lèse-majesté*, and of a criminal attempt against the king's person."

Villemongis bathed his hands in De Raunay's blood; and raising them toward heaven, he cried, —

"Heavenly Father, Thou seest the blood of Thy children! Thou wilt avenge them!"

He fell lifeless as he spoke.

Castelnau, left quite alone, still sang, —

> "Tu nous as fait entrer et joinder
> Aux pièges de nos ennemis;
> Tu nous as fait les reins astreindre
> Des filets où tu nous as mis." [8]

The Duc de Nemours had been lavish with his gold in furtherance of his hope of saving Castelnau. The clerk and even the executioners were interested in his salvation. The first executioner said that he was exhausted; and there was a necessary interruption while the other was preparing to relieve him.

Gabriel took advantage of it to urge the duke to renewed efforts.

Jacques de Savoie thereupon leaned toward the Duchesse de Guise, with whom he was said to be on the very best terms, and whispered in her ear. The duchess had much influence over the mind of the queen.

She at once rose, as if she could not bear any more of the sad spectacle, and said loud enough for Mary to hear: "Ah, this is too horrible for ladies! Do you see how ill the queen is? Let us go."

But the Cardinal de Lorraine gazed sternly at his sister-in-law.

"A little more firmness, Madame," said he, harshly. "Remember that you are of the blood of D'Este and the wife of the Duc de Guise."

"Ah, and that is just why I am so troubled!" retorted the duchess. "No mother ever had better cause for suffering; for all this bloodshed and all the hatred aroused by this day's work will fall upon our innocent children."

"How weak women are!" muttered the cardinal, who was an arrant coward.

"However," said the Duc de Nemours, "one does not need to be a woman to be touched by this mournful picture. Tell me, Prince," said he to Monsieur de Condé, "are not you moved by it?"

"Oh, ho!" sneered the cardinal; "the prince is a soldier, accustomed to see death in all forms."

"Yes, on the battle-field," replied the prince, courageously; "but upon the scaffold, and in cold blood,—that's quite another matter!"

"Has a prince of the blood so much pity for rebels, pray?" It was again the sneering voice of Charles de Lorraine which asked the question.

"I have unlimited pity and sympathy," retorted the prince, "for gallant officers who have always worthily served their king and country."

What more could the prince do or say in his position, himself the object of suspicion? The Duc de Nemours understood, and addressed himself next to the queen-mother.

"See, Madame, but one remains," said he, without calling Castelnau's name. "Can we not at least save him?"

"I can do nothing," replied Catherine, turning her head away.

Meanwhile the unfortunate Castelnau was ascending the steps to the scaffold, singing as he went,—

> "Dieu *me* soit doux et favorable,
> *Me* bénissant par sa bonté,
> Et de son visage adorable
> *Me* fasse luire sa clarté." [9]

The people, deeply affected, forgot the fear inspired by spies and *mouchards*, and cried as with one voice,—

"Mercy, mercy!"

The Duc de Nemours was struggling at that moment to soften the heart of the young Duc d'Orléans.

"Monseigneur," said he, "have you forgotten that it was Castelnau who, in this same town of Amboise, saved the life of the late Duc d'Orléans, when it was in great danger during an *émeute*?"

"I will do whatever my mother decides," replied the Duc d'Orléans.

"But," said the Duc de Nemours, imploringly, "if you would but address the king; a single word from you—"

"I tell you again," rejoined the young prince, dryly, "that I await my mother's commands."

"Ah, Prince!" said the Duc de Nemours, reproachfully.

He made a motion to Gabriel expressive of discouragement and despair.

Thereupon the clerk read slowly,—

"Michel Jean Louis, Baron de Castelnau-Chalosses, accused and convicted of the crime of *lèse-majesté*, of heresy, and an attack upon the king's person."

"I call my judges themselves to witness," cried Castelnau, "that the declaration is false,—unless, indeed, it be *lèse-majesté* to oppose with all my strength the tyranny of the Guises. If it is to be understood in that way, they should have begun by declaring them kings. Perhaps it will yet come to that; but it will be for those who survive me to deal with that matter."

Addressing the executioner, he said in a firm voice,—

"Now do your office."

But the headsman, who noticed some commotion in the galleries, pretended to be arranging his axe so as to gain time.

"The axe is dull, Monsieur le Baron," he said in a low voice; "and you are surely worthy to die at a single blow. And who knows but that a moment more—It seems to me that something of good omen for you is going on down below there."

Again the people cried,—

"Mercy! mercy!"

Gabriel, losing all self-control at that supreme moment, ventured to cry aloud to Mary Stuart,—

"Mercy, Madame the Queen!"

Mary turned, met Gabriel's heart-rending glance, and understood his despairing cry.

Bending her knee before the king, she said,—

"Sire, this mercy at least; I ask it of you on my knees!"

"Sire," cried the Duc de Nemours, "has not enough blood been shed? And yet, you know, there should be mercy in the king's countenance."

François, trembling in every limb, seemed struck by these words. He seized the queen's hand.

"Remember, Sire," said the stern voice of the nuncio, who wished to recall the king to a more severe view of his duty, — "remember that you are the very Christian king."

"Yes, I do remember it," replied François II., firmly. "Let mercy be shown to the Baron de Castelnau!"

But the Cardinal de Lorraine, feigning to misinterpret the meaning of the king's first phrase, had made an imperative sign to the executioner.

As François pronounced the word "mercy," Castelnau's head rolled upon the planks of the scaffold.

The next day the Prince de Condé set out for Navarre.

> [5] "O Lord, to us be merciful,
> "And bless us with Thy grace,
> "And show unto our humble hearts
> The brightness of Thy face."

> [6] ""O Lord, to us be merciful,
> And bless us with Thy grace,
> "And show unto our humble hearts
> The brightness of Thy face."

> [7] ""Thou hast put us to the proof when we
> To Thy guidance did aspire;
> "Like gold, Thou hast refined us
> By the ordeal of fire."

> [8] ""Into the snare our foes have laid
> Thou, Lord, hast made us fall;
> "And there, fast hound, we lie, and wait
> Thy word, O Lord of all!"

> [9] ""O Lord, to *me* be merciful,
> And bless *me* with Thy grace,
> "And show unto *my* humble heart
> The brightness of Thy face."

CHAPTER XXX
ANOTHER SPECIMEN OF POLITICS

From the day of that fatal execution, the feeble health of François II. grew steadily worse.

Seven months later (at the end of November, 1560), the court being then at Orléans, where the States-General had been convoked by the Duc de Guise, the poor boy-king of seventeen was obliged to take to his bed.

Beside that bed of sorrow where Mary Stuart prayed and watched and wept, a most interesting drama depended for its conclusion upon the life or death of the son of Henri II.

The real question, although others were interested in its solution, lay between a pale woman and a sinister-looking man, who were seated side by side in the evening of December 4 a few steps from the sleeping invalid, and from Mary, who was weeping silently at his pillow.

The man was Charles de Lorraine, the woman Catherine de Médicis.

The revengeful queen-mother, who had at first been as one dead after the struggle which we have related at the accession of her son, had awakened during the last eight months, since the "Tumult of Amboise."

This, in brief, is what she had done in the bitterness of her hatred against the Guises: she had entered into a secret alliance with the Prince de Condé and Antoine de Bourbon; she had effected a reconciliation secretly with the old Constable de Montmorency. Nought but hatred can cause hatred to be forgotten.

Her new and ill-assorted friends, urged on by her, had fomented rebellion in various provinces, had aroused Dauphiné under Montbrun, and Provence under the brothers Mouvans, and had caused an attempt to be made upon Lyons by Maligny.

The Guises, on their side, were by no means asleep. They had assembled the States-General at Orléans, and had taken care to have a majority devoted to them.

Then, too, they had summoned the King of Navarre and the Prince de Condé to attend the States-General, as was their right.

Catherine de Médicis sent warning after warning to the princes to dissuade them from putting themselves in their enemy's power; but their duty called them, and the Cardinal de Lorraine gave them the king's word as a pledge of their security.

Therefore they came to Orléans.

The very day of their arrival Antoine de Navarre was consigned to a certain house in the city where he was kept continually in sight, and the Prince de Condé was cast into prison.

Then an extraordinary commission issued to try the prince; and he was condemned to death at Orléans by the procurement of the Guises,—the very man whose innocence the Duc de Guise himself at Amboise had announced his willingness to answer for with his sword.

Only one or two signatures were still to be procured, which the Chancellor l'Hôpital was delaying, before the sentence would be executed.

The foregoing statement will serve to show how matters stood on the evening of the 4th of December, as regards the party of the Guises, of which Le Balafré was the arm and the cardinal the head, and the Bourbon faction, of which Catherine de Médicis was the secret soul.

Everything depended, for both sides, upon the expiring breath of the anointed youth.

If François II. could only live a few days longer, the Prince de Condé would be executed, the King of Navarre might be accidentally slain in some altercation, and Catherine de Médicis banished to Florence. So far as the States-General were concerned, the Guises were masters, and if necessary, kings.

If, on the other hand, the young king should die before his uncles were relieved of their enemies, the struggle would begin again, with the chances against them rather than in their favor.

Therefore what Catherine de Médicis and Charles de Lorraine were waiting and watching for with such an anguish of interest on that cold night of the 4th of December, in that apartment in the city of Orléans, was not so much the life or death of their royal son and nephew as the triumph or defeat of their cause.

Mary Stuart alone watched over her young, dearly loved husband without thinking what loss his death might entail upon her.

However, we must not think that the bitter antagonism of the queen-mother and the cardinal betrayed itself to outside observers in their manners or their conversation. On the contrary, they had never seemed to be more confiding or more affectionate to each other.

At the moment at which we look in upon them, taking advantage of François's slumber, they were talking in a low voice and in the most friendly way imaginable about their most secret interests and their inmost thoughts.

For the better to conform to that Italian policy of which we have already given specimens, Catherine had sedulously dissembled her underhand proceedings, and Charles de Lorraine had always pretended to know nothing of them.

Thus they had not ceased to converse as allies and as friends. They were like two gamblers, each of whom cheats loyally for his own side, and who openly use cogged dice against each other.

"Yes, Madame," the cardinal was saying,—"yes, that stubborn Chancellor de l'Hôpital obstinately refuses to sign the decree for the prince's death. Ah! you were indeed in the right, Madame, six months ago, to oppose his succession to Olivier so vigorously! If I had only understood you then!"

"What? is it absolutely impossible to overcome his resistance?" asked Catherine, who had in reality instructed the chancellor to resist.

"I have tried flattery and threats," Charles de Lorraine replied, "and have found him inflexible."

"Suppose Monsieur le Duc should try his hand?"

"Nothing will move that Auvergne mule," said the cardinal. "Besides, my brother has declared that he does not propose to meddle in the affair at all."

"It becomes embarrassing," remarked Catherine, secretly delighted beyond expression.

"There is one way, however," said the cardinal, "by resorting to which we can get along without all the chancellors in the world."

"Is there, indeed? What way is that?" cried the queen-mother, uneasily.

"To have the decree signed by the king."

"By the king!" echoed Catherine. "But can he do it? Has he the right?"

"Yes," replied the cardinal, "we have proceeded thus far in this very matter by the advice of the best jurists, who have declared that the matter may be pushed forward to judgment in spite of the prince's refusal to reply."

"But what will the chancellor say?" cried Catherine, really alarmed.

"He will grumble, as he always does," replied the cardinal, calmly; "he will threaten to resign the seals."

"And if he does really carry out his threat?"

"It will be doubly advantageous, for we shall be well rid of a most inconvenient critic."

"When do you propose that this decree should be signed?" asked Catherine, after a pause.

"To-night, Madame."

"And you will cause it to be executed—?"

"To-morrow."

The queen-mother absolutely shuddered, for the blow was sudden.

"To-night! to-morrow! you do not reflect," she replied. "The king is too ill and weak, and his intellect is not clear enough to understand what you mean to ask of him."

"There is no necessity that he should understand, provided that he signs," retorted the cardinal.

"But his hand is not strong enough to hold a pen."

"It can be guided for him," taking keen delight in the alarm which he saw depicted in the expression of his dear foe.

"Listen," said Catherine, very gravely. "I must give you a warning and some good advice. My poor son's end is nearer than you think. Do you know what Chapelain, the first physician, told me?—that he did not think the king would be alive to-morrow evening, unless by a miracle."

"So much the more reason for us to hasten," said the cardinal, coldly.

"Yes," rejoined Catherine, "but if François II. is not alive to-morrow, Charles IX. reigns; and the King of Navarre will perhaps be regent. What a terrible reckoning would he demand for the infamous punishment of his brother? Would you not be in your turn tried and condemned?"

"Oh, well, Madame, he who risks nothing has nothing!" cried the cardinal, with angry warmth. "Besides, who says that Antoine de Navarre will be appointed regent? Who says that this Chapelain is not mistaken? Bah! the king is alive now!"

"Not so loud! not so loud, uncle!" said Mary Stuart, rising in fright. "You will wake the king! See! you have waked him."

"Mary, where are you?" said the feeble voice of François.

"Here, always by your side, dear Sire," replied Mary.

"Oh, how I suffer!" groaned the poor youth. "My head is as if it were on fire; and this pain in my ear is like a continual sword-thrust. Even in my sleep I have continued to suffer. Ah! all is at an end with me; all is at an end!"

"Don't say so! oh, don't say so!" replied Mary, struggling to restrain her tears.

"My memory is failing," said François. "Have I received the Holy Sacrament? I wish to do so as soon as possible."

"All your duties shall be fulfilled, dear Sire; do not be anxious about them."

"I want to see my confessor, Monsieur de Brichanteau."

"He will be with you immediately," said Mary.

"Are prayers being said for me?" asked the king.

"I have hardly ceased since the morning."

"Poor dear Mary! Where is Chapelain?"

"In the next room, ready to answer your call. Your mother and my uncle the cardinal are there also. Do you wish to see them, Sire?"

"No, no; none but you, Mary!" said the dying man. "Turn a little this way—there—so that I may at least see you once more."

"Courage!" replied Mary. "God is so kind! and I pray to Him with such a full heart."

"Oh, the pain!" moaned François. "I cannot see, and can scarcely hear. Give me your hand, Mary."

"There! rest upon me," said Mary, soothingly, supporting the small pale face of her husband upon her shoulder.

"My soul to God! my heart to thee, Mary! Forever! Alas! to die at seventeen!"

"No, no! you shall not die!" cried Mary. "What ill have we done to God on high that He should thus afflict us?"

"Do not weep, Mary," said the king. "We shall meet again above. I regret nothing in this world but you. If I could carry you with me, I should be glad to die. The journey to heaven is even more beautiful than that to Italy; and then, too, I fear that without me you will never know any joy. They will make you suffer,—you will be cold and lonely; they will kill you, my poor dear heart! It is that which afflicts me much more than death."

The king sank back upon his pillow exhausted, and maintained a dejected silence.

"But you shall not die; you shall not die, Sire!" cried Mary. "Listen, I have a great hope. One chance in which I have faith is left us."

"What do you mean?" Catherine de Médicis, drawing near in her amazement, interrupted her.

"Yes," continued Mary Stuart, "the king may yet he and shall be saved. Something within me tells me that all these physicians by whom he is surrounded and wearied to death are ignorant and blind. But there is a skilful man, learned and famous,—a man who preserved my uncle's life at Calais—"

"Master Ambroise Paré?" suggested the cardinal.

"Master Ambroise Paré!" Mary repeated. "They say that this man ought not to have the king's life in his hands, and would himself prefer not to; that he is a heretic and accursed; and that even if he would accept the responsibility of such a case, it ought not to be intrusted to him."

"That is very certain," said the queen-mother, scornfully.

"What! if I intrust it to him myself?" cried Mary. "Can a man of genius be a traitor! A great man, Madame, is always a good man."

"But," said the cardinal, "my brother has not delayed thinking of Ambroise Paré until to-day. He has already been approached."

"Yes, but who have been sent to him?" retorted Mary,—"those who took no interest in the matter, or even his enemies, perhaps. But I sent a trusted friend to him, and he will come."

"It will take some time for him to come from Paris," observed Catherine.

"He is on the way; in fact, he ought to have arrived," rejoined the young queen. "The friend of whom I spoke promised to bring him here to-day."

"Who is this mysterious friend, pray?" asked the queen-mother.

"Comte Gabriel de Montgommery, Madame."

Before Catherine had time to utter a word, Dayelle, Mary's first lady-in-waiting, came in and said to her mistress, —

"Comte Gabriel de Montgommery is below, and awaits Madame's commands."

"Oh, let him come in! let him come in!" cried Mary, eagerly.

CHAPTER XXXI
A RAY OF HOPE

"One moment!" interposed Catherine de Médicis, in a cold, hard voice. "Before allowing that man to enter, pray wait at least until I can take my leave. If it pleases you to intrust the life of the son to him who cut short the life of the father, I, at all events, do not propose to meet the murderer of my husband again, or hear his voice. Therefore I enter my protest against his presence in this place, and withdraw at his approach."

She did, in fact, leave the room without bestowing a glance upon her dying son or giving him a mother's farewell blessing.

Was it because the detested name of Gabriel de Montgommery recalled to her mind the first outrage the late king had put upon her? It may be so; nevertheless, it is certain that she had no such horror as she pretended of the sight of Gabriel and the sound of his voice; for when she withdrew to her own apartment, which adjoined that of the king, she was careful to leave the door half open, and had no sooner closed another door which opened upon a corridor quite deserted at that late hour than she applied both eye and ear to the aperture, in order to see and hear what took place after her abrupt departure.

Gabriel appeared, ushered in by Dayelle, and knelt to kiss the hand the queen held out to him, before making a profound salutation to the cardinal.

"Well?" asked Mary Stuart, anxiously.

"Madame, I have prevailed upon Master Paré," said Gabriel. "He is below."

"Oh, thank you, thank you, my faithful friend!" cried Mary.

"Pray, Madame, is the king failing?" said Gabriel, in a low voice, casting an uneasy glance at the bed, where François II. lay without color or motion.

"Alas! he never seems to gain," replied the queen; "and I was very impatient to see you. Did Master Ambroise object seriously to coming?"

"No, Madame," replied Gabriel. "He had already been sent for, but in such a way, he told me, as to invite a refusal. He was expected to bind himself in advance, upon his life and his honor, to save the king, when he had not even seen him. He was given to understand that, being himself a Protestant, he was open to the suspicion of desiring the death of a persecutor of Protestants. In short, he was treated with such insulting distrust, and such severe conditions were imposed upon him, that unless he had been utterly devoid of self-respect, to say nothing of caution, he must unavoidably have been led to hold himself aloof. He did so, to his great regret, and was not urged any further by those who had been sent to him."

"Can it be that our intentions were thus misrepresented to Master Paré?" the Cardinal de Lorraine hastily interposed. "Yet my brother and myself have sent to him two or three times, and have been always told of his obstinate refusal to come, and his extraordinary suspicions. We believed those whom we sent to seek him to be most trustworthy!"

"But were they really so, Monseigneur?" asked Gabriel. "Master Paré thinks otherwise, now that I have told him your real sentiments toward him, and the queen's kind words. He is convinced that, unknown to you, persistent efforts have been made for some guilty purpose to keep him from the king's bedside."

"It must be so," returned Charles de Lorraine; "I recognize the queen-mother's hand in this," he muttered, "for she is deeply interested that her son should not be saved. But will she thus corrupt all those upon whose devotion we rely? This is a counterpart of the appointment of her friend L'Hôpital! How she does make sport of us!"

Mary Stuart, meanwhile, leaving the cardinal to his reflections upon what had taken place, and his anxiety as to what was to come, was saying to Gabriel,—

"Monsieur Paré did finally come with you, did he not?"

"At my first request," replied the young count.

"And he is here?"

"Awaiting only your gracious permission to enter, Madame."

"Pray let him come in at once!" cried Mary Stuart.

Gabriel de Montgommery went for a moment to the door at which he had entered, and returned with the surgeon.

Sheltered behind her door, Catherine de Médicis was still watching, more engrossed than ever.

Mary Stuart ran forward to meet Ambroise, took his hand, led him herself to the cherished patient's bedside, and said on the way, as if to cut short all complimentary salutations,—

"Thanks to you for coming, Master Paré. I relied upon your zeal to do good, even as I now rely upon your skill. Come quickly; come to the king!"

Ambroise Paré, yielding to the queen's restless impatience, without having time to utter a word, was soon standing by the bed where François II., vanquished by suffering, so to speak, had only sufficient strength to breathe, almost imperceptibly and with a feeble, moaning sound.

The great physician stood a moment gazing at the young face, drawn and emaciated by suffering.

Then he stooped over the king, who was to him only a patient, and felt and probed the terrible swelling of the right ear with a touch as light and gentle as Mary's own.

The king instinctively recognized the touch of a physician, and yielded to it without opening his heavy eyes.

"Oh, such agony!" he moaned piteously; "such agony! Can you do nothing to relieve me?"

The light was too far away for Ambroise's purpose, and he made a sign to Gabriel to bring it nearer; but Mary seized it first, and herself held it for the surgeon while he made a long and careful examination of the seat of pain.

This silent, minute study lasted perhaps ten minutes; at the end of which Ambroise Paré rose to an erect posture again, and let the bed-curtain fall, apparently deeply absorbed in meditating upon his diagnosis.

Mary Stuart, waiting breathlessly, did not dare to ask him a question, lest she might disturb the current of his thoughts; but she scanned his features in an anguish of suspense. What would be his decision?

The famous physician sadly shook his head; and the movement seemed to the distracted queen like a sentence of death.

"Oh!" she exclaimed at last, unable to control her anxiety any longer; "pray tell me, is there no chance of saving him?"

"There is but one, Madame," replied Ambroise Paré.

"Is there even one?" cried the queen.

"Yes, Madame; and although, alas! it is not an absolutely certain one, still it exists, and I should be very hopeful if—"

"If?" asked Mary.

"If the man to be saved were not the king, Madame."

"Oh, that indeed!" cried Mary; "treat him, and save him as if he were the meanest of his subjects!"

"But suppose I fail?" demanded Ambroise; "for God alone is master. Shall I not be accused of having caused his death, being, as I am, a Huguenot? Might not such an awfully heavy responsibility unnerve me and make my hand tremble, when I should be in need of such absolute calmness and self-confidence?"

"Listen," was Mary's reply: "if he lives, I will bless you all my life, and if — if he dies, I will defend you to the death. Therefore make the effort! make the effort, I beg, I implore you! Since you say it is the last and only chance, for the love of God, do not let it pass, for it would be a crime!"

"You are right, Madame," said Ambroise, "and I will try, — that is, if I am allowed; if you yourself will allow me, for I cannot conceal from you that the remedy to which I must resort is an extreme and unusual one, and, so far as appearances go, violent and dangerous."

"Really?" said Mary, trembling like a leaf; "and is there no other?"

"No other, Madame! There is still time to employ it; in twenty-four hours at the utmost, and perhaps in twelve, it will be too late. An abscess has formed in the king's head; and unless it is relieved and discharged by a speedy operation, it will burst upon the brain and cause death."

"Must you therefore operate upon the king immediately?" said the cardinal. "I will not take the responsibility upon myself."

"Ah, you see that you already begin to doubt me!" said Ambroise. "No, I must have the daylight; and besides, I need the rest of the night to think it over, to get my hand in practice, and make one or two experiments. But to-morrow morning, at nine o'clock, I will be here. Please be here then, Madame, and you, Monseigneur; I should be glad if Monsieur le Lieutenant-General would also attend, in order that those whose devotion to the king is well tried may be present; but no others, — as few physicians as possible. I will then explain what I propose to do, and if you authorize me to proceed, with God's grace, I will try the last chance He has left us."

"And is there no danger before to-morrow?" the queen asked.

"No, Madame," said Master Paré. "But it is most essential that the king should rest quietly, and gather strength for the operation he is to undergo. I will mix with the harmless beverage I see on the table two drops of this elixir," he added, suiting the action to the word. "Let the king take this immediately, Madame, and he will at once fall into a deep, untroubled sleep. Watch him carefully, watch him yourself, if possible, to see that his sleep be not disturbed."

"Never fear! I will answer for that," replied Mary. "I will not leave his side to-night."

"That is of the utmost importance," said Ambroise. "Now I can do nothing more here, and I ask your permission to retire, Madame,—still to devote myself to the king, however, and to prepare for my great task."

"Go, good Master, go!" said Mary; "and accept in advance my thanks and blessing. Until to-morrow!"

"Until to-morrow, Madame," replied Ambrose Paré. "Be of good cheer!"

"I shall not cease to pray," said Mary. "And you also, Monsieur le Comte, once more I thank you," she continued, addressing Gabriel. "You are of those of whom Master Paré has spoken, whose devotion to the king has been put to the proof; therefore come to-morrow, I beg you, to give your illustrious friend the moral support of your presence."

"I will be here, Madame," said Gabriel, as he withdrew with the surgeon after respectfully saluting the queen and the cardinal.

"Yes, and I will be here too," said Catherine de Médicis to herself from her post of observation,—"yes, I will be here; for this Paré is quite capable of saving the king's life with his great skill, and of thus destroying his own party, as well as the prince and myself. The imbecile! But I will be here!"

CHAPTER XXXII
WELL-GUARDED SLUMBER

Catherine de Médicis remained at her post for some time, although none but Mary Stuart and the cardinal were left in the king's chamber; but she neither saw nor heard anything of interest. The queen administered the sleeping-draught to François, who seemed, as Ambroise Paré had promised, to fall at once into a more peaceful slumber. Then everything was still. The cardinal, seated in his chair, was deep in thought; while Mary, on her knees, was pouring out her very soul in prayer.

The queen-mother softly withdrew to her own room to imitate the cardinal's reflective mood.

If she had remained a few moments longer, however, she would have witnessed a scene quite worthy of herself.

Mary Stuart, rising from her knees, said to the cardinal, —

"There is no reason why you should stay to watch with me, dear uncle; for I intend to remain here till the king awakes. Dayelle, the physicians, and the servants in attendance will be quite sufficient for any emergency that can arise; so that you may go and take a little rest. I will send to you if it is necessary."

"No," said the cardinal; "the Duc de Guise, who has been delayed by a number of pressing matters, told me that before he retired he would come to learn the latest news of the king, and I promised to await him here. Hark! do I not hear his step now?"

"Oh, don't let him make any noise!" cried Mary, rushing to the door to warn Le Balafré.

The Duc de Guise entered, pale and excited. He saluted the queen, but in his preoccupation did not think to ask for the king's welfare; he went straight to his brother, and led him aside to a window-recess.

"Terrible news!" he began, — "a veritable thunder-stroke!"

"In Heaven's name, what is it?" asked the cardinal.

"The Constable de Montmorency has left Chantilly with fifteen hundred gentlemen," said the Duc de Guise. "The better to conceal his movements, he made a detour around Paris, and came from Ecouen and Corbeil to Pithiviers by the valley of Essonne. He will be at the gates of Orléans with his troop to-morrow; and I have just received warning of his coming."

"That is indeed terrible!" said the cardinal. "The old villain wishes to save his nephew's head. I will warrant that it was the queen-mother who notified him. Oh, this feeling of utter helplessness against that woman!"

"This is no time to proceed against her, but to bestir ourselves in our own interests," said Le Balafré. "What shall we do?"

"Go at once with our forces to meet the constable," replied Charles de Lorraine.

"Will you guarantee to hold Orléans when I am no longer here with my troops?"

"Alas! no,—indeed, I cannot," replied the cardinal. "All the Orléans people are disaffected,—Huguenots and Bourbons at heart. But in any event the States-General are on our side."

"And L'Hôpital against us, remember, my brother. Ah, it is a hard position? How does the king?" the duke asked finally, danger reminding him of his last resource.

"The king is in bad condition," was the cardinal's reply; "but Ambroise Paré, who has come to Orléans at the queen's request (I will explain this to you later), still hopes to save the king by a hazardous but necessary operation to-morrow morning, which may have happy results. Do not fail to be here at nine o'clock, brother, to sustain Ambroise, if need be."

"Surely I will be here," rejoined Le Balafré, "for that is our only hope. Our authority would die with François's last breath; but on the other hand, it would be a fine thing to frighten the constable, and perhaps make him retrace his steps, by sending him, by way of a welcome, the head of his handsome nephew, De Condé."

"Yes, that would be a very eloquent greeting, in my opinion," said the cardinal, reflectively.

"But this infernal L'Hôpital impedes everything!" exclaimed Le Balafré.

"If we had the king's signature upon the decree for the prince's death, instead of L'Hôpital's," suggested Charles de Lorraine, "there would be no further difficulty, brother,—am I not right?—about this execution taking place to-morrow morning before Montmorency's arrival, and before Master Paré's operation."

"That would not be strictly legal; but it would be possible," replied Le Balafré.

"Very well, then!" cried Charles de Lorraine, eagerly. "Leave me here, my brother; there is nothing more for you to do to-night, and you must need rest, for two o'clock will soon strike. You must husband your strength for to-morrow. Retire, and leave me here. I mean to make a desperate effort myself to retrieve our fortunes."

"What is it to be?" the duke asked. "Pray, take no definite step without first consulting me, brother."

"Never fear! If I have what I want, I will wake you before daybreak to perfect our plans."

"Very well," said Le Balafré; "with this assurance I will retire, for it is true that I am exhausted. But be cautious!"

He said a few consoling words to Mary Stuart, and left the room with as little noise as possible.

Meanwhile the cardinal had seated himself at a table, and was making a copy of the decree of the commission, of which he had the original before him.

That done, he rose and walked toward the king's bed. But Mary Stuart stood erect in front of him, and stopped him with a gesture.

"Where are you going?" said she, in a low tone, but firmly, and with signs of growing anger.

"Madame," replied the cardinal, "it is important, indispensable, that the king should sign this paper."

"What is most important, and most indispensable, is that the king should rest quietly," said Mary.

"Let me have his name at the bottom of this writing, Madame, and I will importune you no more."

"But you will awake him," retorted the queen; "and I do not choose that you shall. Besides, he is not capable of holding a pen at this moment."

"I will hold it for him," said the cardinal.

"I have told you that I will not have it!" replied Mary Stuart, authoritatively.

The cardinal stopped a moment, amazed at this obstacle, which he had never dreamed of.

Then he continued in his most insinuating tones, —

"Listen to me, Madame,—my dear niece, listen to me; I will tell you what is at stake. You understand very well that I would respect the king's repose if I were not constrained by the most urgent necessity. It is our fortune and yours, our welfare and yours, which are at stake. Understand me. This paper must be signed before daybreak, or we are lost!—lost, I tell you."

"That does not concern me," said Mary, calmly.

"Indeed it does! Once more I tell you, our ruin is your ruin, child that you are!"

"Even so, what does it matter to me?" the queen replied. "Do you suppose I concern myself with your ambition? My ambition is to save my beloved, to preserve his life if I can, and meanwhile to guard his priceless repose. Master Paré constituted me the guardian of the king's slumber. I forbid you to disturb it, Monsieur! Understand me! I forbid you! If the king dies, my royalty dies too!—it is all one to me! But as long as one breath remains in his body, I will defend it against the hateful demands of your intrigues. I have contributed more than I ought, my uncle, to the strengthening of your power and influence when my François was still well and strong; but I take your power from your hands again as soon as I have to concern myself with forcing respect to be shown to what may be the last hours of peace on earth that God will vouchsafe this poor life. The king, Master Paré said, would need to-morrow all of the little strength he has left. No one on earth, on any pretext whatsoever, shall deprive him of one moment of this refreshing slumber."

"But when the motive is such an important and urgent one?" said the cardinal.

"Upon no pretext whatever shall any one on earth awaken the king," repeated Mary, firmly.

"Ah, but it must be done!" retorted the cardinal, ashamed at last of having been so long delayed by the unaided resistance of a mere child, and she his niece. "The interests of State, Madame, are not consistent with these sentimental considerations. The king's signature is essential to me at once; and I will have it."

"You shall not have it, Monsieur le Cardinal," replied Mary.

The cardinal took a step toward the king's bedside, but again Mary Stuart faced him and barred his passage.

The queen and the minister looked in each other's eyes for an instant, each as excited and angry as the other.

"I will pass," said Charles de Lorraine, in a quick, short voice.

"Do you dare to lay your hand upon me, Monsieur?"

"My niece!"

"Your niece no longer, but your queen!"

These words were uttered in so firm, and withal dignified and queenly a tone, that the astonished cardinal recoiled.

"Yes, your queen," Mary continued; "and if you approach one step nearer, or make another motion, as if to make your way to the king, I will go to that door; I will call those who are on guard there; and though you be my uncle, though you be minister and cardinal, I, your queen, will order your arrest upon the spot, as guilty of *lèse-majesté*."

"Such a scandal!" muttered the cardinal, in affright.

"Which of us is responsible for it, Monsieur?"

The sparkling eye, the inflated nostrils, the heaving bosom of the young queen, and her whole determined bearing were a sufficient guarantee that she would carry out her threat.

And then, too, she was so lovely and so haughty, and withal so touching, that even the priest, with his heart of bronze, felt moved and beaten.

The man yielded to the child; and the affairs of State obeyed the cry of natural affection.

"Well!" said the cardinal, drawing a long breath, "I will wait, then, until the king awakes."

"Thanks!" said Mary, resuming the gentle and melancholy demeanor which had become customary to her since the king's illness.

"But as soon as he awakes—" continued Charles.

"If he is then in condition to hear what you have to say, and do what you wish, I will interpose no further obstacle."

The cardinal was perforce contented with this promise. He returned to his seat at the table, and Mary to her *prie-Dieu*,—he waiting, and she hoping.

The slow hours of that night of watching dragged themselves along, and François II. did not awake. The promise of Ambroise Paré was not a vain one: not for many nights had the king known such long and peaceful slumber.

From time to time he made a slight movement or uttered a feeble moan; sometimes he pronounced a word or a name, generally Mary's. But he would relapse at once into his deep sleep; and the cardinal, who did not once fail to rise in haste at the least sound, would return dejectedly to his seat.

He crumpled in his hand uneasily the useless, fatal decree, which without the king's signature might well serve for his own death-warrant.

He watched the torches gradually burn out or grow pale, as the cold December dawn whitened the windows.

At last, as eight o'clock struck, the king moved, then opened his eyes, and called, "Mary! are you there, Mary?"

"Always at your side," replied the queen.

Charles de Lorraine rushed forward with the paper in his hand. Perhaps there was time even yet; a scaffold is soon erected.

But at that instant Catherine de Médicis re-entered the royal apartments by the door leading to her own.

"Too late!" muttered the cardinal. "Ah, fortune turns her back upon us! Now, if Ambroise does not save the king's life, we are lost indeed!"

CHAPTER XXXIII
A KING'S DEATH-BED

The queen-mother during that night had not thrown away her time. In the first place, she had sent her creature, Cardinal de Tournon, to the King of Navarre, and had settled terms with the Bourbons in writing. Then before daybreak she had received the Chancellor l'Hôpital, and had learned from him of the expected arrival at Orléans of her ally, the constable; L'Hôpital, by her instructions, promised to be in the great hall, which was next to the king's apartments, at nine o'clock, and to have with him as many of her partisans as he could find. Last of all, she had made an appointment for half after eight with Chapelain and two or three others of the royal physicians, whose mediocre talent was the natural-born enemy of the genius of Ambroise Paré.

Having thus taken her precautions, she was the first, as we have seen, to enter the king's chamber just as he awoke. She went at once to her son's bedside, gazed at him for a few moments with bent head, like a grief-stricken mother, pressed a kiss upon his hand, which was hanging listlessly down, and wiping away a tear or two, took her seat in such a position as to have him always in sight.

She, as well as Mary Stuart, was determined from that time on to watch over that bed of suffering, for her own purposes.

The Duc de Guise entered almost immediately. After exchanging a few words with Mary, he walked toward his brother.

"Have you done nothing?" he asked.

"Alas! I have not been able to do anything," was the reply.

"Fortune is turning against us, then," said the duke. "There is a great crowd in Antoine de Navarre's antechamber this morning."

"Have you any news of De Montmorency?"

"None at all. I have tried in vain to learn something thus far. He could not have taken the most direct road, and he may be even now at the gates of the city. If Ambroise Paré is not successful in his operation, farewell to our fortune."

At this moment the physicians who had been summoned by Catherine de Médicis entered.

The queen-mother herself led them to the bedside of the king, whose suffering and groaning had begun again.

The physicians examined the royal patient, each in turn, and then retired to a corner to consult. Chapelain proposed a poultice to draw out the foreign matter; but the others declared in favor of injecting a certain medicated water into the ear.

They were just agreeing on the last-named method when Ambroise Paré entered, accompanied by Gabriel. After having examined into the king's condition, he joined his professional brethren.

Ambroise Paré, surgeon to the Duc de Guise, whose professional renown was already established, was now an authority to be reckoned with. The physicians told him what they had resolved to do.

"The remedy proposed is inadequate, I am sure," said Ambroise Paré, aloud; "but we must make haste, for the brain will be filled sooner than I thought."

"Oh, hasten, then, in Heaven's name!" cried Mary Stuart, who had overheard.

The queen-mother and the two Guises thereupon drew near the physicians, and joined their group.

"Have you any better and more speedy means than ours to suggest, Master Paré?" asked Chapelain.

"Yes," said Paré.

"What is it?"

"We must trepan the king," said Paré.

"Trepan the king!" cried the three physicians, in tones expressive of the utmost horror.

"In what does this operation consist?" asked the Duc de Guise.

"It is little known as yet, Monseigneur," replied the surgeon. "It consists in making upon the top of the head, or rather upon the lateral part of the brain, with an instrument I have invented, called the 'trepan,' an opening about the size of an angelot."

"God of mercy!" cried Catherine de Médicis, indignantly. "Put the knife to the king's head! And you would dare to do it?"

"Yes, Madame," replied Ambroise, simply.

"But it would be murder!" exclaimed Catherine.

"Why, Madame," added Ambroise, "I propose scientifically and carefully to bore a hole in the head, which is only what the blind and heedless do every day upon the battle-field. Yet see how many such wounds are cured!"

"Will you be answerable for the king's life, Master Ambroise?" asked the cardinal; "that is the question."

"God alone has the life and death of mortals in His hand, as you should know better than I, Monsieur le Cardinal. All that I can promise is that this is the last and only chance of saving the king. Yes, it is the only chance; but it is only a chance."

"But you say that your operation may be successful, do you not, Ambroise?" said Le Balafré. "Tell me, have you ever performed it successfully?"

"Yes, Monseigneur," replied Paré,—"only a short time since upon Monsieur de la Bretesche, at the sign of the Red Rose, in Rue de la Harpe; and to mention a case of which Monseigneur may perhaps have some knowledge, I performed it at the siege of Calais upon Monsieur de Pienne, who was wounded while fighting at the breach."

It may have been with intention that Ambroise Paré recalled the memory of Calais. It is certain that he succeeded, and that the Duc de Guise seemed moved.

"Yes, I remember," said he, "I have no longer any hesitation; I consent to the operation."

"And so do I," said Mary Stuart, enlightened, no doubt, by her love.

"But not I!" cried Catherine.

"What, Madame! not when you have been told that it is our only chance?" said Mary.

"Who says so?" demanded the queen-mother. "Master Ambroise Paré, a heretic, forsooth! Besides, it is not the opinion of the physicians."

"No, Madame," said Chapelain; "and these gentlemen and myself protest against the remedy that Master Paré proposes."

"Ah, do you hear?" cried Catherine, in triumph.

Le Balafré, in great agitation, led the queen-mother into the embrasure of a window, and said in an undertone, with clinched teeth,—

"Madame, hearken to me! You wish that your son should die, and the Prince de Condé should live! You are in accord with the Bourbons and the Montmorencys! The bargain is made, and the spoils divided in advance! I know everything! Take care! I know everything, I tell you!"

But Catherine de Médicis was not one of those who are easily intimidated; and the Duc de Guise made a serious mistake. She only understood the better how essential it was for her to adopt a bold course, since her enemy thus removed his mask. She cast a withering glance upon him, and breaking away from his grasp with a sudden movement, ran to the folding-doors, and herself threw them open to their fullest extent.

"Monsieur le Chancelier!" she cried.

L'Hôpital, according to the orders he had received, was waiting in the large hall. He had collected there all of the partisans of the queen-mother and the princes whom he had been able to find.

At Catherine's call he came quickly forward, and the group of nobles pressed inquisitively toward the open door.

"Monsieur le Chancelier," continued Catherine, raising her voice that she might be heard by all, "it is proposed to authorize a violent and desperate operation upon the person of the king. Master Paré proposes to pierce his head with an instrument of his own devising. I, his mother, with these three physicians, protest against this crime. Monsieur le Chancelier, record my protest."

"Close that door!" cried the Duc de Guise.

Despite the remonstrances of the gentlemen collected in the great hall, Gabriel did as the duke ordered.

The chancellor alone remained in the king's chamber.

"Now, Monsieur le Chancelier," said Le Balafré, "be pleased to understand that the operation which has been mentioned is absolutely necessary; and that the queen and myself, lieutenant-general of the kingdom, will be answerable, if not for the operation, at all events for the surgeon."

"And I," cried Ambroise Paré, "at this supreme moment, assume all the responsibility that you choose to impose upon me; yes, I consent that my own life may pay the forfeit if I do not succeed in saving the king's. But, alas! it is full time. Look at the king! look!"

François lay there, livid, without motion, and with dull, lifeless eyes, and seemed to see and hear nothing,—scarcely to exist, in fact. He no more responded to Mary's caresses or her beloved voice.

"Oh, hasten, hasten, in the name of God!" she said appealingly to Ambroise. "Oh, try to save the life of the king, and I will protect yours!"

"I have no right to forbid these proceedings," said the impassive chancellor; "but it is my duty to state the protest of Madame the Queen-mother."

"Monsieur de l'Hôpital, you are no longer chancellor," rejoined the Duc de Guise, coldly. "Go on, Ambroise," he said to the surgeon.

"We will withdraw," said Chapelain, speaking for the physicians.

"So be it," replied Ambroise. "I must have most perfect quiet around me; so leave me, if you please, gentlemen. For the sake of being sole master for the moment, I assume the sole responsibility."

For some moments Catherine neither spoke nor moved. She had withdrawn to a window, and was looking out into the courtyard, where there was a great commotion; but in the crisis that was approaching, no one beside herself paid any heed to the tumult without.

All others, even the chancellor himself, had their eyes riveted upon Ambroise Paré, who had resumed the cool demeanor of a great surgeon, and was making ready his instruments.

But just as he was leaning toward François, the uproar came nearer, and seemed to be in the adjoining hall. A bitter and joyous smile played about the bloodless lips of Catherine. The door was violently thrown open; and the Constable de Montmorency, in full armor, appeared threateningly upon the threshold.

"I arrive most opportunely," cried the constable.

"What means this intrusion?" demanded the Duc de Guise, laying his hand upon his sword.

Ambroise Paré had no choice but to stay his hand. Twenty gentlemen accompanied Montmorency, and poured into the chamber after him. At his side were Antoine de Navarre and the Prince de Condé. Moreover, the queen-mother and L'Hôpital joined them. There was no longer any hope of maintaining the mastery even by force.

"In my turn," said Ambroise Paré, hopelessly, "I withdraw."

"Master Paré," cried Mary Stuart, "I, the queen, command you to proceed with your operation!"

"But, Madame," replied the surgeon, "I told you that most perfect quiet was necessary! and you see!" he added expressively, pointing to the constable and his train.

"Monsieur Chapelain," said he to the first physician, "try your injection."

"That will take but an instant," said Chapelain, quickly. "Everything is prepared."

With the assistance of his *confrères*, he injected his preparation into the king's ear.

Mary Stuart, the Guises, Gabriel, and Ambroise allowed them to do as they chose, and said nothing; they were completely crushed, and as if turned to stone.

The constable chattered away like a madman.

"This is very well!" said he, well pleased with the forced docility of Master Paré. "When I think that if it had not been for me you would have opened the king's head in such fashion! Kings of France are only wounded so upon the battle-field, do you see? The steel of an enemy may touch them, but a surgeon's knife never!"

And then, exulting over the dejected attitude of the Duc de Guise, he continued, —

"It was quite time that I should arrive, thank God! Ah, Messieurs, they tell me that you proposed to cut off the head of my dear brave nephew, the Prince de Condé! But you aroused the old lion in his lair, and behold him! I have delivered the prince; I have addressed the States-General, who are restive under your oppression. I have, as constable, dismissed the guards you stationed at the gates of Orléans. Since when has it been customary thus to furnish guards to the king, as if he were not safe in the midst of his loyal subjects?"

"Of what king are you speaking?" demanded Ambroise Paré; "for soon there will be no king save Charles IX., — for you see, Messieurs," said he to the physicians, "that despite your injection, the brain is already affected, and is beginning to be filled."

Catherine de Médicis clearly read in the hopeless air of Ambroise that all hope was at an end.

"Your reign is over, then, Monsieur," she could not forbear remarking to Le Balafré.

François II. at that moment suddenly raised himself in bed, opened his great staring eyes, moved his lips as if struggling to pronounce a name, then fell heavily back upon his pillow.

He was dead.

Ambroise Paré, with a sorrowful gesture, made the fact known to those present.

"Ah, Madame, Madame! you have killed your son!" cried Mary Stuart to Catherine, leaping toward her in a frenzy of despair.

The queen-mother bestowed upon her daughter-in-law a venomous, icy glance, in which shone all the hatred she had concealed for eighteen months.

"You, my dear," she sneered, "have no longer the right to speak thus, remember; for you are no longer queen. Ah, I beg your pardon!—queen of Scotland. And we will send you over as soon as possible to reign in your land of fogs."

Mary, with the reaction inevitable after her first burst of grief, fell on her knees, exhausted and sobbing bitterly, at the foot of the bed where the king was lying.

"Madame de Fiesque," continued Catherine, calmly, "go at once and bring the Duc d'Orléans."

"Messieurs," she resumed, glancing at the Duc de Guise and the cardinal, "the States-General, which were devoted to you, it may be, an hour since, are now at our service, be assured. It is understood between Monsieur de Bourbon and myself that I shall be queen-regent, and he lieutenant-general of the kingdom; but you are still grand master, Monsieur de Guise. Therefore perform the functions of your office, and announce the demise of King François II."

"The king is dead!" said Le Balafré, in a deep, hollow voice.

The king-at-arms cried aloud on the threshold of the apartment, according to ancient ceremonial,—

"The king is dead! The king is dead! The king is dead! Pray God for the salvation of his soul!"

"Long live the king!" replied the first gentleman of the chamber.

At the same moment Madame de Fiesque brought the Duc d'Orléans to the queen-mother's side, who took him by the hand, and led him out to show to the courtiers, who were lustily shouting,—

"Long live our good king, Charles IX.!"

"Our fortunes are at an end now!" said the cardinal, gloomily, to his brother, as they were left standing almost alone.

"Ours, perhaps, but not that of our family," replied the ambitious Duc de Guise. "We must think now about preparing the way for my son."

"How can we renew our alliance with the queen-mother?"

"Oh, let us leave her to quarrel with her Bourbons and her Huguenots," said Le Balafré.

They left the room by a secret door, still busily conversing.

"Alas! alas!" murmured Mary Stuart, kissing the cold hand of poor François; "there is no one but me to weep for him, my poor darling, who loved me so dearly."

"And me, Madame," said Gabriel de Montgommery, who had thus far kept in the background, but now came forward with tears in his eyes.

"Oh, thanks, my friend!" said Mary, with a grateful look in which her whole soul shone out.

"And I will do more than weep," said Gabriel, beneath his breath, following from afar, with an angry eye, the Constable de Montmorency, who was strutting about beside Catherine de Médicis. "Yes, perhaps I may avenge him, when I begin anew the unfinished work of my own vengeance. Now that this constable has returned to power, the contest between us is not at an end!"

Thus, even in the presence of death Gabriel, alas! kept in view his personal affairs.

Surely Regnier la Planche was right in saying "that it is a bad thing to be king simply to die."

And he was equally right when he added, "During the reign of François II. France was the theatre whereon were enacted many horrible tragedies which posterity will contemplate with wonder and abhorrence."

CHAPTER XXXIV
ADIEU, FRANCE!

On the 15th of August, 1561, eight months after the demise of François II., Mary Stuart was at Calais, on the point of taking her departure for her Scottish kingdom.

During these eight months she had been engaged in an unceasing struggle, day by day and hour by hour, with Catherine de Médicis and with her uncles as well, who were as impatient as the regent, though for different reasons, to have her well away from France; but Mary found it hard to make up her mind to leave behind her that fair land where she had been a queen, so happy and so well beloved. Even in the sorrowful memories which recalled her premature widowhood, these loved spots held for her a poetic charm which made it difficult for her to tear herself away.

Mary Stuart not only felt that poetic charm, but she herself gave expression to it. She not only wept for the demise of François as a loving wife, but she sang of it like one of the Muses. Brantôme, in his admiration for her, has preserved for us the sweet, plaintive verses which she composed in her tribulation, and which bear comparison with the most notable poetry of that age:

> "En mon triste et doux chant,
> D'un ton fort lamentable,
> Je jette un deuil trenchant
> De perte incomparable,
> Et en soupirs croissans
> Passent mes meilleurs ans.
>
> "Fut-il un tel malheur
> De dure destinée,
> Ni si triste douleur
> De dame fortunée,
> Que mon cœur et mon œil
> Voient en bière et cercueil!

"Que dans mon doux printemps,
À fleur de ma jeunesse,
Toutes les peines sens
D'une extrême tristesse
Et en rien n'ai plaisir
Qu'en regret et désir.

"Ce qui m'était plaisant
Me devient peine dure!
Le jour le plus luisant
Est pour moi nuit obscure,
Et n'est rien si exquis
Qui de moi soit requis!

"Si en quelque séjour,
Soit en bois, soit en prée,
Soit à l'aube du jour
Ou soit sur la vesprée,
Sans cesse mon cœur sent
Le regret d'un absent.

"Si parfois vers les cieux
Viens à dresser ma vue,
Le doux trait de ses yeux
Je vois en une nue.
Si les baisse vers l'eau,
Vois comme en un tombeau.

"Si je suis en repos
Sommeillant sur ma couche,
J'oy qu'il me tient propos,
Je le sens qui me touche!
En labeur, en recoy,
Toujours est près de moi.

"Mets, chanson, ici fin
À ta triste complainte
Dont sera le refrain:
Amour vraie et sans feinte
Qui pour séparation
N'aura diminution." [10]

It was while at Reims, to which city she at first withdrew with her uncle De Lorraine, that Mary Stuart produced these melodious and touching strains. She remained in Champagne until the end of the spring. Then the religious troubles which had broken out in Scotland urgently demanded her presence in that country. On the other side, the almost passionate admiration which the boy Charles IX. expressed whenever he mentioned his sister-in law disturbed the suspicious regent, Catherine. Therefore it was necessary that Mary Stuart should resign herself to depart.

She came to pay her parting respects to the court at St. Germain in July; and the marks of devotion, of adoration almost, which were showered upon her there, served only to augment, if that were possible, her bitter regret.

Her dowry, charged upon Touraine and Poitou, had been fixed at twenty thousand livres annually; she also carried many superb jewels with her to Scotland, and it was thought that the hope of obtaining such rich treasure might tempt some freebooter. Still more fear was entertained that her safety might be endangered by some act of violence on the part of Élisabeth of England, who already saw in the young Queen of Scots a dangerous rival. Consequently a number of gentlemen proposed to escort Mary to her own dominions; and when she reached Calais, she found herself attended not only by her uncles, but by Messieurs de Damville and de Brantôme, — in fact, by the better part of that splendid, chivalrous court.

She found two galleys awaiting her in the harbor of Calais, ready to set sail as soon as she should give the word; but she remained at Calais six days, so painful was the final parting from those who had accompanied her thus far on her way.

At last the 15th of August, as we have said, was definitely fixed upon for her departure. It was a gloomy, threatening day, but without wind or rain.

Upon the shore, and before setting foot upon the deck of the vessel which was to bear her away, Mary, as a mark of her gratitude to all who had thus escorted her to the utmost verge of their country, gave each of them her hand to kiss as a last farewell.

They all came forward, and kneeling before her one after another pressed their lips upon her beloved hand.

Last of all was a gentleman who had never ceased to follow in Mary's train since she left St. Germain, but had always kept in the background on the road, hidden by his broad hat and the ample folds of his cloak, and had neither made himself known nor spoken to a soul.

But when he came in turn to kneel before the queen, hat in hand, Mary recognized Gabriel de Montgommery.

"Ah, is it you, Count?" said she. "I am indeed happy to see you once more, my faithful friend, who wept with me for my poor dead king. But why have you never spoken to me, if you were with these other gentlemen?"

"I felt that I must see you without being seen, Madame," replied Gabriel. "In my loneliness I could better collect my remembrances, and enjoy more fully the pleasure that it gave me to perform so grateful a duty."

"Thanks once more for this final proof of your attachment, Monsieur le Comte," said Mary. "I should be glad if I might show my gratitude otherwise than by mere words. I can do nothing more, unless it please you to accompany me to my poor Scotland with Messieurs Damville and Brantôme—"

"Ah, that would be my most devout wish, Madame!" cried Gabriel; "but another duty binds me to France. One who is dearer to me than life, and consecrated in my eyes, and whom I have not seen for more than two years, is expecting me at this moment."

"Do you mean Diane de Castro?" asked Mary, eagerly.

"Yes, Madame," said Gabriel. "By a letter I received last month she requested me to be at St. Quentin to-day, August 15. I shall not be with her until to-morrow; but whatever may have been her motive in summoning me, she will forgive me, I am sure, when she learns that I did not desire to leave you until you were actually leaving France."

"Dear Diane!" remarked Mary, pensively; "yes, she also loved me well, was like a sister to me. Hold, Monsieur de Montgommery; take this ring to her as a remembrance from me, and go to her as quickly as you can. She may need your help; and when her welfare is concerned, I do not wish to detain you. Adieu! adieu, all my dear friends! They wait for me, and I must go,—alas! I must."

She tore herself away from the arms of those who would still have held her, stepped aboard the small boat, and was at once transferred to Monsieur de Mévillon's galley, followed by the envied gentlemen who were to go with her to Scotland.

But even as Scotland could not supply the void left by France in Mary's heart, so those who accompanied her could not make her forget those she had left behind; indeed, she seemed to love the latter the more dearly. Standing at the stern of the galley, she never ceased to wave her handkerchief, wet with tears, to the kinsfolk and friends whom she left upon the shore.

At last they were in the open sea: and Mary's eyes were drawn in spite of herself toward a vessel which was just entering the harbor she had quitted, and which her gaze followed longingly in envy of its destination. Suddenly the vessel pitched forward, as if she had struck beneath the water-line; and trembling from stem to stern, she began to sink, amid the piercing shrieks of her crew. It was all done so rapidly that she was out of sight before Monsieur de Mévillon had time to send a skiff to her assistance. For an instant a few heads could be seen struggling in the water near the spot where the vessel had gone down, but they disappeared one by one before they could be reached, although the men pulled lustily; and the skiff returned without having saved a single one of the poor wretches.

"Oh, Lord! oh, my God! what a fearful omen for my voyage is this!" cried Mary Stuart.

Meanwhile the wind had freshened; and the galley began to attain some speed, so that the crew had an opportunity to rest. Mary, seeing that she was rapidly leaving the shore behind her, leaned against the bulwarks with her eyes fixed upon the harbor, her sight dimmed by great tears, and repeated again and again,—

"Adieu, France! adieu, France!"

She remained in that position nearly five hours,—that is to say, until night fell; indeed, she would probably not have thought of leaving the deck even then, had not Brantôme come to inform her that her presence was awaited at supper.

Thereupon, weeping and sobbing more bitterly than before,—

"Now, dear France," she cried, "I lose thee indeed; since Night, jealous of my last happiness, pulls her dark veil before my eyes to deprive me of my pleasure in gazing at thee. So adieu, dear France! I shall never see thee more!"

Then with a sign to Brantôme that she would follow him at once, she drew forth her tablets, seated herself upon a bench, and wrote these familiar lines by the last rays of daylight,—

> "Adieu, plaisant pays de France!
> O ma patrie
> La plus chérie,
> Qui a nourri ma jeune enfance!
> Adieu, France! adieu, mes beaux jours!
> La nef qui disjoint nos amours
> N'a eu de moi que la moitié:
> Une part te reste, elle est tienne.
> Je la fie à ton amitié,
> Pour que de l'autre il te souvienne." [11]

At last she went below, and said as she joined her shipmates who were awaiting her, —

"I have done just the opposite of what the Queen of Carthage did; for Dido, when Æneas left her, gazed ceaselessly at the waves, while I find it hard to take my eyes from the land."

They urged her to be seated, and to sup with them; but she could eat nothing, and withdrew at once to her cabin, charging the helmsman to arouse her at break of day if the land were still in sight.

On this point at least fortune smiled upon poor Mary; for the wind died away, and the galley scarcely moved during the night, except with the aid of oars; so that when day broke they were still within sight of France.

The helmsman entered the queen's cabin, as she had ordered him to do; but he found her already awake and seated upon her berth, gazing out through an open porthole at the beloved shore.

However, this pleasure was of short duration; for the wind freshened again, and France was soon lost to sight. Mary had only one hope left: that was that an English fleet would appear in the offing, and they would be obliged to turn back. But that last hope proved futile, like the others; a fog, so dense that they could not see from one end of the vessel to the other, came down upon the ocean, — almost miraculously, as it seemed, being midsummer. They sailed on at hazard, incurring the risk of going astray, but avoiding all danger of being seen by the enemy.

At last, on the third day, the fog lifted; and they found themselves close upon a rocky shore, where the galley would doubtless have gone to pieces if they had sailed two cables' lengths farther. The pilot took an observation, and found that he was off the coast of Scotland, and having skilfully extricated the vessel from the breakers which surrounded her, made the port of Leith, near Edinburgh.

The wits who accompanied Mary said that they had landed in a fog in a mischief-making country of marplots. [12] Mary's coming was entirely unexpected; so that she and her suite were, perforce, content to make their way to Edinburgh upon donkeys, wretchedly equipped, many of which were without saddles, and had nought but cords for reins and stirrups. Mary could not refrain from contrasting these sorry nags with the superb French palfreys which she was accustomed to see caracoling about in the hunting-field, or the lists. She shed a few tears of regret as she compared the fair land she had left with that upon which she now stood. But soon, with her fascinating grace, and struggling to smile through her tears, she said, —

"I must bear my ills in patience, since I have exchanged my paradise for a hell."

In such manner did Mary Stuart arrive on British soil. We have narrated elsewhere ("Les Stuarts") the story of the rest of her life and her demise; and how impious England, the arch-enemy of all that France holds sacred, slew grace in her person, as it had already slain inspiration in that of Jeanne d'Arc, and was subsequently to make an end of genius in the person of Napoleon.

[10] "Sad and plaintive is my song
Of the days now gone forever;
And I mourn the whole day long
The loss of him whom I shall never
More behold. In grief and pain, alas!
The fairest years of my life must pass.

"How pitiless and stern is fate!
That I, to fortune born and pleasure,
Must bend beneath the cruel weight
Of pain and sorrow without measure;
While Destiny thus bounds my whole career
By the dark shadow of the funeral bier.

"In the bright springtime of my life,
Of my youth the very flower,
A melancholy, widowed wife,
I sit and sob the weary hour;
Nor can my heart a taste of joy acquire
In aught save vain regret or vain desire.

"That to me now is bitter pain
Whereat my face was wont to lighten;
And God's bright sunshine seeks in vain
The darkness of my night to brighten:
Nor in my sight is aught so fair or fine
As to arouse a wish that it were mine.

"Wheresoe'er my steps may lead,—
Whether through the forest roaming.
Or perchance by flowery mead,
Or at dawn or in the gloaming,—
Still my fond heart doth ceaselessly deplore,
And mourn the loss of him who is no more.

"If to heaven my eyes I raise,
In some cloud-shape, outlined faintly,
I behold my dear one's face
Smiling with his smile so saintly;
If my glance wanders o'er the ocean's wave,
I seem to see him beckoning from the grave.

"If my eyes in slumber close,
I can hear his dear voice calling;
And my soul with rapture glows
At his soft touch so lightly falling
Upon my cheek. Thus is he near me ever,
Whether I toil or rest; nor can grim Death us sever.

"Have done, O Muse, with thy sad strain!
What boots it to be ever singing?
Yet of my song, this sweet refrain
Is ever in my ears ringing:
The love that's true, with adoration blending,
In absence loseth nought; its growth is never ending."

[11] "Farewell to thee, thou pleasant shore,
The loved, the cherished home to me,
Of infant joy a dream that's o'er!
Farewell, dear France! farewell to thee!

"The sail that wafts me bears away
From thee but half my soul alone:
Its fellow-half will fondly stay,
And back to thee has faithful flown.

"I trust it to thy gentle care;
For all that here remains with me
Lives but to think of all that's there,
To love and to remember thee."

[12] It is impossible to translate this passage so as adequately to convey the meaning of the text, "on avait pris terre par un *brouillard* dans un pays *brouillé* et *brouillon*."—TRANSLATOR.

CONCLUSION

Gabriel did not reach St. Quentin until August 16. At the entrance to the town he found Jean Peuquoy awaiting him.

"Ah, here you are at last, Monsieur le Comte!" cried the honest weaver. "I was sure that you would come! But you are too late, alas! too late!"

"What! too late?" asked Gabriel, in alarm.

"Alas! yes. Did not Madame Diane de Castro in her letter ask you to be here yesterday, the 15th?"

"To be sure," said Gabriel; "but no particular stress was laid upon the date, nor did Madame de Castro say why she desired my presence."

"Well, Monsieur le Comte," rejoined Jean, "yesterday was the day on which Madame de Castro—I should say, Sister Bénie—pronounced the words which make her a nun forever, with no possibility of returning to the world."

"Ah!" said Gabriel, turning pale.

"Whereas, if you had been at hand," continued Jean, "you might perhaps have been able to prevent what is now an accomplished fact."

"No," said Gabriel, gloomily, "no, I could not, I ought not, nor would I have attempted even to oppose that step. Providence doubtless kept me at Calais, for my heart would have broken by its helplessness in the face of her sacrificial act; and the poor, dear, afflicted soul which thus gave itself to God's service might have had to suffer more from my presence than she did when left alone at that solemn moment."

"Oh, but she was not alone," said Jean.

"Of course you were there, Jean, and Babette, and the poor and unfortunate, her devoted friends."

"We were not the only ones, Monsieur le Comte," said Jean. "Sister Bénie's mother was also with her."

"Who,—Madame de Poitiers?" exclaimed Gabriel.

"Yes, Monsieur le Comte, Madame de Poitiers herself, who, on receipt of a letter from her daughter, hastened hither from her retirement at Chaumont-sur-Loire, was present at the ceremonial yesterday, and should be with the new nun at this moment."

"Oh!" said Gabriel, in terror, "why did Madame de Castro send for that woman?"

"Why, Monseigneur, as she said to Babette, that woman is, after all, her mother."

"Alas! I begin to think I ought to have been here yesterday," said Gabriel. "If Madame de Poitiers is here, it can be with no good purpose, nor to fulfil any pious maternal duty. Let us go to the Benedictine convent, if you please, Master Jean. I am in greater haste than ever now to see Madame de Castro, for I fear that she needs me. Come, let us hurry!"

Gabriel was shown without objection into the parlor of the convent, where he had been expected since the preceding day.

Diane was waiting in the parlor with her mother. Gabriel, upon seeing her once more after so long a separation, was carried away by an irresistible impulse, and fell on his knees, pale and dejected, before the grating which separated them forever from each other.

"My sister! my sister!" was all he could say.

"My brother!" replied Sister Bénie, softly.

A tear rolled slowly down her cheek; but at the same time she smiled as the angels should smile.

Gabriel, turning his head slightly, met the gaze of the other Diane, Madame de Poitiers. She was laughing, as demons should laugh.

But Gabriel, with careless contempt for her exasperating demeanor, concentrated his regard and his thought entirely upon Sister Bénie.

"My sister!" he repeated eagerly, and with bitter anguish.

Diane de Poitiers at this point coldly remarked, —

"It is as your sister in Jesus Christ, doubtless, Monsieur, that you call by that title her who yesterday was still Madame de Castro?"

"What do you mean, Madame? Great God! what do mean?" asked Gabriel, with a shudder, as he rose to his feet.

Diane de Poitiers, without replying directly to his question, addressed her daughter: —

"The time has arrived, my child, I think, to reveal to you the secret of which I spoke yesterday, and which, in my opinion, my bounden duty forbids me to conceal from you any longer."

"Oh, what can it be?" cried Gabriel, distractedly.

"My child," continued Madame de Poitiers, calmly, "as I have told you, it was not simply to give you my blessing that I have emerged from the retirement in which I have been living for nearly two years, thanks to Monsieur de Montgommery. Pray do not consider my words ironical, Monsieur," she added in a tone of bitter irony in reply to a gesture of Gabriel's. "In truth, I am extremely obliged to you for having torn me away, with or without violence, from an impious and corrupt world. I am happy now! The divine grace has touched me, and my whole heart is filled with the love of God. To show my gratitude to you, I wish to save you from the commission of a sin,—a crime, it may be."

"Oh, what can it be?" It was Sister Bénie who asked the question now with fast-beating heart.

"My child," continued Diane de Poitiers, in her infernal, cool tones, "I imagine that I might yesterday, with a single word, have arrested upon your lips the sacred vows you were about to utter. But was it for me, miserable sinner that I am, and so happy to be free from earthly bonds,—was it for me to steal from God a soul which was about to confide itself to Him, free and pure? No! and I held my peace."

"I dare not guess! I dare not!" muttered Gabriel.

"To-day, my child," the ex-favorite resumed, "I break my silence, because I see from Monsieur de Montgommery's grief and earnestness that you still possess his entire soul. Now he must make up his mind to forget you; he must do it. But if he continues to soothe himself with the fancy that you may be his sister, the daughter of the Comte de Montgommery, he can allow his memory to return to you now and then without remorse. That would be a crime! —a crime to which I, having been converted since yesterday, do not propose to be accessory. You are not the sister of Monsieur le Comte, but are really the daughter of King Henri II., whom Monsieur le Comte so unfortunately slew in that fatal tournament."

"Oh, horror!" cried Sister Bénie, hiding her face in her hands.

"You lie, Madame!" said Gabriel, vehemently. "It must be that you lie! Where is your proof that you speak the truth?"

"Here," replied Diane de Poitiers, in a most peaceful tone, handing him a paper which she took from her bosom.

Gabriel seized the paper with trembling hand, and read it eagerly.

"It is a letter from your father," continued Madame de Poitiers, "written a few days before his death, as you see. He complains of my cruelty, as you will see again; but he submits, as you may also see, reflecting that in any event I shall soon be his wife, and that the lover will have suffered disappointment only to make the husband's happiness more pure and perfect. Oh, the words of that letter, which is signed and dated, are in no wise equivocal! Am I not right? So you see, Monsieur de Montgommery, that it would have been criminal for you to think of Sister Bénie; for you are bound by no tie of blood to her who is now the spouse of Jesus Christ. And in saving you from such impiety, I hope that I have acquitted my debt to you, and have more than repaid you for the bliss I enjoy in my solitude. We are quits now, Monsieur de Montgommery, and I have no more to say to you."

Gabriel, while this bitter, mocking speech was being delivered, had finished reading the baleful but sacred letter. It left no room whatever for doubt. It was to Gabriel like the voice of his father rising from the tomb to make known the truth.

When the wretched young man raised his wild, haggard eyes, he saw Diane de Castro lying unconscious before a *prie-Dieu*.

He rushed instinctively toward her; but the heavy iron bars arrested his steps.

As he turned back he saw Diane de Poitiers, and upon her lips was playing a smile of placid contentment.

Mad with grief, he took two steps toward her with uplifted hand.

But he stopped in terror at his own act; and beating his brow like an insane man, he cried simply, —

"Adieu, Diane! adieu!" and fled.

If he had remained a second more, he could not have forborne to annihilate that blaspheming mother like the viper that she was!

Outside the convent Jean Peuquoy was anxiously awaiting him.

"Do not question me! Ask me nothing!" exclaimed Gabriel at once, in a frenzy of despair.

And as honest Peuquoy gazed at him in sorrowful astonishment, he said more gently, —

"Forgive me! I fear I am almost mad. I cannot collect my thoughts, you see. It is to avoid the necessity of thinking that I propose to go, to fly, to Paris. Go with me, if you will, my friend, as far as the gate where I left my horse. But, in God's name, talk about yourself; say nothing of me or my affairs!"

The worthy weaver, as much to comply with Gabriel's wish as to try to distract his thoughts, went on to tell how Babette was marvellously well, and had recently presented him with a young Peuquoy, — a splendid fellow; how their brother Pierre had established himself in business as an armorer at St. Quentin; and how, only the month before, they had had news from Martin-Guerre, by a Picardy trooper returning home, and had learned that he was still happy with his reformed Bertrande.

But it must be confessed that Gabriel, who was, as it were, made blind and deaf by his grief, did not understand and only partly heard this joyous narration.

However, when he and Jean Peuquoy arrived at the Paris gate, he warmly pressed the honest burgher's hand.

"Adieu, my friend," said he. "Thanks for your affectionate kindness. Remember me most kindly to all your loving circle. I am glad to know that you are happy; think sometimes in your prosperity of me in my wretchedness."

And without waiting for any other response than the tears which shone in Jean's eyes, Gabriel mounted his horse, and set off at a gallop.

When he reached Paris (as if fate had determined to overwhelm him with affliction of every sort at once), he found that Aloyse, his dear nurse, had died, after a short illness, without having seen him again.

The next day he called upon Admiral de Coligny.

"Monsieur l'Amiral," said he, "I know that the persecutions and religious wars will soon begin anew, despite all the efforts to prevent them. Understand that henceforth I can offer to the Reformed cause not only my heart, but my sword as well. My life is good for nothing except to serve you; so take it, and spare it not. Moreover, in your ranks I can best defend myself against one of my enemies, and finish the punishment of the other."

Gabriel had in his mind the queen-regent and the constable.

It is needless to say that Coligny enthusiastically welcomed the invaluable auxiliary whose courage and vigor had been put to the proof so many times.

The count's history from that moment is identical with that of the religious wars which drenched the reign of Charles IX. with blood.

Gabriel de Montgommery played a terrible part in those wars; and at every momentous crisis the mere mention of his name drove the color from the cheeks of Catherine de Médicis.

When, after the massacre at Vassy in 1562, Rouen and the whole of Normandy openly declared themselves for the Huguenots, the Comte de Montgommery was named as the principal author of this uprising of an entire province.

The same year the Comte de Montgommery was at the battle of Dreux, where he performed prodigies of valor.

It was he, they said, who wounded with a pistol-ball the Constable de Montmorency, who commanded in chief, and would have made an end of him if the Prince de Porcien had not sheltered the constable and received him as a prisoner.

Every one knows that a month after this battle, where Le Balafré had wrested victory from the constable's unskilful hands, the noble Duc de Guise was treacherously murdered before Orléans by the fanatic Poltrot.

Montmorency, relieved of a rival, but also deprived of his ally, was less fortunate at the battle of St. Denis in 1567 than at that of Dreux.

The Scotchman Robert Stuart called upon him to surrender. He replied by striking him across the face with the flat of his sword, whereupon some one fired a pistol at him (the constable); the ball pierced his side, and he fell, mortally wounded.

Through the stream of blood which obscured his sight he thought that he recognized the features of Gabriel.

The constable breathed his last the following day.

Although he had now no direct personal foes, the Comte de Montgommery did not lessen the force of his blows. He seemed invincible and immortal.

When Catherine de Médicis asked who had compelled Béarn to submit to the King of Navarre, and had caused the Prince of Béarn to be recognized as general-in-chief of the Huguenots, the answer was—Montgommery.

When, on the day following the massacre of St. Bartholomew (1572), the queen-mother, in her thirst for vengeance, inquired, not as to those who had perished, but as to those who had escaped, the first name mentioned was—Montgommery.

Montgommery threw himself into Rochelle with Lanoue. The town sustained nine fierce assaults, and cost the royal army forty thousand men. In the capitulation which ensued, it retained its freedom; and Gabriel was allowed to depart, safe and sound.

He then made his way into Sancerre, which was besieged by the governor of Berri. He was well skilled, our readers will remember, in the defence of beleaguered towns. A handful of Sancerrois, with no other arms than iron-shod clubs, held out for four months against a body of six thousand soldiers. When at last they capitulated, they obtained the same terms granted at Rochelle,—liberty of conscience and immunity of person.

Catherine de Médicis viewed with ever-growing fury the continual escapes of her old unconquerable foe.

Montgommery left Poitou, which was in a blaze, and returned to Normandy to rekindle the flames which were subsiding there.

Setting out from St. Lo, within three days he had taken Carentan and despoiled Valognes of all her supplies. All the Norman nobility ranged themselves under his standard.

Catherine de Médicis and the king at once put three armies in the field, and proclaimed the ban and the *arrière-ban* in Mans and in Perche. The royal forces were led by the Duc de Matignon.

This time Montgommery no longer fought individually. Lost in the ranks of the Reformers, he devoted himself to thwarting Charles IX., and had his army, as the king had his.

He formed an admirable plan, which bade fair to assure him a brilliant victory.

He left Matignon besieging St. Lô with his whole force, secretly quitted the town, and made his way to Domfront. There François du Hallot was to join him with all the cavalry of Bretagne, Anjou, and the Caux country. With these forces he proposed to fall unexpectedly upon the royal army before St. Lô, which, being thus caught between two fires, would be annihilated.

But treachery conquered the unconquerable. An ensign warned Matignon of Montgommery's secret departure for Domfront, whither he was accompanied by only forty horsemen.

Matignon cared much less about reducing St. Lô than about capturing Montgommery; so he left the siege in charge of one of his inferior officers, and hastened to Domfront with two regiments of foot, six hundred horse, and a strong artillery force.

Any other than Gabriel de Montgommery would have surrendered without entering upon a resistance sure to be of no effect; but he, with his forty men, determined to show a bold front to that army.

In De Thou's history the incredible narrative of that siege may be read.

Domfront held out for twelve days, during which time the Comte de Montgommery made seven furious sallies; at last, when the walls of the town, riddled and tottering, were practically in the enemies' hands, Gabriel abandoned them, but only to ensconce himself in what was called the Tower of Guillaume de Bellême, and fight on.

He had only thirty men with him.

Matignon ordered to the assault a battery of five pieces of heavy artillery, a hundred cuirassiers, seven hundred musketeers, and a hundred pikemen.

The attack lasted five hours; and six hundred cannon-shot were fired into the old donjon.

In the evening Montgommery had but sixteen men left; but he still held out. He passed the night working at the breach like a common laborer.

The assault began again with daybreak. Matignon had received reinforcements during the night, and had under his command around the tower of the Bellême donjon and its seventeen defenders fifteen thousand soldiers and eighteen pieces of artillery!

The courage of the besieged did not fail; but their powder was exhausted.

Montgommery, rather than fall into the hands of his enemies alive, determined to fall upon his own sword; but Matignon sent him a flag of truce, the bearer of which swore in the name of his chief "that his life should be spared, and he should be allowed to depart."

Montgommery thereupon gave himself up, trusting to the oath. He should have remembered the fate of Castelnau.

On the same day he was sent to Paris in fetters. Catherine de Médicis at last had him in her power. It was by treachery, to be sure; but what mattered that? Charles IX. was dead; and pending the return of Henri III. from Poland she was queen-regent and omnipotent.

Montgommery was dragged before parliament, and condemned to death June 26, 1574.

For fourteen years he had been fighting against the wife and children of Henri II.

On the 27th of June, the Comte de Montgommery—to whom, in mere refinement of cruelty, the extraordinary torture had been applied—was carried to the scaffold and beheaded. His body was subsequently drawn and quartered.

Catherine de Médicis was present at the execution.

Thus closed the career of that extraordinary man, —one of the noblest and bravest souls that the sixteenth century had seen. He had never risen above the second rank, but had always shown himself worthy of a place in the first. His death fulfilled to the letter the predictions of Nostradamus,—

"Enfin, l'aimera, puis las! le tuera
Dame du roy."

Diane de Castro did not survive him. She had died the year before, abbess of the Benedictines of St. Quentin.